As a psychiatric social worker, Diane Gaston spent years helping others create real-life happy endings. Now Diane crafts fictional ones, writing the kind of historical romance she always loved to read.

The youngest of three daughters of a US Army Colonel, Diane moved frequently during her childhood, even living for a year in Japan. It continues to amaze her that her own son and daughter grew up in one house in Northern Virginia. Diane still lives in that house with three very ordinary housecats. Visit Diane's website at http://dianegaston.com

Don't miss these other Regency delights from Mills & Boon® Historical romance's bestselling authors!

REGENCY PLEASURES
Louise Allen

REGENCY SECRETS
Julia Justiss

REGENCY RUMOURS
Juliet Landon

REGENCY REDEMPTION
Christine Merrill

REGENCY DEBUTANTES
Margaret McPhee

REGENCY IMPROPRIETIES
Diane Gaston

REGENCY MISTRESSES
Mary Brendan

REGENCY REBELS
Deb Marlowe

REGENCY SCANDALS
Sophia James

REGENCY MARRIAGES
Elizabeth Rolls

REGENCY INNOCENTS
Annie Burrows

REGENCY SINS
Bronwyn Scott

REGENCY
Improprieties

Diane Gaston

WITHDRAWN

MILLS & BOON

Mills & Boon, an imprint of Harlequin (UK) Limited,
Eton House, 18-24 Paradise Road, Richmond, Surrey TW9 1SR

REGENCY IMPROPRIETIES © Harlequin Books S.A. 2011

The publisher acknowledges the copyright holder of the individual works
as follows:

Innocence and Impropriety © Diane Perkins 2007
The Vanishing Viscountess © Diane Perkins 2007

ISBN: 978 0 263 88736 5

052-0711

Printed in the UK
by CPI MacKays, Chatham, ME5 8TD

Innocence and Impropriety

To the 'Roses' in my life:
My sister, Marilyn Rose
(though she was never fond of her middle name)
and my sister-in-law, Rosemarie

Chapter One

London—July 1817

Vauxhall Gardens was not a place Jameson Flynn would have chosen to spend his night hours, but his employer, the Marquess of Tannerton, required his presence.

To Flynn, Vauxhall was all façade. Mere wooden structures painted to look like Greek temples or Chinese pavilions. Revellers were equally as false, wearing masks to disguise whether they be titled, rich, respectable, or rogue, pickpocket, lady of ill repute.

'Have some more ham.' Tannerton handed him the plate of paper-thin ham slices, a Vauxhall delicacy of dubious worth.

Rich as Croesus, Tanner—as he liked to be called—ate with as much enthusiasm as if he were dining at Carlton House instead of a supper box at Vauxhall. Flynn declined the Vauxhall delicacy but sipped his arrack, a heady mixture of rum and Benjamin flower that redeemed Vauxhall only a little in his eyes. It was not unusual for Tanner to seek Flynn out for companionship, but Flynn had no illusions. He was Tanner's secretary, not his friend.

To look at them, you might not guess which one was the marquess. Flynn prided himself on his appearance. His dark brown hair was always neatly in place, his black coat and trousers well tailored. Tanner, a few years older and lighter in colouring, took less care, often giving the impression he'd just dismounted from his horse.

Flynn placed his tankard on the table. 'You brought me here for a purpose, sir. When am I to discover what it is?'

Tanner grinned and reached inside his coat, pulling out a piece of paper. He handed it to Flynn. 'Regard this, if you will.'

It was a Vauxhall programme, stating that, on this July night, a concert of vocal and instrumental music would be performed featuring a Miss Rose O'Keefe, Vauxhall Garden's newest flower.

Flynn ought to have guessed. A woman.

Ever since returning from Brussels, Tanner had gone back to his more characteristic pursuits of pleasure in whatever form he could find it. Or, Flynn might say, from whatever woman. And there were plenty of women willing to please him. Tanner had the reputation of being good to his mistresses, showering them with gifts, houses, and ultimately a nice little annuity when his interest inevitably waned. As a result, Tanner usually had his pick of actresses, opera dancers and songstresses.

'I am still at a loss. I surmise you have an interest in this Miss O'Keefe, but what do you require of me?' Flynn usually became involved in the monetary negotiations with Tanner's *chère amies* or when it came time to deliver the *congé,* Tanner having an aversion to hysterics.

Tanner's eyes lit with animation. 'You must assist me in winning the young lady.'

Flynn nearly choked on his arrack. 'I? Since when do you require my assistance on that end?'

Tanner leaned forward. 'I tell you, Flynn. This one is exceptional. No one heard of her before this summer. One night she just appeared in the orchestra box and sang. Rumour has it she sang again at the Cyprian's Masquerade, but that is not certain. In any event, this lady is not easily won.'

Flynn shot him a sceptical expression.

Tanner went on, 'Pomroy and I came to hear her the other evening. You've never heard the like, Flynn, let me tell you. There was nothing to be done but try to meet her.' He scowled and took a long sip of his drink. 'Turns out she has a papa guarding her interests. I could not even manage to give the man my card. There were too many ramshackle fellows crowding him.'

Flynn could just imagine the top-lofty marquess trying to push his way through the sorts that flocked around the female Vauxhall performers. 'What is it you wish of me?'

Tanner leaned forward eagerly. 'My idea is this. You discover a way to get to this father and how to negotiate on my behalf.' He nodded, as if agreeing with himself. 'You have the gift of diplomacy, which you know I do not.'

Flynn suspected all the negotiating required was to have said, 'How much do you want?' and the lady would have fallen, but he kept that opinion to himself. He would act as broker; he'd performed such tasks for Tanner before, but always after Tanner made the initial conquest. The way Flynn looked at it, he was negotiating a contract, not so different from other contracts he negotiated for Tanner. Flynn negotiated the terms, the limits, the termination clause.

The orchestra, playing some distance from their supper box, its strains wafting louder and softer on the breeze, suddenly stopped. Tanner pulled out his timepiece. 'I believe it is about time for her to perform. Make haste.'

Flynn dutifully followed Tanner's long-legged stride to the Grove in the centre of the gardens where the two-storeyed gazebo held the orchestra high above the crowd. Tanner pushed his way to the front for the best view. He was filled with excitement, like a small boy about to witness a balloon ascent.

The music began, a tune familiar to Flynn, and, amid cheers and applause, Miss O'Keefe took her place in front of the orchestra. She began to sing:

> *When, like the dawning day*
> *Eileen Aroon*
> *Love sends his early ray...*

Her crystalline voice filled the warm summer air, silencing the revellers. Flynn lifted his gaze to her and all the glittering lamps strung on the gazebo and throughout the surrounding trees blurred. Only *she* filled his vision, dressed in a gown of deep red that fluttered in the light breeze.

Her hair, dark as the midnight sky, dramatically contrasted with skin as pale as clouds billowing over mountaintops. Her lips, now open in song, were as pink as a summer garden's rose.

This was Rose O'Keefe, Vauxhall's newest singing sensation? She seemed more like some dream incarnate. Flynn watched as she extended her arms towards the audience, as if to embrace them all. Hers was a graceful sensuality, but earthy and deeply arousing.

> *Were she no longer true*
> *Eileen Aroon*
> *What would her lover do...*

Flynn swallowed against a sudden tightness in his throat. The Irish tune—'Eileen Aroon'—sung with the tiniest lilt, created a wave of emotion such as he'd not felt in years. He squeezed shut his stinging eyes and could almost see his mother at the old pianoforte, his father by her side, his brothers and sisters gathered around. He could almost hear his father's baritone booming loud and his sister Kathleen's sweet soprano blending in harmony. He could almost smell the rich earth, the fresh air, the green of home.

He'd not crossed the Irish Sea in the ten years since he'd sailed for Oxford, filled with ambition, but this singing temptress not only aroused his masculine senses, but also gave him an aching yearning for just one evening of song, laughter, and family.

'Is she not all I said she would be?' Tanner nudged him on the shoulder, grinning like a besotted fool.

Flynn glanced back to her. 'She is exceptional.'

…*Never to love again…Eileen Aroon…*

Tanner also gaped at Rose O'Keefe, unmindful that his frank admiration showed so plainly on his face. Flynn hoped his own reaction appeared more circumspect, even though the heat of frank desire burned more hotly with each note she sang.

She seemed to represent all Flynn had left behind. Country. Family. Joy. Pleasure. It made him wish he'd answered his mother's monthly letters more than three times a year, wish he could wrap his arms around her and his father, roughhouse with his brothers, tease his sisters. He missed the laughter, the gaiety. How long had it been since he'd laughed out loud? Embraced a woman? Sung 'Eileen Aroon'?

Flynn's ambition had driven him away from his past. He'd been the marquess's secretary for six years, but the position was a mere stepping stone. Flynn aimed to rise higher, in gov-

ernment, perhaps, or—his grandest aspiration—to serve
royalty. Tanner supported his goals, taking Flynn with him
to the Congress of Vienna and to Brussels, where powerful
men learned Flynn's name and recognised his talent. The
marquess assured him the time would soon come for a
position suitable to Flynn's ambitions.

Which was why Flynn was shocked at his reaction to
Rose O'Keefe. She propelled him back, not forwards, and
her clear, poignant voice left him very aware of his
manhood. Carnal desire and thoughts of home made an odd
mixture indeed, and a thoroughly unwanted one. Still, at the
moment, he seemed helpless to do anything but let her voice
and vision carry him away.

Later he would plant his feet firmly back on the ground.
He must, because this woman who had temporarily aroused
his senses and unearthed a buried yearning for home was also
the woman he must procure for his employer.

Rose glanced down at the crowd watching her, so silent,
so appreciative! Her audience had grown larger with each performance, and she had even been mentioned favourably in the
Morning Chronicle. She loved hearing her voice rise above
the orchestra, resounding through the summer night air. The
magic of Vauxhall seemed to charm her as well, as if singing
an Irish air in this fanciful place were merely some lovely,
lovely dream.

Mr Hook himself watched from the side of the balcony,
smiling in approval. Rose tossed the elderly musical director
a smile of her own before turning her attention back to her
audience. She was so glad Miss Hart—Mrs Sloane, she
meant—had seen her perform before leaving for Italy on her
wedding trip. Rose's brief time living with Miss Hart had

taught her many lessons, but the one she treasured most was to be proud of who she was. And Rose was very proud this day. Proud enough to feel all her dreams were possible. She believed that some day she would be the celebrated singer all of London raved about. She would sing at Covent Garden, at Drury Lane or—dare she hope?—King's Theatre.

Rose scanned her audience again. Most of the faces lifted toward her in admiration were masculine ones. Since she'd been ten years old, men had been staring at her. At least now she knew how to hold her head up and be unafraid of their frank regard. She'd learned how to talk to gentlemen, how to encourage their interest—or, more importantly, how to discourage it.

Rose's eye was drawn to two gentlemen in the audience below her. They stood close to the balcony, so that the lamps illuminated them. One was very tall, at least as tall as Mr Sloane, but it was not he who drew her attention as much as the one who stood so still, gazing up at her. This man's rapt expression made her heart skip a beat.

She sang the last bar.

Truth is a fixed star. Eileen Aroon...

Applause thundered skywards as the music faded. Rose stole a peek at the gentleman who had captured her interest. He continued to stand, statue-still, his eyes still upon her. She felt her cheeks go warm.

She bowed and threw a kiss, eyes slanting towards her quiet admirer, before beginning her next song. As she continued through her performance, her gaze roved over all her admirers, but her eyes always returned to him.

Soon the orchestra began her final tune of the evening, 'The Warning'.

'List to me, ye gentle fair; Cupid oft in ambush lies...' Rose began softly, animating her facial expressions and her gestures. 'Of the urchin have a care, Lest he take you by surprise…'

She let her voice grow louder and had to force herself not to direct the song at the mysterious gentleman, who still had not moved. She could neither distinguish his features nor see what colour were his eyes, but she fancied them locked upon her, as she wished to lock hers upon him.

Flynn tried to shake off his reaction to Rose O'Keefe, tried to tell himself she was merely another of Tanner's many interests, but he could not make himself look away from her. Had his grandfather been standing next to him and not in his grave these last twenty years, he'd have said, ''Tis the fairies t'blame.'

Perhaps not fairies, but certainly a fancy of Flynn's own making. It seemed to Flynn that Rose O'Keefe was singing directly to him.

An illusion, certainly. There could be nothing of a personal nature between him and this woman he had not yet met. All he experienced while listening to her was illusion, as fanciful as believing in fairies. His role was clear. He must approach Miss O'Keefe's father and convince the man to allow him to plead Tanner's suit directly to the daughter. Perhaps he would also be required to deliver gifts, or to escort her to Tanner's choice of meeting place. He'd performed such errands in the past without a thought.

It was unfortunate that this rationality fled in the music of her voice, the allure of her person. She sang of Cupid, and Flynn understood why the ancients gave the little fellow an arrow. He felt pierced with exquisite pain, emotions scraping him raw.

With one more refrain, her song ended, and, as she curtsied deeply to the applause that erupted all around him, he roused himself from this ridiculous reverie.

'Bravo!' shouted Tanner, nearly shattering Flynn's eardrum. 'Bravo!'

A moment later she had vanished as if she'd been only a dream. Tanner clapped until the principle performer on the programme, Charles Dignum, began singing.

Flynn stared at Tanner, feeling suddenly as if this man who employed him were Cromwell come to seize his lands and take his woman, an even more ridiculous fancy. Flynn's mother was English, though she'd spent most of her life in Ireland. He had as much English blood in his veins as Irish. What's more, Flynn embraced his Englishness. England was where his life was bound. England was where his ambitions lay.

He shook his head, trying to rid himself of this madness. Rose O'Keefe had been a mere fleeting reminder of home, nothing more.

He pressed his fingers against his temple. He would soon recover his sanity and return to serving Tanner with dispassionate efficiency.

But as Tanner grabbed his arm and led him back to the supper box, the sweet voice of Rose O'Keefe lingered in Flynn's ear, an echoing reverie:

List to me, ye gentle fair; Cupid oft in ambush lies...

Chapter Two

Rose peeked through the curtain at the throng of men outside the gazebo, some carrying flowers, others waving their cards, all calling her name. There were so many, she could not see them all. If *he* was there, the man who had watched her with such rapture, she could not see him.

She turned to her father. 'There are more tonight.'

'Are there now, Mary Rose?' Her father placed his oboe in its case.

The woman at his side, a robust creature with ample décolletage—the woman who shared his bed—added, 'We have our pick, I'd say.'

Rose frowned. 'I do not wish to pick, Letty. I am content merely to sing.'

She had known nothing of Letty Dawes when Rose had surprised her father by appearing on his doorstep four months ago. The letters her father had sent to her at the school in Killyleagh made no mention of Letty, but then his letters had never been very informative.

Her father had been very surprised and perhaps somewhat disappointed to see that Rose had come to London with the ambition to sing. He had always told her to stay in Ireland, to remain at the school he'd sent her to after her mother died, the school that had kept her on as a music teacher. But teaching was not for her. Rose burned with the passion to perform, to sing.

Like her mother.

Rose's most treasured memories were of sitting by her mother's sickbed, listening to her tales of the London stages, the excitement of the music, the lights, the applause, the glory of her finest hour, performing at the King's Theatre. Even seven years of schooling and four more of teaching could not extinguish the fire that had been ignited so early within Rose to follow in her mother's footsteps. Rose had saved her pennies until she had enough to make the journey to London.

But any fantasies she'd had about a loving reunion with her father had been thoroughly dashed in those first few minutes of his surprised hugs and kisses. Letty Dawes had appeared from behind him, lamenting the sacrifices they would have to make to house and feed her, laughing at her desire to sing on the London stage. What theatre would employ an Irish country lass? Letty had said.

At first Rose thought her father had married again, but her father explained that entertainers lived by different rules from those she learned in school. He and Letty did not need marriage to share a bed. Then her father offered to pay Rose's way back to Ireland, and Letty exploded in rage at how much it would cost. A huge row broke out between them, and Rose walked out to escape hearing it, knowing she had caused it. She was glad now that she had walked out, because otherwise she would never have met Miss Hart.

It was Miss Hart who brought her to Vauxhall Gardens that glorious night when Rose had another tearful reunion with her father, and he introduced her to Mr Hook. Mr Hook let her sing one song and, seeing as she was not yet twenty-one, asked her father if he might hire her. So when it came time to leave Miss Hart's house, Rose returned to her father and Letty, who suddenly perceived her as a source of more income. To sing at Vauxhall, Rose would endure anything, even living with Letty.

It seemed she must also endure this frenzy of interest from gentlemen, all pressing her father to meet her. It was all part of the profession, her father told her.

He glanced out of the window. 'Perhaps there will be some titled gentlemen among these fellows. That is who you must court if you wish to move ahead.'

'Yes, indeed,' Letty added, putting an arm around Rose's shoulders as if in affection. 'A titled gentleman would be grand. There is no telling how much you might make, Rose. Why, some men even buy houses for their...'

Rose wrenched away. She knew much more about what men expected of women who performed on stage than she had when she first arrived in London. But what of love? Of romance? That was what Miss Hart had found with her Mr Sloane. That was what Rose coveted for herself.

'What men are expecting in exchange for those houses, I have no wish to give,' she told Letty.

Letty broke into shrill laughter. 'Give? If you don't give it, men will just take it anyway. Better to profit, I always say.'

Her father walked up to her and tweaked her chin. 'Never fear, Mary Rose.' He spoke gently. 'Your papa will make certain you are set up like a fine lady. I wouldn't let my little girl go with some penniless rogue, now would I?'

Rose pressed her hand against her throat. All part of the profession, her father had told her.

He hurried away, and she heard him shout, 'Give me your cards, gentlemen…' before the door closed behind him.

Letty shook a finger at her. 'You obey your father. He has your best interests at heart.'

To escape having to talk to her further, Rose peered through the curtain. The men outside flocking around her father appeared spectre-like in the dim light, like a flock of bats in a moonlit sky. She shivered. She loved her newfound singing success. After Vauxhall's season was over, she was certain she could find more employment. She could support herself. She could afford to wait for love to find her.

Rose gripped the curtain in determined fingers. Until she discovered for herself the sort of true love she'd witnessed at Miss Hart's, she must merely sing her songs and fend off all other plans her father and Letty had for her.

As she stared through the gap in the curtain, she wondered if one of the shadowy figures would materialise into the man who'd drawn her attention when she'd performed. Would he be the one? she wondered. The one who might love her? But as her father collected the cards and gifts, she didn't see anyone who could be *him.*

Letty walked up behind her and opened the curtain wider. 'Your father is a smart man to put them off. They'll be willing to pay more if they must wait to win you.' She paused as if wheels turned slowly in her head. 'But not too long. Too much waiting and they will lose interest.'

Her father's arms were filled with small packages and bouquets of flowers. One hand was stuffed with cards. He turned to come back in, but another man stepped forward. Rose could not make out the man distinctly in the dim light, but he was dressed in a dark coat and seemed of similar size to her man in the audience.

She had a melting feeling, like when she'd watched Miss Hart with her Mr Sloane.

Her father and the shadowy gentleman spoke a few words before the man bowed and walked away, and her father re-entered the gazebo.

He dropped the heaps of fragrant flowers and small, ribbon-wrapped packages on to a nearby table and turned to Rose. 'Mary Rose, pull this last card from my hand.'

She pulled the card sticking out from the stack and read, 'The Marquess of Tannerton.'

He let the other cards cascade on to the table. 'I told the fellow he could call tomorrow at four o'clock.'

Letty's eyes lit up. 'That was the Marquess?'

'I'm not sure of it.' Her father smiled sheepishly. 'I was half-stunned, to be sure. Didn't heed what the fellow said, but I heard "marquess" and told the man he could call.' He gave Rose a patient look. 'You must see a marquess, Mary Rose.'

It should hearten her that the marquess might be the man who so captivated her, but somehow it did not. Whatever could exist between a marquess and a songstress would not be love.

Rose sighed. She would just have to discourage this man. She was confident she'd learned enough about gentlemen to fend off unwanted attention. Her priority at the moment was to finish out her summer singing at Vauxhall, and to have Mr Hook put her forth with the highest recommendations to others who might hire her. Rose wanted to keep singing, perhaps on a proper stage this time, part of a real theatre. She wanted to rise some day to the principal roles, to have her name always in the newspapers, her image on playbills, theatre managers clamouring for her to sing for them.

In the meantime, she wanted coin enough to pay her keep

so Letty would not complain that her father allowed her to stay. Until she found where she truly belonged—or with whom—she would not settle for less. She would not engage her heart to a marquess who wanted her for mere amusement. Even if he was handsome. Even if her blood stirred when he looked upon her.

She merely would let her father believe otherwise.

'I will receive the marquess, Papa,' she said.

Flynn stepped out of the hackney coach and walked the short distance up Langley Street to the lodgings where O'Keefe had directed him, a plain enough building from the outside. He took a deep breath and nodded, telling himself again that the previous night's infatuation with a Vauxhall singer had been due to too much arrack. He was clear headed now.

Rose O'Keefe, like Tanner's many other conquests, would be a woman of business, savvy enough to work out that making herself into a hard-won prize would drive up the price. It was Flynn's job to see that Tanner did not pay one pence more than she was worth—and she ought to be worth no more than the others had cost the marquess.

Flynn stared at the door of the building and tugged at his cuffs, straightening his coat. Appearances were always important in negotiations, he told himself. He cleared his throat and opened the door, stepping into a dark hall.

Letting his eyes adjust to the dim light, he waited a moment before ascending the wooden staircase. One flight up, he turned and knocked upon a plain wooden door. As its knob turned and the door began to open, his chest tightened, exactly as if he had run from Mayfair to Covent Garden.

But the sensation passed when Mr O'Keefe admitted him

into a small parlor with threadbare furniture, adorned by luxurious bouquets of flowers on almost every surface. Flynn congratulated himself for forgoing a bouquet of rare blooms. He patted the inside pocket of his coat that held Tanner's offering.

'Good day to you, sir.' Mr O'Keefe bowed repeatedly. 'Good of you to call.'

'How do you do, sir.' A garishly dressed woman curtsied deeply.

Mr O'Keefe took his hat and gloves and gestured to the woman. 'This is Rose's very dear friend and mine, Miss Dawes.'

She curtsied again.

Their deference was extreme. It dawned on him that they thought he was Tanner. 'I did not give you my name last night. I am Mr Flynn, the Marquess of Tannerton's secretary—'

Mr O'Keefe suddenly relaxed. 'Yes, yes,' he said in an almost normal voice. He thrust his hand out to Flynn. 'Good of you to come.'

Flynn accepted the handshake. 'It was good of you to allow me to call.'

O'Keefe gestured to the sofa. Flynn indicated that Mr O'Keefe must sit as well, and the older man, thin as a reed and a good head shorter than Flynn, lowered himself into an adjacent chair.

'I come on the marquess's behalf,' Flynn began. 'The marquess has had the pleasure of hearing your daughter's lovely voice. He is most anxious to meet her.'

Mr O'Keefe nodded, listening intently.

Flynn continued, 'I should like to convey the marquess's high regard to Miss O'Keefe directly, if that is possible.'

'I'll fetch her,' Miss Dawes piped up. 'I have no idea why she has not showed herself.'

'I would be grateful.' Flynn watched her bustle through an interior door.

'Rose!' he heard Miss Dawes say sharply.

Flynn frowned.

'She'll come,' Mr O'Keefe said in a reassuring tone.

Flynn did not wish to negotiate with the father. Experience had taught him that it was preferable to deal with the woman herself.

'Here she is,' chirped Miss Dawes from the doorway. She quickly stepped aside.

Rose O'Keefe entered the room, so graceful she seemed to glide above the floor. Up close, with daylight illuminating the room, her beauty robbed his lungs of air. Her face, so fair and fine, was framed by raven-black tendrils, her skin translucent. But it was her eyes that captured him and aroused him again. They were as green as the rolling hills of County Down.

He stood.

Before he could speak, she said, 'You are?'

Her father rose from his chair and walked over to her. 'Mary Rose, Mr Flynn is secretary to the Marquess of Tannerton.'

Her glorious green eyes widened slightly.

Flynn bowed. 'Miss O'Keefe.'

She seemed to recover from any surprise, saying coolly, 'You were wanting to speak to me, sir?'

Flynn heard the lilt of Ireland in her speech, not quite as carefully eradicated as his own. He began, 'I come on behalf of the marquess—'

'I see,' she interrupted. 'What is it a marquess wants of me that he cannot be asking himself?'

Flynn blinked.

'Mary Rose!' her father pleaded. 'Mind your tongue.'

'Obey your father!' Miss Dawes scolded.

Miss O'Keefe darted Miss Dawes a defiant glance. This was going badly, Flynn thought. It was beginning to seem as if her father and this Dawes woman were forcing her into this. Tanner never desired a woman be compelled to share his bed. Flynn needed to deal directly with Miss O'Keefe. He must be assured she would be a willing partner.

And, at the moment, Miss O'Keefe looked anything but willing.

'I will speak with Miss O'Keefe alone, sir,' he said in a smooth voice.

Mr O'Keefe looked uncertain.

Miss Dawes wagged her finger towards the daughter. 'Talk to him, Rose. Be a good girl.' Then she hustled the father out of the room.

Flynn turned back to Miss O'Keefe. Her green eyes were strained.

'I would not distress you, miss,' he said softly.

She waved a graceful hand in the air. 'It is of no consequence.'

He paused, composing his next words.

She spoke first. 'You came for a reason, Mr Flynn?' Her voice was high, and tiny lines appeared at the corners of her perfectly sculpted lips.

His brows knitted. This girl seemed not at all eager to hear an offer. 'Indeed. About Lord Tannerton.'

'Would you care to sit, sir?' she asked with forced politeness.

He inclined his head, waiting for her to sit opposite him before he lowered himself into the seat.

'You were saying, Mr Flynn?'

He began again, 'I was saying, the marquess has heard you sing—'

'And you, Mr Flynn? Have you heard me sing?' She seemed bent on interrupting him.

'Yes, Miss O'Keefe, I have had the pleasure.'

A genuine smile fleetingly appeared. 'Were you liking my singing?' She dipped her head and he noticed that her lashes were long and luxurious.

'Very much,' he said, regaining his wits.

She folded her hands in her lap. 'Flynn…it is an Irish name. Where are you from, Mr Flynn?'

Flynn did not usually lose such total control over a conversation. It disturbed him, nearly as much as perceiving her reluctance disturbed him. Nearly as much as her eyes disturbed him.

'Where am I from?' he repeated.

'Yes, where in Ireland are you from?'

He could not remember the last time he'd been asked this. 'County Down, near Ballynahinch.'

Her bewitching eyes sparkled. 'I attended school in Killyleagh.'

'So did my sister.' Those words slipped out.

'Oh!' She turned thoughtful for a moment. 'Could she be Siobhan Flynn, by any chance? There was a Siobhan Flynn two years ahead of me.'

Siobhan's name propelled him back to Ballynahinch. Little Siobhan. She'd been eleven when he'd last seen her. How old was she now? Twenty-one?

It meant Miss O'Keefe was naught but nineteen. No wonder her papa hovered near.

'She may have been the same,' he said.

Miss O'Keefe's eyes danced with excitement. 'How does she fare? I rarely heard news of any of the girls after they left.'

Flynn realised he had barely heeded news of Siobhan in his mother's letters. 'She is married and has two sons.'

Miss O'Keefe sighed. 'How nice for her!'

Flynn began again. 'About the marquess—'

'Oh, yes, the *marquess*.' Her false tone returned. 'He sent you. You did not come to speak with me about home.'

Home. Home. It repeated in his ears.

'The marquess is anxious to make your acquaintance, Miss O'Keefe. He is prepared to become your friend.'

'My friend?' She glanced away. 'He knows so much after listening to a few songs?'

He opened his mouth to respond with lavish compliments.

She spoke first. 'Are your friendships so easily made, Mr Flynn?'

'My friendships?' He was repeating again. He disliked that she distracted him from his intent, making him think instead of friends, long-ago boys who explored crumbling castle ruins with him or fished in crystalline streams.

He forced himself to meet her gaze directly. 'I assure you, Miss O'Keefe, the marquess chooses his friends judiciously, and none would complain about the connection.'

She did not waver. 'And is he usually sending you to inform his new friends of their good fortune?'

Flynn wrinkled his brow. She did not seem pleased at all at Tanner's interest. Why? Her father and that other female certainly relished the potential connection.

He must convince her she would do well under Tanner's protection. She would certainly have more freedom than she appeared to have in her father's house, with the shrill Miss Dawes bullying her.

But the image that rose in his mind was not of her with Tanner, but of her standing on a green hillside, wind billowing through her skirts and hair.

He mentally shook himself. Somehow he maintained his direct gaze. 'The marquess involves me if he feels it would best please the lady to do so.' He reached into his coat pocket. 'To show his good intentions, the marquess wishes to bestow upon you a small gift.'

Flynn pulled out a velvet box. She glanced in alarm at the door behind which her father and Miss Dawes were certainly eavesdropping. She stilled his hand. 'No gifts,' she whispered, slanting her eyes towards the door again. 'Please.'

Flynn's hand paused in mid-air, her touch branding his skin. Silently he nodded, slipping the box back in his pocket.

'A gift would be very nice indeed,' she said, raising her voice.

'Then you shall have one very soon,' he said.

Rose returned her hand to her lap, her breath coming rapidly. Her hand still tingled from touching him, and all her insides felt like melted candle wax.

He had played along with her wish not to have her father or Letty hear of a gift. If he had not, Letty would be badgering her for days to get her hands on a gift from a marquess. And to keep peace, her father would implore her to give in. The other gifts gentlemen left for her—gifts that ought to have been returned—made their way into Letty's possession or were sold to buy some other trinket she desired.

Rose tried to show Mr Flynn her gratitude with a look, but had to avert her gaze from the intensity of his startling blue eyes.

When Letty had come to fetch her, saying the marquess's secretary had arrived, Rose had been relieved she would not have to refuse a marquess to his face, especially if he were indeed the man who'd so captivated her. But the man who captivated her was his secretary and was Irish, and, even more wonderful, he'd become a momentary ally.

He was very handsome up close, with his commanding gaze. His hair and brows were nearly as dark as her own. She loved the firmness of his jaw and the decisive set to his sinfully sensuous mouth. What would it be like to touch her lips to his?

Rose mentally shook herself. She was thinking like a romantic, making this into a story like the novels she enjoyed reading, the ones that wove wonderful stories of love. This man had not come to court her, but to procure her for his employer.

Even so, his blue eyes continued to enslave her.

'The marquess is a good man, Miss O'Keefe,' he said.

She peered back at him. 'Mr Flynn, why do you tie this up in pretty words? Do you not mean the marquess is wishing me to be his mistress? Is that not what this is about? Is that not the kind of "friend" he wishes me to be?'

A muscle flexed in Mr Flynn's jaw, but his gaze held. 'To be such a friend of this man has many advantages. He can assist you. Protect you.'

Rose's gaze slipped back to the door that hid her father and Letty. They both certainly wanted her to accept the marquess's protection. And his money.

He looked to the door, as well. 'Will you need protection, Miss O'Keefe?' His voice was soft and low. And concerned.

She glanced back in surprise and gave a light laugh. 'I shall experience no difficulties, I assure you.'

Letty was as unpleasant as a woman could be, and her father was completely under her thumb, but Rose did not feel they yielded that much authority over her. She liked living with her father, making up a little for all the years that had separated them.

'You could allow the marquess to help you,' he said.

She reached over to grasp his hand in reassurance but stopped herself midway. 'I'll be needing no help.' She added, 'All I want is to sing…'

He seized on those words. 'Lord Tannerton could help you—'

She put up her hand, regretting she had spoken. 'I require no help. Do not be worrying yourself over me.'

Their eyes connected, and it felt like butterflies took possession of her insides.

'Thank the marquess for me,' she said in a loud voice. 'It was good of you to come.' She stood and walked towards the door.

It took a moment for him to follow her. 'I do not understand you, Miss O'Keefe,' he said, his voice no more than an urgent whisper. 'Why do you hesitate?'

She handed him his hat and gloves. 'Good day to you, Mr Flynn.' She opened the door.

He started to walk through it, but turned and grasped her hand in his. 'Welcome or not, Miss O'Keefe, you do have a friend.'

He released her and swiftly took his leave. Rose brushed her hand against her cheek, wishing the friend were not the marquess but Mr Flynn himself.

Chapter Three

Flynn paused a moment when he reached the street, puzzled by this experience. The times he'd risked huge amounts of Tanner's wealth on some tenuous business matter, he'd been in better control. Nothing had gone as he'd expected. Worse, his senses were still awhirl. Merely looking at the girl had been enough to throw his rationality out of the window.

With no idea what to tell Tanner, he straightened his hat and started walking in the direction of Covent Garden to find a hack.

'Mr Flynn!' he heard behind him.

Turning, he saw Mr O'Keefe running toward him. Flynn stopped.

The older man caught up to him, breathing hard. 'Letty said—I mean—I wanted a word with you.'

Flynn merely waited.

'Tell…tell the marquess how flattered we are—my daughter is, I mean—at his kind interest.'

'I will tell him.' Although, if Flynn did tell Tanner this, he'd be lying. The daughter did not seem flattered in the least.

Mr O'Keefe's mouth twisted into an apologetic smile.

'My Rose is a sensible girl,' he said, a fond look appearing in his eye. 'She'll just need some persuading.'

Flynn regarded this man who looked as if a strong wind might blow him away. Flynn could not see him persuading his daughter about anything. The unpleasant Miss Dawes, however, was another matter.

'I must leave.' Flynn turned away.

'Do try again, sir,' Mr O'Keefe cried as Flynn walked away.

Flynn looked over his shoulder. 'I shall tell the marquess you said so.'

Mr O'Keefe nodded vigorously, and Flynn hurried on his way to a row of waiting hackney carriages.

He soon reached Tanner's Audley Street town house, returning to the familiar opulence, the order, the civility.

The footman who opened the door said, 'His lordship wishes you to attend him in the game room straight away.'

Not even a moment to collect himself, nor to plan an explanation of his incredible meeting with Miss O'Keefe.

'Thank you, Smythe.' Flynn handed the man his hat and gloves and made his way to the game room.

When he entered, Tanner was leaning over the billiard table, lining up a shot. Flynn stood in the doorway until the ball cracked into another one, sending it rolling across the green baize and landing successfully in the pocket.

'Flynn!' Tanner waved him in. 'Come, tell me all about it. I am most anxious. Could think of nothing else since you left.'

Tanner settled himself in one of the leather chairs by the window and gestured for Flynn to pour them some claret from the decanter on the side table.

'Well, did you see her?' Tanner asked as Flynn handed him a glass of claret. 'Of course you did or you'd have been back sooner. What did she say? Did she like the gift? What the devil did you purchase for her?'

Flynn poured wine for himself, but did not sit. 'I purchased a matched set of gold bracelets.'

'And?' Tanner grinned eagerly.

Flynn took a sip before speaking. 'She refused the gift.'

Tanner half-rose from his seat. 'Refused?'

'I fear so, my lord,' he admitted.

Tanner waved his hand dismissively. 'It was the wrong gift, then, but I am sure you assured her there would be more gifts. What of a meeting?'

Flynn averted his eyes.

The marquess sank back in the chair. 'Do not tell me she refused to meet me?'

'She did not refuse exactly, but neither did she agree.' Flynn's powers of diplomacy had escaped him with Miss O'Keefe, but perhaps they would hold him in better stead with Tanner.

Tanner raised his brows. 'What the devil happened then? What did you talk about?'

Of home. Of Ireland. But Flynn was not about to provide this as an answer. 'I explained the advantages of your… friendship, and she listened.'

'That is all?' The marquess's forehead wrinkled in confusion.

'That is all.'

Tanner slowly sipped his wine, finishing it, while Flynn could not even put a glass to his lips.

He placed his still-full glass on the table and reached for the decanter. 'More, sir?'

Tanner shook his head, still silent.

All of a sudden Tanner burst into a wide grin and thrust out his glass. 'She is playing a deep game, is all. Gold bracelets? You were too cheap, man. The girl wants more and she knows she can get it!' He laughed. 'You must deliver a more valuable gift.'

Flynn refilled Tanner's wine glass, not wanting to explain that giving Miss O'Keefe a gift was not so simple a task.

'Give her emeralds next time, to set off her eyes. An emerald ring!' Tanner's own brown eyes sparkled. 'What the devil, offer her patronage as well—an allowance. A generous one. Show her I am willing to pay her price.'

As a business move, Flynn typically would have advised against this. The next offer in a negotiation ought not to be so high. But in Rose O'Keefe's situation, he was more than willing to try to get her away from the bullying Miss Dawes.

Flynn nodded. His heart raced at the prospect of seeing her again, even though to see her was merely a function of his duty to Tanner. Still, he could not erase from his memory the sensuous grace of her figure, the irresistible tint of her lips, the eyes that beckoned him home.

He took his leave from Tanner. There was much to be done to carry out the next phase of the marquess's plan.

The very next night Flynn stood below the gazebo's balcony at Vauxhall Gardens, again listening to the crystalline sound of Rose O'Keefe's voice filling the evening with song. He'd secured a private box and supper for Miss O'Keefe, leaving a message to her father to escort her to the box when the orchestra broke and Signor Rivolta, the man who played six or eight instruments at once, performed. He trusted her father would approve of the meeting.

She wore the wine-red gown again, the colour of passionate nights, and her fair skin glowed against its richness. Flynn convinced himself he merely admired her beauty, the way he might appreciate the beauty of a flower or a painting or how the house in Ballynahinch shone golden in the light of the setting sun.

He watched until she made her final curtsy and disappeared into the dark recesses of the balcony. He then made his way to the supper box to ensure all was as he'd planned— a supper of light delicacies, nothing too fancy, but all very tasteful. Assured everything was prepared and ready, he spent the rest of the time pacing, his breath catching whenever the music ceased, and easing when it resumed again.

Finally the orchestra was silent. Flynn continued pacing until he heard the O'Keefes approach. Unfortunately, it was Miss Dawes's piercing voice that gave him warning. He ought to have expected her.

'Behave yourself, miss. I'll not have you ruining this for your father—' The woman's speech cut off when she saw Flynn. 'Mr Flynn!' She switched to a syrupy tone.

'Good evening,' Flynn said to them all, but to the one who wore a hooded cape that nearly obscured her face, his voice turned husky. 'Miss O'Keefe.'

She nodded. 'Mr Flynn.'

'This is so very kind of you, sir.' Mr O'Keefe tiptoed into the box and hesitated before accepting Flynn's outstretched hand. O'Keefe's hand was bony, but his handshake warm.

'So kind,' O'Keefe murmured. He turned to his daughter. 'Is that not so, Mary Rose?'

She merely glanced at her father before turning to Flynn. 'Is the marquess here?'

Both Mr O'Keefe and Miss Dawes wore hopeful expressions, but Miss O'Keefe seemed anything but eager.

'He regrets not being at liberty to come,' Flynn prevaricated. He directed them to the table. 'But please sit and have some supper.'

Mr O'Keefe and Miss Dawes hurried to the round table set with porcelain china, crystal glassware and silver cutlery. Flynn pulled out the chair for Miss O'Keefe, and she glanced into his eyes as she sat down. He signalled the footman to bring another chair and place setting, after which the food was served: tender capons and a rich assortment of cheeses and fruit. The footman uncorked a bottle of champagne, pouring it into all four glasses.

'Oooh, bubbles!' exclaimed Miss Dawes in her coarse voice. 'I love the bubbly wine.'

Rose picked up her glass and took a sip. She had tasted champagne before at Miss Hart's, so its fizzy taste was not a surprise.

She watched Letty dig into the prettily displayed food as if she had not consumed a large dinner a few hours before. Mr Flynn's food was fine, Rose thought, nibbling more delicately. The cheese tasted good with the strawberries and cherries.

Mr Flynn sat himself next to her and she discovered that she was very aware of each small movement he made. In a way she was glad she could not see his eyes. It was hard to be thinking when she could see his eyes.

Signor Rivolta's lively music drifted over to their ears, his gay tune seeming out of place in the tension-filled supper box.

'When is the marquess going to make his offer for our Rose?' Letty bluntly asked.

Rose stilled, hating that Flynn would be associating someone so ill mannered with her.

Flynn paused, just one beat, before directing his answer to her father. 'To speak of an offer is premature, sir, but I should like to discuss with Miss O'Keefe a possible meeting.'

'Oh, there will be an offer all right,' Letty broke in, waving her fork at Rose. 'Look at her! What man could resist our lovely Rose?'

She reached over and not so gently patted Rose on the cheek. It was all Rose could do not to flinch.

'I am most interested in my daughter's welfare,' her father added in an earnest voice. 'This must be worth her while.'

Rose disliked being discussed like this, as if she were goods to barter.

Mr Flynn put down his fork. 'I am instructed to tell you, Mr O'Keefe, that the marquess insists I speak with the lady herself in such matters. He must be assured his interest suits her before he proceeds in the negotiation. I am sure you understand.'

Her father's brows knitted. 'But I must also agree to any arrangements. She is still my responsibility, sir.'

'She knows what is expected of her,' added Letty.

Rose knew exactly what Letty expected. Letty expected a great deal of money to come into her pocket by way of this marquess. She glanced at her father. His motives were more unselfish, but still distasteful.

'We will speak later,' Flynn said to her father.

Rose rather liked the way Flynn simply passed over Letty, as if she had no say in the matter, which she certainly did not.

'She's still young, Mr Flynn,' her father added, sounding genuinely worried.

Flynn turned to Rose with a question in his eyes, but Rose had no idea what he was asking. 'I will see no harm comes to her.' His gaze changed into something that made her feel like fanning herself.

She glanced down at her food. Imagine that a mere look from a man could make her feel like that.

Signor Rivolta's music ended and the faint sound of applause could be heard. Soon the orchestra would play again.

'I must get back.' Mr O'Keefe rose.

Flynn stood as well. 'Miss Dawes will wish to go with you, I am certain.' He walked over to help Letty from her chair, giving her no oppportunity to argue. 'I will safely deliver Miss O'Keefe to you before the night is done.'

Mr Flynn escorted them both out of the box, then returned to the table, sitting opposite her this time.

Rose gazed at him with admiration. 'You do have the silver tongue, do you not, Mr Flynn? I believe Letty thought she wanted to go with Papa.'

He frowned. 'Only one of many talents,' he said absently.

He'd rattled her again, making her wonder what had suddenly made him frown. She picked up a strawberry and bit into it, slowly licking its juice from her lips.

Mr Flynn's eyes darkened and he looked even more disturbed.

Rose paused. Could it be she had captured Mr Flynn's interest? That idea made her giddy.

She took another sip of champagne and lowered her eyes to gaze at him through her long lashes. He reached over to retrieve his glass, downing the entire contents.

Rose felt light headed.

He gave her an intent look. 'We must talk, Miss O'Keefe.'

But she was not finished flirting with him. She leaned forward, knowing it afforded him a better glimpse of the low neckline of her gown. 'Will you not call me Rose?'

His eyes darkened again. 'Rose,' he repeated in a low voice that resonated deep inside her.

Their heads were close together, his eyes looking as deep

a blue as the Irish Sea. The air crackled between them and he leaned closer.

A reveller, one who no doubt had been drinking heavily, careened into the supper box, nearly knocking into the table. The footman quickly appeared and escorted him out, but it was enough to break the moment between them.

He frowned. 'I apologise for that.'

She hoped he meant the drunken man. 'You could not help it.'

He gazed at her in that stirring way again. 'I could not help it.' He set his jaw. 'About the marquess—'

But Rose could not bear losing this new, intoxicating connection between them. She daringly put her hand upon his arm. 'Let us not speak of the marquess. Let us simply enjoy this beautiful night.'

He stared at her hand for a moment. Slowly he raised his head. 'Your father—'

'I will tell my father that I put you off, but that you will be back.' She squeezed his arm. 'What say you? Can we walk through the gardens? I have seen so little of Vauxhall. I have been confined to the gazebo, really.'

He stared at her, then released a long breath. 'Very well.'

With a leaping heart, she finished the rest of her champagne. She grasped his hand in hers and led him out of the supper box. He offered his arm. 'Hold on to me, Rose. I must keep you safe.'

It was a fair warning. Vauxhall could be a dangerous place for a woman alone, but that did not keep Rose from enjoying the feel of his muscle beneath his sleeve.

They joined the throngs of people enjoying the clear, warm night. The music of the orchestra filled the garden, the sound ebbing and flowing on the summer breeze. Night had fallen and the lamps glowed like bright stars. Flynn escorted her through the arches painted to look like the Ruins of Palmyra. He showed her the Pavilion with its allegorical paintings. They strolled down the Colonnade past the fountain sparkling in the lamplight. What had seemed false to him two nights ago now seemed magical. He was under her spell again, he had to admit, but that last exchange with her father gave him pause. Her father treated her as if she'd just come out of a schoolroom.

As if she were an innocent.

If she were an innocent, negotiations were at an end. Even if Tanner would accept a girl who'd been un-touched—and he would not—Flynn could never involve himself in such an arrangement. It was almost a relief. An end to this madness.

They paused by the fountain, and she dipped her fingers into the cool water, a gesture so sensuous it belied his earlier thought.

'Rose! Rose!' A young woman ran towards her, bosoms about to burst from a revealing neckline, flaming red hair about to tumble from a decorative hat. A rather mature gen-tleman tried to keep pace with her. 'Rose, it is you!' The two women embraced. 'I've been here every night you've sung. I thought I'd never talk to you.'

'Katy.' Rose pressed her cheek against her friend's. 'I have missed you so much.'

This Katy broke away to eye Flynn up and down, making him feel like a sweetmeat in a confectioner's shop. 'And who is this?'

'This is Mr Flynn, Katy.' Rose turned to him. 'My dear friend, Katy Green.'

Flynn somehow managed to keep the shock from his face.

Her friend could only be described as a—a doxy. No innocent would greet a woman like Katy Green with such undisguised affection.

He bowed. 'I am charmed, Miss Green.'

The young woman gave a throaty chortle and turned to Rose. 'Where did you find this one? He's quality, I'd wager a guinea on it.'

'Oh, Mr Flynn is a very important man.' Miss O'Keefe slanted an amused look at him. 'But, it is not what you are thinking, Katy.'

'Isn't it?' The doxy's expression was sceptical. 'What a shame…'

As the two young women talked of even more acquaintances, Flynn was left standing with the older gentleman.

He recognised the somewhat ramshackle fellow who was said to be one step from River Tick. 'Good evening, Sir Reginald.'

The man was still catching his breath. 'Flynn, isn't it? In Tannerton's employ, am I right?'

'You are, sir.'

Sir Reginald poked him in the ribs. 'Doing very well for yourself, ain't you, my boy? Rose is a looker.'

Flynn did not reply. He was still in the throes of confusion. Rose O'Keefe could not be an innocent. Sir Reginald, a man on the fringe of society, knew her. A doxy knew her. She must be of their world. It made sense—the way she moved, the expression in her eyes, the timbre of her voice. That sort of sensuality made for arousing a man's needs, enough to bewitch him, that was for certain. But she also brought him an aching yearning for the green hills of Ireland, the warmth of family, and the pure, unspoiled days of his boyhood in Ballynahinch. How did he explain that?

Illusion, he told himself. Again. In any event, none of this should matter to him. Rose O'Keefe could be nothing to him.

'I am working for Tannerton,' he explained to Sir Reginald.

'Aha!' The man wagged his brows knowingly, but this only disturbed Flynn more, as if by his innuendo the man were crushing the petals of a flower. A rose.

A bell sounded, announcing the illuminations were about to begin.

'Come,' cried the red-haired Katy. 'We must get a good spot!' She seized Sir Reginald's arm and pulled him through the crowd.

Flynn held back until Katy and Sir Reginald disappeared. He wanted Rose to himself, wanted the illusion to return, even if she was not supposed to mean anything to him.

But he was thinking only of himself. He turned to Rose. 'Do you wish us to find your friend?'

She shook her head and gripped his arm again. Together they walked to the illuminations. People jostled and pushed them, all trying to find the perfect spot to see the fireworks. It seemed natural for Flynn to put his arm around her and hold her close, so that she would not become separated from him.

The whoosh of a rocket signalled the first of the bursts of light and colour, and the explosions sounded like several muskets firing at once.

'Oh!' Rose gasped as the sky lit up with hundreds of shooting stars.

She turned her smiling face towards him, the hood of her cape falling away. Their gazes caught. The illuminations reflected in her eyes, and he was truly bewitched, lost, drowning in the sparkling lights. He bent his head and she lifted hers so that there could be no more than an inch separating their lips. Flynn wanted, ached, to close the distance, to feel the soft press of her lips against his, to taste her, to hold her flush against him. His body demanded more of her, all of her.

But he forced himself to release her, to break the contact with her eyes.

What had he been thinking? This was Tanner's woman, as sure as if Tanner had given her his name. What sort of suicide was it for Flynn to even gaze at her as he had done?

Tanner might appear affable, but he was a formidable adversary if crossed. If Flynn, a mere secretary, a mere employee, took liberties with a woman Tanner had selected for himself, not only his position would be lost, but his entire future.

Her smile disappeared and she turned her head to watch the pyrotechnic display. Flynn kept his arm wrapped around her. Indeed, he could not bring himself to move it. She felt soft and warm against him, and he wanted to hold her through eternity.

The illuminations, however, came to an end.

'I must return you.' He slipped his arm from her back as the crowd dispersed, and glimpsed her friend strutting away, Sir Reginald in tow.

Rose—Miss O'Keefe, he should call her—nodded, taking his arm in a more demure fashion. Still, he could not hurry to the orchestra's gazebo where he must leave her. He did not wish to let her go.

She stopped when they reached the door. 'Thank you, Flynn, for the lovely tour of the park and the illuminations. I am most grateful to you.'

No, he could not release her yet. It was too soon.

Flynn remembered he had not given her the emerald ring still in his coat pocket. He had not spoken to her of Tanner's willingness to be a generous patron. He had done nothing that his employer had sent him to do.

But even Tanner's disappointment in him could not compel him to rectify this lapse in efficiency at the present moment.

'Miss O'Keefe, may I call upon you tomorrow?' Tomorrow he would do his duty, what his employer required of him.

She stared into his eyes, not answering right away. She inhaled sharply as if her decision had been a sudden one. 'Not at my lodgings. Take me for a drive in the park.'

He nodded. 'Two o'clock?' Neither of them belonged in the park during the fashionable hour when the highest rung of society took over. Two o'clock should be early enough.

'Two o'clock,' she repeated.

'There she is!' a man's voice shouted, and other voices joined him.

A throng of men started towards them. Flynn quickly rapped loudly on the door. It opened immediately, and she disappeared inside.

Flynn faced the group of men, unreasonably angry at their pursuit, unreasonably wanting to claim her for himself. Had he been alone that first night, not with Tanner, he might have been among men such as these. 'She is spoken for, gentlemen. Abandon your pursuit.'

There were grumbles and arguments, but they all eventually dispersed. Except one man, elegantly attired in a coat that could only have been made by Weston. Flynn recognised him as the Earl of Greythorne.

'You are Tannerton's man, are you not?' the earl asked.

'I am,' Flynn responded. He started toward the Grand Walk.

The earl fell in step with him. 'And is the alluring Rose O'Keefe claimed by Lord Tannerton?'

'She is.'

Flynn tried to remember what he knew of the gentleman, besides the fact that Tanner thought him a 'damned prig.' Greythorne's estate was in Kent, but he possessed properties in Sussex and somewhere up north as well. He frequented the *ton* entertainments. Belonged to White's. Still, there was something he was forgetting. Some rumour about the man.

Greythorne chuckled. 'A pity. I fancy her myself.' His arm swept the area. 'As do others. Tannerton may be in for a serious contest.'

Greythorne possessed enough wealth to pose a threat. If he offered a great deal of money to put Rose under his protection, Flynn had no doubt Miss Dawes would bully O'Keefe into accepting. She'd have no qualms about selling Rose to the highest bidder.

Flynn regarded the man. 'I am certain, as a gentleman, you would not covet what another man has claimed as his.'

Greythorne's slippery smile remained. 'Her father does not seem to agree with your perception. He seemed to indicate the game was still in progress.'

It was as if dark clouds suddenly gathered. 'The deal is all but made,' Flynn said.

Greythorne continued walking. 'I would be the last man to encroach,' he assured Flynn. 'But if the deal is not made, I'm prepared to play my hand.'

Chapter Four

The next day was as sunny as any summer day could be in London as Flynn navigated the streets of Covent Garden on the way to Rose's lodgings. Tanner had wholeheartedly endorsed this escapade, especially after hearing of Greythorne's interest.

'Something about that fellow,' Tanner had said. 'I have always detested the man. Damned natty, for one thing. Never a speck of dirt, or a wrinkle in his coat. Every hair in place. Devilish odd.' Tanner had shuddered. 'Something else, though. I shall endeavour to discover what it is.'

Tanner had insisted Flynn take his curricle and the matched chestnuts, which had cost him a fortune at Tattersalls.

Flynn brought the curricle to a halt in front of Rose's building. He tossed a coin to a boy passing by, asking the lad to hold the horses. As he climbed the stairs to knock upon Rose's door, his excitement grew, an excitement he had no right to feel.

The door opened and there she stood, green paisley shawl draped over the same dress she'd worn when he last visited these rooms, hat and gloves already on. If she could appear this beautiful in a plain dress, think of how she would look in all the finery Tanner could buy her.

He frowned as she turned to close the door. He must keep Tanner in mind. Wrest control over this tendency to be bewitched.

But his resolve frayed as his hands spanned her waist to lift her into the curricle. And frayed more when she smiled down at him.

He climbed up next to her, and the boy handed him the ribbons. 'Hyde Park, is that correct?' he asked her.

'It does not have to be Hyde Park,' she replied in a breathless voice.

'Where then?'

The sun rendered her skin translucent, and he had the urge to pull off his gloves and touch her with the tip of his finger.

'Anywhere you wish,' she whispered.

They stared at each other.

'Hyde Park, then,' he said finally.

He flicked the ribbons and the horses started forward. He drove through the riders, wagons, carriages, and hacks on Long Acre towards Piccadilly. 'Your father gave you permission for this outing, I trust.'

'He and Letty are out,' she responded. 'So there was no objection.'

She had not really answered him, he realised. He thought of asking for an explanation. Why did she appear to be under her father's control, yet also out in the world with the likes of her friend Katy Green?

'It is a fine day,' he said instead.

'Yes, it is.' She changed positions and her hand brushed his leg as she readjusted her skirt.

He felt her touch long after her hand closed upon the bench to steady herself.

Flynn mentally shook himself, and concentrated on what he intended to accomplish. He must give her Tanner's gift, the finest emerald ring Flynn could find at Rundell and Bridge. He must offer her Tanner's patronage and propose a time and place for her to meet Tanner.

And he must ensure she spurned Greythorne.

As the curricle reached the Hyde Park gate, Flynn felt back in form. 'Have you driven through the park before, Rose?'

'Oh, yes,' she replied, with no elaboration.

He was again reminded that she was no green girl, but it only forced him to wonder who her former escorts had been.

The fine day had brought many others to the park. Governesses with young children, servants and shopworkers, all taking respite from their toil. Fine gentlemen drove carriages accompanied by gaily dressed female companions—their mistresses, no doubt. Flynn knew some of these men, though he knew better than to nod in greeting. Later in the day some of these same gentlemen would return to this same carriage path to drive their wives or some respectable miss they were courting.

It occurred to Flynn that, if he did his job successfully, Tanner would soon be sitting in his place in this same curricle with Rose beside him. He frowned.

'What makes you unhappy?' she asked.

He started and looked over to see Rose staring at him, her lips pursed with concern.

'I am not unhappy, I assure you.'

One brow arched. 'You looked unhappy, I was thinking.'

With effort he composed his features into their usual bland

expression. 'I am not unhappy. Merely concentrating on driving.'

She faced forward again to watch the few carriages approaching them at a leisurely pace. 'Yes, it is so treacherous here.'

He ignored her teasing and changed the subject. 'Do you enjoy carriage rides?'

'I do,' she replied, smiling again.

'The marquess has several carriages,' he said, dutifully promoting Tanner's interest. 'This one, of course, and a phaeton, a landaulet—'

'How nice,' she said without enthusiasm.

He persevered. 'He also has been known to purchase carriages for special friends.'

'Yes. Special friends.' She showed no increased interest.

Flynn gave her a sideways glance. Most women would leap at the chance to receive this man's regard. The advantages were inestimable. 'He is a generous man, Rose. I can provide you many examples to prove it, if you wish.'

She gave him an imploring look. 'Please do not.'

He frowned again, pretending to concentrate on the horses and the carriage path. Finally he asked, 'What is it, Rose? Every time I mention the marquess, you put me off. Perhaps if you could explain why, I would proceed in a manner to please you.'

Two spots of colour dotted her cheeks. 'Oh, I have nothing against the man…'

Flynn waited for her to say more. The horses waited, too, almost slowing to a stop. He flicked the ribbons and they moved again. The Serpentine came into view, its water glistening in the afternoon sun.

'It is pretty here,' she said after a time.

He forgot about Tanner. Against the green of the grass,

lushness of the trees and blue of the Serpentine, she looked like a Gainsborough portrait. He wished he could capture her image, frame it and hang it upon a wall to gaze at for ever.

He closed his eyes. This was madness, coveting his employer's intended conquest.

He drew a breath, steeling himself again to perform his task. 'I should like to speak for Lord Tannerton, if you will permit me.'

Rose wiped an escaped tendril from her forehead. She'd been pretending Mr Flynn had called upon her like a suitor. A foolish notion. He merely wanted to talk of the marquess.

The rhythmic sound of the horses' hooves on the gravel path seemed louder while she delayed her answer. How could she explain to him that she was not wanting a marquess's money? She was wanting what every girl wanted.

Love.

She set her chin firmly. 'Later perhaps we can speak of the marquess.'

'But I ought—' he began, but clamped his mouth shut. He blew out a long breath and continued in a resigned tone. 'What do you wish to talk about, Rose?'

The knot inside her uncoiled. She could pretend a bit longer. 'Oh, anything…' She smiled at him, suddenly light hearted. 'Things people talk about.'

Things she longed to know about him.

She took a breath. 'Have…have you been in England long, Flynn?'

It took him a moment to respond. 'Since I was eighteen.'

'And how long is that, then?' she persisted.

'Ten years.'

She had discovered his age! Twenty-eight. 'What brought you to England, then?'

'I came to attend Oxford.'

'Oxford? That is where gentlemen go, is it not? To become vicars and such?'

He laughed. 'Yes, and other things.'

'Your family was high enough for Oxford?'

He stiffened. 'It was.'

She'd offended him. 'I should not have spoken so.' She blinked. 'I hope you'll forgive me.'

His expression softened. 'My father is gentry, Rose, a fairly prosperous landowner. He was well able to send me to Oxford.'

Rose relaxed again. 'And what after Oxford?'

'I came to London in search of a position. Lord Tannerton took a risk hiring me.'

'You must have impressed him.'

He gave a half-smile. 'More like he took pity on me, I should think. But I have learned much in his employ.'

She felt bold enough to ask more. 'Have you been back to Ireland, then?'

He shook his head, and the frown reappeared on his face.

Oh, dear. She'd made him unhappy again. She cleared her throat. 'I've only been in England a few months.'

'And why did you come, Miss O'Keefe?' His response sounded more automatic than curious and, oh, so formal.

'The school was willing to keep me teaching. The school near Killyleagh, I mean. But I had this desire to sing, you see.' She paused. 'Like my mother.'

'Your mother?'

She nodded. 'My mother sang in London in her time. She died long ago.'

He looked at her with sympathy, pricking a pain she usually kept carefully hidden.

She swallowed. 'In any event, my father was working in

London, so I came here.' She glanced away. 'He could not afford to keep me at first, but then Mr Hook hired me to sing.' She skipped over a lot of the story, perhaps the most important parts. 'And when I'm done singing at Vauxhall, I'll find another place to sing.'

'Where?' he asked.

'Oh, somewhere. I'm thinking there are plenty of theatres in London.'

'There are theatres in Ireland as well,' he said.

She shrugged. 'Not like in London. London has King's Theatre and Drury Lane and Vauxhall nearby. Plenty of places. My mother once performed in King's Theatre.'

'That is impressive,' he said.

She laughed. 'Not very impressive, really. She was in the chorus, but she did sing on the stage at King's Theatre.'

'Do you wish to sing in the King's Theatre?' he asked.

She sighed. 'I do. More than anything. It must be the most beautiful theatre in the world.'

He smiled. 'It is quite beautiful.'

'You've seen it?' She turned to him eagerly.

'I've accompanied Lord Tannerton there on occasion.'

'You have?' She would have loved to just walk inside the building, see the boxes and the curtain and the stage. She sighed again.

He continued to smile at her.

She could not help but smile back at him, thinking how boyish he looked when he let his face relax.

A carriage came in the other direction and he attended to the driving again. They lapsed into silence.

She searched for something else to ask him. 'What work do you do for Lord Tannerton, then?'

'I manage many of his affairs—' He cleared his throat.

'His *business* affairs. Tend to his correspondence, arrange his appointments, pay bills, run errands and such.'

'Ah, I see.' But she really did not understand the business of a marquess.

He went on, 'You might say I attend to all the tedious details, so the marquess is free for more important matters, and so his life runs smoothly.'

Such work would give Rose the headache. 'Are you liking what you do?'

He nodded. 'I have learned much about the world through it. About politics. Money. Power—'

Such things were mysteries to her.

'I have even been to Vienna and Brussels and Paris with Lord Tannerton.'

Her eyes widened with interest. 'Have you now?'

'The marquess assisted in the diplomacies, you see. And I assisted him.' He spoke proudly.

She liked seeing his pride. 'Were you there for the great battle?'

'In Brussels, yes, but we were not at Waterloo.' His face became serious. 'The marquess helped with the aftermath, assisting in the logistics of the wounded and in any other way of being at service.'

Rose did not know what 'logistics' were, but she knew there were many wounded in the battle. Many Irish soldiers had fought and died at Waterloo. She was glad Flynn had been there to help those who survived.

He gave a dry laugh. 'But it must be tedious to hear of such things.'

'Oh, no,' she assured him. 'I confess I do not understand all of it, but you were meaning, I think, that you were in important places, doing important things.'

'That is it,' he agreed. 'In the centre of things. A part of it all.'

'I'm supposing it is a little like being a performer, isn't it? Performing is not so important, perhaps, but it is being a part of something. I mean, the singing is only one piece of it. There are the musicians, too, and the conductor and all. Everyone together makes the performance.'

He looked at her so intently her insides fluttered. 'Yes, it is precisely like that. One feels good about one's part in it.'

'Yes.' She quickly glanced away and spied a man crossing the park with a bundle on his shoulder. 'And that man there is doing his part, too, isn't he? We don't know what it is, but without him it would not happen, would it?'

A smile flitted across his face, disappearing when he gazed into her eyes again. 'Yes, I expect you are very right.'

Her breath quickened, like it had when he'd almost kissed her under the illuminations the night before.

'So what, Flynn, is your King's Theatre?' she asked, needing to break the intensity, just as he had broken away when he almost kissed her. 'Or have you reached it already?'

'My King's Theatre?'

'What you want more than anything.'

His eyes darkened, making her insides feel like melting wax again.

The horses stopped, and his attention turned to them, signalling them to move.

'What I want more than anything…' he repeated as if pondering the question. 'To be a part of something important,' he finally replied. 'Yes, that is it.'

She waited for more.

His brow furrowed. 'Lord Tannerton is an excellent employer, an excellent man, Rose, but…' His voice faded, although his face seemed lit with fire.

'Something more important is what you are wanting?' she guessed.

He nodded. 'To work for government. For a diplomat, perhaps. Or the Prime Minister. Or for royalty.'

'Royalty?' she exclaimed.

He flicked the ribbons and shook his head. 'It is daft.'

She put her hand on his arm. 'It is not daft! No more daft than me wanting to sing in King's Theatre.' But it did seem so impossible, and somehow it made her sad. 'It would be important, wouldn't it? So important you'd not be seeing the likes of me.'

He covered her hand with his and leaned towards her. The horses drifted to a stop again.

'Move on!' an angry voice shouted.

A young man driving a phaeton approached them from behind. Flynn put the chestnuts into a trot, but the phaeton passed them as soon as the path was wide enough.

They finished their circuit of the park, not speaking much. Their silence seemed tense, holding too many unspoken words, but Rose still wished the time to go on endlessly. Soon, however, other carriages entered the park, driven by gentlemen with their ladies. The fashionable hour had arrived, and they must leave.

As Flynn turned the curricle on to her street, he was frowning again. 'What is it, Flynn?' she asked.

'I have not talked to you of Tannerton,' he said. 'My reason for seeing you. And there is something else, Rose.'

She felt a pang at the reminder of his true purpose. 'What is it?' she asked in a resigned tone.

He gave her a direct look. 'Another man will be vying for your favours. He is Lord Greythorne. He is wealthy, but some unpleasant rumour hangs about him.'

'What rumour?' She had no intention of bestowing her favours on whoever it was, no matter what.

'I do not know precisely,' he said.

She shrugged. 'I thank you for the warning, Flynn.'

'It is important that you not choose Greythorne.'

She did not wish to choose any man, not for money or the gifts he could give her. She wanted to tell Flynn he could tell them all to leave her alone. Let her sing. That was all she wished to do, even if he were making her imagine other possibilities.

Her father had been drumming it into her that to be a success on the London stage, she must have a wealthy patron. It seemed all anyone wanted of her—her father, Letty, the marquess, this Greythorne.

Flynn.

He was still talking. 'Lord Tannerton would be good to you, Rose. I would stake my life on it.'

But she did not *love* Lord Tannerton. That was the thing.

With such a lofty man, she could never have what Miss Hart had with Mr Sloane.

She needed time. 'I will think on it some more, Flynn.'

Langley Street was empty in front of her building. He jumped down from the curricle and held her waist as he lifted her down.

She rested her hands on his shoulders a moment longer than necessary, not wanting to say goodbye to him. Wanting to see him again. 'I…I will be singing at Vauxhall tonight. If you've a mind to come.'

He stood still, but it seemed as if his eyes were searching hers. 'I will be there.'

'Come to the gazebo door. You'll be admitted, I promise.' Her spirits were soaring again. He wanted to see her. *Her*.

He grasped her hand and held it a brief delicious moment. 'Tonight, then.'

Feeling joyous, Rose entered the building and climbed the stairs to her father's rooms.

When she opened the door, Letty stood there, hands on her hips. 'Were you with that Flynn fellow? Has he given you a meeting time with the marquess?'

She ought to have been prepared. 'It is not set, Letty. But soon, Mr Flynn tells me.'

'Where did you go, Mary Rose? I was wondering.' Her father sat in the chair near the fireplace.

Rose walked over and gave him a kiss on the top of his bald head. 'A drive in the park, is all.' She headed for her room.

Letty blocked her way. 'This Flynn. Did he tell you how much the marquess will pay?'

Rose looked her in the eye. 'I thought you would be proud of me, Letty. I put him off. Did you not say that would increase the price?'

'Well, I—' Letty began, but Rose brushed past her to disappear into the little room that was her bedchamber.

Returning from the mews where he'd left Tanner's curricle and horses, Flynn ran into Tanner walking back from St. James's Street.

Tanner clapped him on the shoulder. 'How fortuitous! You have been on my mind all the afternoon. What progress, man? Do tell.'

Flynn had nothing to tell.

'Out with it, Flynn. What the devil happened?'

As they walked side by side, Flynn used what Rose had called his *silver tongue*. 'You must trust me in this matter, my lord. The lady is not the usual sort. You were correct about diplomacy being required.'

Tanner put a hand on his arm, stopping him on the pavement. 'Do not tell me she disliked the emerald ring!'

Flynn had forgotten it was in his pocket. 'I did not present it to her, sir.'

'You did not present it?' Tanner looked surprised.

It was difficult to face him. 'She would have refused it.'

Tanner started walking again. 'My God, she is a strange one. What woman would refuse such a gift?'

One who bewitches, thought Flynn, but he replied, 'She is a puzzle, I agree.'

'You do not think she prefers Greythorne, do you?' Tanner asked with a worried frown.

'She was unaware of Greythorne's interest.'

Tanner looked aghast. 'And you told her of him? Now she will know there is competition!'

Flynn countered, 'Now she knows to come to us to top any offer he makes.'

After a few paces, Tanner laughed. 'She is a rare one, isn't she? I am unused to exerting myself. This is capital sport.'

Tanner, of course, had not exerted himself at all beyond charging Flynn with the work. 'I need some time to gain her trust, I think. I shall see her again tonight at Vauxhall.'

Tanner clapped him on the shoulder again. 'Excellent! I have a previous engagement, otherwise I'd join you.'

Flynn felt only a twinge of guilt for being glad of Tanner's previous engagement.

'Did you discover anything about Greythorne?' Flynn asked.

'Not a thing,' replied Tanner.

Later that evening when Flynn strolled down the Grand Walk of Vauxhall Gardens, he thought about Greythorne, trying to place his finger on who'd spoken ill of the man.

He had at least an hour to ponder the puzzle before the orchestra played. He knew she would have arrived by then, and he could then present himself at the gazebo door.

He thought about simply knocking on the door now, but he really did not want to chance encountering her father, or, worse, being plied with questions about Tanner by Miss Dawes.

Flynn stopped at one of the restaurants in the gardens instead. Sitting at an outside table, he sipped arrack amid the laughter and buzz of the people walking by. He could feel the velvet box containing the emerald ring still in his pocket. It kept him grounded. A reminder of Tanner, of Greythorne, of what his duty must be.

As he idly watched the passers-by, he let his mind drift to how it had felt to walk through the gardens with her, her arm through his, how the illuminations lit her face, how tempting her lips had been.

He took a longer sip of arrack.

'Well, look who is here!'

Flynn glanced up to see Rose's friend, Katy, striding his way.

'Mr Flynn! Fancy meeting you here again!' She flung herself into a chair even before he could rise. 'You must be here for Rose. Imagine, our little Rosie catching the eye of a marquess! Not that I'm surprised. She barely needed lessons with that face and figure. Just enough to get rid of the accent and learn to put herself forward.' She reached for his glass and took a sip.

Flynn felt as if he were caught in a whirlwind. 'Lessons?'

Katy laughed, patting his arm. 'Never mind that.'

Showing no signs of leaving, she commandeered his glass for herself. He signalled for more for both of them.

She rested her elbows on the table. 'Tell me about this marquess. Sir Reginald says he is an important man.'

Flynn pursed his lips, wishing he'd said nothing to Sir Reginald. 'You must understand, Miss Green, this is not a matter I am free to discuss.'

'Miss Green?' She laughed again. 'Well, aren't you the high-and-mighty one! Call me Katy. Everyone does. I tell you, it's a marvel how well Rosie's done. Here I thought I was the only one. Not that Sir Reginald is anything. He takes me around and I meet people. I'm going to rise higher myself, I am.'

Katy's words were like puzzle pieces scattered on a table. They made no sense. 'How do you know Miss O'Keefe?'

'Rose, you mean?' She grinned, then tried to compose her animated face. 'You might say we were…schoolmates.' Her voice trembled with mirth on this last word, and she dissolved into gales of laughter, slapping the table and causing several heads to turn their way.

He raised his brows, but she did not elaborate. Their arrack came and she finished his first glass before reaching for the next one.

'Are you here to see Rose?' she asked.

'Yes,' he answered, somewhat reluctantly.

'And where is this marquess? I've a fancy to set eyes upon this paragon.' She looked around as if Lord Tannerton might suddenly appear.

'He is not here.'

She shrugged, taking another gulp of arrack. 'I'll be on tenterhooks 'til I see him, I expect. I might fancy a marquess myself, though I didn't aim to look so high. Miss H— Well, I mean, we were told to think high of ourselves, but I keep my feet on the ground, so to speak.'

Flynn was no closer to understanding her. Rose and Katy schoolmates? Not in Killyleagh.

The discordant chords of the orchestra tuning up reached his ears, and he interrupted Katy's unrestrained volubility. 'Forgive me, Miss Green. I must go.' He stood.

'Go?' She rose as well. 'Where are you off to, Mr Flynn?'

He hated to tell her, but feared she would follow him no matter what. 'Miss O'Keefe said to meet her at the gazebo.'

'Oh?' She clapped her hands. 'That is splendid. I'll go with you. Give her another hello.'

So, with the gaily dressed, red-haired young woman hanging on his arm, Flynn strolled to the orchestra's gazebo.

Miss Dawes opened the door. 'Mr Flynn! Come in. Come in.' She noticed Katy behind him and gave a scowl.

Katy grinned at her. 'How do you do?'

Some mischief took hold of Flynn, making him give precedence to the obvious harlot, Katy. 'Miss Green,' he said in his most formal voice. 'May I present Miss Dawes, a friend of Mr O'Keefe's.'

Miss Dawes looked like thunder, but Katy rose to the occasion. 'A pleasure, ma'am,' she said in an uncannily ladylike voice.

Miss Dawes ignored her. 'I'll fetch Rose.' She huffed out of the room, almost tripping over a jumble of instrument cases the musicians had left.

A minute later Rose walked in, the lamplight softening her lovely features.

'Katy!' she said in surprise.

Katy danced up to her and gave her a hug. 'I hope you don't mind, Rosie. I talked Mr Flynn into bringing me here. Met that dragon, Miss Dawes, too. Who does she think she is?'

Rose looked bewildered. 'Are…are you here with Mr Flynn?' Her glance slid over to him.

Katy laughed, but it was Flynn who answered, 'She merely wished to say hello to you.'

Katy released her. 'That I did.' She chattered on about Miss Dawes and how all the men would admire Rose when she sang.

Rose turned to Flynn, anxiety in her eyes. 'If you wished to spend time with Katy—'

'Goodness!' Katy exclaimed. 'I am meeting Sir Reginald, who has promised to introduce me to some rich fellow.' She swayed up to Flynn and pressed herself against his arm. 'Unless that marquess would be interested in me?' Without waiting for his reply, she returned to Rose to give her a peck on the cheek and flounced out of the door.

Rose looked at him. 'I…I thought you were with her.'

'I was not,' Flynn said.

Her face relaxed. 'Would you like to stand in the balcony while I'm singing?'

'I should like that,' he responded truthfully.

They talked of inconsequential things until she was called to perform. Flynn stood in a dark corner of the balcony, able to see her in profile, though she turned to smile at him before beginning her first tune, an old Irish ballad he remembered his sisters singing as a duet. She continued with 'O Listen to the Voice of Love.'

His gaze wandered to the audience. It was still light enough to see the people staring spellbound as she sang. She captivated them all, he thought, scanning the crowd.

He caught sight of Lord Greythorne and scowled. But Greythorne was not looking at Rose. Flynn followed the direction of the man's gaze across the span of people. He froze. At the edge of the crowd stood a familiar tall figure, arms crossed over his chest, face tilted toward the lovely Rose O'Keefe.

Lord Tannerton.

Chapter Five

Flynn listened to Rose's final notes drift into the night air and watched her take her final bow. Tanner's 'Bravo!' sounded above all the other voices.

It was good he was here, Flynn told himself determinedly, because Flynn needed to remember that his task was to get Rose to accept Tanner's protection. He needed to be certain Tanner won her over Lord Greythorne. The more time Flynn spent alone with her, the more bewitched he became, as if he were also vying for her regard.

Rose came over to him, smiling. She grasped his hand. 'We must go below.'

He let her lead him to the room below stairs.

'How was I?' she asked him, as the voice of Charles Dignum reached their ears. 'I felt myself straining here and there. Was it noticeable, do you think?'

She still held his hand. He stared at it a moment before answering. 'I noticed no imperfection.'

She smiled and squeezed his fingers. 'What shall we do now? The night is lovely and I must wait for my father and

Letty. I know you wish to talk to me, but could we do so while we explore the gardens again? Go see the hermit?'

The hermit illusion was located at the far end of one of the darker, less crowded paths well known for dalliance. Flynn could just imagine leading her into one of the private alcoves, holding her in his arms and finally tasting her lips.

He forced himself to face her. 'Lord Greythorne is here,' he said. 'As is Lord Tanner.'

Her eyes flashed. 'Lord Tanner? You did not tell me he would be here.'

'I did not know,' he quickly explained. 'He was engaged elsewhere, but I saw him in the audience. He is here.' Flynn held her shoulders. 'Allow me to present you to him. You might see for yourself the man he is.'

She stared into his eyes. 'Oh, Flynn.' It took her a moment to go on. 'Not so soon. I mean, I…I am not ready to meet him. I have not decided yet that I should.'

He tilted his head toward the stairway leading to the orchestra's balcony, to where her father played his oboe. 'Your father wishes it, does he not? The marquess will not wait for ever, and Greythorne is very willing to step in.'

Her eyes turned anxious. 'Time, Flynn. Can you be procuring me a little more time?'

He nodded, knowing he should not.

Tanner would take care of her. Take her away from the unpleasant Miss Dawes and the drab set of rooms shared with her father. Tanner would protect her from men like Greythorne, anyone who might mistreat her. It would be best for her to simply meet Tanner. See the man he was, and make her decision. Then Flynn could go back to a sane life.

'I shall see you have more time,' he said.

'Thank you.' She grasped his hand. 'Call on me tomorrow,

Flynn. Share supper with me. I do not perform tomorrow. You could come after my father and Letty leave. I will be more prepared to think.'

He stepped closer to her. What could one more day matter? Her beautiful face turned up to his. It seemed natural to slide his hand down her arm, lift her hand to his lips. Even through her glove he could feel its warmth, taste the allure of her.

He released her. 'I will call tomorrow, then.'

'Eight o'clock? Papa and Letty will have left by then.'

He nodded.

He walked over to the door, but before he opened it, he turned back to her. 'I had forgotten. I must give you this tonight. From Lord Tanner.' He pulled out the small velvet box from his coat pocket.

She held up her hand to refuse it.

'Accept it, Rose. It is a trifle to him, but I can no longer find excuses for not giving it to you.' He placed it in her hand.

She opened the box, revealing the ring, a sparkling emerald surrounded by tiny diamonds, in a setting of carved gold. 'This is not a trifle, Flynn,' she said, trying to hand it back to him.

'It is to Tannerton.' He closed her fingers around it. 'Take it, Rose. It does not obligate you to him, I promise.' He kept his hand over hers for too long. 'I must leave.'

He quickly pulled away and opened the door.

'Goodnight, Flynn,' he heard her say as he hurried through the doorway into the night.

Adam Vickering, Marquess of Tannerton, sat in a supper box with his friend Pomroy and the party of high flyers and dashers Pomroy always seemed to collect.

Pomroy filled his glass with arrack. 'You're like a besotted fool, Tan—' He paused to belch. 'Never thought you the sort who let a woman lead him by a string.'

Tanner gulped down half his arrack. 'I'd be dashed pleased to be led by this one, if I could only get near enough to secure her.' He looked heavenwards. 'You heard her, Pomroy. She is an angel.'

'Ha!' his friend barked. 'I'd say she's devilish crafty. Has you eating out of her hand and all without speaking a word to you. She's going to play you against Greythorne, you know, like bidders at Tattersalls.

'Got to admit, it is good sport.' Tanner's grin turned to a scowl. 'What have you discovered about Greythorne?'

'He courted Amanda Reynolds, all the rage a year ago. Everyone thought they would marry. She spurned him, though.'

'Left him for another man?' Tanner asked.

'Some soldier, I believe.' Pomroy shrugged.

'Her head turned by a man in regimentals?' Tanner concluded. 'Not unheard of, you know.'

'Yes, but there was more to it, I'm certain,' Pomroy said. 'She could have had anyone. Don't you remember her? She was perfection.'

Tanner conjured up an image of a cool blonde, the sort who would pine for routs and balls and dreadful *musicales*. He took another mouthful. 'Always disliked that fellow Greythorne. Looks the whole day like he'd just left his valet.'

Pomroy was summoned by one of the prime articles he'd found in the Gardens. Pomroy would no doubt enjoy her company all night through, but such females held no interest for Tanner. While his friend attended to the pretty thing,

Tanner leaned back on his chair, balancing it on its rear legs. He raised his drink and gazed out into the crowd.

With any luck he'd catch sight of his secretary and have him wrangle a meeting with Miss Rose O'Keefe. Even if luck was not with him, he could still congratulate himself for escaping Lady Rawley's tedious *musicale*. Half an hour of the soprano she'd hired had nearly done for him. He wished half the fashionable set would leave Town and go rusticate in the country. Leave him free of their tiresome invitations. Let them all go rusticate, in fact.

Not that he had any intention of burying himself in such boredom. He paid his managers well so he would not have to put in an appearance at any of his properties until hunting season.

Tanner swished his arrack in the glass. Ordinarily he'd be in Brighton this time of year, but the elusive Rose O'Keefe had kept him in town.

Tanner's eyes narrowed as a pristinely attired gentleman swinging a walking stick strolled up to the supper box.

'Why, if it is not Tannerton.' Greythorne tipped his hat in an elegant gesture that seemed to mock Tanner's boyish balancing act.

Tanner perversely accentuated his lack of gentility by stretching his arms to the back of his head. 'Greythorne.'

Behind Tanner Pomroy laughed and one of his female companions squealed. Greythorne eyed them with ill-disguised contempt.

He directed his gaze back to Tanner. 'I hear we are rivals of a sort.'

'Rivals?' Tanner gave a dry laugh. 'I highly doubt that.'

Greythorne ignored his barb. 'For the captivating Rose O'Keefe. I quite covet the girl, you know.'

'Really?' said Tanner in a flat voice.

Greythorne tapped the wall of the supper box with his stick. 'Your secretary tells me she is yours, but I confess I see no signs of it.'

'Eyes bothering you?' Tanner remarked.

Greythorne brushed at his coat, as if a piece of dirt dared mar his appearance. 'You are amusing, Tannerton.' He glanced in the direction of the Grove where Miss O'Keefe had performed. 'Perhaps I shall amuse you when the young temptress is mine.'

'No fear of that.' Tanner lifted his glass to his lips. 'Doubt you've ever been amusing.'

Greythorne's lips thinned and Tanner actually fought the need to laugh.

'To the victor go the spoils,' Greythorne said, making a salute before strolling off.

'Trite bastard,' Tanner muttered to himself.

Pomroy twisted around. 'Did you say something?'

Tanner did not reply, because he saw someone else in the crowd. He propelled himself out of his chair, sending it clattering to the ground, and vaulted over the supper-box wall.

'Flynn!' he called, pushing through the people to catch up. He grabbed Flynn's arm and pulled him to the side. 'When do you meet with her, Flynn?'

His secretary regarded him in his usual unflappable manner, not even showing surprise at his presence. 'I have done so already,' Flynn answered.

'To what result?' Tanner asked eagerly.

Flynn paused, only briefly, but enough to try Tanner's patience. 'I was able to give her the ring,' Flynn finally said.

'Excellent!' Tanner's eyes lit up. 'Did she like it?'

'She said it was more than a trifling gift.'

That was all? 'Well, I suppose that is something.' Tanner grasped Flynn's arm. 'We need more progress, man. That

snake Greythorne is slithering around. He just spoke to me.'
Tanner gave a mock-shiver. 'I'd hoped for a meeting tonight.'

'I did not expect you tonight, my lord,' Flynn said in a
bland voice.

Tanner grinned. 'That is so. I escaped some ghastly
musicale with some equally ghastly soprano to come here. I
could not resist. I tell you, Miss O'Keefe's sweet voice was
balm in comparison.' He rubbed the back of his neck. 'This
business is taking an intolerably long time.'

'Patience is required.'

'Well, we both know how little of that commodity I
possess.' Tanner clapped him on the arm. 'That is why I
depend upon you, Flynn. If it were up to me, I'd go there now
and demand she see me, but I suspect you would advise
against it.'

'I would indeed.'

Tanner blew out a frustrated breath. 'I wonder what Greythorne will do. I trust him about as far as I can throw him.'
He thought about this. 'Make that as far as he could throw
me.'

'I can assure you she shows no partiality toward him,'
Flynn said.

Tanner grinned. 'That is good news. What is next for us
then?'

'I shall dine with her tomorrow.'

Tanner gaped at him. 'Dine with her? Well done. Very well
done, indeed.' His secretary was clocking impressive amounts
of time with her. Things were looking up.

Flynn gave him a wan smile.

'Tanner!' Pomroy was standing in the supper box,
waving him over.

Tanner glanced at him. 'Pomroy beckons. I suppose I must

go. He's managed some entertaining company, no one to remark upon, but anything is better than that ghastly *musicale.*' He rolled his eyes. 'Enjoy yourself, Flynn. Might as well see what pleasures the garden can offer, eh?'

'Thank you, sir,' Flynn replied.

Tanner headed back to the supper box, not noticing his secretary did not heed his advice. Flynn turned towards the Kennington Lane gate where he could catch a hackney carriage back to Audley Street.

The next evening Rose said goodbye to her father and Letty, watching from the window until they were out of sight. Waiting a few minutes longer to be sure they had time to get in a hack, she donned her hat and gloves, picked up a basket, and hurried outside. She walked the short distance to the Covent Garden market past youngbloods who whistled and made lewd remarks. The theatres had not yet opened their doors, but the street was teeming with well-dressed gentlemen casting appraising glances at gaudily dressed women who only pretended to have some destination in mind.

Rose listened for the pie man's call and made her way to him to purchase two meat pies. She also bought strawberries, a jug of cream, and a bottle of Madeira wine. It would be simple fare, but the best she could manage without the means to cook and without her father and Letty suspecting. She returned home, setting the pies near the small fire in the parlour fireplace. She moved the table they used for eating and found a cloth to cover it. She set two plates, two glasses, and cutlery and stood back to survey her work.

It was not elegant, nothing, to be sure, like a marquess's table set with porcelain china and silver, but it was the best she could do.

All the day she'd felt out of breath, not from nerves at hiding this from her father, but anticipation of seeing Flynn.

She'd been so disappointed at Lord Tannerton's appearance the night before, forcing her to forgo Flynn's company. She'd had girlish fantasies of walking with Flynn down the Dark Walk, where lovers could be private, where lovers could kiss. Tannerton had spoiled it.

She was determined Tannerton would not spoil this evening, even if Rose must talk about him with Flynn. She intended to spend some part of the evening merely enjoying being alone with him. In school she'd learned it was not proper to entertain a man alone in one's lodgings, but here in Covent Garden no one expected proper behaviour. She planned to take advantage of that fact.

While she checked the kettle to see if there was water enough to heat for tea, the knock sounded at the door. Rose wheeled around, pressing her hand against her abdomen to quiet the flutters. She hurried to the door and opened it.

Flynn stood with a small package in his hand. 'For you, Miss O'Keefe.'

She hesitated. Another present from Tannerton. Letty had already discovered the ring and was at this moment wearing it on her finger. Rose took the package into her hand and stepped aside so Flynn could enter.

Flynn placed his hat and gloves on the table near the door and turned to her, pointing to the package. 'It is a token,' he said. 'From me.'

From Flynn? That made her happy. She eagerly untied the string and opened the box. Inside was an assortment of sweetmeats, all prettily arranged. She thought she had never seen anything so lovely, nor received such a wonderful gift.

She smiled at him. 'Thank you. I will serve them with our

tea.' Or leave them untouched to treasure for ever. 'Please come to the table.'

She poured him a glass of Madeira. 'I know it is customary to have conversation before dinner is served, but I thought it best for us to eat right away.'

'Whatever you desire, Rose,' he said, still standing.

He waited until she had fetched the meat pies from in front of the fire and placed them on the plates, then held her chair for her. She smiled up at him.

'Our meal is rather plain,' she apologised.

'I do not mind.' He settled in his seat and took a forkful. 'I do not know when I last ate meat pie.'

She felt her cheeks warming. 'I am sorry to serve you such poor fare.'

'Oh, no,' he said. 'I meant it is a rare treat.'

She gave him a disbelieving glance. 'There goes your silver tongue again.'

'Truly, Rose.' He looked so sincere she was tempted to believe him.

She glanced back down at her plate. 'You know, in my grandparents' house this would have been a luxury. There's more meat in my pie here than they ate in a week sometimes.'

A faint wrinkle creased his brow. 'Their lives must be difficult.'

'Oh,' she said, 'they died a long time ago, soon after my mother. After that my father put me in school in Killyleagh.'

He glanced up again. 'You had other family, certainly.'

'Not of my mother's family, but there are plenty of O'Keefes.' She took a sip of her wine. 'My father's family never was accepting of him being a musician, so I never really knew them.'

Flynn took another bite of the pie he was truly enjoying.

He remembered how poor some were in Ireland. He had not realised she'd been one of them. Tanner's generosity could give her a secure, comfortable life. This was the perfect opportunity to convince her of the advantages of accepting his offer. If he could even convince her to meet Tanner, she would learn this for herself.

'We need to discuss your meeting with Tannerton, Rose,' he ventured.

She stared down at her plate. 'Yes. I have promised you we would do so.' She looked up at him. 'So speak. I shall listen.'

The force of her eyes drove all words from his mouth. 'Perhaps after our meal,' he said.

She smiled. 'Tell me more of King's Theatre, then. Tell me of its interior.'

So he talked of King's Theatre, Drury Lane, Covent Garden, as well as other smaller theatres he'd attended. He told her of the sopranos he'd seen: Catalani, Camporese, Fodor, among them. She listened, eyes dancing in delight at his descriptions, and he found himself wishing he could share such experiences with her.

She served him a simple dessert, strawberries and cream, and after she cleared the dishes away, she said with a twinkle in her eye, 'Shall we retire to the drawing room, then?' She gestured to the two cushioned chairs near the fire. 'I'll make tea.'

He sat while she poured hot water from the kettle into a teapot. Though their conversation had been comfortable before, they now lapsed into a strained silence, broken only by her questions of how he took his tea.

She sat opposite him and poured, placing one of the sweetmeats he'd given her on the saucer.

'Rose…' he began.

She attempted a smile, but it vanished quickly. 'I know. We must talk.'

His brow furrowed, and he felt like whatever silver tongue he might possess had been badly tarnished. 'Let me arrange a meeting with Lord Tannerton, Rose, before Greythorne becomes more of a problem.'

She frowned at him. 'Do you mean *meet* Lord Tannerton, or something else?'

He picked up the sweetmeat, but could not bite into it. He returned it to the saucer. 'A meeting only. You are not obligated for more.' It was becoming torturous to think about the *more* that would eventually transpire once she accepted Tanner.

She stared into her teacup. 'And later?'

He could not look at her. 'If you find him…agreeable, there is no limit to what he might do for you.'

'Ah, but it is what I must do…' she murmured, her voice trailing off.

He gave her a puzzled look. What was her reluctance? She was not without experience in such matters. She was friends with Katy Green, after all, whose station in life was very clear. Katy seemed to take the marquess's interest in Rose as nothing unusual. And Rose had alluded to other liaisons— those gentlemen who drove her in Hyde Park, for example. A connection with a wealthy marquess ought to be eagerly sought after. Unless…

He straightened his back. 'Rose, is there another man…?'

'Interested in me, do you mean?' She pointed to a tray of cards on the table where he'd placed his hat and gloves. 'Those fellows, I suppose.'

He shook his head. 'I mean a man who interests you.'

'Me?' It took a moment for comprehension to dawn. 'Oh!' She blinked rapidly, then raised her liquid emerald eyes to his. 'No, Flynn,' she said in a soft, low voice. 'There is no one else.'

He stopped breathing.

Finally she averted her gaze. 'Why do you ask such a thing?'

He picked up his cup. 'You have persistently avoided talking about the marquess.'

'So you thought it must be another man.' She regarded him with an ironic expression. ''Tis not enough I might not fancy being bartered like some fancy item in a shop.'

He stared at her. 'You are not being bartered.' Though he feared she had captured the essence of the matter.

'Of course I am,' she said, her tone pragmatic.

But why did she dislike it, if she would come out the winner?

She stood. 'Never mind it. I'll meet your marquess.' She crossed the room. 'Tell me when.'

He walked over to her, making her look at him. 'Are you certain?'

She cocked her head. 'I'm certain. But I'll not be obligating myself further than that. And I'd prefer Letty and my father not be a part of it.'

He had no difficulty agreeing with that.

'And no gifts, if you please.'

That was unexpected, but easily done.

'And you must be present.'

He gave her a surprised glance. 'I?'

'Yes, and it would not look very well if I were the only woman with two gentlemen, so I would like Katy Green to come as well.'

He nearly winced. 'Miss Green?'

She looked up at him through her thick lashes. 'I do not want to be alone.'

'I will arrange it,' he said in a resigned tone. He'd not imagined being forced to watch Tanner charm her.

She gave him a brave but false smile. 'Good. That is settled. No need to talk of it further.'

She drummed her fingers on the long wooden box that rested on a table in the corner of the room where they stood. 'Let me show you something,' she said suddenly.

He raised his brows.

She smiled with mischief. 'Watch.' She opened up the box to reveal a small pianoforte. 'Isn't it a treat?'

He laughed. 'Yes, a surprise as well.'

She ran her fingers lightly over the keys. 'It belonged to my mother. To take with her when she travelled in those days she was singing. It is in fine sound, too. Listen.'

She pulled up a small stool and rested her fingers on the keys, playing random chords until she began a tune he recognised only too well, though he had not heard it for over a decade: 'Shule Agra.' She sang:

> *His hair was black, his eye was blue*
> *His arm was stout, his word was true*
> *I wish in my heart, I was with you...*

He'd sung the song of a sweetheart slain for the Jacobite cause with the rest of his family at his mother's pianoforte. When Rose came to the chorus, Flynn could not help but join her.

'Shule, shule, shule agra...'

He closed his eyes and let the sound of their melding

voices float around him and seep into his skin, sending him back to Ballynahinch, to home and family.

'Go thee, thu Mavourneen slaun,' they sang, holding the last note for several extra beats.

She rose and turned to him and their gazes held. 'Beautiful,' he said, bewitched.

Without thinking, he brushed his fingers across her cheek. Her eyes darkened and she leaned closer to him. His nostrils gratefully inhaled her sweet clean scent, like the flowers in his mother's garden. She tilted her face to him, so close he could feel her breath against his skin.

He lowered his head slowly, wanting for just one brief moment to find home again in her lips. She remained perfectly still, waiting. His lips came closer, so close their breath mingled. A half-inch more and he would taste her—

Voices sounded in the hallway, someone entering one of the other rooms, but enough to jar him from his reverie.

He dropped his hand and stepped away.

'Flynn?' she whispered. Her eyes reflected his own wrenching need.

'This is madness,' he rasped. Madness for him to covet the woman his powerful employer laid claim to.

She tried to come closer, but he held up his hand. 'I must go.'

She blocked his way to the door. 'Why is it madness, Flynn?'

He had no choice but to touch her. He put his hands on her arms and eased her aside so he could collect his hat and gloves.

She stepped closer again. 'Why is it madness?' She scooped up the calling cards that had been piled next to his gloves. 'It is what Tannerton and Greythorne and all these gentlemen want, is it not?' She let the cards cascade from her fingers. 'Why can it not be between you and me?'

'Because of my employer, Rose.' He pulled on his gloves. 'It would be the ruin of my future. Yours as well. Do you not see that?'

'But he need never know,' she countered.

'*I* would know. After all he has done for me, I would not repay him so.' Did she think he could make love to her one day and face Tanner the next?

He opened the door, but turned back to her. 'You are indeed like your friend Katy, are you not? Do not tease me further with talk of needing time. I will not believe you.' He started through the door but swung around again, leaning close to her face, as close as when he almost kissed her. 'You are just what you seem, Rose. A fancy piece.'

Her lips parted in surprise, but they remained as enticing as before. With a growl of frustration, he wrenched himself away and hurried down the staircase.

Rose leaned against the doorframe, arms wrapped around herself. She squeezed her eyes shut. His words stung, but she knew he'd been correct. She'd behaved badly. Wantonly.

She re-entered the room, shutting the door behind her and hurrying to the window. She watched him leave the building, his pace as quick as if pursued by lions.

Leaning her forehead against the cool glass, she sang, 'I wish in my heart, I was with you…'

Vauxhall was not nearly as pleasant this night without Rose O'Keefe singing. Greythorne grimaced as Charles Dignum began. He stalked out of the Grove and strolled towards the Transparency. Out of the corner of his eye he glimpsed one of Vauxhall's many delights—a woman with flaming red hair, laughing on the arm of that fool Sir Reginald, pulling him through the crowd.

He sucked in a breath. That laughter gave him a twinge.

He blew out the breath and walked on, scanning the crowd. He wanted a woman. Needed a woman. It had been a long time since he'd invited a woman into his den of pleasure. What harm to pluck another flower while he waited to win the elusive Rose from that—that—*Corinthian* Tannerton?

Blood surged through his veins. He'd win Rose O'Keefe and show her his special set of delights, and once under his control, she would forget all about Tannerton's pursuit.

Greythorne wiped his face, grateful to the Diamond, Amanda, who had spurned him and lost the opportunity to experience his special talents. Because of the Diamond, he'd pushed himself to dare new delights. New heights. Nearer and nearer the brink.

He'd also had to take more care. There were some who knew his brand of pleasure, and he dared not risk more exposure. He rubbed his hands together. The more secretive he became, the more daring as well. There were no limits in anonymity.

He grinned, imagining this girl's laughter fading, her eyes widening, mouth opening, cries ringing against the walls of his special room.

He donned the mask he kept in his pocket, the mask that protected him, the mask that freed him. The red-haired woman might be occupied this night, but there were other blooms to be plucked.

And Greythorne loved to cut flowers.

Chapter Six

The message from Flynn arrived for Rose the following afternoon, delivered into her father's hands. 'Mary Rose, it is from that marquess's fellow,' he said.

Letty, interrupted from admiring how the emerald ring sparkled on her pudgy hand, ran to his side. 'Well, what is it? What does he say?'

Letty snatched the letter from her father and walked over to read it by the light from the window. 'He wants to meet her! Two days hence.' She dropped the letter on the table. 'Did I not say it would be so?'

Rose picked up the paper, reading that the selected meeting place was King's Theatre, to see a performance of Don Giovanni. She pressed the paper against her beating heart. Flynn was giving her King's Theatre. A real opera, too, with performers singing out the whole story. It was almost exciting enough to forget that he'd pushed her away, accusing her of acting like a harlot. Or that she must meet the man who wanted her to be his harlot.

Letty snatched the paper from Rose's hand. 'Let me read

it again.' Her lips moved as she went over the words. She handed it back to Rose. 'He is saying that Miss Green must come with you.'

'I asked that she be invited. She is one of the girls I lived with.' Rose had never explained much to her father about living in Miss Hart's house. She never explained anything to Letty.

'Where do you meet the marquess?' Her father took another sip of gin.

'She will ruin it, I know she will,' Letty grumbled, crossing the room to pour more gin for herself, drinking it alone in a sulk.

'At King's Theatre, Papa,' Rose replied.

He smiled at her. 'Your mother sang at King's Theatre. Did you know that, Mary Rose?'

'I did, Papa.'

He put his hands on her shoulders. 'Daughter, you are saying you want to sing. Here is your chance!'

She laughed. 'Papa, I am to watch the opera. And the marquess will not be asking me to sing.'

'I keep trying to tell you the way of things.' He put his arm around her and sat her down in one of the chairs. He sat opposite, still holding her hand. 'A woman in the theatre gets work by pleasing the right people, if you get my meaning. This is the life you chose.' He reached over to pick up his glass of gin from the table. 'The marquess has a lofty title and money. 'Tis said he is very generous to his girls.'

'Papa,' she entreated. 'I'm certain I can make money singing. The newspapers said nice things about me. I'm sure to get another job after the Vauxhall season is over.'

Her father took a sip, then shook his head. 'You'll be hired to sing if you have someone asking for you. Like I could ask Mr Hook for you, being in the orchestra and all. But in the theatres, you need a patron, Mary Rose. And if this marquess wants you to sing, you will be finding work.' He took her hand again and made her look at him. 'If you displease such a man, if you spurn him, you'll never work again. All he has to do is say the word.'

Rose glanced away. Flynn had said as much. The marquess had the power to dash her dreams.

Her father squeezed her hand until she looked at him again. 'Listen, your own darling mother might have risen to greatness. She had the voice, the prettiest voice you'd ever be wanting to hear, and she was as lovely—you favour her, Mary Rose.' He smiled sadly. 'She caught the eye of such a man as your marquess. An earl, I'm remembering he was. But she was wanting me, instead.' He shook his head as if he could still not believe it. 'The earl was mighty angry, as you can imagine. And then neither of us could find work anywhere. By then you were on the way, and I took her back to Ireland. It was a long time before the earl forgot, and I could return to Englad to earn good money again. And then, of course, your mother got sick...' His voice faded.

Rose bowed her head, her emotions in a muddle. Her beautiful mother had been faced with such a choice? Her mother had chosen love. Had that not been right?

Her father's eyes filled with tears. 'She got sick, but I was here in London. Working. Never to see her again—' He lowered his head, his shoulders shaking.

Tears poured down Rose's cheeks as well. If she had not been born, perhaps her mother might have returned to the stage. Perhaps she would have become the darling of the London theatre. But her mother had chosen marriage and childbirth and poverty. If she had chosen that earl, perhaps she would have lived.

Rose put her arms around her father. 'Well, I'm meeting the marquess, so there's nothing to fear.'

He lifted his head again and gave her a watery smile.

Rose returned a fond look. She wanted to sing, not only for herself, but for her mother. Let her mother live again through her.

Letty called from her corner of the room. 'What are you talking about, Alroy? I hope you are telling your daughter to get off her duff and take what this marquess wants to offer us.'

'I have convinced her, I think.' Her father sniffed and patted Rose's hand again.

'I'll meet the marquess, Papa,' she repeated.

He smiled again and raised his glass to his lips. Rose left her chair and went to her bedchamber to don her hat, gloves and shawl. When she returned to the parlour, Letty was busy talking with her father of where they might live when the marquess's money was in their pockets.

'Henrietta Street, I'm thinking,' Letty was saying. 'But a proper house, not three rooms—'

'I'm going out, Papa,' Rose broke in.

Her father looked up. 'There's a good girl, Mary Rose. Watch out for yourself.'

'That's right.' Letty laughed. 'We don't want you damaged.'

Rose walked out the door and down to the street. It was a grey day, and she hoped it would not rain. She headed for Covent Garden to find a hackney carriage.

She had never visited Katy, who now lived at Madame Bisou's gaming-house. Madame Bisou had invited Katy to live there after they left Miss Hart's. The other girls had chosen love, Rose reminded herself.

Rose wanted success, now more than anything.

She found a carriage and told the coachman, 'Bennet Street, please.

He let her off at the junction of Jermyn Street and Bennet Street and she walked to a sedate-looking house where anyone might have lived. A large footman answered her knock.

'Good day to you,' Rose said. 'Would you please be telling Miss Green that Miss O'Keefe has come to call?'

The footman put a finger to his cheek. 'Miss Green?' His confusion suddenly cleared. 'Oh. Katy. Just a moment.' When he returned he said, 'Follow me.'

He led her above stairs to a sitting room. Both Katy and Madame Bisou sprang to their feet when she entered.

'Rose! How good to see you.' The *madame* kissed Rose on both cheeks. 'You've not been here since Katy moved in.'

'Forgive me, Madame,' Rose responded, only now realising how much she had missed this woman with her false French accent. The girls had quickly figured out Madame Bisou was not really French. The *madame*'s hair colour, an unnatural red, was false as well.

There was nothing false about her large breasts, pushed up to show to best advantage in her low-cut dress, nor about her generous, loving nature. Rose gave her a heartfelt hug.

Katy came over and Rose also hugged her. 'Who'd have thought you would visit? Vauxhall's newest flower doesn't need a gaming hell.'

Madame Bisou stepped out of the room to arrange for tea and Katy pulled Rose on to a settee.

'So why are you here?' Katy asked. 'Have you met up with the marquess? Have you come to tell us about it?'

'Not exactly,' Rose said. 'But you are not far wrong.'

'I knew it!' said Katy.

Madame Bisou walked back in. 'Tea will be coming, but I must not stay, Rose. I must get back to Iris.'

Katy turned to Rose. 'Iris was badly hurt last night.'

Rose did not know the girl. 'I am sorry to hear of it.'

'She went with me to Vauxhall,' Katy cried. 'But I left her with some fellows when Sir Reginald showed up.'

'It was not your fault, Katy,' Madame Bisou said. 'These things happen.'

'What happened?' Rose asked.

Katy's eyes flashed. 'She went with some man. A gentleman, she thought, because he had fine clothes, but he tied her up and used a whip on her—'

'Used a whip!' Rose exclaimed.

Madame Bisou crossed her arms over her chest, squeezing out even more décolletage. 'I ought to have told you girls of this, but, how could I?'

'Told us what?' Rose asked.

Madame Bisou sat down, facing them. 'Some men seek their pleasure not in the usual way.' She paused. 'Some get their senses aroused by inflicting pain.'

Rose glanced to Katy. 'Pain?'

'Oh, I see,' Katy said. 'Whips and things.'

Rose looked to Madame Bisou. 'Men get pleasure from using whips?'

'Well, it's a rare one that does—not that you don't find plenty, mind you,' Madame Bisou went on. 'Most men, you know, are easily led if you make them think they are seducing you, but some…some get an arousal when they hurt a girl. It is their pleasure to inflict pain. Like a bully, *n'est-ce pas?*'

Rose felt sick at the thought.

'A Frenchman wrote a book about it,' Madame Bisou added.

Rose put her hand on her chest. 'Oh, Katy, you must take care!'

Katy waved a hand. 'I can handle myself.'

'Do you know who hurt the poor girl?' Rose asked the *madame.*

She shrugged. 'Iris said he wore a mask.' She patted Rose's hand. 'I assure you, we do not allow such men in this gaming hell. If we hear of such a man, or if one dares mistreat one of the girls, Cummings tosses him out.'

Rose shook her head. 'But Katy is out and about. At Vauxhall, where so many men wear masks.'

Katy laughed. 'Do you think I cannot spot a viper like that?'

Madame Bisou cautioned her. 'It is sometimes difficult. You cannot tell merely by looking at a man.' She stood. 'I must go.' She took Rose's hand briefly. 'Katy has told me of your marquess. That is good for you, Rose. Tannerton is a good man.'

Even Madame Bisou sang his praises.

Katy settled back in her seat. 'Tell of the marquess. That is what I wish to hear.'

Rose could not help but think that Katy needed the marquess more than she did, no matter what her father said of the theatre. If Katy had enough money, she could abandon this dangerous life.

'I hope you will like it,' Rose said. 'I am to meet with him in two days. His guest at King's Theatre.'

'At a theatre?' Katy seemed unimpressed.

Rose continued. 'The best news is, you are to accompany me.'

Katy's mouth dropped open. 'Me?'

'Yes. I asked if you could come with me.'

Her friend looked at her as if her wits had gone begging. 'But why?'

Rose hesitated before answering. 'I was not wanting to go alone. Mr Flynn is to be there, too. If you do not come, I'll be the only woman with two gentlemen.'

Katy laughed. 'You did not want two men all to yourself? If your marquess is half as handsome as your Mr Flynn, it would be heaven to have them all to yourself.'

Rose felt her cheeks grow hot.

Katy's eyes filled with mischief. 'Why not bring Letty Dawes with you?'

Rose returned a withering glance. 'You must be jesting.'

Katy laughed. 'Oh, I'll go. I have a fancy to meet this marquess who pines for you so strongly. Wish I could play it cool like you do, Rose. Never could disguise wanting a man as much as he might want me.'

Rose gave her a stern look. 'Did not the *madame* always instruct you to dampen such liveliness? Do you not remember?'

'That's like asking a tiger not to have spots,' Katy responded.

Rose could not help but smile.

When the night arrived to attend the opera at King's Theatre, Rose went to Madame Bisou's to dress. The *madame* had insisted on hiring a hairdresser to fix their hair, and Rose and Katy each wore Paris gowns Miss Hart had given them. Katy's was a rich green silk gown that set off her red hair to perfection. Rose wore silk in a pale blush with white lace adorning the bodice and hem. The hairdresser threaded a strand of pearls through her hair, and Madame Bisou lent her pearls to wear around her neck and on her ears.

As Rose and Katy stood next to each other, surveying their images in a full-length mirror, Rose thought they looked tasteful. She had no wish to look like a harlot, even if that was what everyone wished her to be, what Flynn had accused her of being. She looked pretty, but she was nothing compared to Katy. What man could resist Katy's vibrant beauty? Perhaps, if Rose were very lucky, the marquess would transfer his interest to Katy. And Flynn would forgive her.

Gentlemen were already arriving at the gaming-house at the time the marquess's coach was to pick them up. Perhaps they would think her a new girl at this place, not much better than a bawdy house.

She shook her head. She must accustom herself to men thinking of her in this carnal way. It was part of being in the theatre, her father would say. She glanced at Katy, whose excitement just enhanced her lively beauty. How could she not impress the marquess?

Soon the footman came to tell them a gentleman waited for them in the hall.

'Well, you are off, then,' Madame Bisou said, nearly as excited as Katy. 'I wish you good luck.'

She squeezed both their hands, and the two young women descended the stairway. Some men in the doorway of the gaming room stopped to watch them, their sounds of approval reaching Rose's ears. She felt herself blush.

Rose purposely let Katy go first so Katy would make the first impression.

'Why, if it isn't Mr Flynn,' declared Katy halfway down the stairs. She extended her hand so he could assist her on the last few steps. 'Where is the marquess?'

Flynn's eyes followed Rose's slower progress as he answered, 'He will meet us at the theatre.' When Rose reached Katy's side, he said a curt, 'Good evening, Rose.'

'Flynn,' she answered, fearing matters would never be easy between them again.

'Well.' He looked at Katy, but only fleetingly glanced at Rose. 'You look very charming. I am indeed most fortunate to escort you.'

Katy took his arm, holding on to him much too close. 'Let us be off, then. We do not want to keep a marquess waiting.'

Flynn offered his other arm to Rose. Her fingers trembled as they lighted on his sleeve.

In the coach, Katy's lively chatter filled the air, so Rose could excuse it that Flynn did not speak to her. He said a word here and there to encourage Katy to rattle on, but his attention to her friend only made Rose feel worse.

Soon the coach pulled up to King's Theatre. As Flynn escorted them in, Rose forgot everything, even the admiring stares of gentlemen, as she took in the beauty of its grand hall, all marble and gold gilt. Flynn led them up carpeted stairs and past doors to what must be the boxes. They did not go far before he stopped at one and, after making a quick knock, turned the knob.

Katy nearly jumped up and down, but Rose held back, so it was Katy who first entered the darker interior of the box, where Rose could just make out the figure of a man.

He spoke. 'Good evening. You must be Miss Green.'

Katy replied, 'You are correct, sir. I presume you are Lord Tannerton?'

'I am indeed.'

When Rose's eyes adjusted to the dimmer light, she realised the marquess was the tall man she had seen standing near Flynn that first night at Vauxhall, the one with the casual air and affable expression.

'I've seen you at Vauxhall,' Katy said, as if speaking Rose's thoughts.

The marquess smiled. 'I have seen you too, Miss Green. Someone as lovely as yourself cannot be missed.'

Katy laughed, but softly this time. 'I thank you. But you must meet Miss O'Keefe.'

She stepped aside, exposing Rose, and the marquess turned his eyes on her. 'Miss O'Keefe, I am delighted you have come.'

Flynn stepped forward. 'Miss O'Keefe, may I present Lord Tannerton.'

Rose dropped into a curtsy. 'My lord.'

Tannerton extended his hand to her to help her rise. She had no choice but to accept it. 'It is my pleasure to meet you,' he said, holding her hand only a second longer than was comfortable.

He stepped back so that they could come farther into the opera box. Katy moved to the back, as did Flynn.

The Marquess spoke to Rose alone. 'We shall have some refreshments at the intermission, but I have arranged for wine now. Would you care for a glass?'

She needed something to calm her. 'Yes, thank you,' she said.

Flynn immediately poured the wine, but Lord Tannerton handed Rose's glass to her.

'It is French champagne. Bottled before the conflict, but I managed to acquire a case very recently.' He took his own glass. 'May I propose a toast?'

Rose inclined her head, wondering why a marquess would ask her permission.

'To new friends,' he said, turning to include Katy, but letting his gaze linger a bit longer on Rose.

'To new friends,' repeated Katy.

Rose did not speak, but she took a sip.

'Come now,' Tannerton gestured to two front chairs. 'Sit and be comfortable. The performance should start at any moment.'

Rose turned towards Katy. 'Perhaps Katy—Miss Green— would like to sit up front as well?'

Katy ignored Rose's silent plea. 'I'll sit behind you. Keep Mr Flynn company.' For emphasis she laced her arm through Flynn's.

'Come,' Tannerton repeated.

He settled Rose in an elegant brocade chair and sat beside her. For the first time she looked out into the opera house.

'Oh, my!' she exclaimed.

The theatre curtains were rich red with a gold fringe as long as she was tall, with the King's crest, also in gold. The curtains spanned nearly the whole distance from ceiling to floor, a space high enough for several tiers of boxes all around. Light blazed from huge chandeliers close to the stage and from candles all around the edges of the boxes. The orchestra floor was busy with people talking and laughing and moving around. Several of the boxes were empty, but in those that were not, elegant gentlemen were seated with ladies dressed in beautiful gowns. Some were looking straight into their box, pointing and whispering to their companions.

'It is rather thin of company.' Lord Tannerton smiled at her. 'But I hope you like it.'

'It is lovely,' she responded, trying not to think of what the other theatre-goers might be saying about her. 'Much larger than I even could have imagined.' She'd only read of theatres like this one. The closest she'd been to seeing one was when Miss Hart had taken them to Astley's Amphitheatre, but that was an entirely different sort of place. This was the best of theatres.

'I am pleased to be the first to show it to you. Flynn said you had a wish to see it.'

Flynn.

Flynn had made this happen for her. He alone knew how much she desired it. He must have forgiven her wanton behaviour, to give her such a gift. 'I did indeed.'

It had seemed natural to Rose to tell Flynn all about her mother singing in King's Theatre, about her mother's dashed dreams and shortened life. She had no such impulse to tell the marquess.

The musicians entered and took their seats, the violinists tuning their strings, horn players testing their instruments' sound. Though none played at full volume, the notes filled the huge room, and Rose found she was eager to hear the performance, especially the singing.

'Do you fancy yourself singing in this theatre some day?' Tannerton asked her.

Rose shot a glance at him. Had Flynn told him this as well? It seemed a betrayal of confidences. 'Why do you think so?'

He shrugged. 'King's Theatre is the pinnacle, is it not, for singers? At least others have told me so.'

Perhaps Flynn had not told him all her secrets, after all. She heard Flynn behind her talking quietly to Katy and wished he would speak loud enough so she could hear what he said.

Katy disappointed Rose, acting so subdued Tannerton would never notice her. In fact, Katy seemed more determined to have Flynn's company.

Tannerton handed her a paper. 'Here is the programme telling who sings tonight. I will get you a candle if you cannot read it.'

She took the paper and stared at it even though she could read but little in the dim light. It gave her an excuse not to talk to him.

'Thank you,' she said belatedly, briefly glancing at him.

Tanner smiled at her. He had a boyish handsomeness, she had to admit. An open countenance. He was tall and athletic and looked out of place in this elegant theatre, as if he would prefer hunting or whatever gentlemen did in the out of doors. By appearance, and so far by manner, he did not threaten, but Rose could not forget her father's warning. This was a man who possessed the power to ruin her ambitions. She turned back to staring at the programme.

'I think it is about to begin,' Tannerton said.

She glanced at the stage. The conductor of the orchestra took his place. The musicians quieted, but the audience seemed as noisy as ever. The music began. Rose could make out that the opera was one of Mozart's, but she had never heard the music before. Her school had not owned these sheets of music. She poised herself to listen and watch, not wishing to miss a bit of it.

When the curtain opened, she even forgot who sat beside her. The set was magical, looking so real she could barely believe she was not looking through some window. She heard singing voices like she'd never heard before, big voices, bigger than her own, big enough to fill this huge theatre. When the soprano sang, Rose held her breath. She wanted to open her mouth and mimic each note, to try to make her voice bigger, like this one.

She could understand none of the words. She was not even sure what language they were singing. It did not matter, however. The performers showed her the story, a shocking one, really. Don Giovanni was a seducer of women, a man who made conquests and who cared little of what havoc he wreaked in people's lives. When the character Elvira sang, Rose could hear her heartache and her rage. Elvira loved and hated Don Giovanni. Rose wanted to weep for her. How thrilling it would be to sing one's emotions like that.

When the intermission came, Rose felt bereft. She wanted to go on listening. She wanted to step on to the stage and be a part of it, to raise her voice with the others in the beautiful music they created.

Instead, a footman brought in some cakes and fruit and other delicacies.

'At intermission one often calls upon others in other boxes,' Tannerton told her. 'But I have asked the footman to stand outside and explain we do not wish to be disturbed.'

That was kind of him. The last thing she wanted was to have the magic of the performance interrupted by curious people come to see who sat next to the marquess. She was desperately trying to hold on to the music, replaying it in her head, silently singing, wishing she could sound like those wonderful performers.

They took refreshment around a small table. Flynn, sitting directly opposite Rose, poured more champagne.

'How do you like the performance, Miss Green?' Tannerton asked.

Katy grinned. 'It is fun, is it not? Don Giovanni is a clever rogue. I hope he escapes.'

'We shall see,' said Tanner, eyes crinkling into a smile.

Tanner turned to Rose. 'And you, Miss O'Keefe. What do you think of it?'

Rose looked up to see Flynn watching her. He quickly averted his eyes. She could barely speak. Words were not enough to convey what she felt. 'I have never heard such singing,' she said reverently. 'I like it very much.'

'Then I am happy.' Tannerton grinned boyishly. 'I have pleased you both.'

The second half of the opera was every bit as magical. Rose felt the music inside her. She was transported by its beauty, affected by its emotion, and invigorated by possibilities she had not known existed. To sing with such power and feeling. She could hardly wait to try to mimic their sound.

Too soon it was over, the music making its last crescendo. Rose felt as if her soul had been dropped from a great height back into her own body. She applauded with all the energy she possessed.

When the performers took their final bow, the only sounds that could be heard were the scuffling feet and muffled voices of people leaving the theatre.

Lord Tannerton put his hand on her arm. She had forgotten him, forgotten her purpose for being there.

'Time to go, Miss O'Keefe,' he said.

Chapter Seven

Flynn watched Tanner touch Rose's arm. His own hand tingled, as if it were he, not Tanner, who touched her. He stretched and flexed his fingers, trying to dispel the illusion, but it did no good, because Tanner touched her again, escorting her out of the box on his arm. He had known it would be difficult to see her with Tanner. He had just not anticipated how difficult.

There was no doubt in Flynn's mind that he'd chosen well when he'd picked King's Theatre as the place for Tanner to meet Rose. Tanner had grumbled—the man hated opera—but Flynn knew that this place would be more precious to Rose than a whole cask of emerald rings. She would never forget the man who gave her King's Theatre.

Flynn ought to be congratulating himself all round.

But every time Tanner had looked at Rose or leaned towards her or spoke to her it was like daggers were being thrust into Flynn's flesh. He was surprised that the champagne he'd consumed had not spurted out of him like from a water skin poked with holes.

They found Tanner's carriage among the line of vehicles outside. Tanner lifted Rose into it, holding her by the waist. He assisted Katy in the same manner. Flynn was the last inside, taking his seat next to Katy. His gaze met Rose's, and she smiled, gratitude shining in her eyes.

He would not regret giving her this evening, no matter that it signified the loss of a brief, fanciful, mad dream.

The carriage made the short trip to Bennet Street in good time. As it pulled up in front of the gaming-house, Katy said, 'You must all come up for some supper. Madame Bisou has arranged a nice treat.'

'But—' Rose glared at Flynn.

He shook his head. He knew nothing of this.

Tanner gave the answer, agreeable as always. 'Of course we will. Very generous of the *madame*.'

So they all entered Madame Bisou's house and were escorted to a private parlour. The Madame was there to greet them.

'Good to see you, *chérie*.' She offered her cheek for Tanner to kiss. 'You have not favoured us with your presence in an age.'

'That is so.' He smiled apologetically. 'I must rectify that, mustn't I?'

Like two old friends, Tanner chatted with Madame Bisou while she ushered the others into chairs, joining them herself.

They were served cold meats and fruits and cakes and more wine. Tanner began to mellow from the drink.

'And what do you think of our Rose?' Madame Bisou asked him.

Rose stared at her plate, a blush staining her cheeks.

Tanner gazed at her. 'I think she is as lovely as her name.'

The words twisted in Flynn's gut.

Tanner continued to gaze at Rose in frank admiration. 'Do you sing at Vauxhall tomorrow night?' he asked. He

gestured to the clock on the mantel. Dawn was not long
away. 'Tonight, I mean.'

'I do, sir,' she responded in a quiet voice.

Tanner continued, 'Would you do me the honor of sharing
a meal with me at the gardens tomorrow? We can arrange
something, can we not, Flynn?'

Flynn nodded. He could arrange whatever Lord Tannerton wished. That was his job.

Rose glanced at Flynn with a silent panic he did not comprehend. She turned to Tanner. 'I hope you will not mind, sir,
if we include the others present in that invitation? Miss
Green, Mr Flynn and Madame Bisou?'

Flynn admired her skill in turning the invitation around,
making it appear as if chiding Tanner for poor manners. Her
reticence towards Tanner still bewildered him, however. Now
that she'd met him, she could have no further objection to
him.

Flynn noticed Katy flashing her eyes at Rose. Apparently
Katy did not understand such behaviour any better than he
did. Rose gave her a plaintive look in return.

Tanner's face showed dismay, but he answered in his
typical affable tone. 'They shall be included if you wish it.'

Katy rolled her eyes.

Madame Bisou put a hand on Tanner's arm. 'Sweet of you
to include me, *chérie,* but I have a business to attend to.' She
stood. 'In fact, I must check on the gaming room now. I wish
I could accept your invitation.' She smiled at Rose. 'I miss
hearing our Rose sing.'

The connection between Rose and this mistress of a
gaming hell was not lost on Flynn. Rose must not always have
been under her father's thumb. The whole thing was a mystery,
but the real mystery was why it disturbed Flynn so greatly.

Flynn and Tanner stood to bid Madame Bisou adieu, thanking her for the meal. She tweaked Tanner's chin playfully and headed for the door, stopping to look back at him. 'Come play my tables, Lord Tannerton. Come join your friend Pomroy. I believe he is here tonight.'

'Pomroy is here?' said Tanner with interest.

Before the gentlemen could sit again, Katy stood, stifling a yawn that did not look quite real. 'I hope you will forgive me,' she said in a ladylike voice. 'But I must bid you goodnight as well.' She curtsied to Tanner. 'It was a pleasure, sir.'

He gave her a charming smile. 'I will see you in a few hours, Miss Green.'

Katy grinned back. 'You will, won't you?'

Rose also got up from her chair. 'I should retire as well.'

Tanner looked disappointed. 'Must you?'

She nodded. 'I must get some rest if I am to perform.'

'May I escort you to your room?' Tanner asked, somewhat hopefully.

Flynn flinched, preparing for her to say yes.

Rose barely looked at Tanner. 'I do not live here, sir.'

'That is so.' Tanner responded. 'Flynn said you live with your father. Do we return you to your father or do you stay here this night?'

She glanced at Flynn, not Tanner. 'I should prefer to return home.'

Tanner's face fell, but he recovered quickly. 'We will take you home then, will we not, Flynn?' he said in a cheerful voice.

'Indeed,' Flynn responded, trying very hard to keep his voice bland.

If Rose had allowed Tanner to come with her to a room here, her acceptance of his interest would have been secured, and only the financial arrangement would remain for Flynn to manage. The matter would be at an end.

So how was it he was relieved she had not accompanied Tanner to a bedchamber abovestairs?

He followed Tanner as he walked with Rose out of the parlour. As they passed the game room, Tanner hesitated. 'I should like to greet my friend who is here.' He turned to Rose. 'Would you care to come in the game room a moment, Miss O'Keefe? Or would you prefer to have Flynn see you home directly?'

'I prefer to go home,' Rose replied. She extended her hand to Tanner. 'Goodnight, sir.'

He brought her hand to his mouth and kissed the air above it. 'I shall look forward to seeing you at Vauxhall.'

'At Vauxhall,' she said.

Flynn descended the stairway with Rose and collected their things from the footman. Neither of them spoke. Flynn ought to have manoeuvred Tanner to take Rose home. He could have done so with a judicious word. Dear God, why had he not?

He had done this to himself. He wanted to be alone with her in the dark confines of the carriage.

Rose felt a flare of excitement as Flynn assisted her into the carriage. She had been pining to speak with him, to thank him for this wonderful night. To share with him her reaction to the opera. She had so many questions.

He did not sit beside her, but rather took the back-facing seat. She could barely make out his features in the dim light that filtered in from the carriage lamps outside.

As soon as the carriage moved, she leaned toward him. 'Flynn, thank you for this night. I do not know how to express my gratitude.'

'My duty,' he responded curtly.

His stiffness took her aback.

He went on in a dry voice, 'I take it Lord Tannerton was pleasing to you.'

'Lord Tannerton?' She shook her head in confusion. 'I was not speaking of him, but of the opera! Of King's Theatre. I know that was your doing. You knew what it meant to me.'

He did not immediately respond. 'I thought only of what would best facilitate my employer's wishes.'

'That's foolishness you are talking,' Rose retorted. 'You gave me the opera. I know you did.' She hugged herself with remembering it. 'It was so grand! I've never heard such singing! The voices, Flynn. How did they make their voices so big?'

'Big?'

'You know, their voices seemed to come from deep inside them. The sound filled that huge theatre. How did they do that?' Even the mere memory of it excited her. 'I want to learn to do that. Do you think I can, Flynn?' She sang a note, experimenting. 'That is not it, is it? I long to understand how it is done.'

She wanted to practise right now.

'I am sure it can be learned.' His voice turned softer.

'I long to learn it,' She went on. 'I wish I could return to hear them again. I wish I could remember the music and the words. I could not understand the words. Was it Italian? I do not know languages. Just a little French and Latin, but very little.'

'It was Italian,' he said.

'Think how it must be to know what all the words meant.' Some day she would learn Italian, she vowed. 'I wish I had the music. I would memorise every part of it.'

'Lord Tannerton will be gratified that he pleased you.'

He'd not been listening to her. She'd been talking of the

music, not Lord Tannerton. She closed her mouth and re-treated to her side of the carriage, making herself remember the music.

He broke the silence. 'Did you find Lord Tannerton agree-able, Rose?'

'Everything agreeable,' she answered dutifully, trying to recall the melody Elvira sung.

But he'd broken the spell, and she remembered that she'd agreed to see Tannerton again that evening. 'At Vauxhall tonight. How shall I find you?' she asked.

'I will collect you from the gazebo when your perfor-mance is done.'

'Letty will be there. Come alone to fetch me, not with Lord Tannerton.' She did not need Letty speaking directly to Lord Tannerton.

'I will come alone, then,' he agreed. He talked as if they were discussing some manner of business, like paying Tan-nerton's bills. It was business, really. 'Will you see that Miss Green is also there?'

'I will.'

They rode in silence the rest of the way. When the coach came to a stop in front of her lodgings, Flynn helped her out and walked her to the door.

'I will walk you inside,' he said.

There was only one small oil lamp to light the hallway, and Rose heard mice skitter away as soon as their footsteps sounded on the stairs.

In front of her door they were wrapped in near-darkness, a darkness that somehow made him seem more remote and made the music in her mind fade.

'Goodnight, then.' She was unable to keep her voice from trembling.

'Goodnight,' he responded. He turned and walked to the head of the stairs.

She put her hand on the doorknob.

'Rose?'

She turned back to him.

'I am glad you enjoyed the opera.' Before she could reply, he descended the stairs.

That night Greythorne stood in the shadows of the Grove, watching and listening to Rose O'Keefe sing. If anything, her voice was richer this night, especially passionate. Such passion ought to be his, he thought. He'd be her conductor. She would sing only for him, notes only he could make her reach.

He spied Tannerton in the crowd. His adversary, a man who'd struck the initial claim. Greythorne would not let that impede him. It would only make the prize more precious to know he'd stolen it out from under the nose of the Marquess of Tannerton. The man was all Greythorne disdained, a Corinthian who cared more for horses than for the cut of his coat. Who would know they could share the same tailor? If it were not for Weston, the man would look like a ruffian on the street.

After Miss O'Keefe finished, Greythorne watched Tannerton say something to that secretary who always seemed to be about. The two men parted. Something was afoot. If not for a woman, neither he nor Tannerton would spend this much time in London with summer upon them, not when other pleasures beckoned at places like Brighton or even Paris.

Greythorne wondered what it would be like to take Miss O'Keefe to Paris, far away from familiar people or influences. Perhaps that was what he would do, but first he must discover what Tannerton planned for this night.

He followed Tannerton, but the man walked aimlessly, stopping to speak to the few persons of quality who were present at the gardens this night. He ought to have followed the secretary instead. That Flynn fellow ran the show. Greythorne hurried back to the gazebo in time to glimpse the secretary escorting two women, one wearing a hood. He tried to keep them in sight, but lost them in the crowd.

Cursing silently, he continued to search the line of supper boxes where Tannerton had dallied.

Finally he discovered them.

In one of the more private supper boxes, half-obscured by trees near the South Walk arch, sat Tannerton with the hooded lady. Greythorne wagered the woman was Miss O'Keefe. Greythorne waited for the moment he could make himself known.

His eyes narrowed as he watched Tannerton talking to the chit as if she were already his. The marquess had made progress, perhaps, but Greythorne was not ready to concede defeat. His little interlude of two nights before had quite fired his blood for more. He was more than ready to pluck another flower.

A Rose.

Greythorne left the shadows and sauntered across the walk up to the supper box. 'Good evening, Tannerton.' He tipped his hat.

'Evening,' Tannerton reluctantly responded, making no effort to change from his slouch in his chair.

'Forgive me for intruding.' Greythorne made certain to use his smoothest, most ingratiating voice. 'I could not resist the opportunity to tell this lovely creature how much I enjoyed her performance.'

Miss O'Keefe, who had been hiding behind her hood, gave a start. Though he could not see her clearly, he made out the tiniest nod of acknowledgement.

'Kind of you, I am sure,' Tannerton said in an unkind voice.

Greythorne tipped his hat again. 'Perhaps we will meet again, Miss O'Keefe.'

At that moment, the other woman in the box stepped forward, bringing a glass of wine to the lovely Rose. It was Greythorne's turn to be surprised. She was the red-haired harlot whom he had seen with Sir Reginald, the one whose laughter had fired his blood. He widened his eyes in interest, an interest she caught.

She gave him an appraising look in return. 'Good evening, sir.'

He smiled most appealingly and doffed his hat to her. 'Good evening, miss.'

Tanner glanced up at the woman. 'Greythorne was just leaving.'

Greythorne did not miss a beat. 'Regretfully leaving,' he said in his smoothest voice. He tipped his hat again to Rose. 'Miss O'Keefe.' And to the redhead. 'My dear.'

He sauntered back to the South Walk, heading in the direction of the Grove. Not defeated. Exhilarated. Two flowers to pluck instead of one. He'd have them both and rub Tannerton's nose in it.

Rose shuddered. 'That was Lord Greythorne?'

'Who is Lord Greythorne?' Katy asked, still watching him walk away.

'He's a man who…who has asked my father about me,' Rose told her.

Tannerton's open countenance turned dark. 'Not a gentleman worth knowing.'

'Do you say so, Lord Tannerton?' Katy said lightly. 'He seems a fine gentleman to me.'

Tannerton grimaced. 'Something about the fellow. Can't remember it and neither can Flynn.' He turned to Flynn. 'Right, Flynn?'

'Indeed, sir,' Flynn replied.

Katy gave Tannerton's shoulder a playful punch. 'You are just saying that because he wants our Rose.' She laughed. 'Do not tell me you fear a little competition?'

Tannerton sat up. 'I relish competition.'

Rose glanced in the direction where the man had disappeared. He had given her a shiver. She turned to Flynn to see his reaction, but his back was to her. He'd barely spoken to her again tonight, but he spoke easily enough to Katy.

Katy came back to him, grabbing his arm and squeezing it. Rose turned away.

Tannerton regarded Rose with a hopeful expression. 'The dancing has begun. Shall we?'

Rose glanced at Flynn, but he was still thoroughly occupied with Katy. 'Of course,' she said to Tannerton, taking his arm.

By the time they had entered the Grove, the lively country dance had ended, and the orchestra struck up a waltz. Tannerton took her by the hand, twirling her under his arm before placing his other hand at her waist. He led her into the steps with great energy, joining the other couples, who created patterns of wheels within wheels.

Tannerton held her with confidence and moved her skilfully. Rose had had little experience with dancing, less with the waltz, but she was aware of his grace and the allure of his physicality. This was a man who did not take a misstep, a man secure being a man.

Such virtues ought to persuade her to succumb to him. Unfortunately, she spied Flynn leading Katy into the dance, and all Rose could think of was how it would feel to be in Flynn's arms, to be staring into Flynn's eyes as they twirled under the magical lamps of Vauxhall.

When the dance was done, Tannerton did not release her hand. 'Come walk with me,' he urged.

She held back. 'Please, no. I…I have a thirst. From the dancing.'

He gave her a rueful smile that should have melted her heart, but did not. 'Then we must return to the supper box for more refreshment.'

Katy and Flynn entered the box behind them. 'Was that not fun!' Katy exclaimed, giving Flynn another affectionate squeeze.

Rose could barely look at her, she was so filled with envy. 'Next waltz you should dance with Lord Tannerton,' she blurted out.

The marquess paused only a moment before affably agreeing. 'A capital idea. We shall trade partners.'

Rose was mortified that she had spoken so impulsively. She tried to tell herself that she had done it because she wanted Tannerton to transfer his affection to Katy. But that would be a lie. She'd merely been jealous.

Mr Hook did not keep them waiting long for another waltz, understanding his audience's preference for the more intimate dance, where the man held the woman in his arms.

Flynn did not seem as eager this time to follow Tannerton to the dancing area. Rose felt another wave of guilt for pushing herself on him when he had placed her off limits to him, but Katy had so easily taken her place.

All such thoughts were forgotten when she faced him and stared up into his blue eyes. He swung her into the pattern of twirling couples, not nearly as skilfully as Tannerton, but it hardly mattered. Rose settled into his arms with the feeling she belonged there.

He did not speak, but neither did he take his eyes off hers. Rose's vision blurred everything but him, and for this small space of time, she pretended that there was no one in the world except the two of them. At first he held her lightly, as if not wishing to touch her at all, but with each turn he seemed to pull her closer to him. She wished they would turn and turn and turn until their bodies touched and they moved as one. She wished she could burst into a joyous song that would never end.

But the music did end. Flynn still held her.

'Thank you, Flynn,' she murmured, gazing into his eyes.

His eyes were dark and needful, and the blood raced through her veins in response. She felt herself pulled to him, closer and closer, just as the twirling of the dance had drawn them close.

He held up a hand and stepped back. 'Tannerton will be waiting.'

Chapter Eight

Two days later Flynn once more stood before the door of Rose O'Keefe's lodgings. Tanner had charged him with giving Rose something that would induce her to accept him. Something more precious to her than emerald rings. Something that was her heart's desire. Something that would ensure his winning over Greythorne.

Flynn had arranged it.

He listened to the voices of Mr O'Keefe and Miss Dawes inside, and hesitated a moment before rapping on the door.

'Answer the door,' Miss Dawes shouted from within.

Footsteps sounded across the floor. The door opened.

'Yes?' O'Keefe broke into a smile when he saw Flynn standing there. 'Why, it is Mr Flynn, is it not? Come in, sir. Come in.'

Flynn entered the room.

'Mr Flynn...' Miss Dawes's voice was syrupy '...it is a pleasure to see you.'

'I come to call upon Miss O'Keefe, if you please,' Flynn said.

O'Keefe looked hopeful.

Miss Dawes said, 'I hope you have come to make an offer. We cannot wait for ever.'

Flynn disliked such brashness. 'I would urge more patience. The marquess is taking the next step. That is why I have come.'

'Rose is at the market, shopping for dinner. She will be home shortly.' Miss Dawes gave a frustrated gesture, and Flynn spied the emerald ring on her finger.

Flynn frowned. 'I must take my leave. I shall return when Miss O'Keefe is home.'

Before they could object, he was out of the door, heading to the market in hopes of finding her. He passed stall after stall of fruits and vegetables, each owner loudly attesting that his wares were the finest. One stall even sold hedgehogs, an animal some Londoners fancied as a pet, mainly because of its appetite for beetles.

Covent Garden was also the 'den of iniquity,' the place where dolly-mops and lightskirts congregated, displaying themselves much like the colourful oranges, limes and lemons on the fruit stalls. Had Flynn wished for some female company, he had only to nod and show his coin, but he was intent on finding Rose.

He spied her at a stand where herbs were displayed, lifting a fragrant bundle of lavender to her nose. He navigated his way through the shoppers to reach her.

She saw him approach and put the lavender down. 'Flynn.' She gave him a cautious smile.

He tipped his hat. 'Good day, Rose.'

'What a lovely surprise.' Her smile fled as she glanced over to a group of doxies loudly hawking themselves. 'Are…are you here to shop?'

He saw the direction of her gaze and realised she thought he might be looking for female company. 'I came looking for you.'

'For me?' Her emerald eyes looked cautious.

'Come, let us walk together.' He reached for the basket she carried on her arm.

They strolled past the stalls in the direction of her lodgings, entering a quieter part of the street.

'Why did you look for me, Flynn?' She asked in a soft voice.

'Lord Tannerton has a gift for you.'

She blinked and looked away. 'I do not want a gift.'

'You will like this one,' he assured her.

She tossed him a sceptical glance.

'Lord Tanner has arranged for Signor Angrisani and Miss Hughes of King's Theatre to give you lessons in voice—'

She clutched his arm. 'You do not mean it!'

He tried to keep his face composed, but her excitement resonated inside him. 'Indeed. And if your voice is suitable, Lord Tanner has convinced Mr Ayrton to use you in the chorus, for at least one performance.'

'Mr Ayrton?'

'The musical director,' he explained.

Her eyes grew as large as saucers. 'I would perform on the stage of the King's Theatre?'

'Yes.'

'Oh, Flynn!' Her voice cracked and her face was flushed with colour. Every muscle and nerve in his body sprang to life.

'It is wonderful!' She twirled around, but stopped abruptly. 'Oh.'

'What?'

She stared into the distance as if unable to speak. Suddenly she turned back to him. 'Lord Tannerton arranged this?'

He opened his mouth to answer, but was silenced by another transformation of her features.

An ethereal smile slowly grew on her face, and she seemed to glow from within. She lifted her jewel-like eyes to his. 'You arranged this, Flynn.'

Both gratification and guilt engulfed him. He'd pleased her, as he longed to do, but she must believe it was on Tannerton's behalf.

She touched his arm, the sensation of her fingers on his sleeve radiating through all parts of him.

'*You* arranged this for me.' Her voice was awed. 'Oh, Flynn!'

Rose took in Flynn's handsome, too-serious features, her heart swelling in her chest. He alone had known what this meant to her. Flynn was giving her what she'd dreamed of for as long as she could remember.

'You have arranged for my fondest wish to come true,' she whispered, gazing into the depths of his eyes.

Four young bucks staggered toward them, holding on to each other and swaying with too much drink. One of them grinned. 'You plucked a right rose,' he said to Flynn. 'M'hat's off to you.' The young man tried to reach his hat, but the lot of them nearly toppled over as a result. With his companions cursing him for nearly knocking them down, they stumbled away.

'They think I am your doxy,' she said to Flynn.

She'd received other frank remarks from men in the market that afternoon, remarks that made her cringe with discomfort and hurry on her way, but somehow she did not mind so much to be thought of as Flynn's doxy.

But he looked pained, so she changed the subject. 'Tell me where I am to go, what time, what I am to do.'

'If you are able, the *signor* and Miss Hughes will see you at King's Theatre tomorrow, at two o'clock.' He spoke stiffly, as if he were scheduling some appointment for the marquess. 'I shall come to escort you there.'

'You will?' That made her even happier. She wanted to share her dream with him.

They walked the rest of the way to her lodgings, she in happy silence. All she could think of was walking in to King's Theatre on Flynn's arm. Perhaps he would stay and listen to her sing. Perhaps he would escort her home and she could talk to him about each moment of the lesson.

Her building was in sight, and she was loathe to leave him, even though his expression was as hard as chiselled granite. This gift he would give her came with strings attached, she knew. The time was approaching when she must repay Lord Tannerton for what Flynn had done for her.

As they neared the door of her building, Flynn slowed his pace. 'I spoke with your father and Miss Dawes,' he said. 'They are pressing for Lord Tannerton to make his offer.'

She nodded.

'It is your move, Rose, but I urge you not to delay. Your father may accept another offer not to your liking.'

'With Greythorne?'

'Yes.'

Rose knew he spoke the truth.

'I must accept Tannerton,' she said in a resigned voice. 'I know this.'

His eyes seemed to reflect her pain. 'Soon,' he said.

The next day Rose and Flynn stood in the hall of King's Theatre with Mr Ayrton, the musical director of *Don Giovanni*.

'So pleased to meet you, Miss O'Keefe. Any friend of the marquess is certainly a friend to us. He is the most generous of men...'

He escorted them through the pit of the theatre to the stage, where, standing next to a pianoforte, were two men and a woman.

'I am to go on the stage?' Rose asked in wonder.

'Indeed,' replied Mr Ayrton. 'What better place to examine the quality of your voice?'

Flynn held back, and Rose twisted around to give him one more glance before she followed Mr Ayrton to the stage entrance.

She was presented to Miss Hughes. 'Hello, my dear,' the woman said in her melodious Welsh accent.

'You played Elvira!' Rose exclaimed, stunned that this ordinary woman had transformed herself into that character, so much larger than life.

'That I did.' Miss Hughes smiled.

'I confess I am surprised you are not Italian. I could not tell, to be sure.'

The next person introduced to her was Signor Angrisani. 'And you were Don Giovanni,' Rose said, as he gave her a somewhat theatrical bow.

'That is so,' he said smoothly. 'And I am Italian, unlike Miss Hughes.'

The third man was the pianist, a Mr Fallon, who merely nodded.

'I shall leave you to these excellent teachers,' Mr Ayrton said. 'But I assure you, I shall listen with Mr Flynn.'

Rose's nerves fluttered, and she was grateful Flynn would be with her the whole time. She gazed out into the theatre, but it was too dark to see him.

She turned back to Miss Hughes and Signor Angrisani. 'Thank you both for taking your time to teach me.'

'Oh—' Miss Hughes laughed '—we have been amply

rewarded, I assure you. Shall we warm your voice and discover your range?'

They began by having her sing what she could only describe as nonsense sounds, exercise for her voice.

'Some scales, if you please,' Angrisani said, nodding to the pianist, who played a scale pitched in middle C.

Rose sang the notes, concentrating on each one. They made her sing them again, and then went higher until Rose could feel the strain. They asked the same thing, going lower and lower.

Then Miss Hughes handed her a sheet of music. *In qulai eccessi* she read.

'I do not know these words,' Rose said.

'Do not distress yourself.' The *signor* patted her arm. 'Speak them any way you wish.'

She examined the sheet again, mentally playing the notes in her head as if plucking them out on her pianoforte.

She glanced at Miss Hughes. 'This is your song from the opera.'

'It is, my dear,' the lady responded. 'Now, let us hear you sing it.'

Rose tried, but stumbled over the foreign words and could not keep pace with the accompaniment.

'Try it again,' Miss Hughes told her.

The second time she did much better. When she finished she looked up to see Miss Hughes and Signor Angrisani frowning.

The *signor* walked up to her. 'You have a sweet voice, very on key and your…how do you say?…your diction is good.'

She felt great relief at his compliment.

'But your high notes are strained. You are breathing all wrong and you have poor volume,' Miss Hughes added. 'You must sing to the person in the farthest seat.'

Rose nodded.

'Sing louder,' Miss Hughes ordered.

She sang again, looking out into the house, thinking of Flynn sitting in the farthest seat. She sang to him.

But it did not please the *signor* and Miss Hughes. They fired instructions at her. 'Stand up straight.' 'Open your mouth.' 'Breathe.'

There was so much to remember.

'Breathe from here.' Miss Hughes put her hand against Rose's diaphragm. 'Not here.' She touched Rose's chest. 'Expand down with your muscles. You will get the volume.'

Rose attempted it, surprised when she sounded louder.

For the high notes, Signor Angrisani told Rose to lift the hard palate in the roof of her mouth. 'Inhale,' he said. 'As if you are about to sneeze. Drop your tongue. Now push out through your nose.'

She was dismayed at how many tries it took to co-ordinate all these instructions. When she succeeded, the notes came out crystal clear.

It seemed as if the lesson were over in the wink of an eye. Her mind raced with trying to remember everything they had told her. She must not have done too badly, because they invited her back in three days' time. As Signor Angrisani walked her back to the pit, Rose put her hand to her throat, wanting to protect it for the next lesson, hoping she would not strain it by singing at Vauxhall in a few short hours. She would fix herself some hot water flavoured with lemon juice to soothe it.

As the *signor* walked her through the theatre, she saw two men standing at the back. She could hardly wait to reach Flynn.

'I shall bid you good day.' Signor Angrisani stopped halfway through the theatre. He kissed her hand.

'Thank you, *signor,*' she said, trying to use the proper accent.

He smiled. 'Eh, you shall do well, did I not say?'

He had not said, but she was delighted to hear it now.

She felt like skipping the rest of the way to where Flynn waited.

As she got close, she saw that the gentleman standing next to Flynn was not Mr Ayrton, but Lord Tannerton.

She lost the spring in her step.

'Lord Tannerton,' she said as she neared him. She dropped into a graceful curtsy.

He smiled at her. 'How did you like your lesson?'

She darted a glance to Flynn, who stood a little behind him. 'I liked it very much, sir. I am indebted to you for your generosity.'

He waved a dismissive hand. 'Ah, it was nothing. Glad to do it if it gives you pleasure.'

'Great pleasure, my lord.'

Rose had no doubt the marquess could easily afford whatever sum it took to make Mr Ayrton, Miss Hughes and Signor Angrisani so agreeable, but she did not forget that it was Flynn who had made this happen.

'As much pleasure as I receive hearing your voice, I wonder?' His expression was all that was agreeable.

She cast her gaze down at the compliment.

'May I have the honor of escorting you home, Miss O'Keefe?'

She glanced up again. 'Oh, I would not trouble you. I am certain I might easily find a hack.'

'It is no trouble,' he reassured her. 'My carriage should be right outside. It shall give me the opportunity to hear your impression of your tutors.'

She'd been eager to tell Flynn everything, but now she could think of nothing to say about her lesson.

There was no refusing the marquess now, or, she feared, when he asked for more intimate favours. 'Very well, my lord.'

'I shall see you back at Audley Street, Flynn.' Tannerton said this affably, but it was still a dismissal.

Flynn nodded, but said nothing. He turned and walked out of the theatre.

Rose was alone with the marquess.

'Shall we go?' He offered his arm.

When they made their way to the hall, Rose saw Flynn just disappearing through the doors. By the time she and the marquess reached the street, she could not see Flynn at all.

'My carriage, Miss O'Keefe.' As he spoke, the carriage pulled up to the front of the theatre.

King's Theatre was located in Haymarket. She would have several minutes of riding alone with him to Covent Garden. He gave his coachman the name of her street and helped her into the carriage.

'And how did you find the lesson?' he asked after they were settled in and the coach began moving.

'There seems much to learn,' she replied.

'I suspect you will be a good student.'

He asked her other questions about the lesson, about what she thought she needed to learn, about singing in general. It was the sort of conversation intended to put a person at ease. She admired his skill at it. She had to admit his interest in her likes and dislikes seemed genuine, though she could not imagine him burning with ambition, as she and Flynn did. He could not possibly understand what it meant to her to sing, not like Flynn understood.

Rose glanced at him. He was a handsome man, more

handsome, perhaps, than Flynn, whose features were sharper and his expression more intense. But Lord Tannerton did not make her heart race. When he gazed upon her, he did not seem to see into her soul.

'I have strict orders from Flynn not to walk you inside your lodgings,' Tannerton said as they passed Leicester Square. 'I gather he does not wish me to encounter your father.'

She almost smiled. More likely Flynn was protecting him from Letty.

'Mr Flynn is a careful man,' she said.

'Oh, he is exceptional, I'll grant you that,' Tannerton agreed.

'How long has Mr Flynn been your secretary?' She knew the answer, of course, but she would rather talk about Flynn than anything else.

He paused, thinking. 'Six years, I believe.' They walked on. 'Not that I expect him to remain,' he added.

This was new information. 'Oh?'

He gave her a sly glance. 'Can you keep a secret, Miss O'Keefe?'

'Of course I can.' She kept many secrets.

He leaned closer and whispered. 'Our Flynn burns with ambition, you know. He wants to rise higher than his present employ and deserves to, I believe. I have lately spoken to the Duke of Clarence about Flynn. His Royal Highness will come around, I think. God knows, he could use a man like Flynn.'

Flynn to work for royalty. For a Royal duke? All Rose knew about the Prince Regent's second brother was that his mistress had been Mrs. Jordan, a famous actress. But that poor lady had died not long ago. It was said the Duke would marry now. He would become more serious about his station in life.

Flynn would serve the Duke well, no doubt, Rose thought. Such employment meant the fulfilment of his dreams.

Both their dreams would come true. She ought to be happy. Only, at this moment, it merely made her sad.

'This is my street,' she said, looking out of the window. 'The coachman should stop here.'

He rapped on the roof of the carriage, and it slowed to a stop. He got out and helped her descend.

She pointed to a building two doors down. 'That is my building.'

He turned to see which one she meant and spoke suddenly. 'What the devil is that fellow doing here?'

She saw a man walk out of her building and turn in the opposite direction from where the carriage had stopped.

Greythorne.

Chapter Nine

Tanner asked his coachman to follow Greythorne. The man walked only a short distance before jumping into a hack, but luck was with Tanner—Greythorne left the vehicle at White's. He could not have picked a better place for an accidental meeting.

'I'll not need you,' Tanner told his driver. 'Take the horses back.' He glanced up at the threatening sky, wondering if he'd regret that decision if caught in a downpour.

He entered the gentleman's club and greeted the doorman by name, divesting himself of his hat and gloves. Sauntering into the dining room, he spied Greythorne alone at a table, placing his order with the footman. Tanner acknowledged the few other gentlemen in the room who gestured for him to sit down, but instead made his way to Greythorne.

'Well, look who is here,' said Greythorne, watching him approach.

Tanner grinned. 'I'll take that as an invitation to join you.' He signalled the servant for some ale and lounged in the chair opposite his rival.

'Ale?' Greythorne sniffed.

Tanner cocked his head. 'I like ale.'

Greythorne lifted his nose. 'To what do I owe this…honour?'

'Thought I would see how our game is going.' He leaned forward. 'Making any progress?'

Greythorne sneered. 'Do you think I would tell you?'

Tanner sat back again. 'Actually, I did. I mean, if you have won the girl, you would be more than happy to tell me.'

The servant brought Tanner his ale and brandy for Greythorne.

'So,' Tanner went on, 'you have not won the girl, but neither have you given up, I'd wager.'

Greythorne scowled at him. 'I am progressing nicely, if you must know.'

'Indeed?' Tanner said. 'So am I. What is your progress?'

Greythorne swirled the brandy in his glass and inhaled its bouquet before taking a gentlemanly sip. Only then did he answer, 'I believe I shall not tell you.'

Tanner lifted his tankard and gulped some ale, licking his lips of the remaining foam. 'Then I cannot very well report my progress either, can I? We are at a stand.'

Greythorne eyed him with disgust. 'I am sure it makes not a whit of difference to me.'

Tanner leaned forward again. 'Does not the competition fire your blood, man? The prize becomes more precious for knowing another covets it.'

'For you, perhaps,' Greythorne said with a casual air Tanner did not believe in the slightest.

'Where is your fighting spirit?' Tanner taunted. 'This is a manly challenge, is it not? Who will win the fair maid?'

Greythorne gave a sarcastic laugh. 'Shall we joust for our little songstress? Shall we don our chainmail and armour and wave our banners?'

Tanner pretended to seriously consider this. 'The Tanner-ton armour will not fit me. Too small.' He eyed Greythorne. 'Might fit you, though.'

The barb hit. Greythorne's eyes flashed with anger as he took another sip of his brandy.

Smiling inwardly, Tanner went on, 'No a joust would not do. How about fisticuffs?'

The man nearly spat out his drink. 'Do not be absurd!'

Tanner pretended to be offended. 'You proposed a physical contest, not I.'

'I am not going to engage in a physical contest to see who wins the girl,' Greythorne snapped.

Tanner lifted his tankard. 'I beg your pardon. I misunder-stood you.' He took one very protracted gulp, knowing he kept Greythorne hostage during it. Finally he set the tankard back on the table and continued as if he'd never interrupted his conversation. 'So no physical contest for the girl. I do agree. That seems rather trite. How about a physical contest to learn this progress we each have made?'

Greythorne looked aghast.

Gratified, Tanner went on, 'If you win, I tell you what we have achieved in conquest of the girl. If I win, you tell me the progress you have made. Agreed?'

'No, I do not agree!' Greythorne looked at him as if he were insane. 'You would have us pound at each other with our fists over such a trifle? I assure you, I would do no such thing.'

Tanner did not miss a beat. 'Oh, not fisticuffs. That would not be a fair fight at all. I've no real desire to injure you—well, not much of a desire anyway—or to injure my hands.' He looked at his hands as if admiring them.

Greythorne's eyes shot daggers.

Tanner returned a sympathetic look. 'We could tame this for your sake. Perhaps a game of cards, if a physical contest is too fearful—I mean, if it is not to your liking.'

The man straightened in his chair. 'I am well able to defend myself, if the sport is a gentlemanly one.'

'Oh?' Tanner lifted his brows. 'A race, perhaps? On horseback or phaeton?'

Greythorne grimaced.

'No? Too dirty?' Tanner said. 'What then?'

He waited, enjoying the corner he'd put Greythorne in.

Finally Greythorne answered, 'Swords.'

Tanner grinned. 'Swords it is!'

When they walked out of White's, leaving a rustle of voices discussing what was overheard, it had started to rain. Greythorne opened an umbrella, not offering its shelter to Tanner as they walked from St. James's to Angelo's Fencing Academy next door to Gentleman Jackson's Boxing Club on Bond Street. To thoroughly annoy Greythorne, Tanner sustained his friendly conversation the whole way, as if they were fast friends instead of adversaries.

When they entered the Academy, Tanner received a warm greeting from the third-generation Angelo to run the establishment. Tanner and Greythorne both stripped to their shirtsleeves.

'Choose your weapon,' Tanner invited.

'Épée?' responded Greythorne. 'And shall we forgo masks?'

Tanner approved of that bit of bravado. He preferred clearly seeing the expression on his adversary's face. In Greythorne's case, he assumed it would be like reading a book.

'How many touches?' Tanner asked.

Greythorne thought a moment. 'Five.'

Tanner nodded.

With Angelo and a few others watching, they saluted and faced each other *en garde*. Tanner gave Greythorne invitation, carefully watching how the man moved. Greythorne engaged his sword, and the sound rang throughout the room. Parrying the thrust, Tanner executed his riposte with just enough speed and skill to keep Greythorne attacking.

Again and again, Greythorne lunged and engaged. The man was light on his feet and had a supple wrist. He also had confidence in his skill. Tanner had to concentrate to keep up his defence. Greythorne managed a clever glissade, sliding his blade along Tanner's, creating music not unlike a bow across a violin. The point of his sword hit Tanner's shoulder.

'Touché,' cried Greythorne.

'Bravo,' someone called from the sidelines. Gentlemen from White's, who had overheard the challenge, took their places to witness the fun.

Tanner acknowledged the touch, while a flurry of bet-making commenced among the onlookers. As near as he could tell, the odds were not in his favour.

He and Greythorne walked back to the middle of the room. Tanner glanced over and saw his friend Pomroy standing next to Angelo. Pomroy regarded Tanner with raised brows. Tanner lifted a shoulder and gave Pomroy a rueful smile.

He took position opposite Greythorne again.

'You will lose both this and our other little competition,' Greythorne boasted, as his épée clanged against Tanner's blade, driving Tanner backwards. Tanner allowed alarm to show on his face as Greythorne looked more and more self-assured. Greythorne whipped the blade upward, its edge catching Tanner's face before the point pressed into his neck.

'*Touché*,' Greythorne repeated.

Tanner felt a trickle of blood slide down his cheek. Greythorne's eyes shone with excitement, a change in demeanour Tanner did not miss. He swiped at his cheek with his sleeve, staining the cloth red.

The contest resumed, and the shouts of their onlookers grew louder. The épées touched in a flurry of thrusts and ripostes, clanging louder and louder. Salty sweat dripped down Tanner's face and stung the cut on his cheek. Greythorne sweated as well, his pace slowing, but his skilled work with the sword continued to keep Tanner on alert. When Greythorne earned one more touch, his laughter at the feat lacked force. Three *touchés* to Tanner's zero. The odds against Tanner winning went up.

Tanner breathed hard as they stood *en garde* again. Greythorne began the same pattern of thrusts and parries he'd executed before with great success. This time, however, they merely informed Tanner exactly what would happen next. At Greythorne's counter-riposte, Tanner parried and lunged, forcing Greythorne's blade aside. He quickly attacked again, the point of his épée pressing at Greythorne's heart.

The onlookers applauded, and the wagering recommenced. Greythorne's eyes widened in surprise.

They began again. This time Tanner went on the attack. He picked up the pace of his swordwork, then slowed it again, until Greythorne's brows knitted in confusion and he began making simple mistakes. Tanner drove Greythorne back again and again, each time striking a different part of his body, all potentially lethal had the épées not been affixed with buttons to prevent the sword from running straight through the flesh. He earned three more *touchés*.

With the score four *touchés* to Greythorne's three, Greythorne rallied, giving the contest more sport and increasing the frenzy of betting among the onlookers. The blades sang as they struck against each other, the sound much more pleasing to Tanner's ear than what he heard in King's Theatre or Lady Rawley's music salon. He relished it all. The strategy and cunning, the rumble of the onlookers, the danger, the sheer exertion.

He and Greythorne drove each other back and forth across the floor as the onlookers shouted louder and louder, odds changing with each footstep. Greythorne engaged more closely in an impressive display, the look of victory on his face. He lunged.

Tanner twisted around, parrying the attack from behind. He continued to spin, lifting Greythorne's blade into the air, forcing him off balance. Tanner made the circle complete as he swung his blade back to press against Greythorne's gut. The surprised man stumbled and fell backwards to the floor.

'That was five! Five *touchés!*' someone cried from the side.

Tanner continued the pressure of the dulled tip of his blade on the buff-coloured pantaloons Greythorne wore. The fabric ripped.

'You've damaged my clothes!' Greythorne seethed.

Tanner flicked the épée slightly and the tear grew larger. 'What say you?'

Greythorne moved the blade aside with his hand and sat up. He did not look at Tanner.

'What progress?' Tanner demanded.

Greythorne struggled to his feet. 'I am to dine with her tonight at Vauxhall.'

The onlookers had not attended to what must have seemed to them an epilogue to the drama. Wagers were settled and the onlookers dispersed, a few gentlemen first coming up to Tanner and clapping him on the shoulder. The winners of the betting, he surmised. Pomroy waited while he dressed. After thanking Angelo, he and Pomroy walked to the door. Greythorne was just ahead of them.

Outside rain was falling as if from buckets.

'My clothes will be ruined!' Greythorne snarled.

He held back, but Tanner and Pomroy did not hesitate to step out into the downpour, breaking into laughter as they left Greythorne in the doorway.

'Damned prig!' Pomroy said.

They ducked into the first tavern they came to, already crowded with others escaping the weather, including some of the gentlemen who had witnessed the swordfight. Tanner accepted their congratulations good naturedly. He and Pomroy pushed their way to a small table in the back.

When they were settled and some ale was on the way, Pomroy said, 'What the devil was that all about?'

Tanner grinned. 'I exerted myself to discover what Greythorne next planned in his conquest of Miss O'Keefe.'

'Such a trifle?' Pomroy pointed to the cut on his cheek. 'There was not an easier way to come upon that information?'

'And miss that sport?' Tanner felt his injury with his finger.

A harried tavern maid brought them their ale, and Tanner took a thirsty gulp.

'I discovered something about your fashionable adversary,' Pomroy said.

Tanner sat forward. 'Tell me, man.'

His friend took a sip of his ale instead. Tanner drummed the table with his fingers while he waited. Pomroy placed the tankard down and brushed the moisture from his coat sleeves, merely to delay and to annoy Tanner.

'I discovered…' he finally began, pausing to give Tanner a teasing smirk '…that your friend is not welcome at several of the brothels in town.'

'This is all?' Tanner took another drink.

His friend waved a finger in the air. 'Think of it. Why would a man be barred from a brothel?'

'Not paying?' Tanner ventured. 'Emitting too great a stench?'

Pomroy shook his head. 'He has been barred because of cruelty. He inflicts pain.'

Tanner recalled Greythorne's eyes when his sword drew blood. He frowned. 'I remember now. Morbery went to school with him. Told me once Greythorne passed around de Sade's books and boasted of engaging in his practices.' He halfway rose to his feet. 'Perverted muckworm. I must take my leave, Pomroy. The devil is set to dine with her this night.' He dug in his pocket for some coin, but sat back down. 'Dash it. I'm spoken for tonight. Clarence again.'

'Send the ever-faithful Flynn,' drawled Pomroy.

The rain settled into a misty drizzle that Flynn did his best to ignore as he stood under the scant shelter of a tree bordering the Grove at Vauxhall. There were a few other hearty souls who had braved the weather to listen to Rose sing, but Flynn had not seen Greythorne among them.

He'd listened with alarm to what Tanner had told him about Greythorne. A devotee of the Marquis de Sade, the man who said 'the only way to a woman's heart is along the path of torment.' Flynn knew the man's works. De Sade's books were more popular at Oxford than the texts they were meant to study. Flynn had read the forbidden volumes as assiduously as the other Oxford fellows. De Sade had a brilliant mind and a perverted soul; if Greythorne meant to practise his brand of pleasure on Rose, Flynn would stop him—no matter what he had to do to accomplish it.

As he listened to her, Flynn thought Rose's singing altered. She sang with less emotion, less energy, perhaps due to the rain, or Greythorne, or strain from her voice lesson. He could tell she was attempting to put her newfound knowledge into practice, trying to breathe as they'd taught her, to sing the highest notes as they'd taught her, but she seemed self-conscious, as if fearing her knuckles would be rapped at any moment if she made an error.

He missed the undisguised pleasure that had come through in her voice before, but he well understood her determination to improve. His own ambition was as keen. They both burned with the need to rise high, as if achieving less than the highest meant total failure.

Flynn knew Tanner would let him open doors for Rose, like the one he'd opened for her at King's Theatre. The marquess had the power to fulfil her dreams.

When she finished singing her last note and curtsied to the audience, the applause was nearly drowned out by the sound of the rain rustling through the leaves and hissing on the hot metal of the lamps' reflectors. Flynn quickly made his way to the gazebo door. A few other admirers also gathered there.

He knocked on the door and gave his name and card to the servant who answered it. When he was admitted, he heard another not so fortunate fellow say, 'How did he get in?'

The servant left him alone in the gazebo's lower room, and a moment later Rose came rushing in, directly into his arms.

'Oh, Flynn! I hoped you would come!'

He could not help but hold her as she clung to him and buried her face in the damp fabric of his caped greatcoat. When she finally pulled away, tears glistened on her dark lashes.

'When does Greythorne come?' he asked.

She glanced up in surprise. 'You knew of it?'

He nodded.

A faint smile flitted across her face. 'He cancelled. Postponed, I mean.'

He gazed at her. 'Let us go somewhere we can talk.'

She went to take her cloak off a hook on the wall. When they walked out, the bedraggled men outside could be heard saying, 'That's her!' and 'Dash it! He's cut us out.'

He whisked her away, leading her down the Dark Path. It was dotted with small classical structures where couples could be private. Flynn tried the knob of the first one they came to, and, finding it unlocked, brought her inside. Rushlights lit the interior. A table was set with wine and two glasses.

'I am guessing this party has been cancelled,' Flynn said, gesturing to the table. 'Come.' He led her to the single *chaise-longue,* the only place to sit. 'If they do show up, we will make an apology and leave.'

He unfastened her cloak and laid it aside with his greatcoat, hat and gloves before coming to sit next to her. Taking her hand in his, he pulled off her gloves, one finger at a time.

She could barely breathe for the feel of his bare hand upon hers. 'Greythorne gave my father money for my company.'

He held both her hands in his.

She stared at them. 'But…but when the rain came he… begged off. He sent a message. So I do not know when I shall be required to meet him. I do not wish to meet him at all, Flynn!'

He nodded, squeezing her hands. 'Have no fear. I will think of some way to help.'

Rose gazed at him, feeling relief and something even more

powerful. She could not believe he had come to her, rain and all. Now that his hands folded over hers, tethering her with his strength, she had not realised how keenly she needed him.

But he released her and stood, turning his back to her. 'Lord Tannerton is prepared to better any offer Greythorne makes.'

She bowed her head. Tannerton again. Standing between them. 'When?' She felt the gloom descend upon her.

He answered in a low voice. 'I must go to your father with Tannerton's offer. If he accepts right away and does not wait for Greythorne to make a counter-offer, then it would still take me a week to make arrangements.' He turned back to her. 'Two weeks, perhaps.'

'Two weeks,' she whispered.

He came to sit next to her again. 'There is no other choice, Rose.'

Her mind had accepted this. She wanted to sing. She wanted some day to sing Elvira's part in Don Giovanni, to be a name everyone knew, like Catalani, and she wanted nothing to stop her. She wanted to live the life her mother had lost.

Only her heart warred with that ambition. Her heart pined for love. For Flynn.

She pulled away from him and rose from the chaise. 'I do not want to stay here, Flynn. I…I feel as if I am trespassing.'

She bent down to pick up her cape. He came to her and took the cape from her hands, wrapping it around her. He fastened it under her chin and pulled the hood up to cover her head. She had difficulty breathing, he was so near. She dared not lift her chin to look into his eyes, because she wanted so dearly for his eyes to burn with the same desire raging inside her.

But she could not help herself. She tilted her head back. His eyes were dark with passion. The joy of it caused her knees to go weak. All she need do was close the distance between them and place her lips on his. What harm to taste his lips just once? Everyone expected her to be a wanton, why not behave like one now? She longed to be the wanton with Flynn.

'Flynn,' she whispered.

Rising on tiptoe, she touched her lips to his, lightly at first. When he did not move away, she slid her arms around his neck and increased the pressure. His lips parted, and she darted her tongue into his mouth where he tasted warm and wet and wonderful.

A low groan escaped him, and as she felt his breath cool her mouth, she grasped him tighter. His arms encircled her and he slammed his body against hers, his fingers pressing into her soft flesh. All sensation raced to where he ground himself against her, urging her on, thrilling her with the feel of his manhood hard beneath his clothes.

He wanted her, it meant. She was glad she'd learned about what was happening to him. And to her.

'Flynn,' she repeated, this time with urgency.

One of his hands slid around her body to her breast, rubbing and fondling until Rose thought she would cry out with the pleasure of it.

He unclasped her cloak and let it slide to the ground. Picking her up in his strong arms, he carried her to the chaise. She kissed his lips, his cheeks, his neck, anywhere she could reach.

'Make love to me, Flynn,' she begged.

He placed her gently on the *chaise* and positioned his body over hers. He bent towards her, closer and closer, and she thought she would burst from need of him.

Suddenly he broke away, so abruptly she looked to see if someone had pulled him off her, but there was no one there.

'You are bewitching me,' he rasped, grabbing her cloak from the floor. This time he merely tossed it to her and walked over to pick up his greatcoat and hat. 'I will take you back to the gazebo.'

Outside it rained harder than before. The Dark Walk was darker and more deserted than ever now that the hour had advanced and clouds hid the moon. She could barely see where she was going, and she nearly slipped on the slick path trying to keep up with him.

She reached for him, grabbing his arm. 'Flynn! Stop.'

He stopped, but did not look at her. 'Rose, this attempt to seduce me was a mistake, do you understand? It must never happen again.'

'Seduce you?' she cried, 'You seemed willing enough, Flynn. Do not make the fault all mine.'

He turned to her. 'I will not betray Tanner.' Even in the darkness she could see his eyes flash at her. She took a step toward him, but he backed away. 'No, Rose.'

She lifted her trembling chin. 'You've already betrayed him, have you not, Flynn? By wanting me? You cannot be telling me you do not want me, because I know you do.'

'Wanting and taking are not the same thing,' he said through gritted teeth.

He started walking again. As she hurried to stay with him, he stopped again, so abruptly she nearly collided with him.

He whirled on her. 'What I do not understand is why you behave like a loose woman with me, but act as if bedding a marquess would be the worst torture in the world.'

'A loose woman!' she cried. 'Is that what you think of me?'

He did not appear to hear her. 'Do not tell me you merely

want more money, because you do not behave as if you want any money at all. If you wanted another man, it would make sense, but why throw yourself at me—'

'I did not throw myself at you!' She swung her hand to slap his face.

He caught her by the wrist.

'You were the one who chose the Dark Walk, Flynn, who brought me into that room. You chose that private place, and you dare accuse me of being the seductress?' She tried to twist away, the hood of her cape falling from her head.

He grabbed her other wrist and struggled with her, losing his hat and pulling her closer and closer until her body was flush against his and their faces were only a hair's breadth away, the need burning in his eyes.

'How do you explain this, Flynn?' Her voice shook. 'I am not throwing myself at you now, am I?'

He did not release her right away, but held her, his breath rapid, his flesh so hot it seared her senses. Then he released her and ran a ragged hand through his hair.

Rain battered their uncovered heads and streamed down their faces. Slowly, however, the flames of their anger and passion fizzled in the damp air, as if turning to ashes. To gloom.

Rose whispered to him, her words competing with the rain. 'What are we to do, Flynn?'

He did not answer, but his eyes shone an intense blue in the dim light, and the rain curled his usually neatly combed hair. He looked boyish. Vulnerable. He reached for her hand.

'We left our gloves back in that room,' he said, rubbing his bare thumb against her palm.

'Oh…' Rose closed her eyes at the exquisite feel of his touch '…I must retrieve mine. I have no other pair.'

He nodded and they started back, trudging through the

puddles forming in the gravel of the walk. When they reached the small structure, he entered it alone and came out with both pairs of gloves.

They walked back in silence, Rose holding his arm.

''Tis odd the orchestra is not playing,' Rose said as they neared the gazebo. The paths were deserted. The supper boxes empty. 'Everyone has left.'

They hurried to the gazebo door. Inside the servant was sweeping the floor.

His broom stilled when he saw her. 'Miss O'Keefe, your father told me to tell you to ask the gentleman to escort you home, for Mr Hook told everyone to go home because of the rain and so your father did.'

Rose nodded. 'Thank you, Mr Skewes.'

The thin wiry man grinned. 'He said as long as it was the fellow that was here before—' he nodded to Flynn '—he'd not worry about you and neither was I to worry.'

'You are kind,' she said. 'We had better be off, then.'

She and Flynn walked back out into the rain.

There were a few other stragglers walking to where the hackney coaches waited beyond the gate. Rose's cloak felt heavy from the soaking rain, and she shivered.

'You are cold.' Flynn started to unbutton his greatcoat.

'No.' She put up a hand. 'Your coat is as soaked as mine. I will be fine once we are in the carriage.'

They waited in a queue until it was their turn. Flynn lifted Rose into the hack and called out her direction to the jarvey.

They sat closer together than was wise, given how easily passion had sprung up between them. Rose shivered again, more from frustration than the chilling damp, but he unfastened her cloak and bundled it out of the way. Then he shrugged out of his greatcoat and wrapped an arm around her to warm her.

She snuggled close to him and rested her head on his shoulder. The passion that had nearly driven them to a frenzied coupling had settled into something more intimate and infinitely more sorrowful. In silence they held each other all the way across the new Vauxhall Bridge, up the roads skirting the river to the Strand, and into Covent Garden.

When the vehicle stopped on Langley Street, Flynn wrapped Rose in her cloak again and helped her out. Asking the jarvey to wait, he walked her inside her building.

'Will you be all right?' He put his hand on her arm as they reached the top of the stairs. 'Your father will not be angry?'

Rose shook her head. 'Remember, he said he would not worry if I was with you.'

His fingers tightened around her arm.

He dropped his hand. 'I must go.'

She did not move.

He started to turn away, already grasping the banister, but he suddenly turned back to her. She ran to him, and he caught her face gently in both hands, kissing her, a slow, savouring kiss more steeped in sadness than in the fires of passion that had earlier burned them both.

Without speaking another word, he released her and hurried down the stairs.

Chapter Ten

By the next morning, the rain had cleared and the day promised to dry up some of the damp. Still, Flynn was grateful Rose was not scheduled to sing that evening, and she had assured him no plans to dine with Greythorne would be made.

Flynn needed the respite from the turmoil raging inside him, but, more than that, he needed a very quiet place. He closeted himself in Tanner's library, busying himself with the most tedious of his many tasks.

Tanner breezed into the room, humming a tune, and causing Flynn to lose the tally of the long line of figures he was tabulating.

'I trust I am not interrupting something important,' Tanner said.

Flynn had done something uncharacteristic the night before. After leaving Rose, he availed himself of one of Tanner's bottles of brandy and downed the entire contents in the privacy of his own room. He now paid the price with a killing headache and a foul mood.

Head throbbing, he put down his pen and recapped the inkwell. 'Did you have need of me?'

Tanner picked up a ledger Flynn had left on the side table. 'No need, really.' He leafed through the ledger, slammed it closed, and dropped it with a thud that ricocheted in Flynn's brain. 'I did wonder how it went with Greythorne—and Miss O'Keefe, of course.'

Flynn's mood became blacker. 'He cancelled because of the rain.'

Tanner laughed, a loud guffaw that rattled painfully in Flynn's throbbing head. 'The fribble. He'd give her up to keep his coat dry.' He laughed again, then drummed his fingers on the wooden table. 'Did he set another date?'

Flynn gripped the edge of the desk, trying to remain composed. 'Not as yet.'

'Rain is good for something besides crops,' said Tanner cheerfully.

Flynn tried to look composed. 'It appears he is putting pressure on her father. He paid a sum for the opportunity to dine with her.'

'Ah ha!' Tanner cried.

Flynn pressed his fingers against his temple.

'We have more in our arsenal of weapons besides money, do we not, Flynn?' Tanner laughed again.

Flynn had not a clue what Tanner meant, but he would rather not ask and prolong this loud conversation.

But Tanner showed no inclination to be quiet. 'We have cunning, and we have friends in high places.'

'Indeed,' muttered Flynn, who did not care what the deuce Tanner meant, if he would only stop talking.

'Any fellow can throw money at a woman and win her, can he not?' Tanner went on, walking to and fro as he spoke, his footsteps pounding on the carpet. 'But we think of voice lessons and opera performances!'

'I am not getting your point, Tanner,' Flynn said tersely.

Tanner glanced at him quizzically, then peered at him more closely. 'You look ghastly, Flynn. What the devil is wrong with you? You look as though you are going to shoot the cat.'

Flynn's stomach did not react well to this reference to vomiting. 'I have a headache.'

'A headache from too much drink,' Tanner concluded. 'What did I miss last night?'

'Nothing. You missed nothing.' Merely a near-betrayal of all Tanner's trust in him.

Tanner continued stomping around the room. 'Good, because it was very fortunate that I was in the company of his Royal Highness, the Duke of Clarence, you know. Friends in high places!'

Flynn gave him a direct look. 'Am I supposed to understand you?'

Tanner laughed again, this time a loud, barking, brain-joggling laugh. Flynn pressed his temples.

'No need to heed me.' Tanner winked.

Did not Tanner need to meet someone at White's or bid on a horse at Tattersalls, or something? 'If you require my services, sir, I will endeavour to oblige you, but I was working on these sums…'

Tanner sidled up to the desk and leaned over Flynn to look at the numbers on the page. 'I trust nothing is amiss?'

Flynn could feel Tanner breathing down his neck. 'All is as it should be—but I have not tabulated the whole list.'

'I despise sums.' Tanner lumbered away, pulling books off the bookshelves, opening them, then slamming them shut again, and shoving them back into place.

Flynn closed his eyes and waited for the wave of hammering in his head to subside.

'So!' said Tanner, so loud Flynn thought his head would blow apart. 'What is next in this game of ours? I say, this is more like a chess game every day, except not so ghastly tedious.'

A chess game, indeed, thought Flynn. The Queen was the prize. And after his behaviour the previous night, Flynn was a rook. 'It is time to deal with the father. Make the offer.'

Tanner stood before him, hands on his hips, head cocked. 'I had surmised more pursuit was in order. The girl hardly seems willing.' He looked pensive. 'I knew she'd be a challenge. She should come around after Ayrton puts her in the opera. How long do you think that will be?'

'I believe he thought she could carry off a small part in the chorus in two weeks' time,' Flynn told him.

Ayrton had been impressed by Rose's natural talent, but he'd also confided to Flynn that she did not have the voice for the principal roles. For all her quick learning, Flynn was inclined to agree. In Flynn's opinion, she excelled at the sort of singing she did at Vauxhall, songs with words the common folk could understand. Flynn thought her voice belonged in English opera, in one of the smaller theatres where audiences could see her and hear every word.

'So, what say you?'

Flynn shook himself. 'I beg pardon, sir, I was not attending.'

Tanner walked over to the decanter and poured a bumper. He thrust the glass under Flynn's nose. 'Drink it. It is the only sure remedy.'

The mere smell made Flynn wish to cast up his accounts, but he did as his employer ordered. He took the glass in his hand and drank it down.

Tanner settled himself in a chair. 'I can see I shall have to exert myself even more. I shall have to make the plan.'

As far as Flynn could tell, Tanner had not exerted himself

at all, except to wangle the information about Greythorne's dinner plans, although Flynn did not know how he accomplished that feat. He'd jokingly said he'd fought a duel and won, but that was nonsense, even if he had come home with a cut on his cheek and no other explanation of how it got there.

Truth was, if Tanner would exert himself, he'd be happier. He had acted with dispatch in Brussels after the great battle. Had got his hands dirty there or, rather, bloodied, lifting the wounded off the wagons and carrying them into the makeshift hospitals he'd worked at setting up.

All of this made no difference, however. Flynn had already told him what needed to be done. The exertion would, no doubt, be Flynn's. The result, Tanner's conquest of Rose.

'Here is the plan.' Tanner poured himself half the amount of brandy he'd poured for Flynn. 'No more of this mucking around with voice lessons and such. We make a generous offer to the father, money for himself and that woman of his. An annuity, perhaps, and some sort of lodging—'

'For the father?' This seemed like an unnecessary extravagance.

Tanner looked at him. 'Well, you did say that Dawes woman was the greedy one. Give her money enough to keep her out of mischief and out of Miss O'Keefe's hair. It goes without saying that you will offer the lovely Rose her own money and lodgings. A pretty little house off St James's or something. The thing is, we bid high and leave Greythorne in the dust. The deal is done.'

Flynn's headache was already receding. 'You would do this without having won her favour?'

Tanner waved his words away. 'Gratitude is an effective aphrodisiac.'

Yes, Flynn agreed silently. Rose had been grateful to Flynn and look where it had almost led them.

'You would buy her lodgings, buy her father lodgings, and give both money for life with no guarantee?'

Tanner grinned. 'It does sound foolish.' He shrugged. 'It is a gamble. In any wager there are risks. We will just chance it. Cannot have Greythorne win, now, can we?'

On that point Flynn heartily agreed.

That evening Lord Greythorne prowled the paths of Vauxhall, stepping around the puddles that still threatened his boots. It was not his custom to trudge muddy paths, but Tannerton had raised his ire, and Greythorne needed a release.

Curse Tannerton. Ungentlemanly of him to force the swordfight in the first place, then to resort to trickery. Fencing was supposed to be elegant, like a dance of violence, with rhythm and grace. Not that back-and-forth business Tannerton engaged in. Ripping a perfectly good pair of pantaloons— Greythorne could never forgive that.

He scowled as he scanned the path. Tannerton had won a minor victory, but Greythorne would win the prize—Greythorne had plans for Miss Rose O'Keefe, and Tannerton did not figure in them.

He rubbed his hands and admired how the supple leather of his gloves moulded to his fingers. Gazing around at the women nearby, he imagined his fingers wrapping around a delicate cream-coloured neck, squeezing—

His excitement and his need grew. He began his search in earnest. Rose O'Keefe would wait for another day. This night Greythorne had hopes for another bloom to appear. She was present almost every night. He'd been watching. Tonight he was determined to get her alone.

He scanned the crowd, assured she would be easy to spot. He made a second circuit of the Gardens, running into some ladies and gentlemen of his acquaintance. He stopped to pass pleasantries with them. They could not know he had a mask in his pocket, no inkling that when he donned it he would engage in delights beyond which they could not imagine.

But at the moment, irritation battled with such delicious anticipation. If he failed to find the girl—

He heard the laughter behind him and paused by the Octagon temples to see who would pass by.

There she was, on the arm of that fool, Sir Reginald, again. Her auburn hair flaming loose over her shoulders, her gait bawdy and inviting. He stepped into the shadows and affixed the black cloth mask over his face. Then he followed her, biding his time. He knew it would come. It must come.

It did. Sir Reginald walked away from her to speak to another gentleman, and Greythorne made his approach.

'Are you left alone, miss?'

She turned, looking him up and down, too frank and bold for her own good. 'I am rarely alone for long, sir. Are you looking for company?'

He bowed. 'It would give me considerable pleasure to have your company, miss.'

She tossed her head. 'Call me Katy. Everyone does.'

'Katy,' he murmured, making sure he looked into her eyes. She returned a curious look, then smiled again.

He glanced toward Sir Reginald. 'Will your gentleman there object to my speaking with you?'

'Sir Reggie?' She looked amused. 'Do not worry over him.'

He took her arm and walked a few steps away from her former escort. 'I fear I desire more than conversation, my dear Katy.'

'Do you, sir?' She batted her eyelashes. 'I would desire

more than conversation, too, but I'm holding out for a man of wealth.'

He took her hand and slipped it inside his coat to the pocket where he kept his coin purse. He let her feel the coins.

Her eyes crinkled in satisfaction. 'Shall we go, sir?'

He wrapped her arm through his and led her through the Colonnade. 'Let us not couple in some damp structure on the Dark Walk. I have a house, a wine cellar, a place where we might dally the night away. It will be as you have never before experienced. You reward will surpass your wildest dreams.'

She laughed, the laugh that had attracted her to him in the first place. He took her cheeks between his leather-sheathed fingers and squeezed, placing a wet kiss on her full, eager lips.

'My coach awaits.'

On Sunday morning Rose dressed for church, enduring Letty's taunts about pretending to be better than she ought. She needed to be outside, in some semblance of fresh air. She needed to do something to take her mind off of Flynn.

He'd consumed her thoughts all the previous day and night. She wanted him, needed him. This was what Miss Hart found with Sloane and what her other friends had found as well.

Love.

But like her mother's love, Rose's was doomed. For her love to flower would mean the ruin of Flynn's career and hers. If the marquess even knew Flynn had kissed her and almost bedded her, he would dash arrangements for Flynn's employment with the Royal Duke. Flynn's dream.

No matter if Rose were willing to choose love and risk her own career, she would not risk Flynn's.

Still, she wanted him, felt empty without him. She missed

him with every fibre of her being, even to be deprived of his company for one short day. Her only consolation was knowing he would call on her tomorrow to take her to her singing lesson. It seemed an eternity to wait.

She walked to St Paul's nearby and sat in one of the back pews. The atmosphere was peaceful, and she enjoyed blending her voice with other voices in hymns so familiar she needn't use the hymnal. She recognised some women there. She'd seen them parading in Covent Garden. Their dresses were more modest and subdued this day, their faces scrubbed clean and nearly obscured by the brims of bonnets. This was their parish church, a place they ought to feel they belonged rather than looking so unsure of their welcome.

Were they praying for forgiveness, Rose wondered, for the Magdalene lives they led? Or were they praying for the chance to leave such lives behind, as Mary Magdalene had done? Rose was uncertain for what she should pray, so she merely sang the hymns and read the hymnal and listened to a sermon about love. God's love, but about love all the same.

After the service ended, she slipped out of the church, as did the other women sharing the back pews. She could not bear to return to Langley Street, so she walked the distance to call upon Katy, hoping the hour would not be too early.

Her knock at the door went unanswered for several minutes. The large footman finally appeared, looking as if his waistcoat had been hastily buttoned. He rubbed his eyes.

'I have come to call on Katy.'

He nodded and trudged up the stairs. The house seemed very quiet, and Rose regretted this impulsive visit. What if Katy were asleep? What if she were entertaining a gentleman?

But the footman appeared on the stairs with Katy behind him in a morning dress.

'Hello, Rose,' Katy said in a flat voice. 'Come on up.'

'I woke you,' Rose said apologetically.

Katy shook her head. 'I could not sleep.'

Katy led her into the dining room, where Madame Bisou stood talking to another girl. The girl left, and Madame Bisou walked over to them.

'Rose, how good of you to come.' She bussed both cheeks and turned to Katy. 'Should you not be in bed, dear?'

'In bed?' Rose asked.

Katy shook her head. 'I wanted to get up. Could not lie there, thinking all day.'

The *madame*'s lips pursed.

'Are you ill, Katy?' Rose asked.

'Naw.' Katy lifted her hand to brush her hair away from her face.

Rose gently held her wrist. It was circled by reddish bruises and scrapes. 'What happened to you?'

Katy pulled her hand away and laughed. 'It is nothing.'

'Not nothing,' Madame Bisou said. 'And I could strangle that Sir Reginald—'

'Sir Reginald did this to her?' Rose said in alarm.

'Of course not,' Katy cried.

'But Sir Reginald was supposed to be looking out for you,' Madame Bisou scolded. 'You knew a man at Vauxhall hurt Iris! And you went with this one?'

Katy rolled her eyes. 'I know. You have said so repeatedly,' She put her hand on the back of a chair as if to steady herself.

'Come sit.' Rose put an arm around her.

Katy flinched.

She let go. 'I hurt you?'

'The man used a whip on her. Welts all over her,' Madame Bisou exclaimed. 'And those marks on her wrists are from leather straps.'

'Katy!' Rose eased her into a chair. 'Sit here. I will fix you a plate. What do you want?'

'I'm not hungry,' Katy said.

'I will bring you something none the less.'

Rose selected a dish of raspberries and some toasted bread and jam for Katy. She returned to the sideboard, selecting much the same for herself. Madame Bisou poured tea.

'What happened?' Rose asked as she sat down.

'I met this fellow at Vauxhall. He seemed respectable enough. Nice clothes and all,' Katy said. 'So I went with him.'

Madame Bisou crossed her arms over her chest, squeezing out even more décolletage than usual. 'It was like I said, he was one of those men—'

'Who enjoy hurting a girl.' Rose finished the sentence, remembering Madame Bisou's warning not so long ago. Rose placed her hand on Katy's. 'I cannot bear that this man hurt you. He whipped you?'

'Well, he did a little, until I got my hands free and grabbed him where it hurts.' Katy gave a brave smile, looking more like herself. 'He fell to the floor, he did, and I gathered my clothes and ran. Didn't care if I was naked. I found a place to put on my dress, though, so it wasn't so very bad.'

'Oh, Katy!' Rose squeezed her hand.

Katy pulled it away. 'I think the welts will heal. I don't think I'll have too many marks.'

'Where did he hurt you?' Rose asked.

Katy looked down at the table. 'He had rooms. Not a fancy house, I'm sure, but there was a cellar.'

'I meant where on your body?'

'Oh!' Katy shook her head at her misunderstanding. 'On my belly mostly. He was trying to hit my privates.'

Rose left her chair and hugged Katy, very gingerly. 'I am so sorry this happened to you.'

'I am sick over it.' The *madame* shook her head.

Katy pulled away from Rose, blinking rapidly. 'It is over and done. Not something to dwell on.' She cuffed Rose on the arm. 'But tell us. Have you accepted the marquess? Is that what you have come to tell us?'

Rose felt her cheeks flush. 'Not yet.'

Katy peered at her. 'You are not still acting like a wooden stick with him, are you?'

'She's just being coy,' the *madame* told Katy. 'Remember what I taught you, Katy. Act as if you care nothing for the man and he will give you the moon.' She turned to Rose. 'What has Tanner given you? Jewels? Has he offered a house yet? Tanner is an extremely generous lover. You are very fortunate.'

Rose could barely look at her. 'He has given me voice lessons at the King's Theatre. If I do well, I might perform there.'

'Voice lessons!' Katy gave a derisive snort.

'How odd,' agreed Madame Bisou.

'He gave me a ring, too, and I…I think more is forthcoming.' Rose paused. 'I am afraid my father will select this other man. Lord Greythorne.'

'Bah! Tell him not to,' said Madame Bisou. 'Greythorne is a bad one. He is one of those men like we have been discussing. I do not allow him in this place.'

Rose's eyes widened.

Madame Bisou rose. 'I must leave. Accept Tanner, *ma petite*. You cannot do better. He is generous. All the girls I have known have profited very well by the connection.' She stroked Katy's cheek. 'We must get you in front of some wealthy men, Katy. Vauxhall is not the place. You will not go back there unless it is with someone I trust. Not Sir Reginald. Bah! You must stay in the game room. I know the men who play there.'

Katy smiled. 'I'll keep an eye on who is winning, that is what I'll do.'

As soon as Madame Bisou left, Katy turned to Rose. 'The man wore a mask, Rose, but I knew who he was! He was that Lord Greythorne.'

Rose felt her face drain of blood. 'You are certain?'

Katy nodded vigorously. 'I never forget a body. Do not ever be alone with him, Rose.'

She did not wish to worry Katy. She would say nothing about her obligation to dine with Greythorne.

She said, 'I think he should be stopped, Katy. I should tell Flynn about him.'

Katy gave her a quizzical look. 'Flynn? What can he do?' She shook her head. 'Do not tell anyone about him, Rose. Promise me.'

'Why? We could stop him.'

'No,' she cried, rising from her chair. 'Nobody would believe me over an earl. But word would get out, and men would think I like that sort of thing. I could not stand it.'

'But—'

Katy's eyes pleaded. 'Promise me, Rose! You must promise me!'

Rose hugged her. 'Very well. But you have told Madame Bisou, surely?'

'No,' Katy said. 'You heard her. She knows enough about him. I'm only telling you to warn you.'

'If this is what you wish,' she murmured.

She changed the subject and cajoled Katy into eating. They talked about Miss Hart and the others and the fun they'd had together. Eventually Katy relaxed and laughed again and seemed more her vivacious self. When it came time for Rose to leave, she hugged her friend with great care and saved her tears of sympathy until she was back outside on her long walk home.

The streets were full of people now, and the hustle and bustle distracted her a little. She stopped by the market stalls and picked out some food for dinner. Her arms were laden with packages and she had to shift them all into one hand to get into the building, and then shift them again to enter their rooms.

'Here she is!' chirped Letty as Rose kicked the door closed behind her.

Lord Greythorne rose from a chair.

'Come in, Rose, dear,' continued Letty. 'We have a caller.'

Lord Greythorne crossed the room to her. 'Allow me to relieve you of your burdens.' He took the packages from her hands.

'I will take them, m'lord,' her father said, hurrying over.

Letty glared at Rose. 'For goodness' sake, take off your hat and gloves. Make yourself presentable.'

Rose left the room for her bedchamber, for once grateful to Letty for ordering her about. Her heart pounded with anger and fear. She had no desire to face this monster who had used whips and leather straps on her friend.

She took as much time as she dared taking off her gloves and hat and putting her hair in a cap. When she could delay no longer, she returned to the parlour.

Greythorne stood again. He now had a wine glass in hand.

Letty stomped over to her and snatched the cap off her hair. 'Go sit with our guest,' she hissed.

'Lord Greythorne has come himself to set a new date for dining with you,' her father said cheerfully.

'I am at your service.' Greythorne bowed to her. 'Name the day, the place, the time.'

Refusal was impossible. Her father had already accepted the money. She lifted her chin and glared at him. 'I will dine with you at Vauxhall on Tuesday, but I insist upon an open supper box.'

His smile stiffened. 'Of course. Vauxhall it shall be.'

She returned a smile equally stiff. 'If it does not rain, that is. I presume you will beg off if it rains.'

Some dangerous emotion flashed through his eyes. 'Indeed. We do not wish our clothing damaged by the rain.'

Rose thought of Flynn, hatless, heedless of the rain pouring down, soaking through his greatcoat.

'Sit down, my lord,' Letty said with exaggerated politeness, and more sharply to Rose, 'You, too, Rose. Entertain our guest.'

Greythorne waited until she sat in the chair near him.

'Our Rose has aspirations to sing in King's Theatre, my lord,' said her father in a proud tone.

'Do you, Miss O'Keefe?' Greythorne looked amused. 'You want bigger and better things than Vauxhall Gardens?'

'I am very grateful to be singing at Vauxhall, sir,' she replied. 'And I will be grateful for the chance to sing in King's Theatre as well.'

'What role do you hope to sing?' he went on.

His gaze was riveted on her, his expression conveying total interest, but the lack of feeling in his eyes frightened her.

She swallowed. 'Merely the chorus, sir.'

'A woman of your talents should desire more,' he said. This time when his eyes flicked over her, she felt as if he were seeing under her clothes.

It angered her more. 'Do you know so much of singing?'

'I know what I like.' His look was even bolder.

'Well, I think it is all foolishness,' Letty said. 'Singing in a chorus when she has been a soloist. One should never go backwards. I am sure you will agree, my lord.'

Greythorne glanced at Letty, than back at Rose. 'To enjoy the experience is the important thing.'

Rose had the feeling he was not referring to singing opera.

A knock sounded on the door.

'Now who could that be?' said Letty testily.

Rose's father walked over to the door, and Rose was glad for a reason to look away from Lord Greythorne. She twisted around as her father turned the knob and opened the door.

'Good afternoon, Mr O'Keefe.'

Flynn stood in the doorway.

Chapter Eleven

Greythorne's eyes narrowed as he spied Tannerton's man Flynn standing at the door. He was heartily sick of that cursed sycophant Irishman turning up everywhere.

'Oh, Mr Flynn…ah…do come in.' The simpleton O'Keefe shuffled aside.

At least O'Keefe acted as if this appearance was not expected. Greythorne detested anyone who withheld information from him. He knew the father would play him off against Tannerton, but he'd not be made the fool.

Flynn stepped into the room, stiffening when he saw Greythorne. Greythorne smiled inwardly in satisfaction. He'd knocked the oh-so-efficient secretary off kilter.

O'Keefe's woman laughed. She might be the commonest sort, but she had her eyes open. Greythorne made a mental note of the fact.

'Good day, Miss Dawes.' Flynn bowed, giving her more courtesy than such a base-born woman deserved. He turned to the daughter, the prize Greythorne coveted. 'Miss O'Keefe.' And finally to Greythorne. 'Sir.'

Insolent cur.

'Mr Flynn,' Rose responded in her melodious voice, no tension apparent.

Greythorne clenched his fingers around his glass. It appeared Tannerton had made headway. His Irish lackey had been treated to none of the reserve she'd shown him, to whom she'd acted as skittish as a colt. No matter. The way to win this woman was through her cowardly father and the money-grasping woman pushing him. Once won, he could make her sing a different tune.

Flynn turned back to O'Keefe. 'Forgive my interruption. I must speak with you, sir. If you name a time that would be convenient for you, I will be pleased to accommodate.'

Miss Dawes grabbed O'Keefe's arm, grinning. The man replied, 'Ah…ah…tomorrow, perhaps? Before I must leave for Vauxhall.'

'Excellent,' Flynn said.

Greythorne eased the pressure on the glass, though he'd much rather have shattered it. Tannerton was ready to make an offer, he surmised. Greythorne would discover some means of outsmarting the man. Perhaps he would devise the plan before supping with the girl two nights from now.

Flynn directed a worried glance in his direction. Good. The man ought to worry.

Rose stood up, bringing Greythorne to his feet as well. 'Would you like some tea, Mr Flynn?'

Flynn quickly glanced from him to Rose and back again. The man was rattled, Greythorne was gratified to realise.

But he frowned when Flynn's expression set with sudden decision. Flynn turned his eyes back on the girl. 'I fear there is no time. Lord Tannerton's carriage is waiting. He is most eager for your drive today. Are you quite ready?'

'Oh!' she exclaimed. 'How…how foolish of me. I shall get my hat and be with you directly.'

'You did not tell us of this, Rose!' Miss Dawes shrieked after her, but the lovely Rose had already disappeared through the doorway.

Flynn stood with a perfectly bland expression, which Greythorne would have liked to strike off his face with the slap of his leather gloves. Tannerton was moving in. Greythorne swore silently.

'Well…' Mr O'Keefe mumbled into the tension of the room.

Wheels seemed to be turning in Miss Dawes's head. She, no doubt, was trying to calculate how she might profit from this game's new hand.

Rose came rushing back into the parlour, still tying the ribbons of her hat. 'I am ready, Mr Flynn.'

Greythorne stepped forward, blocking her way. 'It has been my pleasure to pass these brief moments with you, Miss O'Keefe.' He took her hand and lifted it to his lips. 'Until we meet again.'

'Good day to you, sir.' She pulled her hand away and stepped around him.

'Where are you going, missy?' the shrill Miss Dawes cried. 'You had better behave yourself or you'll answer to your father!'

Flynn spoke up. 'A mere carriage ride, Miss Dawes. I assure you there is no reason to be concerned.'

Rose took his arm, and the two of them walked out of the door.

Greythorne swivelled to O'Keefe and his woman. 'You will receive an offer from that man. I will top it. But I warn you, do not cross me on this, if you value your lives. I mean to be the winner and I'll let no one stand in my way.'

Flynn almost carried Rose down the flight of stairs to the outside door, feeling as if the very devil was at their heels.

Greythorne.

When they reached the street, he paused.

She looked around. 'Where is the carriage?'

'There is no carriage,' he admitted. 'I invented the tale to get you away.'

'Lord Tannerton is not waiting?' she asked.

'No.'

She smiled and clutched his arm tighter.

'We had best move out of view, though. I would not put it past Greythorne to follow us.' He glanced around. 'Shall we walk to the river?'

They crossed through Covent Garden and continued to the Strand, where Flynn slowed the pace.

More private now, Flynn asked, 'What did Greythorne want? Did he make his offer for you?'

'I was not party to the whole of his conversation.' She stopped and looked at him worriedly. 'Oh, Flynn! I must take supper with him at Vauxhall on Tuesday night. I could not think how to avoid it.'

He frowned. 'You shan't be alone with him.'

'But I will,' she cried. 'I am to go alone with him!'

He touched her cheek, saying more softly, 'You shan't be alone with him. I will be nearby.'

Her eyes searched his. A breeze lifted her bonnet and played with a wayward curl. He tucked it under the brim and laced her arm through his again. They continued walking.

'I am thinking he is a bad man, Flynn.' He felt her shudder as she spoke.

When Greythorne had touched her hand, Flynn wanted to punch his face into a bloody pulp.

'I promise I will be there, Rose. You may not see me, but I will not leave you alone with him.'

She lay her cheek against his arm.

They walked down Savoy Street to the water's edge, standing below the new Waterloo Bridge that had just opened on the anniversary of the great battle. They stood side by side watching the wagons, carriages and riders cross. Flynn was only too aware of his desire to wrap his arm around her and to savour this closeness. They did not speak for a long time.

'Why did you call upon my father, Flynn?' she finally asked.

He could not look at her. 'To make Tannerton's offer.'

She moved away, ever so subtly, but suddenly a gap as wide as the Thames seemed to separate them. 'I see.'

'Lord Tannerton will make so generous an offer, Greythorne will not top it,' he said. 'We will not let him win you, Rose.'

She merely nodded.

He faced her, stroking her arms. 'Greythorne will not plague you again.'

She looked into his eyes. 'What do you know of him?'

He paused, unwilling to share the sordid details of Greythorne's perversions. 'As an eligible and wealthy earl,' Flynn said, 'he is welcome in the best houses. But he is essentially a cruel man.'

She seemed to weigh this scanty information. He thought she would speak, but she did not.

Her lids fluttered and she gazed up at him. The lock of her hair came loose again to play in the wind. The clatter of the vehicles crossing the bridge sounded in his ears almost as loud as the pounding of his blood.

He leaned down, knowing he should not, but unable to help himself. With gentle fingers he lifted her chin, and she rose on tiptoe. He knew now how soft her lips were, how warm they felt, how she tasted. He placed his lips on hers and came home. He cupped her cheeks with his hands, fearing she would pull away before he'd taken his fill. There was nothing chaste about the kiss, although only their lips touched. It awakened his body and all his senses and sent him soaring into the heavens.

Finally, like a man waking reluctantly from a dream, he broke the contact.

'Flynn,' she whispered, sounding out of breath.

What was he to do with this passion he had neither the strength nor the desire to control? He might be betraying the man who employed him, who believed in him, and trusted him implicitly, but Rose brought him back to life, to home. With Rose, he felt like a boy again, running across emerald hills. He wished to raise his voice in song. He felt himself bursting to be free.

But he needed to bury himself again to play the dispassionate negotiator with her father, the faithful assistant with Tanner. What was painful now, merely watching Tanner talk with her, would soon become torturous when Tanner took her to his bed.

Flynn gritted his teeth. 'Tomorrow I must speak to your father. Make Tannerton's offer.'

The next day Rose waited for Flynn to call, knowing he would not escort her to King's Theatre for her lesson. Rather, he would closet himself with her father and determine her fate. When his knock sounded upon the door, she felt the familiar thrill at the prospect of seeing him, of feeling his gaze upon her like a soft caress. But she also felt despair.

Her father admitted him to the parlour. He looked so ashen, Rose feared for his health.

'Lord Tannerton is waiting below to take you to King's

Theatre,' he told her. She hoped her father and Letty did not perceive the tone of doom in his words.

So, after an aching, shared, agonised glance, Rose left him standing with her father.

When she reached the outside, Tannerton walked up to her, smiling. 'Good day, Miss O'Keefe. Are you ready for your lesson? I thought you might enjoy a sporting ride to the theatre.' He gestured to the waiting vehicle, a high-perch phaeton drawn by two horses black as night and held in tow by a small man in livery.

She delayed. 'How am I to even get up there?'

He grinned. 'I will assist you.'

He climbed on to the seat and reached his hand down to her. She grasped it, and he pulled her into the seat as if she were made of feathers. As soon as she was settled, he took the ribbons in his hands, and the tiger, who had been holding the horses, ran to the back and hopped on.

He glanced at her. 'I hope you do not mind only two horses. I've raced the vehicle with four, but four on these busy streets make the journey tedious.'

'I am sure I do not know if I mind,' she responded. 'I've not been riding in a phaeton before.'

From the high, open seat Rose could see everything on the street. The novelty of it almost distracted her, but her mind was back with Flynn speaking to her father.

'Forgive me for not calling for you at your rooms. Flynn gave me strict orders to stay away.' Tannerton's expression was serious.

Perhaps his mind, too, had turned in the same direction.

'I see,' was all she could think of to say.

He gave her a wry smile. 'I suppose Flynn thought I would bollix the whole matter.'

'Bollix it?'

'I've no head for such things,' he explained. 'Flynn is the negotiator. I either say I'll pay the moon just to get the tedious business over with or wind up in fisticuffs.'

Somehow neither choice seemed to flatter her.

'Do not fear.' His voice turned kind and he placed a hand upon hers. 'Flynn will see everything turns out.'

He made a neat turn on to St Martin's Lane, tucking the phaeton between a hackney carriage and a curricle driven by a young man concentrating fiercely. Rose spun around to look at him. It was Robert Duprey, her friend Mary's husband! They must have returned from Bath. He did not notice her, however, being too intent on his driving.

'I have what I hope will be good news for you.' Tannerton looked as casual holding the ribbons as Duprey had been tense.

'Yes?' she said politely.

He cast her a quick glance. 'We have spoken with Ayrton…'

Rose could guess the *we* meant Flynn had spoken to Ayrton.

'Miss Hughes and Signor Angrisani will rehearse you for the chorus. You will perform with the opera.'

This was what she had dreamed about, but the expected elation did not come. 'Thank you.'

He stopped the phaeton in front of King's Theatre and helped her down from the high perch. Though his hands spanned her waist, she felt none of the thrill she experienced at Flynn's touch. He walked into the theatre with her and sat in the back while she made her way to the now-familiar stage.

Her lesson was gruelling, but, as before, so filled with learning she did not mind it. She almost forgot about Flynn and her father. Miss Hughes and the *signor* taught her how a chorus must sing with one voice, how she must meld her voice with the others, like she had done in church. The girl whom Rose would be replacing came to sing the part with her.

During a break, Rose asked her, 'Do you mind if I take your place for one performance?'

The girl looked stunned at the question. 'Good heavens, no. I will make more money not performing.'

Flynn would pay the girl generously so Rose might have a dream come true. Rose corrected herself. Flynn might hand the money to the girl, but the money came from Tannerton. She wondered how much each of these people was being paid so she could sing at King's Theatre.

As the lesson came to its end, Signor Angrisani said, 'You must attend the performance tonight and as many times as you are able so you will see how you should move. Mr Ayrton has scheduled you to sing this next Saturday.'

Her life would thoroughly change.

When she walked back through the theatre to where Tannerton waited, her heart skipped a beat. Flynn was with him. She felt his eyes upon her as she made her way to him.

'Flynn?' she asked as soon as she came close.

He knew precisely what she asked. 'The offer is made,' he said. 'Your father has been compelled to wait for Greythorne before accepting.'

'Compelled?' she asked.

'Not a thing to be concerned about,' Tannerton interjected. 'Greythorne will be dealt with.'

The marquess was pacing the aisle, looking as if he were eager to leave the place. 'Shall we go?'

She nodded. He strode quickly to the entrance, leaving her to fall into step with Flynn.

'What does he mean, "Greythorne will be dealt with"?' she whispered.

Flynn shrugged. 'I presume he means we shall win. He dislikes losing.'

The phaeton was not out at the front of the building. She presumed the tiger was walking the horses around. Tannerton looked a bit more at ease out of doors.

He walked back to Flynn and Rose. 'Are you able to attend the opera tonight?' he asked her.

'Yes.' She thought she would attend even if she had to walk to the theatre and back.

'Good. Excellent.' The phaeton rounded the corner, and he walked back to the street. As it pulled up, he said, 'I believe I shall charge Flynn to take you.' He gave her a rueful smile. 'I cannot sit through the same opera twice. I hope you will forgive me.' He turned to Flynn. 'Are you able to do it? Are you able to escort Miss O'Keefe tonight?'

Flynn gave Rose a burning glance before answering, 'If you wish it.'

Greythorne had made certain he watched at the hour the secretary was to arrive at O'Keefe's lodgings. He watched the man arrive with Tannerton, watched the lovely Rose drive off with the marquess. Then he waited until the secretary left the lodgings again. Tannerton's offer was made, then.

Greythorne then had called upon O'Keefe and his avaricious woman. He'd put the devil's fear into them, telling them he would match Tannerton's offer.

The sums the marquess was prepared to settle on the beauteous Rose and her father were insane. Greythorne had no intention of paying so much. After the woman became a bore, he would cut off the money and seize the property. What could she or her father do? Go to the magistrate? Ha! Let her run to Tannerton then. He could pay for what was left of her.

Greythorne smiled inwardly, remembering the look of terror on O'Keefe's face at his parting words. A little menace always put a proper seal on a business transaction.

Chapter Twelve

That evening when Flynn helped Rose into Tanner's carriage for the trip to the theatre, her excitement was less for the performance than for being alone again with Flynn. She needed to talk to him. About the offer to her father. About singing in the opera. About kissing him.

She frowned when he did not sit next to her, taking the backward-facing seat. She looked at him questioningly.

'We must take care, Rose,' he said. 'It is madness to—to—'

'To kiss?' she said.

'Yes,' he agreed. 'To kiss.'

She stared at him, wanting to protest, but she saw the suffering in his eyes. She turned to the carriage window without attending to what she saw there. 'Tell me of your interview with my father.'

He explained the offer, and her jaw dropped in disbelief. Surely no man paid so much for the favours of a woman? Flynn explained that Tannerton wanted to ensure Greythorne bowed out.

* * *

By the time they sat in the opera box, Rose forced herself to attend to the performance. Flynn sat no closer to her there than in the carriage, but close enough that she could share with him all the impressions, all the questions, all the wonder she had kept inside the first time she had seen *Don Giovanni*. They paid particular attention to the chorus, to the role she would play, a role so small she suspected no one else in the audience gave it the slightest heed.

Rose contented herself with Flynn's company and his conversation. It might be all she had left of him.

On the ride home, he asked her, 'Do you prefer the opera, Rose? Would you rather perform there or at Vauxhall?'

She thought about it. 'The opera is so grand.' She thought of standing on the same stage as her mother had—only it was not the same stage, because that theatre where her mother performed had burned down. Still, she felt as if it were her destiny to stand in her mother's place, to sing as her mother had done, and perhaps realise the dreams her mother had harboured in her heart until childbirth had robbed her of her health.

'Which do you prefer?' she asked him, needing to stop thinking of this.

He did not hesitate. 'Vauxhall.'

Her brows rose in surprise.

'The opera is grand spectacle, I grant you,' he explained. 'But there is nothing more beautiful than you singing at Vauxhall.'

Her insides melted.

The warm feeling remained with her the rest of the carriage ride, to the door of her lodgings, to the door of her father's rooms.

She turned to him, extending her hand, keeping within the boundaries he had set for them. 'Thank you, Flynn.'

He took her hand in the dim hallway, but used it to pull her to him, to where she truly belonged. In Flynn's arms.

He kissed her, long and hard, like a man returning home from a long journey.

Tannerton sat in one of the comfortable chairs near the bay window at White's, nursing a brandy and mentally tabulating his winnings at whist. It was hopeless. He could not remember how much he started with, how many vouchers he'd written, then torn up, how much his last hand had netted him. Suffice to say he'd come out ahead. Let Flynn do the sums.

The door opened and he heard an angry voice call, 'Where is Tannerton?'

Tanner grinned. He'd wondered how long it would take. He sat tight until the man rushed towards the card room. He imagined him searching the coffee room, the game room, the privy. He started to hum, swinging his leg, watching in the direction from which the man would return.

He caught himself humming that ghastly tune those opera people had Miss O'Keefe sing over and over until Tanner thought he'd go mad if he heard it one more time. Now it was still plaguing him. He was not putting up with another voice lesson. Let Flynn take her. Flynn actually liked that ghastly music. Why could they not sing the kind of music found in dark taverns smelling of ale and the sweat of men who actually toiled for a living? Give him a bawdy song any day. At least a bawdy song had some wit.

A few moments later the man came rushing back. He grabbed one of the servants walking by. 'Where is Lord Tannerton?' he demanded.

The servant merely turned his head about five degrees and said, 'There, m'lord.'

Tanner lifted his glass in salute.

Greythorne glared at him and pushed the servant out of the way.

'Come here for some sport?' Tanner said affably. 'Or is today not your lucky day?'

'I came here looking for you and well you know it.' Greythorne's face was an alarming shade of red.

'Oh, I doubt I could guess the workings of your mind.' He pointed to one of the chairs. 'But now you've found me, have a seat and tell me what I can do for you.'

Greythorne hesitated, obviously thinking to sit would be too cordial in his advanced state of rage. But he did finally lower himself into a chair.

'We can get you some brandy, I am sure, if you have a little patience.' Tanner looked around, but the servant had left the room. 'Or some ale.'

'Never mind that,' Greythorne growled.

'Not thirsty?' Tanner acted surprised.

Greythorne looked daggers at him. 'You play an unfair game, Tannerton.'

Tanner feigned shock. 'Do you accuse me of cheating at cards? Please do not, or I shall have to call you out. I have no wish to kill you.' He reconsidered. 'Well, perhaps, not a very big wish to kill you.'

'Cut line, sir,' Greythorne cried. 'You know very well what I am talking about. You have overstepped the bounds of what is gentleman-like behaviour in contests such as this.'

'There you go again.' Tanner shook his head. 'Accusing me of not being a gentleman would also force me into a duel. With my luck I'd kill you, but be hanged for it. That seems like a terrible waste to me. The hanging part. Of course, I could have Flynn attend to it. Then I suspect it would come out satisfactorily—'

'Enough!' Greythorne's eyes bulged. 'You have used an unfair advantage to win this contest, and I will not hear of it!'

Tanner leaned forward and gave him a level stare. 'Yes, enough, sir. I have used all the cards at my disposal, and it is not my problem if you lack a full deck.'

Greythorne shot to his feet. 'I will win her, Tannerton. That is something you may depend upon. You forget I have her all to myself tomorrow night.'

But Tanner could trust Flynn to make certain Greythorne had company. 'I am shaking in my boots,' said Tanner.

'You are a disgrace.' Greythorne trembled with indignation. 'Wearing boots in the evening.'

With one last scathing look at Tanner, he stormed out of the club.

Tanner stared down at the black boots on his feet, a bit scuffed after wearing them all day. He looked over to the door through which Greythorne had fled and started to lift his glass to his lips, stopping halfway. He glanced down at his boots again and burst into laughter, a loud boisterous laugh that rang throughout the gentleman's club.

When Rose stood on the balcony to sing the next evening, she tried to find Flynn among the onlookers, but she could not see him. She found Greythorne easily enough, looking at her as if she were the meal he would be eating that night. Her eyes did not linger long on him.

She had warmed up her voice as Miss Hughes and Signor Angrisani had taught her, and she rehearsed how to breathe.

There were so many new things to think about when she sang, she almost forgot the words. She sang her usual tunes, but concentrated on her breathing and the volume of her voice. She was not happy with the result.

Still, her audience applauded when she finished, and she curtsied to them.

As she was walking to the stairs, Mr Hook stopped her. 'What is it, Rose? You are not singing as usual.'

She bowed her head. 'I know. I did not do well, did I?'

The music director gave her a stern look. 'No, you did not. You sing the words without the meaning behind them as if they were just notes on a page.'

'I have been taking lessons, Mr Hook,' she explained. 'Learning to breathe and to make my voice carry better. I was thinking of those things.'

He put a fatherly hand on her arm. 'Sing the words, Rose. Make them mean something. That is what they want.' He gestured in the direction of the audience.

'I shall try, Mr Hook,' she said. 'I shall do better to-morrow.'

He patted her arm. 'I am sure you will, child.'

He returned to the orchestra, and she started down the stairs, pausing halfway. She did not wish to disappoint Mr Hook, who had believed in her and had given her this important job. She began to question if she could sing at all. Would she make a fool of herself at the opera? Could one chorus member ruin a performance?

She took two more steps and stopped again, remembering that Greythorne would be waiting for her. Flynn said he would be here to protect her, that Tannerton would send two of his footmen as well. She wished she had seen Flynn. Something very easily could have prevented him from coming. Like a carriage mishap. Or an errand for Tannerton. Or a sudden fever.

She leaned against the wall for support. If he ever were hurt or sick, she could not bear it! She must not think of such things. She must handle Greythorne by herself. Madame Bisou had taught her how to fend off unwanted advances, not quite as effectively as Katy had used on Greythorne, but Rose would not allow matters to advance that far.

She entered the downstairs room, and Greythorne stood waiting there for her.

Letty rushed up to her, carrying her cloak. 'What kept you so long, Rose? It is not polite to make a gentleman wait.'

She took the cloak from Letty. 'Mr Hook stopped me.'

Letty turned to Greythorne. 'See, m'lord. 'Twas nothing at all. Mr Hook is the director, you see. It is he who employs her.'

Greythorne bowed and directed his gaze at Rose. 'I was not worried in the least.' He held out his hand. 'Shall we go, my dear?'

Rose avoided his hand by busying herself with donning her cloak. As she walked to the door, Letty hurried behind her and pulled up the hood to cover Rose's head.

'Wait,' Letty said. 'Let me see who is outside.' She slipped out of the door, only to return a minute later. 'If you leave right now, no one will see you.'

'Then shall we?' Greythorne offered his arm and Rose could think of no way to refuse it.

As they reached the outside, she shook her head so that her hood fell away and Flynn would be able to see her better. She glanced around, but could see no one watching.

'I hope you have honoured my wishes to remain in the open, sir,' she said.

He reached across and covered her hand with his own. 'I assure you, my dear, I am determined to please you.' He rubbed her hand with his thumb, a slow seductive touch.

She wanted to pull away and run from him, but he let go and acted as if nothing had happened.

'I have engaged a supper box,' he said in a smooth voice. 'And we shall have all the delicacies Vauxhall can offer.'

As they crossed the Grove, a voice called out, 'There she is!' and she heard footsteps hurrying behind her.

Her heart beat faster in the hopes that she would see Flynn behind her, but it was a younger man who caught up with them.

He doffed his hat. 'I enjoyed your performance, Miss O'Keefe,' he said, walking sideways to keep pace.

'Thank you, sir.' Unlike other nights, she was glad to be accosted by an admirer, especially since there was no sign of Flynn.

'Would—would you accept my card?' He extended it to her.

'Yes…' She reached for it.

Greythorne pulled her away. 'Leave her,' he snapped.

He hurried her to a supper box as private as one could get in the Gardens, the last one on the Grand Walk. Fewer people would pass by and those who did would be interested only in their own company, not what occurred in a nearby box. The three supper boxes next to this one were also empty, and Rose suspected he had rented those as well.

'I asked for a public place and you have made this one private.' She had no reason to speak politely to him.

He had the gall to give her a wounded look. 'I assure you, it was not my intention. This is what was offered to me.'

She did not believe him.

The thin slices of ham and tiny chickens were waiting on the table, as was a bottle of wine. There was not even a servant in sight. Several lamps lit the walk in front of them, but only one inside the supper box. She suspected it would be difficult to see into its recesses. The table had only two chairs, side by side.

He must have seen her looking at them. He said, 'I instructed the servant to place the chairs so we might watch the passers-by, and so you will feel more…chaperoned.'

So he might be close enough to take liberties, she feared. He escorted her inside the box and pulled out the chair for her to sit. When he sat in his chair he moved it even closer to hers. With a show of solicitude he poured her wine and placed some ham on her plate. She ate and drank because it saved her from speaking to him.

'Is the food to your liking?' He leaned a bit closer.

'It is satisfactory,' she replied in a flat voice.

He leaned forward even more. 'You sound unhappy, Miss O'Keefe. Tell me how I might please you?'

She faced him directly. 'It was not my choice to be here, but my father's. You paid him money for my presence. I had no choice but to comply.'

The smile on his face stiffened. 'You are not yet twenty-one. You must do your father's bidding.'

'Yes, I must,' she retorted. 'But I do not enjoy your company.'

His eyes flashed. 'Perhaps you will learn to enjoy it.'

She swept her arm over the area. 'It does not help that you choose a secluded spot when I requested a public one. Or that you arrange the chairs so I cannot move away from you. That there is not even a servant here. How am I to enjoy myself when you do everything in your power to see I do not?'

He averted his gaze for a moment, then with a sudden resolve moved his chair farther away, glancing at her in a silent question.

'That is better,' she said.

'How else might I please you?' he asked. 'Would you like to walk through the park?'

She feared Flynn would never find her if she did not stay in one place. 'No, I would not.'

'Your pleasure,' he said with some irony in his voice.

Just then the young man who had stopped her earlier came into view, dragging a friend with him. 'See? She is here. I told you she was.'

The friend came over to the box, leaning on the wall. 'Miss O'Keefe! It is you! I have come every night to Vauxhall in the hopes of meeting you.'

Rose would have been embarrassed at the admiration, except she was so relieved to see other people. 'You are too good, sir.'

He stuck out his hand into the box. 'I have this for you.' In his hand was a pretty pink rose.

She left her chair to accept it. 'Thank you, sir. I shall keep it.'

The young man put his hand over his heart in a dramatic gesture. 'It is I who should thank you!'

Greythorne also stood up. 'Run along now and leave the lady in peace.'

It was their presence that gave her peace.

The two young men backed away, throwing her kisses as they went.

'Come, sit.' Greythorne's tone was unfriendly.

She remained where she was. Where was Flynn?

Greythorne walked back to his chair and waited for her. 'I dislike them annoying you,' he explained.

She returned to her chair and he refilled her wine glass. She sipped it, her eyes on the walk. A man crossed in front of her, walking alone. She hoped that was one of Tannerton's footmen, but it could have been anyone.

Charles Dignum finished singing, and the dance music began. She listened to the first set, a country dance, and watched the walk. Once in a while a couple strolled by, but no one else.

He poured her more wine.

The ham and her nerves had made her thirsty. She sipped this third glass, but felt the wine's effects and decided she should drink no more.

'You like to dance, I think,' he said, smoothly. 'You made a pretty figure with Tannerton last week.'

'Were you watching me?' The idea made her shiver.

He widened his smile, showing his white, even teeth. 'I am not so different from your two young admirers. As smitten as they. Perhaps more.'

'Somehow I do not think those two young men would have paid my father to spend time with me.' She lifted her glass to her lips.

He gave a soft laugh, but one with no cheer in it. 'I suspect they would not have thought of it, nor had the funds.' He leaned towards her again. 'I did what would achieve my aims, Miss O'Keefe. I desire your company above all things and will do what I must to have it.'

She finished her wine after all.

He stood and extended his hand to her. 'We shall dance.'

She glanced out at the walk again, but there was no one in sight. Nothing but trees, dark and shadowy where the lamplight did not reach. At least the Grove would be filled with people.

She took his hand, feeling dizzy from the wine as she stood. Her limbs felt like malleable clay as they walked to where the dancing took place under the gazebo. She glanced up and could see her father holding his oboe, waiting for the signal to start, but he was oblivious to her distress.

The waltz began, and she had to endure Greythorne's hands upon her. As he twirled her into the dance, she felt nauseous and unsteady. He swung her around, and she had difficulty remaining upright. The lights blurred and blackness filled her vision.

Suddenly he was walking with her down a path. She must have fainted, she thought, assuming he was taking her back to the supper box.

'I would rather go back to the gazebo,' she mumbled, but he paid her no heed.

The path got darker and darker, and she realised this was not the way to the supper box.

'Let me go.' She fought to stay alert.

He pulled her into the trees where no one could see. 'I have won you, Rose. Tannerton thinks he has foiled me, but he has not.' He gripped her so tightly she could barely move.

In the vice of his arms, he put his lips on hers. Her stomach swam with nausea, and she hoped she would vomit all over him. As she struggled he rubbed against her and she felt his arousal. 'It is time to claim you—'

He started to lift her skirt. She tried to kick upwards with her knee or free her hand to hurt him as Katy had done, but to no avail. Her muscles would not obey, and he held her too tight.

'I will have you now, right here, and then I will take you with me. Tannerton may be slow to act, but I am not—'

She wrested one hand free and grabbed for his throat, squeezing as hard as she could. His grip loosened.

Just as she was about to push away, she glimpsed someone behind him, a man in a mask. The man grabbed him by the collar and pulled him off her, sending him rolling on to the still-damp ground.

Rose propelled herself into the masked man's arms. She knew it was Flynn. Greythorne slipped as he tried to pick himself up, swearing about the damage to his clothes.

'Come.' Flynn half-carried her, while Greythorne shouted obscenities behind them. Waiting on the path were her two young admirers. Tannerton's footmen, she realised.

They did not slow their pace until reaching the supper boxes along the South Walk. They paused under the last arch.

'You came,' she murmured to Flynn, blinking hard to keep herself awake.

'Do you think he knows who you were, Mr Flynn?' one of the men asked.

'I hope not.' Flynn pulled off his mask. 'But what can he do? No one would show him sympathy for forcing himself on her.'

Flynn, arm still around Rose, shook hands with the two footmen, who said they would stay in the Gardens and keep an eye on Greythorne.

'Thank you,' Rose mumbled. After they left, she put a hand to her head. 'I feel dizzy.'

'He must have drugged you, Rose.' Flynn's arms around her kept her from sinking to the ground. 'I am taking you out of here now.'

Chapter Thirteen

Flynn refused to take her to her father's rooms, to the man who had taken money and compelled her to accept Greythorne's company. He told the jarvey of the hackney carriage to drop them off at the only other place he could think of, Madame Bisou's.

In the coach she snuggled against him, her head resting over his heart. She fell asleep even before they'd pulled on to the road. Occasionally she mumbled something incomprehensible, assuring him she was asleep and not unconscious.

Even through his worry, he savoured the feel of her so trustingly nestled in his arms. He relished the warmth of her body, the sound of her even breathing, the chance to hold her without apology.

When the hackney stopped on Bennet Street, Flynn did not rouse her from her sleep, but carried her to the door. The footman answered his knock right away, recognising them both.

'What is wrong with the miss?' he asked.

Flynn did not wish to explain the whole. 'She's ill. Drugged, I suspect. Is there a bed for her?'

'Drugged!' exclaimed the large footman. He seemed to be cogitating on that. Very slowly.

'I need a room for her,' Flynn repeated. 'Tell the *madame*. Quickly!'

The man nodded. 'Follow me. There's a room up the stairs.'

Flynn followed him up three flights of stairs to a room with a bed, card table and chairs. His arms straining at this point, he placed her on the bed, while the footman lit two candles from the lamp in the hallway.

'I'll alert Madame.' The man left.

Flynn unfastened Rose's cloak and unwrapped it from her body. He pulled off her elbow-length gloves and removed her shoes. Lastly he took the pins from her hair, combing out the tangles with his fingers.

There was a brief knock on the door, and Madame Bisou entered. 'What has happened?'

'She was in the company of a man who must have drugged her wine. I found her in time,' he told her.

'Mon Dieu,' she cried. 'I thought we taught her of such dangers! Was she not listening?'

Flynn did not understand, but this was no time to ask what she meant. 'May she stay here?' he asked. 'It was her father who arranged this meeting with the man, you see. I cannot take her back to him.'

'That ruddy bastard,' she mumbled, French accent gone. 'Of course she may stay here.'

The door opened, and Katy burst in the room. 'Cummings said Rose was sick!'

Madame Bisou put her finger to her lips. 'Shh! She is not sick. She's been drugged.'

'Drugged!' cried Katy, so loud Rose stirred on the bed. 'What happened?'

'I think we should give her water,' Flynn said. 'To dilute what she has ingested.'

'I'll fetch some.' Madame Bisou rushed out.

Katy knelt at the bedside. 'What happened, Mr Flynn?' she asked more quietly.

'Her father arranged for her to take supper with Lord Greythorne. I—the marquess, I mean—was suspicious of him, so we put a guard on her. Greythorne paid her father for her company. He put something in her wine and tried to take advantage of her.'

Katy looked directly at him. 'Greythorne,' she repeated in a low flat voice. 'To the devil with him.'

'Indeed,' Flynn agreed. 'We—Lord Tannerton, that is— must protect her from him.'

Katy glanced away. 'Well, it is about time the marquess did something. Where is his lordship? I did not see him here.'

'I am here on his behalf,' Flynn answered her.

She turned her attention back to Rose. 'Let's get her clothes off so she can rest comfortable.'

He did not move. Undress her?

She smiled. 'Do not fear, Flynn. I'll do the undressing. You do the lifting.'

Katy removed Rose's stockings and they rolled her over on her stomach. Katy wore elbow-length gloves on her hands, so it was difficult for her to unfasten the tiny pearl buttons along the back of Rose's dress, the same dark red dress she'd worn when Flynn first set eyes on her. Flynn undid the buttons.

'This is a Paris dress,' Katy said in admiring tones.

Where had Rose purchased a Paris dress?

'Now lift her a little.' Katy bunched the skirt in her hand. 'I'll pull it over her head.'

Rose murmured when Flynn lifted her and Katy pulled the dress off. Katy unfastened her corset next. Flynn could not help but watch. Katy caught him looking, but merely grinned.

'She's a beauty, our Rose.' She sounded proprietary. 'The prettiest one.'

Flynn lifted her again, her curves soft underneath her thin muslin shift. Katy turned down the bedcovers. They soon had her tucked into the bed.

Madame Bisou returned. 'I've brought some water.'

Flynn sat on the bed, propping Rose up with one arm and putting the glass to her lips, giving her a little at a time.

Madame Bisou regarded her with pursed lips. 'We shall watch over her well, Mr Flynn. No need for you to stay.'

He felt stricken. How could he leave her without knowing for certain she would wake in the morning and be recovered?

'Oh, let him stay, if he has a mind to,' Katy said.

Flynn hastily added, 'I think Lord Tannerton would insist upon my staying.'

Katy winked at him.

'Very well.' Madame Bisou looked around the room. 'If you need anything, Katy can get it for you. I had better return to the card room.'

'Thank you, Madame,' he said.

After she left, Katy stood. 'Something tells me you would fancy a tall tankard of ale, am I correct? And maybe some bread and cheese?'

He gave her an appreciative smile. 'You are indeed correct.'

When she brought back the food, they sat at the table, eating and watching Rose.

'I did not realise I was hungry and thirsty,' Flynn said. 'Thank you, Katy.'

She gave him a pleased expression. 'Figured you had not eaten, if you were watching out for Rose.'

'I had not even thought of eating.' He'd thought of nothing but of keeping Rose safe from Greythorne.

Rose stirred, and they both waited until she settled herself again.

Katy spoke. 'You are worried about her?'

He did not quite meet her eyes. 'Well, yes. I mean, Lord Tannerton has charged me with her care. I would be remiss in my duties—'

She grinned over the rim of her tankard. 'Duties my mother's uncle. You look at her as if your breathing is about to stop, Flynn. You don't do that because your marquess told you to.'

His gaze returned to Rose, but he did not speak.

Katy persisted. 'My guess is that you've fallen head over noggin for her, haven't you?'

He tried to keep his expression impassive.

Her eyes softened. 'Must not be a treat to fall in love with the woman your employer wants you to procure for him.'

She made it sound so sordid. He was not procuring Rose for Tanner. If anything, he was trying to ensure her future. To protect her through Tanner.

He stared at her friend.

'Very well, don't admit it, but I know it's so.' She glanced back to Rose. 'She's lucky, she is. Our Rose. Lucky you were there to save her from that blighter.' Still watching her, she went on, 'You know, of all of us, Rose seemed the most— what's the word? When you don't listen but look like you are thinking about something else?'

'Distracted?' he suggested.

'Yes! That's it! Distracted.'

Flynn took a sip of his ale, trying to make some sense out of this. 'What do you mean by "of all of us"?'

She reddened. 'Lawd, I meant nothing. Nothing at all.'

He peered at her. 'Come clean, Katy. How do you and Madame Bisou and Rose know each other?'

She merely stared at him.

He persisted. 'You told me before that you went to school with Rose, but it doesn't fit. Rose has not been in England for very many months, and I would wager a pony you have never been to Ireland.'

Her eyes widened. 'I'm not supposed to tell.'

'Tell *me*, Katy. If I am to help her, I must know about her.'

She tapped on the table, still staring at him.

He glanced away and back again. 'If you believe what you do about me, you must know I would do nothing to hurt her or anyone she cares about.'

She took a long time thinking, squirming in her chair, eyes darting about the room. Suddenly she leaned forward. 'Well, it is a secret, and you must swear on your mother's grave that you won't tell anyone.'

'My mother isn't in her grave. She's alive and well in Bal-lynahinch.' At least he hoped she was. She was when her last letter arrived three weeks ago. Flynn promised he would reply to the letter this very day.

Katy puzzled over his words. 'Well, then, swear on your mother's grave for when she's in it. Some day.'

He was Irish enough to think that would bring bad luck. 'How about I swear on my grandfather's grave? He's the sort who would rise out of it if I broke my word.' Flynn had a flash of the old man giving him a tongue lashing that stung worse than a switch to his buttocks.

'Very well.' She screwed up her face as if it would be hard

to force the words out. 'Me and Rose did go to school together. It was not that Irish school of hers. It was a…' she paused and took a deep breath '…a courtesan school.'

'A what?'

'A courtesan school. A school to teach us to be courtesans and not merely girls in a bawdy house. This lady—and I'll never give her name, I don't care how many graves you swear on—she started the school, so as we would wind up better than we was—I mean, than we were.'

Flynn was not certain he heard correctly. 'A *lady* ran this school?'

Katy nodded. 'Right in her home on—never mind what street. See, her maid was wanting to run away to a bawdy house, but the lady did not want her to. She said girls were better off to be courtesans, like Harriette Wilson. We met Harriette Wilson, too. She came to the lady's house.'

Flynn gave her a sceptical look. The famous courtesan received in a lady's home? It was not to be believed.

'Anyway,' Katy said. 'Mary and me—Mary and I—ran away from the house where we were working because we heard the lady talking about it to Mrs Rice and we found our way to the lady's house where she had the school.'

'Mrs Rice?'

Katy narrowed her eyes. 'The abbess who ran the bawdy house. She was a bad lot.'

'Rose was in a bawdy house?' He did not want to believe this.

'Not in our bawdy house,' Katy replied. 'Truth to tell, I'm not sure where she came from. Ran away from her father, I think. She heard Mary and me talking on the street, and she came with us to Miss H—' She clamped her mouth shut.

'So the three of you went to this lady's house because she

had a courtesan school?' He was still trying to comprehend this.

She gave him a patient look. 'Well, there was her maid and that made four of us. The school was started for us, and Madame Bisou was hired as our tutor.'

'But…why?'

'I told you why.' She sounded exasperated. 'Because the lady thought a courtesan had the best kind of life. A courtesan could pick and choose what men to bed, and make lots of money, too, and no man could take her money away from her, like a husband can do.'

There was some logic to this. It was, after all, the excuse he made to himself when he'd negotiated with Tanner's mistresses in the past.

Flynn took a long sip of his ale, trying to digest this still incomprehensible information. He'd only fleetingly harboured the illusion that Rose was an innocent—she'd too often alluded to a past, after all—but if she had so single-mindedly pursued the life of a courtesan, why did she hesitate to accept Tanner's interest? Tanner was a courtesan's dream.

He looked at Katy. 'How is it that Rose did not come here with you? Why was she with her father?'

Katy threw up her arms. 'You ask me that? I cannot know. You might as well ask me why the others chose to get married. Especially Mary, running off with that numskull, Du— I mean, getting married was one of those things we were taught not to do. Why shackle yourself to some man who takes your money and then goes off and gives it to a mistress? Better to be on the other side.'

Another all-too-true statement, Flynn thought.

They fell silent until Katy said, 'Come to think of it, Rose met up with her father that night we all went to Vauxhall. That's when Mr Hook let her sing. I think the old man talked her into coming back to live with him. If she'd asked me, I'd have told her she was daft.'

They finished eating, and Flynn moved his chair closer to Rose's bedside. He gave her more water, propping her up again with his arm. Her eyes opened and she smiled.

'Flynn,' she whispered.

She drank a few sips, licking droplets from her lips. He returned the glass to the bedside table and helped her settle under the covers again. Her eyelids soon grew heavy again, fluttering closed finally in sleep.

He glanced up to see Katy watching him, sympathy in her eyes.

Rose struggled awake, eager to escape disturbing dreams of dark shadows and sinister creatures.

She forced her eyes to open, though the light from the window hurt them. She blinked. The room was strange. She sat up in alarm.

Flynn was there, rising from a chair next to the bed. 'It is all right, Rose. You are safe.'

'Flynn!' She reached for him and he enfolded her in his arms. In his embrace, she indeed felt safe.

He released her and gestured to the table in the centre of the room. Katy, head resting on her arms, was fast asleep.

'I brought you to Madame Bisou's,' he told her. 'I could think of no other place.'

'Greythorne?' she rasped.

'I am certain he cannot know where you are.' He brushed her hair away from her forehead.

There was so much she could not remember. She recalled

the supper box and Greythorne asking her to dance. She recalled feeling dizzy, then all was dark and she struggled to free herself.

'You rescued me.' She remembered the masked face that had been Flynn's.

His expression acknowledged this. 'Greythorne does not know who rescued you, although he may suspect. We must decide what to do about him, but that can be attended to later. How do you feel?'

She grabbed his hand and held on to it. 'My head aches.' She took in his face, the stubble of beard shadowing his jaw. He was dressed only in his shirtsleeves, neckcloth untied, waistcoat unbuttoned.

He sat in the chair next to the bed, still holding her hand. She glanced down at herself and realised that she was dressed only in her shift. She ought to be embarrassed at her dishabille—and his—but she was not. It seemed natural they should be together this way.

She glanced over at Katy. 'Katy stayed all night, too?'

He nodded.

'Is she feeling well enough?'

He looked puzzled. 'Yes, she seemed well.'

Rose tried to clear the muddle from her mind. 'Did Greythorne put something in my wine?'

He nodded. 'Laudanum, most likely.'

'I'm thirsty.'

He took his hand from hers and poured her some water. She drank eagerly.

When she handed the glass back to him, she reached up to run her finger along the scratchy beard on his jaw. 'Thank you, Flynn. For everything.'

She slid her hand around the back of his neck and urged

him toward her, her heart racing at the anticipation of his lips upon hers.

There was a rustling behind him. 'Aw, I fell asleep!' Katy cried.

Rose let go and Flynn sat back in the chair.

Katy stretched. 'Are you awake, Rose?'

'Yes,' she said. 'But I only just woke. Flynn said you stayed with me the whole night. I hope that was not too much for you, Katy.'

'Naw.' Katy grinned. 'I figured you needed a chaperon.' She stood and stretched again. 'Anybody hungry? I'm hungry as a duck.'

'Would you like some breakfast, Rose?' Flynn asked.

She nodded. 'Some tea would be lovely.'

'Can we bring her some?' Flynn asked Katy.

'No,' Rose said, putting her hand on his arm. 'I would rather get up.'

Katy walked over and leaned her elbows on Flynn's shoulders. Rose narrowed her eyes at this intimate gesture.

'Tell you what,' Katy said. 'I'll find you a nice dress to wear, and we'll get you fixed up to come to the supper room. Mr Flynn can join us there.'

Katy breezed out of the room.

Flynn stood. 'Forgive my appearance.'

Rose thought he had never looked so handsome.

He turned his back and hurriedly buttoned his waistcoat. As he reached for his coat, he caught her gaze again. It was just as if he'd touched her, the sensation was so intense. She wished he would cross the room to her. She wished he would share her bed in the way men share with women, the way he wanted her to share with Tanner.

Instead he put his coat on and sauntered over to the window.

Katy returned, carrying a pale pink day dress. 'Now off with you, Flynn. Ask Cummings to give you a razor. You look a fright.'

Rose wanted to protest, but he gave a wry smile. 'I must indeed.' He glanced at Rose again, a look that seared her senses. 'I will see you in the supper room.'

Before she could form a reply, he left.

Katy started to help her out of bed. 'Are your legs wobbly?'

'My knees feel a bit weak,' she responded.

Katy laughed. 'My knees would be weak too, with a man like that looking at me.'

Rose peered at her. 'What man?' she asked.

Katy looked at her as if she were a lunatic. 'Flynn, of course. He looks at you like a cat looks at a dish of cream.'

'Oh, Katy!' Rose leaned against her friend. 'Do not say it. He merely acts for Lord Tannerton.'

Katy hugged her. 'Do not try to flummox me, Rose. The two of you look like April and May. The thing is, what are you going to do about it?'

Rose sighed, pulling away and walking over to the pitcher of water and washing bowl. 'There is nothing to do about it. Flynn is employed by Tannerton, and Tannerton wishes to offer for me.' So long as Tannerton held the key to Flynn's future success, she could not risk turning him against Flynn.

Rose dampened a towel and wiped her face.

Katy went on. 'Tannerton's no fool, you know. He's bound to catch on.' Katy tapped her forehead. 'I know! What you do is take Tannerton up on his offer, get a house out of him and who knows what else, and then when he tires of you, you'll have the all-clear with Flynn, plus a tidy sum to live on, too.'

Katy's practicality sounded sordid.

Rose washed herself off, while Katy fetched her corset, saying, 'I tell you, if that Flynn took a fancy to me, I might give him a jolly run for his money.'

Rose felt as if she could not breathe, although it had nothing to do with Katy tightening the corset's laces. It was probable Flynn would turn to some other woman. Why not Katy, so lively and bright and sympathetic?

'Are you interested in Flynn, Katy?' Rose tried to sound calm, but her voice wobbled.

Katy laughed and gave her a quick hug. 'I'm interested in any man, long as he has money.'

It was not a particularly reassuring answer.

Katy helped her on with the dress and brushed her hair, tying it back in a ribbon. They were soon entering the supper room. Flynn, clean-shaven again, was seated with Madame Bisou.

The *madame* sprang from her chair and hurried over to Rose. 'How are you feeling, Rose, *ma petite?* What a fright you gave us.'

'Just a little shaky, Madame,' she said.

Flynn stood and pulled out a chair for her. 'I will fix you a plate. What would you like?'

'Some toast and jam, perhaps?'

Flynn brought her the food, and Madame Bisou poured the tea. They said little while she nibbled on her piece of toast. She ate slowly, feeling a touch of nausea.

Flynn finally spoke. "We must consider what to do next. I confess, I do not want you to go back to your father's house.'

'Of course she must not go back there!' cried Madame Bisou.

'My father will be worrying about me,' Rose said.

'Mr Flynn can send word to him that you are in a safe place.' The *madame* grasped her hand and squeezed. 'You must stay here, Rose, dear, for as long as you like.'

Flynn nodded in approval.

'I…I thank you, Madame,' Rose said, moved by the woman's generosity. She glanced at Flynn.

Flynn gave her a steady look. 'You must let me deal with your father. He will want to follow Lord Tannerton's wishes. Trust me, Rose. We will keep you safe.'

With Tannerton's name and Flynn's energies, Rose had no doubt anything could be done.

Chapter Fourteen

When Flynn walked into the Audley Street town house, Tanner was just descending the stairs.

'Where the devil have you been?' Tanner's typical affable tone was notably absent.

Flynn glanced at the footman in the hallway who was making an ill-disguised effort to appear as if he were not listening to every word. 'I'll tell you the whole, if you have a moment. In the library?'

Tanner led him directly to the library. He turned to face Flynn as soon as Flynn closed the door. 'My men said you left them in Vauxhall and that you had Miss O'Keefe with you.'

Flynn answered, 'That is so. Wiggins and Smythe told you about the rescue, no doubt. Greythorne drugged her wine. I brought her to Madame Bisou's and stayed to make certain she was recovered. I thought that a better plan than taking her to her father's residence.' Flynn felt a pang of conscience. His actions had been more complicated by emotion than this dispassionate explanation implied.

Tanner gave him a level gaze. 'You could not have sent word to me of this last night?'

Flynn felt his face grow hot. 'I confess, I never thought of doing so.' His mind had all been on Rose.

Tanner waved his hand. 'It is of little consequence. She is well, I hope.'

'Yes. She's unharmed.'

Tanner sank into a chair. 'I was up half the night imagining Greythorne had done you an injury. Finally sent one of the men to his residence, but all was as I had intended.'

'Greythorne seemed more worried about his soiled clothing than about chasing us.'

Tanner grinned. 'That is what Wiggins said. He said, "the man was cursing something awful, m'lord."' Tanner mimicked his footman's accent perfectly.

Flynn peered at Tanner, the earlier comment just registering in his brain. 'You sent someone to Greythorne's residence?'

Tanner crossed his legs and leaned back in the chair. 'I do occasionally rouse myself to have a thought or two. If Greythorne had done a mischief, I wanted to be prepared to deal with it.'

Or to send someone else to deal with it, Flynn thought.

Tanner absently swung one leg up and down, certainly not exerting himself at this moment to think through what they must do next. Flynn felt out of patience with him, although Tanner was truly not behaving at all out of the ordinary.

Flynn spoke more sharply than he intended. 'We must make plans, my lord. There is Greythorne to consider. He is certain to try again. And we cannot return Miss O'Keefe to her father. He is not strong enough to protect her.'

Tanner grinned. 'Oh, we need not fear Greythorne.'

Easy for Tanner to make light of this. He had not seen Greythorne's hands all over Rose.

Flynn frowned. 'He is an unpredictable enemy, Tanner. He cannot be expected to behave like a gentleman.'

Tanner laughed. 'Indeed!'

'Some gravity, if you please, sir.' Flynn started to pace. 'Miss O'Keefe's well being is at stake.'

Tanner's leg swung up and down, up and down. 'It is not as bad as all that. You might be shocked to discover, my dear Flynn, I have actually exerted myself to deal with Greythorne.' He looked heavenward. 'An inspired solution, I might add.'

Flynn stopped pacing. 'What did you do?'

Tanner uncrossed his legs and leaned forward, mischief in his eyes. 'I asked his Royal Highness, the Duke of Clarence, to *require* Greythorne's company.' He pulled his timepiece from his pocket and opened it. 'In fact, they ought to be on the road to Brighton this very hour.'

Flynn gaped at him. 'You asked the Duke what?' He laughed. 'Greythorne must accompany the Duke to Brighton?'

Tanner grinned. 'His Royal Highness is somewhat of a romantic, you know, so he was quite willing to foil Greythorne's ungentlemanly interference in my interests. Greythorne was mad as a hornet about it. Saw him at White's.'

Flynn gaped at his employer. 'I am all admiration. That was well done, indeed.'

Tanner's expression turned pensive. 'Not quite so well done. I fear my machinations precipitated that rash act of his. I had not thought he would sink so low.'

Flynn frowned. Luckily they'd known enough to keep watch over her.

'I need to speak to her father.' Flynn started pacing again, half-frustrated, half still annoyed at Tanner. 'It is that Dawes woman who is the real problem there, however.'

Tanner shrugged. 'Give them money.'

Flynn turned around.

Tanner gave him a patient look. 'Regard me, Flynn. Miss Dawes is motivated by greed, and the father is weak. If we cut them out, the woman will remain a thorn in our sides, plaguing us, Miss O'Keefe and her father from now until the girl reaches her majority. I say give the father an outrageous sum of money, send them off to Bath, and be done with them.'

Tanner's approach would be effective. It was a rare problem that could not be solved by throwing great sums of money at it. It was typically Flynn's job to find some more economical solution.

Flynn would be happier to see Greythorne—and Miss Dawes—transported to Botany Bay, although the law would likely not consider their offences as warranting such a punishment. The rights of one minor girl were practically non-existent, after all.

'You are certain you wish me to spend your money in this way?' Flynn asked.

Tanner shrugged. 'Send them to Bath. Unless you think you can pack them off to Scotland.'

Scotland? There's an idea, thought Flynn.

'I'll attend to it right away.'

After donning clean linen, Flynn set off for Langley Street to confront Rose's father. He entered the building and climbed the stairs with determination. As he neared the door, he heard voices and sounds of movement inside.

He knocked and all sounds ceased. 'Mr O'Keefe?' he called through the door. 'It is Flynn.' More silence. 'Please open, sir. You will want to see me.'

He put his ear to the door and could hear footsteps approaching.

'Are you alone?' O'Keefe asked through the closed door.

'I am alone,' Flynn replied.

Flynn stepped back from the door and watched a shadow darken the keyhole. O'Keefe was peeking through it. The door opened a crack, and Mr O'Keefe peered out before opening it wider.

'So sorry. I must be careful, Mr Flynn.' O'Keefe said.

'Careful of what?' Flynn asked.

O'Keefe stepped aside to let the younger man enter. 'Do you know where my daughter is?' he asked. 'She went off with some fellows last night.'

'She's safe,' Flynn assured him.

Her father patted his arm, his eyes moist.

Flynn walked in. The room was in disarray. Clothes strewn about. A trunk half-filled. Papers piled on tables. Letty Dawes, looking haggard, walked out from the bedchamber carrying a portmanteau.

'You are leaving.' Flynn surmised.

'Indeed we are.' Miss Dawes gave a dramatic huff. 'No thanks to that girl of his.' She gestured angrily towards O'Keefe. 'Ran off last night, she did. Left that rich Lord Greythorne, mud all over him, spitting mad, I'll tell you. He said he'd make good his threat and I've a mind he means it.'

'His threat?' Flynn asked.

Mr O'Keefe spoke up. 'Threatened our lives if Mary Rose did not return and accept his money—'

'He was going to give us money, as well. More than that

marquess,' added Miss Dawes. 'Just like her to go off with some no-good fellows. Common blokes, his lordship told us. Flirting with her while she was supposed to be cosying up to him. I tell you, she did it on purpose, just to cut her poor father out.'

O'Keefe looked away, shamefaced.

'I am beginning to understand.' Flynn frowned. 'But I cannot yet comprehend why you are leaving.'

O'Keefe glanced at him. 'He said he would kill us if we don't give him my Mary Rose.' His voice broke.

'As if we knew where to find the girl.' The wattles on Miss Dawes's neck shook with emotion. 'In some common man's bed, giving it away just to spite us! If that marquess of yours had only made his offer sooner. I do not care if he is rich and has a lofty title, he is a slow-top and a fool!'

'Letty,' O'Keefe said in a low voice. 'Mr Flynn says Mary Rose is safe.'

'Hmmph!' She put her fists on her hips. 'Well, that does not help us, does it?'

Flynn barely maintained his bland, negotiating demeanour in the face of this outrageous woman. 'You feel Greythorne will make good his threat?'

Miss Dawes wailed, 'Of course he will! That girl has all but destroyed us, and what do we have to show for it? The paltry sum his lordship gave us for her to be nice to him last night. And trinkets!' She thrust her hand in his face, the emerald ring still on her finger. 'I've half a mind to take her dresses with us and sell them. If we had a bigger trunk that is exactly what I would do, but that trunk she had in her room is much too small.'

Flynn spoke quickly, thinking even faster. 'I am certain the marquess would lament this turn of events. He is a sympathetic man.' This was a deal Flynn never guessed he'd be making.

'We will die of starvation!' Miss Dawes cried. She flung herself into a chair.

'Now I can still work, Letty, dear.' O'Keefe patted her shoulder.

'I concur that you must get away,' Flynn broke in. 'The marquess with help you. Where would you like to go?'

'Where can we be safe?' wailed Miss Dawes.

'Glasgow,' said Mr O'Keefe in a quiet voice. 'It is a big city.'

'Glasgow?' Miss Dawes huffed.

'I could find work there,' said O'Keefe.

Flynn dipped his hand into his coat pocket. 'The marquess will help you.' Flynn withdrew the money he'd been carrying. 'Five hundred pounds.' He handed it to Mr O'Keefe. They could survive on the interest of five hundred pounds.

Miss Dawes snatched the notes from O'Keefe's hand and counted.

'Glasgow,' Flynn repeated. There was opportunity in the Scottish city. Many a merchant there became rich from the city's easy access to shipping, and would want a rich man's entertainment. A musician like O'Keefe might well find work.

'Glasgow.' Miss Dawes smiled, clutching the bank notes to her ample breast.

Later that afternoon, Rose gazed out of the bedchamber window where she'd spent the night. Flynn had assured her she need not miss her voice lesson if she felt well enough to attend. Her head ached just a little, but not enough to keep her away.

She caught sight of Flynn crossing the street at the end of

the road. Leaning against the window frame, she watched his progress. He moved with such purpose, tension in his stride, as if he were so intent upon where he was going, he never stopped to think if that was where he wanted to be.

As he approached the door, Rose could no longer see him without hanging out of the window. She stepped away and smoothed her skirt. She hurried to the mirror, checked her hair, and pinched her cheeks to add some colour to her face. After one more quick look in the mirror, she left the room. As she descended the stairway, she heard laughter. When she reached the hall, Katy had her arm through Flynn's.

Katy glanced up and saw Rose. 'Look who is here, Rose! I'm trying to steal him away, but he'll have none of it.'

Rose found no humour in Katy's jest. 'Mr Flynn goes where he pleases, I am sure.' She bit her tart tongue.

Katy laughed some more. 'He ought to go where he pleases.'

Katy released Flynn. Rose felt her insides melt as his gaze followed her progress down the stairs.

'I am ready,' Rose said in a quiet voice.

'Are you certain you feel well enough?' His expression was full of concern.

She nodded. 'I want to attend the lesson.'

'Let us go then.' He offered her the arm that Katy relinquished.

'Enjoy yourself, Rose!' Katy exclaimed.

Feeling guilty for her jealous thoughts, Rose stepped away from Flynn and hugged Katy.

When they were outside, Flynn said, 'We should find a hack.'

'Can we walk?' she asked.

The day was warm, but it felt good to be free of the

confines of the four walls. Besides, it would give her more time with him.

'As you wish,' he said.

They started on their way and, while they walked, he told her about his visit to her father.

'Is my father in danger?' she asked, her brow furrowing.

'I doubt it.' He pulled her arm tighter through his. 'Greythorne is no fool. Murder would be a foolish risk.'

Rose thought Greythorne very capable of murder. Anyone who could do what he did to Katy...

'I am glad my father is leaving,' she said. 'I am wanting him to be safe. But Greythorne will come after me, will he not? He will be coming to Vauxhall.'

Flynn placed his hand upon hers where she clutched his arm. 'No need to fear. He is gone for the moment.' He explained the trip Lord Tanner had arranged for Greythorne.

She widened her eyes. 'Lord Tanner knows the Prince so well to ask such a favour?'

'I suppose he does,' Flynn said.

Then surely Tannerton would be successful in convincing the Prince to employ Flynn.

Flynn went on, 'All that remains is to find you lodgings and hire servants to attend you.' His voice was matter of fact, but Rose felt like a door was slamming.

'I have sent one of Tannerton's maids and a footman to your father's building to pack up your clothes and your pianoforte and have them sent to Madame Bisou's.'

He had remembered her most precious possession—her pianoforte. 'Thank you, Flynn.'

It was bittersweet to have Flynn walking next to her, the man she wanted to love her, when she was more and more destined to be in the bed of another. She delighted in Flynn's touch, his scent, and how the sun lit his face. The memory of how he'd looked that morning, rumpled and unshaven, made her tremble.

At King's Theatre Miss Quinn and Signor Angrisani were all smiles at her progress. They rehearsed her in the chorus part, walking her through it, showing her where she would stand, how she should move. She would perform on Saturday. She would perform in King's Theatre, as her mother had done.

When the lesson was over, Mr Ayrton escorted her through the theatre, but instead of finding Flynn waiting for her, Lord Tannerton stood there. Flynn was nowhere in sight.

'My lord.' Rose curtsied.

'Miss O'Keefe.' Tannerton smiled at her.

Mr Ayrton spoke to him. 'She must practise each day this week, but she is welcome to join the chorus on Saturday.'

'So I heard you say.' Tannerton offered his hand to the man. 'Thank you.'

When Ayrton left them, the marquess said, 'My carriage is waiting. I came to escort you to Madame Bisou's.'

She could not refuse. It was time for her to accept what he offered.

Inside the carriage, she said, 'I have much to thank you for, my lord.'

He waved a hand. 'I assure you, all was easily done.'

Easily done by Flynn. She caught herself in the unfair thought, remembering what Tannerton had done. 'Greythorne is far away, because of you,' she said. 'Flynn said you asked the Duke of Clarence.'

He laughed. 'Flynn told you of that, eh? It was an inspired idea, I'll agree.'

She could not contain her curiosity. 'And did you convince his Royal Highness to employ Mr Flynn?'

'I did,' he said proudly. 'Have not told Flynn yet, however.' He gave her an impish look. 'You must keep the secret a little longer.'

'Yes, my lord.'

She could not help but be disappointed that he'd been successful so soon. As long as Flynn remained in Tannerton's employ, she'd at least be able to see him, even if it was as Tannerton's mistress. When Flynn went to a Royal palace to work, she would never see him again.

Tanner smiled at her. 'Would you allow me to escort you to Vauxhall this evening? Perhaps afterwards we could eat supper there.'

Of course she must accept this invitation. It would be churlish not to. Would he think she was accepting more?

'My lord,' she began, 'so much has happened. I…I am not certain I am…'

He seemed to take no offence at her discomfort. 'If you like, Flynn and your friend Katy can come as well.'

She released a relieved breath. 'Then I would most graciously accept.'

Chapter Fifteen

The next two days followed the same routine. Flynn arrived to take her to her lesson, and Lord Tannerton escorted her back. They all four went to Vauxhall and supped afterwards. Rose consoled herself with the pleasure of having at least one dance with Flynn each night.

She forced herself to think only of performing in the opera in her tiny chorus part.

On the Saturday of her performance, Flynn brought her to King's Theatre early where the rest of the company rehearsed with her. One of the girls let it slip that they had been paid well for their time.

Flynn had been very quiet on the walk to the theatre, and she'd sensed the pent-up emotion inside him. Was he suffering as much as she? She was afraid to ask. Once in the theatre, he wished her luck, giving her a kiss on the forehead she could feel still, though hours had passed and the performance was about to begin.

Then she was onstage performing her minor part in *Don*

Giovanni. Rose imagined her mother walking a stage much like this one, looking out into the same vastness of the theatre audience, wearing the same heavy paint on her face and the same sort of costume. Though Rose's nerves jangled throughout the performance, she did not miss a cue and she remembered all the lyrics.

Lord Tannerton, Flynn and Katy were in Tannerton's box, Rose knew. Tannerton—through Flynn, of course—had even included Madame Bisou. Rose could imagine them in their seats watching her. She knew Flynn's eyes would be upon her the whole time. She knew he wished her well.

She managed to get through the entire performance without a mistake. When the final curtain call brought shouts of 'Bravo!' for Miss Quinn, Signor Angrisani and the other principals, Rose felt a rush of relief. She had done it. She had performed in King's Theatre.

Afterwards, dressed again in her own gown, the other girls took her with them to the theatre's green room, the room where gentlemen came to meet the female performers. She endured many frankly admiring glances from the waiting gentlemen before she saw Lord Tannerton standing with Mr Ayrton.

'Ah, here she is.' Tannerton stepped forward to take her hand.

She dropped into a curtsy.

'You did very well, Miss O'Keefe.' Tannerton smiled at her. 'At least as much as I know of it. Flynn said so, in any event, and he knows of such things. I can only say I enjoyed it.'

Mr Ayrton bowed to her. 'I have been speaking to the marquess, as you can see. We have made a nice arrangement. If you should like to remain in the chorus, it will be my pleasure!'

Rose surmised the 'arrangement' meant some sort of monetary compensation for having her perform with the company, employment based on the fact that she had a wealthy and generous patron.

She managed an appreciative expression. 'How kind of you, sir.'

Tannerton offered his arm. 'Shall we be going? Our party awaits.'

She walked out on Tannerton's arm, eager to see Flynn, wanting to explain to him how she'd expected her spirits to soar with joy at having her dream come true. She was happy to have performed at King's Theatre, but it had not compared to the first time she sang at Vauxhall, that magical evening when Mr Hook let her sing one song. Flynn would understand.

As they walked down a hallway, the marquess leaned down to her, his eyes twinkling. 'I have a surprise for you.'

She was not sure she wanted more surprises.

They turned a corner and there waiting with Flynn and Katy were Mary and Lucy, the girls she knew at Miss Hart's, and their husbands. Rose was speechless in disbelief.

Tannerton whispered in her ear, 'Surprise.' He gave her a little nudge.

She ran towards them, Mary, Lucy, and Katy meeting her halfway with hugs and tears.

'Madame Bisou sent us messages that you were performing,' Mary said. 'What a lovely surprise!'

'It was grand!' Lucy said. 'I've never seen the like, and to think you were there on that big stage!'

'Oh, never mind that!' Rose cried. 'How are you both faring? Is there any news from Miss Hart—I mean, Mrs Sloane?'

Lucy gave a shy smile. 'I call her "Miss Hart," too. Can't help it.'

'Lucy has a letter. Tell her, Lucy!' Mary said.

'Later,' Lucy said. 'I have it with me. But say hello to Elliot!'

Mr Elliot, Lucy's husband, stepped forward and Rose could not help but give him a hug, and Mr Duprey, Mary's husband, as well.

'So good,' Duprey said. 'Nice performance. First-rate.'

'Thank you.' Rose wiped tears from her eyes. 'I'm thinking it is good to see you, too. I have missed you so. I did not know you had returned to town.' The Dupreys were to have spent the summer in Bath, and the Elliots at Mr Sloane's country estate.

'Come, let us depart.' Lord Tannerton shooed them on. 'They are to dine with us, Miss O'Keefe. You shall have plenty of time for conversation.'

At Madame Bisou's, Tannerton and Flynn talked with Elliot and Duprey while Rose read Miss Hart's letter, all the way from Venice. Her friends looked on.

'Oh, she is increasing!' Rose exclaimed, the news oddly making her feel like weeping.

Mary leaned over to her and grasped her hand. 'I am, too.'

'As am I!' Lucy added.

Tears did spring to her eyes then. Her three friends, all to have babies. She hugged them again.

The meal was a lively affair, with much conversation and many toasts, most led by Tannerton, who seemed bent on making the ladies laugh. Rose noticed that Mr Elliot and Flynn were often conversing together. After the meal she found herself near Elliot.

'Do you know Mr Flynn, then?' she asked Elliot, who was Mr Sloane's secretary.

He answered her, still sipping a glass of wine, and more tipsy than she'd ever seen him. 'We've met a time or two. He's a good man.'

That made Rose feel proud, though she had no right to pride about Flynn.

Elliot went on, 'They say he's destined to great things. An MP or something. It is known that Tannerton is grooming him for more.'

For a prince, thought Rose.

She glanced over at Flynn, at the moment talking with Duprey. Flynn looked up at the same time. Their eyes met.

After Elliot moved away, Katy sidled up to Rose. 'What will you do?'

Rose blinked. 'About what?'

'About him.' Katy cocked her head in Flynn's direction.

Rose looked at Katy, unable to disguise her emotions. 'I do not know, Katy. I do not know.'

When the first light of dawn appeared in the city sky, the party broke up. A very sleepy Mary and Lucy left in the arms of their husbands. Rose watched them. They both had chosen not to become courtesans. Instead they had fallen in love.

Now they were both so happy.

Tannerton walked up to Rose. 'I'll bid you goodnight, Miss O'Keefe.' He swayed from too much drink.

She dropped into a formal curtsy. 'Thank you again, my lord.'

He took her arm to make her rise and spoke with good humour. 'None of that. I'd rather a kiss.'

Rose panicked. He wanted her to kiss him? She glanced wildly around the room for Flynn, but he was busy assisting Katy to stand. Katy laughed shrilly and wrapped her arms around Flynn's neck.

Rose glanced up at Tannerton, still smiling down at her. She lifted her face to him.

He gave her a kiss on her lips. His lips were as soft as Flynn's. They were as moist and as warm. They even tasted of the brandy he'd been drinking. But that was all.

He broke contact and gave a crooked grin. 'Flynn will make the next arrangements.'

She knew what he meant, and her heart depressed to a cavernous state. She glanced over at Flynn again. Katy was no longer wrapped around him, but could be seen staggering out of the room. Flynn gazed back at her, eyes burning into her, his anguish unguarded and as clear to her as her own.

In the next few days, Flynn walked around like an automaton, winding himself up in the morning and wearing down by nightfall, falling into bed with eyes open, unable to sleep.

His task had been to find a house for Rose. A place convenient for Tanner, who preferred his mistresses to be in easy walking distance. There were plenty of such residences close by St James's Street and the gentlemen's clubs. The difficulty was finding one for sale or lease, one that would provide the comfort Flynn wished Rose to have.

Even more difficult was examining bedchamber after bedchamber and having to imagine Rose and Tanner sharing the bed. The images were too vivid, as vivid as the memory of Tanner kissing her, a now nightly occurrence Flynn was forced to witness when they escorted Rose to Vauxhall, then back to Madame Bisou's.

To his dismay, Flynn discovered a small set of rooms on Great Ryder Street, tucked away and private, but not too far from White's or Madame Bisou's, which should please Rose. Two parlours on the main floor, a bedchamber and sitting room on the first floor. Maids' rooms above that. The kitchen was in the basement, as well as more servants' rooms. The place was furnished so tastefully not a thing need be changed—except to find a corner for Rose's pianoforte.

He made the deal, even managing to get the price lowered significantly, a last-ditch effort to sabotage himself that failed. His success made him inexplicably furious.

She could move in within days. It had been equally as easy to line up servants, a housekeeper, a cook, a housemaid, a lady's maid, and a footman. She had one more week to sing at Vauxhall. She could move in before that week was over, and then she would be Tanner's.

But as long as she performed at Vauxhall, he could see and listen to her as he had that first night. Perhaps if she accepted the offer at King's Theatre, he could watch her there, where her beautiful voice would be lost in the meld of other voices. The thought did not cheer him.

Still, on stage she could be a dream, but everywhere else she must be Tanner's mistress. The very idea seemed to unleash some deep Celtic rage, heretofore lying dormant in Flynn's Irish soul. Perhaps Tanner would even send him on errands for her, purchasing and delivering gifts, arranging and cancelling meetings.

His fury burned hotter.

Flynn thought of the letter he'd posted that morning, addressed to his mother, informing her he was coming home. He had been ready to do battle if Tanner protested, but Tanner approved the request without question. Flynn planned to be gone no more than two months. Surely he could recover from this madness in two months.

Feeling as if he would combust from the inside, he walked back to Audley Street to inform Tanner the residence was acquired.

He entered the game room where the Marquess, in his shirtsleeves, played at billiards.

Upon seeing him, Tanner threw him a cue stick. 'Join me in a game.' He set up the red ball and aimed his cue ball for it. It hit, the red ball missing the pocket by a hair.

Flynn was determined Tanner would not win the game. He placed his cue ball on the table and made the shot, nicking the red ball just enough to put it in.

'Lucky shot.' Tanner grinned.

As Tanner lined up his next shot, Flynn said through gritted teeth, 'I have found a residence for Miss O'Keefe.'

Tanner looked up. 'Oh? Where?'

'Great Ryder Street. Complete with furnishings and at a good price.' Flynn tried to keep the anger from his voice.

He tried to remind himself that Rose was better off with Tanner, the Englishman who could make her dreams come true, than with the likes of Greythorne, who merely wanted to hurt her. What could the Irish Flynn offer her? Nothing.

Besides, he tried to console himself, he still had his ambition. Where he wanted to go, a courtesan songstress would not be welcome. An Irishman especially must be above reproach if he was to achieve high goals, and that would be true of his wife, as well. Rose would be shunned, a fate she did not deserve.

This was all useless pondering. Nothing had changed, Tanner had won Rose. Not Flynn.

Flynn frowned as Tanner replaced the red ball on to the table. "I must alert the servants I hired. All will be ready within a week."

'Ah.' Tanner sounded as if he were barely listening. Flynn had lately seen him more excited by the purchase of a new hunter at Tattersalls. Somehow this merely made Flynn angrier.

Flynn took his next shot, hitting both the red ball and Tanner's cue ball, but did not pocket either one.

'By the way…' Tanner took his turn '…I am dining with Liverpool tonight, so I must beg you to escort Miss O'Keefe alone.' He knocked both balls into the pocket, flashing Flynn a grin. 'The man is bent on keeping me busy for a few days. I do hope he does not prose on about Blanketeers and habeus corpus.'

Habeus corpus—the right of a detainee to appear before a court—had been suspended by Parliament that year, because of protests such as the Blanketeers and the mobbing of the Prince Regent's carriage.

'These are important matters,' Flynn responded, but now the blood had begun to race through his veins.

'I know. I know.' Tanner gestured for him to take his turn. 'It is just that Liverpool is so damned repressive and he proses on for hours. It becomes tedious after a while.'

Flynn had stopped listening. All he could think was he would be escorting Rose without Tanner.

That evening, when he knocked on the door to Madame Bisou's gaming-house, he vowed to do nothing to spark the tinder of his passion for Rose. He would simply enjoy her company.

The footman Cummings admitted him, and soon Katy came into the hall. Katy would act as chaperon, Flynn reminded himself. Her presence would assist him in maintaining his proper place.

'Is the marquess waiting in the carriage?' she asked.

'He shall not attend tonight.' Flynn did not explain. Katy would have less wish to hear of Blanketeers than Tanner did.

Her brows rose. 'So you are alone?'

'I am.'

She stared at him, her hands on her hips. Finally, she blurted out, 'I cannot go to Vauxhall either. I have a…a gentleman who is meeting me here. I am expecting Sir Reginald. You met Sir Reginald before, didn't you, Flynn?'

'Katy…' he began, but Rose appeared on the stairway, lovely in her deep red gown. She held her cloak over her arm.

'I can't go with you, Rose,' Katy called to her. 'So sorry.' Katy did not sound sorry in the least.

Rose was putting on her gloves. 'But, Katy—'

Katy interrupted her. 'The marquess isn't going either, so Flynn is going to escort you. You do not mind, do you?'

Rose turned her eyes on Flynn, and the desire he was so intent on dampening flared into life.

'I am thinking I do not mind.' Her voice was low and sultry.

Flynn took the cloak from Rose and wrapped it around her shoulders. Without a word, they hurried out of the door to Tanner's carriage.

He lifted her inside, his hands spanning her waist. Her eyes were dark, her lips tantalisingly parted. He climbed in and signalled the coachman to start. As soon as the carriage moved off, Rose launched herself on to his lap, into his arms.

'Flynn,' she cried as her lips rained kisses on his neck and cheek. 'I never thought to be alone with you again.'

He was a lost man. He sought her lips with all the hunger that had built up over the days he'd barely dared to look at her. He tasted her and pressed her hard against his groin. Nothing existed for him but Rose, her scent, her softness, the urgent sounds she made in the back of her throat.

Flynn wanted them both free of clothing, no barriers to impede them, but the confined space of the coach made this difficult. He freed her breasts from her low-cut dress and let his tongue play on the pebbled skin of her nipples. She moaned with pleasure. He no longer cared if the space was confined. He began to pull up her skirts.

The coach hit a rut and tipped suddenly, throwing her off him. It righted itself immediately, but the jolt was enough to return him to his senses.

'We must stop this,' he said. 'It is madness.'

In the dim light of the coach's interior, he could see her eyes still wide with passion, her breath still rapid. Slowly, like a sleeping child awaking, she nodded.

She fussed with the bodice of her dress.

'Did I damage it?' he asked, knowing he'd been close to tearing it off.

'No.' She looked up at him and smiled. 'I'm just needing to put myself back in it.'

After setting herself to rights, she straightened his neck-cloth and waistcoat, and then laid her head on his shoulder. 'And don't you be saying you regretted that, Flynn. Because you know you did not.'

No, he did not regret it. His only regret had been stopping.

Chapter Sixteen

Rose whispered to Flynn to secure one of the rooms on the Dark Walk for them, while she prepared herself to perform, and to watch her sing from the place where she first saw him. While she warmed her voice like Miss Hughes and the *signor* had taught her, Mr Hook walked by, looking displeased at her. She could not care. This was her night with Flynn. Her only night with Flynn. Nothing would make her unhappy.

When she stood in her place on the balcony facing the audience below, she immediately looked to the spot where Flynn would stand. He was there, face lifted towards her, as he had been on that first night. She smiled down at him.

The music began, and, like that first time, she sang 'Eileen Aroon.' Though she swept her gaze around the crowd, she returned to Flynn, and sang:

> Changeless through joy and woe
> Only the constant know...

She would be constant to him in her heart, even though she must release him into the world where he would achieve great things. She would take whatever brief time they had together and make it enough to last a lifetime. This was not a night for grief, but a time for joy and for love, and she poured these emotions into her song, forgetting how to breathe, forgetting how to project her voice.

Her song filled the night air, and the one after that, and the one after that. She listened to her voice as she sang. The sound was richer, fuller, louder. It was the sound of joy.

She would strive for this always, in each performance. For Flynn. It would be her own secret way to celebrate the love she had for him, her own way to hold on to him.

She finished with a sad song, 'The Turtle Dove Coos Round My Cot,' a widow's song. She would be like a widow, she thought, after this night, but for now she intended to live and love.

The audience burst into applause with shouts of 'Bravo!' for her. She glanced at Flynn, who stood as still as a statue, as rapt as he'd been throughout. She blew him a kiss, then blew other kisses to cover what she had done.

Finally, filled with happiness and anticipation, she turned and moved towards the balcony stairs.

Mr Hook stopped her. 'Much better, my dear.'

She grinned and impulsively kissed him on the cheek before hurrying away, knowing she would soon be with Flynn.

'There's more fellows out there tonight,' said the servant, Skewes. 'And yer father is not here to deal with ''em.'

She peeked through the curtain. 'I will deal with them myself.'

She opened the door and stepped out. The men were so surprised they gasped and fell back.

'How kind of you all to come,' she said. 'I am engaged for

the evening, but if you wish, I will accept your cards and flowers, but, please, no gifts.'

The men came forward, but with such politeness and reserve, she wondered why she had ever been frightened of them. As she accepted cards and bouquets of flowers, she spied Flynn watching her at the fringe of the group. She felt giddy at seeing him, as if she could flutter above these men like a butterfly.

'Thank you,' she said to each of them.

Some of the young ones—her age, she supposed—were more frightened of speaking to her than she could ever have been of them. She laughed as her arms were piled with flowers. Some slipping to the ground. The throng thinned, and Flynn stepped closer, picking up the fallen blossoms.

Finally, they drifted away, and Rose turned to go back into the gazebo's waiting room.

'One moment, miss!' a voice cried. A young fellow humbly dressed hurried up to her. He bowed. 'A gift for you.' He handed her a box, about the size of a glove box, only deeper. Its red ribbon had come loose, the ends dangling over the edge.

'I do not accept gifts,' Rose told him.

The man looked stricken. 'I've orders to give this to you and I dare not say I failed.'

'Who gives you the orders?' Flynn asked.

The man glanced around anxiously. 'He…he was here-abouts a minute ago. I don't know his name and he paid very well, but he said I must give this to you.'

'Oh, very well,' Rose said, reaching for the box and placing it on top of her mountain of flowers. 'You have done your job.'

The man bowed again and hurried off.

Flynn opened the gazebo door and followed her inside. 'You needn't have gone out there. I would have played your father's part, you know.'

She grinned impishly at him. 'I do not wish you to be fatherly with me. Besides, it was not so terrifying as it once seemed. I do not know why I feared it so.'

The orchestra was playing a very loud piece, the drum making the walls shake. Rose was eager to leave with Flynn. She walked over to a table and dropped the flowers and box on to its surface. She let the cards slide out of her hand, and reached for her cloak on a peg on the wall.

When she swung the cloak around her shoulders, it knocked some of the flowers and the box to the floor. Flynn stooped down next to her to help pick them up. The box had fallen on its side, its top off. When Rose reached for it, a foul smell made her blink, and something wrapped in a scrap of thin muslin rolled out of the box. Rose picked it up and lifted a corner of the cloth.

She screamed and flung it away.

'What? What is it?' Flynn was right there, holding her.

She shook her head, unable to speak. Skewes bent down to look.

'Eucch!' he said, standing up again.

'What is it?' Flynn still held Rose.

'It is a ring,' said the servant. 'With the finger still in it.' He kicked it toward Flynn.

It was not just any ring. It was the ring Tannerton gave to her, the one Letty had snatched away and placed upon her own finger.

'It is Letty's finger, I think,' Rose managed.

The servant picked up something else. 'This looks like a reed.'

Rose glanced at it and turned to bury her face into Flynn's chest. 'My father's. For his oboe.'

Flynn released her long enough to retrieve the finger and the oboe's mouthpiece, wrap them in the cloth, and return them to the box.

'He is out there, isn't he, Flynn?' she rasped.

Flynn stood. 'I fear so. I am taking you home immediately.' He scooped up all the cards the men had given her and stuffed them into his coat pocket.

'I'd as leave you keep me out of this!' cried Skewes.

'If you speak of it to no one,' responded Flynn. 'Can we depend upon it?'

'Well…' the man prevaricated '…times is fairly tough…'

Flynn reached into another pocket and pulled out some coins. 'Will that do?'

The man snatched them from his hand and nodded, apparently satisfied.

'We leave now, Rose.' He picked up her cloak and put it around her.

She did not argue, but clung closely to him as they hurried through the gardens, heading to where the carriage would be waiting.

From the shelter of nearby trees, Lord Greythorne watched the door of the gazebo open again, the cloaked figure walking out on Tannerton's secretary's arm. Disappointing. The gift had been intended for Tannerton as well as for the chit. Greythorne had counted on shocking Tannerton with the return of his own gift in a most dramatic manner.

Greythorne frowned, touching the mask that hid his identity. Once again Tannerton had spoiled his carefully made plans. Surreptitiously following the hurrying pair, Greythorne consoled himself. They rushed as if the devil himself were chasing them.

He chuckled, enjoying himself in the role of the devil. If the lovely Rose thought his little gift frightening, she could anticipate so much more. He would show her fear. She would not escape like that strumpet friend of hers. She would experience the fullness of his wrath. The thought made him tremble with excitement.

As he anticipated, they were leaving the gardens, to return to that gaming hell where she'd gone to live, he suspected. He disliked her selling her favours to other men, but he was reasonably certain that Tannerton had not yet bedded her. Not if his spies reported accurately.

When they headed to where the carriages waited, Greythorne decided not to follow. The time was not yet right to escalate the tension. Let her live in fear of him for a while. The secretary would inform Tannerton, Tannerton would know who was the craftier. He'd know Greythorne would win.

Tannerton surely did not think he would stay in Brighton with the Prince, did he? The Royal Duke was easily fooled. All Greythorne had to do was come down with a disease of the contagious sort, and the Duke wanted him nowhere near. Greythorne paid his footman to impersonate him, to stay in his rooms at Brighton, having meals sent up and his valet to attend him. Good that both men were as loyal as money could buy. They would be well compensated for this little charade.

The only distasteful part had been dressing in his footman's clothes and returning to London in a common post chaise. He knew better than to return to his town house, so he went to the other place, to where he was not known as Greythorne, but merely as Mr Black, a man with plenty of coin and a willingness to pay for whatever needed doing.

He had easily discovered Miss O'Keefe's whereabouts after the…departure…of her father and his odious woman. Greythorne smiled again at that memory. Even he had not anticipated the heady exhilaration of wielding power over life and death. Even now he was hungry to experience the feeling again.

He'd had a watch kept on Rose, had seen her perform at King's Theatre, had been present at Vauxhall. He wanted the coveted Rose, the one men pined for as she sang into the cool Vauxhall nights. She had looked exceptionally desirable this night. He wanted her because the Marquess of Tannerton had dared to compete with him. He would show the marquess that Greythorne never lost.

Except once. He'd lost the Diamond once, but he would not repine over that, a mere trifle compared to the delights now ahead of him.

Greythorne turned back to the Grand Walk, filling himself with need again. He could prowl through the gardens looking for some willing girl who could be lured by a few coins, or he could stoke the fires within him, letting them build into white-hot fervour, striking when the time was perfect.

He decided to scour the gardens. Maybe that pretty little red-haired harlot would be in the gardens again. He needed to settle a score with her, did he not? And if he could not find her, he would simply feed his fantasies of all he might do in a few days' time, when his revenge on Tannerton would be complete.

He laughed aloud, and people turned to stare at him. He stared back until they hurried away. When the devil sought revenge, there would be nothing Tannerton could do to stop him.

Flynn reluctantly left Rose at Madame Bisou's, in the care of the *madame* and her burly footmen. He did not trust anyone but himself with her care at such a time, but there was much to do to ensure her safety. He was only sorry the hour was too late to go directly to the magistrate.

Not that the magistrate could do much until Greythorne's whereabouts were established and more of a connection between the severed finger and the earl could be ascertained. He shuddered to think what treachery Greythorne had committed, but the fate of Mr O'Keefe and Miss Dawes was fairly clear. Rose had said so as well.

Flynn had underestimated the danger from Greythorne, and his guilt over Rose's father and Miss Dawes scraped him raw. He should have seen they needed more safeguarding.

Flynn entered Tanner's town house carrying the box containing the gruesome gift. Wiggins attended the door.

'Has Lord Tannerton returned?' Flynn asked.

'Not as yet, Mr Flynn,' the footman replied.

Flynn gave Wiggins his hat and gloves. 'When he comes in, tell him to come to the library. I need him.'

Wiggins nodded, following Flynn into the library, lighting the candles for him. Flynn set the box on the desk and thanked the footman, who left the room.

Flynn poured himself a glass of brandy from the decanter on the side table. His mind was busy, planning what they must do to find Greythorne and to keep Rose safe.

After an hour, Tanner walked in. 'Flynn? Wiggins said you wanted me.'

'Rose—Miss O'Keefe received a gift tonight after her performance.' Flynn did not know how to convey the horror to Tanner other than to show it. 'The box is on your desk.'

Tanner's brows rose in curiosity. He walked over to the box and opened it, unfolding the muslin to see what was inside.

He stared at it a long time. 'This, I assume, is the ring you purchased for Miss O'Keefe?'

'It is.' Flynn poured Tanner some brandy and placed the glass on the desk for him. 'We must surmise that the finger belonged to her father's companion. The other object is the mouthpiece to an oboe, presumably Mr O'Keefe's.'

Tanner closed up the box. 'Revolting. And loathsome.' He pulled out his handkerchief and rubbed his hands with it, even though his fingers had not touched the objects. 'Are we to assume Greythorne is behind this?'

'Who else?' Flynn responded.

'Indeed.' Tanner picked up the glass of brandy and backed away from the desk. 'I had not imagined he was so dangerous.' He crossed the room to the chairs, but did not sit. 'Why did his Royal Highness not send word Greythorne was not in Brighton?'

Flynn shrugged, knowing Tanner did not expect an answer. 'The man obviously made good his threat to O'Keefe and Miss Dawes.'

Tanner curled one hand into a fist. 'I dislike underestimating an adversary.'

'Madame Bisou's footmen will be guarding Miss O'Keefe.'

Tanner stopped. 'Yes, very good. She is in danger, certainly. How does she fare?'

Flynn thought of her frightened eyes and her stoical insistence she would be all right. 'More frightened than she chooses to reveal.'

Tanner nodded. 'I will send Wiggins and Smythe to help guard her. We must show the magistrate this appalling gift.'

'I agree. We can inform him of Greythorne's threat.' Flynn disliked the idea of identifying Rose. The newspapers thrived on stories such as this one. 'I say we go to the magistrate with this evidence. We cannot keep Rose's name out of it, so we say she has many admirers, Greythorne included.' Flynn reached into his pocket and pulled out the cards Rose had been given. 'I can make a list of these men and add Greythorne's name to it.'

Tanner rubbed his chin. 'Perhaps it would be best to keep my name out of it, Flynn. God knows, having a marquess mixed up in this business will bring on the gossip-mongers.' He frowned as he thought. 'I have it. We tell the magistrate you are Miss O'Keefe's admirer, not I. You have been seen with her more often than I, so that should be no difficulty.'

Flynn could not argue that fact, though it was closer to the truth than he dared to admit.

Tanner went on, 'I will go to the Bow Street Runners and engage them to find Greythorne. They will have the skills to prove Greythorne is behind this dastardly plot.' Tanner gained energy with each step of his plan. 'Explain to Miss O'Keefe that I will not be much in her company for a few days.'

Flynn would have more time alone with her? He dared not think about that. 'What of her new residence? In three days' time, she is expected to move in.'

Tanner shrugged. 'Let her move in, if she wishes it. I see no reason to deny her that comfort. Besides, I can visit her in her own lodgings more discreetly than at Madame Bisou's. Might be easier to guard her there, as well.'

He can visit her. Flynn knew what that meant. He poured himself another brandy.

Tanner watched him drink it. 'I endangered her,' he said in solemn tones. 'And got her father and his woman friend killed.' He shook his head. 'Ghastly.'

The next morning, as early as he deemed practical, Flynn made his way to the magistrate. At the same time, Tanner headed for Bow Street.

The magistrate listened to Flynn's story, peered at the dis-membered finger, and began to shuffle papers on his desk.

'Ah.' He held one paper to his nose, peering at it through his spectacles. 'This is the one.' He handed it to Flynn.

It was a report of the bodies of a man and a woman found in an alley two days ago. One finger was missing on the woman's hand. Evidence of torture was gruesomely detailed.

'They've not been buried yet.' The magistrate restacked his papers and folded his hands on the desk. 'We thought to wait a few days to see if someone would claim them, and here you are. Would you be so good as to take a look?'

Flynn had no choice but to agree. He followed the magis-trate's man to the cellar of a building nearby.

'They were stripped naked, they were,' the man said con-versationally. 'Most are, you know. Especially anywhere near a rookery. I'd say these two were meant to be discovered, just left in an alley, easy enough to see.'

The bodies lay on a large wooden table and were wrapped in roughly woven cloth stained with God-knew-what. The man waved to Flynn to lift the cloth. Holding his breath from the overpowering stench, Flynn lifted one, then the other.

They were, indeed, Mr O'Keefe and Miss Dawes. Or what death had done to them. He glanced to the man and nodded, and they quickly vacated the room.

Flynn returned to the magistrate and finished the business, such as it was. When the magistrate learned Rose lived at Madame Bisou's and sang at Vauxhall, he gave Flynn a knowing look and accepted the list of men Flynn had compiled from Rose's Vauxhall admirers.

'You say the Earl of Greythorne threatened to kill these two if the father did not sell the girl to him?'

It was bluntly stated, but accurate. 'I do, sir.'

'Seems a great deal of fuss over one fancy piece.' His gaze was frankly sceptical. 'They told this to you, eh?'

Flynn flinched when the magistrate called Rose a fancy piece. 'That is the gist of it, sir.'

'Bring the girl to me,' he told Flynn. 'I must question her.'

Flynn agreed to do so.

Before he left, Flynn made arrangements for proper shrouds for the bodies, wooden coffins and a Christian burial. They would be buried that very day, the magistrate's man assured him.

With the scent of death still lingering in his nostrils, Flynn made his way to Madame Bisou's.

Rose received him alone in a small parlour. When the door closed, Rose came into his arms, not in passion like the night before, but in need of comfort, which he was glad to provide.

'How do you fare, Rose?' he asked when they finally broke apart. He held her hands and searched her face.

'I did not sleep well.' She gave a wan smile. 'But, I suppose that should be expected. Katy was a dear and stayed with me all night.'

He stroked her cheek with the back of his hand. 'I am glad you were not alone.'

They stared into each other's eyes for a long moment, before she turned away. 'There is tea. Shall I pour for you?'

'If you like,' he said.

'I remember how you take it.' She sat in the nearby chair, putting in the cream and sugar.

He sat near her, waiting for her to finish pouring.

'I have news,' he said in a tight voice.

She nodded and met his eyes.

'Your father and Miss Dawes have been found. They are dead, Rose.'

She nodded again.

'I...I saw them.' He could not think of words to speak, unwilling to tell her the horror of what he'd seen.

'Were they whipped?' she asked.

'Whipped?' Her question was odd, but the bodies had indeed been riddled with whip marks.

She blinked. 'I mean, do you know how they died?'

Yes, he did know. The magistrate's report listed every cut on their bodies, including on their genitals. A physican had concluded they bled to death.

'Stabbing,' he abridged.

She turned away and moaned.

He took her hand in his. 'I've arranged for a proper burial, Rose.'

'Must I attend it?' she asked in a shaking voice.

'No, you do not have to attend it.'

'My poor father!' Her face crumbled, and he took her in his arms again, holding her until her sobbing slowed, holding her still. 'I know he did not seem like much of a father, Flynn, but he paid for my schooling. He wanted me to have a good life.'

He stroked her hair. 'When I last spoke to him, Rose, his concern was all for you.'

She nestled against his chest. 'I'm thinking I killed him. And Letty, too. They would be alive, if not for me. They wouldn't have suffered—'

He felt her shudder in his arms. 'You are not responsible for this, Rose. Greythorne did this, and it is he who should hang for it.'

'Oh, Flynn.' She pulled away and looked at him with eyes of pain. 'I'm thinking I could have stopped him. I...I knew about him, you see, but I promised not to tell.'

His gaze flew to hers. 'You knew about him? What did you know?'

She inhaled a ragged breath. 'I knew he liked to hurt women.'

Flynn glanced away. 'We knew it as well, Rose. Tanner and I. We did not stop him.' He did not know if he could forgive himself that lapse. All he knew was, Greythorne would be stopped now, before he hurt Rose. He looked at her again. 'How did you discover this about him?'

'I...I cannot tell you. All I can say is, I knew someone hurt by him. Whipped by him. I'm thinking if I had not promised to be quiet about it, maybe he would have been put in prison.'

He stood, drawing her to her feet and enfolding her in his arms again. 'We are all thinking we might have stopped him. We will stop him now, though. I have to take you to the magistrate, Rose. He will ask you questions...'

He explained to her all that he and Tanner had discussed, how Tanner would set the Bow Street Runners on Greythorne, how she would be guarded at all times, how they would pretend it was he, Flynn, who was her protector, not Tannerton.

'You are my protector, Flynn,' she murmured. 'I'll not forget.'

Chapter Seventeen

⟨∾∾∾∾∾∾⟩

Rose walked with Flynn through St James Park after her interview with the magistrate. The trees and grass and lake were calming, and she could almost forget everything but being on his arm.

The magistrate had questioned her about admirers. Rose left out Tannerton's name, but was required to speak of Lord Greythorne's interest in her. The magistrate produced the list Flynn had compiled from the cards she had received. He then asked her how many of these men she had 'been with.' His implication had been clear.

This was the life she had chosen, she could almost hear her father say. Her eyes pricked with tears again. Her poor, poor father. Her father had loved her in his way, but now he was gone, lost for ever.

And soon Flynn would be lost to her, too.

Flynn's eyes darted to and fro, alert, she knew, for any danger. The park was blessedly peaceful, however, and she was convinced she would be safe in daylight as long as she was not alone. She was safe with Flynn. Rose always felt safe with Flynn.

'I neglected to tell you something,' Flynn said in an ominous tone, a sombre contrast to the colourful riot of flowers they strolled by.

Not more bad news. Could she beg him to withhold it? She had been trying to forget everything but walking with him, like the other couples who strolled in the park as if without a care.

She sighed. 'What is it?'

'I have found rooms for you.' He seemed to force some cheer into his voice. 'A nice little place on Great Ryder Street, not too far from Madame Bisou's.'

'When must I move in?'

'A few days.' There was tension in his tone.

They walked in silence along the lake where swans and geese glided past.

Her throat grew tight. 'What is to happen, then?'

'Happen?' He paused. 'What is to happen is Lord Tannerton will have fulfilled the terms agreed upon.' He spoke like a stranger, like she imagined a man of business might sound. 'The contract will be complete—'

'Yes, I know that,' she broke in. 'I was thinking, what will happen to us?'

They stopped at the water's edge. The swans swam to them in the hopes they carried crumbs in their pockets.

He stared out at the water. 'We have been through this, Rose. It will be over.'

It had been foolish of her to ask when she knew the answer, like rubbing salt into a wound. She watched the swans swimming in pairs. At school she'd learned that swans mated for life. How did they select each other? she wondered. Did they know so quickly, as she'd known with Flynn?

As if in silent agreement, she and Flynn turned and started walking on the path leading out of the park.

Rose took a last look at the swans and turned to face him. 'I'll miss you, Flynn.'

They entered a part of the path where the trees formed a canopy, blanketing them with shade and sheltering them momentarily from view.

Flynn stopped suddenly and pulled her into the shrubbery. 'Rose,' he murmured, folding her in his arms.

She hungered to taste his lips, and he obliged her, kissing her with desperation and need. She forgot where they were, or did not care. Knocking his hat off, she buried her fingers in his thick dark hair. He leaned her against the tree, pressing himself against her, lifting her a bit so she fitted against the hard shaft she felt under his clothes. He kissed her face, her neck, the bare expanse of skin exposed by her gown's neckline.

How could she bear this with any other man?

Laughter and voices sounded, coming closer. He released her. The moment had passed. She straightened her clothing while he retrieved his hat. The people on the path walked by and their voices faded into the distance.

Rose forced Flynn to look at her. 'There's no denying this between us, Flynn.' All her desire was reflected in his eyes. 'I'm thinking we must do this. Just once, perhaps, but we must do it. I'm not Lord Tannerton's yet. I'm still a free woman. I'll honour my obligation to him, but first—' she broke off, her voice cracking '—first I want to be with you.'

He wrenched away from her and stood, his gaze averted from her, arms crossed over his chest. Finally his arms dropped to his sides and he turned back to her. He nodded and the ache inside her eased.

'Tomorrow.' His voice was deep and resonant. 'Tomorrow I will show you your new residence. The servants do not come until the following day, and you may move in the day after that—'

The day Lord Tannerton would visit her, no doubt.

'But tomorrow we will be alone.'

She stepped towards him, putting her arms around his neck. He held her again, and they clung together for a long time.

The next day, no one at Madame Bisou's questioned it when Flynn arrived to take Rose out. Although it was an earlier hour than usual, his escort of her was too common-place to remark upon. Katy, too, was silent, but Katy had been silent and preoccupied since Greythorne had killed and was supposed to be lurking about.

Flynn had hired a hackney carriage, even though her new rooms were an easy walk. He instructed the jarvey to drive around the streets, a precaution against Greythorne discovering her new address.

But Rose did not wish to think of Greythorne. She was in such a fever of excitement she could hardly sit still. Only knowing they had the whole day together kept her hands off him.

They switched vehicles at Westminster Abbey, its grey towers rising majestic above them. Some day she'd like to look inside the Abbey. It was said there was much to see there—old tombs and altars and things—the sort of experience she'd like to share with Flynn.

But she had no desire to dwell on the fact that this would be her one precious day with Flynn. She would merely savour it.

The hackney let them off near the Mason's Yard on Duke Street. All they had to do was turn a corner and they were there, on a private little street one could almost miss unless looking for it. No one would see her enter with Flynn, she was certain, and just as certain no one could take heed of their leaving. She did not sing at Vauxhall this night, so they might stay as late as they wished.

Inside, however, she felt suddenly sheepish. As she untied her bonnet, she glanced around the small hall, noticing the narrow stairway in front of her, the one that undoubtedly led to the bedchamber.

Flynn, as well, seemed to take his time removing his hat and gloves. He rubbed his hands together. 'Shall I show you the rooms?'

'Very well,' she responded, leaving her things on the table next to his. Rose cared little about the rooms, but perhaps by the time the tour was done the shaking inside her would stop.

'Let us start at the bottom.' He showed her to an even smaller staircase that led to the basement rooms. In the small kitchen was a basket of food. Fresh bread, cheeses, wine.

Flynn said, 'I thought we might get hungry.'

She smiled at him. He thought of everything.

She peeked into the servants' rooms and followed him back to the main floor. In the front was a pretty little drawing room, behind it, a smaller parlour set up for dining.

Flynn stared at her. 'Shall we go abovestairs?'

A thrill rushed through her. She nodded.

His eyes darkened and he took her hand, leading her up the stairs. He first brought her into a cosy sitting room, its main piece of furniture an elegant *chaise-longue,* large enough for two.

'The bedchamber is next,' Flynn told her. He lifted her hand to his lips, and she felt the kiss echo in every part of her. He backed toward the doorway, pulling her along. When his hand rested on the doorknob, he paused. 'Are you sure of this, Rose?'

Her nerves had fled with his kiss. 'I am sure.'

He opened the door.

Prominent in the room was the loveliest bed she had ever seen. Its wood was dark and it had four posts and beautiful ivory brocade bed curtains and bed cover. It was every bit as pretty as the bed in Miss Hart's room in Mayfair, but Rose had never thought to sleep in one like it.

The thought that she must share this bed with Tannerton flitted through her mind, but she ruthlessly chased it away. Today there was no one but Flynn.

He looked at her questioningly.

She laughed and pulled him into the room. 'I'll not be changing my mind, Flynn.'

She kicked off her shoes and tugged him over to the bed.

He lifted her hand to his lips. 'I'll not change my mind either, Rose, but I want this to be right for you. We have all day for lovemaking…'

She unbuttoned his waistcoat and spread her hands on his shirt. 'I was thinking the same.'

His eyes were fixed on hers as he shrugged out of his coat, letting it fall to the ground. Rose slipped off his waistcoat and turned around so he could undo the laces of her dress. It seemed right for him to touch her, to remove her clothes. She marvelled that it could feel so right.

In the courtesan school, all the talk of undressing had seemed silly to her, but now she understood its power. Every layer removed brought them closer, and she wanted to be close to Flynn. Katy had always insisted that lovemaking brought pleasure. Rose could now agree and they'd barely begun.

Her dress slipped to the floor, and he worked next on the laces of her corset. When that too was tossed to the floor, he stood behind her and removed the pins from her hair. As her hair cascaded down her back, he combed it with his fingers. Nothing could feel so glorious, she thought—until he reached around her and cupped her breasts. Glorious was too tame a word for the sensations he created. Suddenly even the thin muslin of her shift seemed too thick.

She turned. 'Sit on the bed and I'll remove your boots,'

This task was harder than she'd imagined, and she had to tug hard to free his feet, almost falling backward when the second boot came loose.

She laughed, hurrying back to him. She'd suddenly re-membered more of what she'd been taught at the courtesan school.

'Watch me!' She slowly pulled off her shift. Standing before him naked, she was exhilarated by the appreciation in his eyes. She lifted her arms and did a joyous pirouette. 'Your turn,' she cried playfully.

He gave her a wry look. 'I cannot compete.'

She climbed on the bed and sat cross-legged, pretending to appraise him. He made a show of removing his stockings, his shirt, his pantaloons, and finally his drawers. Her lively mood fled for a moment as she ran her eyes over him. He was lean and muscular—and, she noted, a smile growing across her face, very aroused.

'Do I disappoint?' he asked, his voice rumbling and low.

She slowly shook her head and lay back against the bed's pillows. 'Never.'

He climbed upon the bed, but did not touch her, taking time to simply gaze at her. Rose realised what happiness could be. Happiness was being alone with Flynn, knowing he was hers, all hers for the moment.

He smiled and very slowly brought his lips to hers in a slow lanquid kiss that made her feel as pliant as grass on the hills of Killyleagh. She savoured the warmth of his lips, the stroking of his tongue, the scent and taste of him, as she might relish a whole day to wander the countryside, no hurry to rush home.

His hand skimmed her bare skin, easing any remnants of tension. Time seemed to stand still, and she had the notion her precious day would never end.

He broke off the kiss, letting his lips slide downward, to the sensitive skin of her neck and to the now-aching flesh of her breasts. His mouth closed over one nipple and sensation shot deep inside her, making her arch her back and knead her fingers into his buttocks. It surprised and delighted her that his muscles were firm.

The delicious things he did to her breasts made her writhe beneath him. Need grew, and suddenly the slow pace seemed torturous.

'Flynn,' she rasped, her tone urgent.

'Soon,' he murmured as his kisses trailed farther down her body.

The pleasure was excruciating. She flung her arms over her head, unable to bear another moment.

'Why not now, Flynn? Now, please?' she begged.

He lifted himself above her in all his glorious manhood. She was breathless with anticipation, every nerve in her body throbbing with need of Flynn, to unite with him, be one with him, to bind herself to him for ever, even though she would lose him again in a day's time.

No, she would not think of losing him now, not when he sought that private part of her, not when he sought to join her as completely as she could imagine.

Her legs spread and his pace slowed again. He entered her with a gentleness that she knew was borne of his love for her.

She urged him on, wanting him inside her totally, unable to be still when it seemed ecstasy was so near.

With one final thrust, he plunged into her. She cried out with the pain of it and felt the moisture of her blood.

He froze, still inside her. 'Rose? What the devil?'

'Do not stop, Flynn,' she said, moving beneath him, the need returning as quickly as the pain fled.

But he pulled out of her and sat up. 'You are a virgin!'

Rose sat up as well. 'Was a virgin,' she corrected, misery invading. 'But I'm not understanding why that means anything.'

'It means a great deal!' His voice rose in pitch.

Flynn rang a ragged hand through his hair. He felt a pang of guilt for shouting at her, but nothing to compare with the guilt of taking her innocence. His emotions were scattered helter-skelter, but the raw physical need of her still pulsed within him.

She was a virgin. Not a courtesan. Not an experienced girl.

He got off the bed and padded over to a small bureau in the corner. From the pitcher that rested on top of it, he moistened a towel. He had prepared the water and the towels, but not for this purpose. Not to wipe away blood.

He handed the towel to her and moistened another one for himself.

She looked as if she might weep. 'You must explain to me, Flynn, why it means anything at all, because I'm not understanding still.'

He could not even heed her question. 'You deceived me, Rose.'

'Deceived you?' She blinked rapidly. 'How? You never asked me, Flynn. I would have told you.'

'The devil with that. You were trained to be a courtesan. What else was I to think?'

She gaped at him. 'You knew about the courtesan school?'

He glared back at her. 'Katy told me. She told me you were trained by Harriette Wilson, for God's sake. What *virgin* is trained by the most notorious courtesan in London?'

She looked away. 'She only called upon us the one time.'

'Katy met you on the street, she said.' He was still trying to make sense of this. It changed everything for him. Everything.

She pulled off the bed linens and wrapped them around herself. 'I'm thinking there are many virgins who walk to the shops. That is where I met Katy and Mary.'

He shook his head. 'You told me yourself you had been with other men.'

She blinked. 'I never did.'

He took a step closer, suddenly realising he was still naked. He snatched up his shirt and wrapped it around his waist. As he was tying it, he gave her an accusing glance. 'You told me you had gone driving in the park.'

'And you thought that meant I was bedding a man? It was an outing for us. Robert Duprey took us in turns.'

He stared blankly. He'd assumed she was a seductress from the moment he'd first seen her upon the balcony at Vauxhall.

God help him. He had almost delivered a virgin to his employer. Worse, he'd deflowered her himself.

She lifted her chin. 'I went to the courtesan school because I had nowhere else to go. Letty had a terrible row with my father about me and I needed to be somewhere. And, besides, I was thinking I needed the polish Katy and Mary were talking of when I overheard them. I was thinking it would help me on the stage, and so it did, because Mr Hook thought I was worth hiring.'

He refused to bear the total responsibility for what

happened between them. He gave her a level stare. 'You pushed yourself on me, Rose. Almost from the beginning. Were you trying to practise with me, so you would be ready for a marquess? Or did they not teach you in your courtesan school that virgins command a higher price?'

She rose to her knees, eyes flashing. 'I was not so foolish, Flynn, to be thinking I could sing on stage and not lose my virtue some time. Lord knows, at school—at Killyleagh—they drummed into us what girls like that were. Trouble was, I wanted to be one of those girls. My mother was one of those girls. All I was hoping was the man I bedded would be— would be someone I could have regard for. Like in the story-books, you know. Romantic. Do you see?'

'So I was to be your hero in some blasted Minerva Press novel?' He gave a dry laugh.

She lifted her chin. 'I thought you a man I could have regard for.'

He bowed his head. Not only had he taken her virtue, he'd stolen her affection as well.

With great dignity, she climbed off the bed and reached for her shift. Turning away from him, she let the bed linens slip from her body, revealing her creamy skin and a figure that was sheer perfection. The image of her dancing playfully for him just a few moments before returned. He'd felt joyous at seeing her. Had rejoiced at holding her in his arms, at making love to her. He'd held at bay the shattering knowledge that it would be Tanner making love to her in two days' time. How could he pass her off to Tanner now?

He whirled on her. 'If you have such regard for me, how can you go from my bed into Tanner's in the space of a few days?'

She looked as if she were glass about to shatter. 'What choice do I have?'

He was forced to avert his eyes.

Her voice was quiet. 'What they did not teach me in courtesan school was that your feelings for a man was what made you want to have intimacies with him.' She gave a choking sound. 'I want this with you, Flynn. Maybe I will never truly want it with another man, but I want it with you.' She swallowed. 'I only had this one chance.'

He felt as if he'd been pushed into a dark pit and was still falling, deeper and deeper into blackness. Everything she said made painful sense. It was he who had transgressed, the smart, ever-efficient Flynn who never missed an opportunity to be with her. He even used her dreams as a reason to tie her closer to him. Had he wished, he could have done his employer's bidding without making himself so indispensable.

'I am sorry, Rose,' he said in a soft voice. 'I've wronged you and I am sorry. I did not mean the words I've said to you. I am merely angry at myself for not knowing…'

The air seemed to go out of her, and he wanted to wrap his arms around her and never release her. Like a shaft of light, it came to him what he must do. What he most desired to do.

It took all his effort to keep from shouting it out loud to her. He must not be heedless. He must not tell her now. He must show her first.

'Rose?'

As her shift slipped down over her body, she turned her head.

'Are you still wanting me, Rose O'Keefe?' he asked, using the brogue he'd so carefully erased from his speech.

Her eyes widened in surprise. She answered him in a serious voice. 'I'm still wanting you, Jameson Flynn.'

Chapter Eighteen

Flynn crossed the room to her, lifting her chin with his fingers. He leaned down and kissed her, hoping she could feel his apology, his promise.

Their gaiety had fled, but had turned into something far more precious to him. He was no hero in a Minerva Press novel, but his heart had finally been opened. He'd been telling himself it was mere base desire, borne of hearing her sing a song.

'Cupid oft in ambush lies…' She'd sung those words that first night, and the cherub had certainly struck Flynn with his arrow, but he'd not known until now that the arrow carried love.

He would give his love back to her, show her with all the passion exploding inside him. Passion for her and for life. It had been so long since he'd wanted merely to celebrate life.

He tore his shirt away and lifted her on to the bed. Lying next to her, he slipped his hands under the skirt of her shift, lifting it higher and higher until he pulled it over her head. This time he explored her reverently, gently. She was subdued and wary, and he mentally kicked himself for making her so.

She accepted his touch, but passively, and he could not blame her. He would not rush her, though, because they would have plenty of time to retrieve the joy he'd chased away.

Slowly she came alive beneath his touch, her back arching, her lips returning his kisses, but he still waited, allowing her to show him when she was ready.

She made an urgent sound and grasped at him, and he knew the time was right. He positioned himself over her again, but gazed into her eyes.

'I love you, Rose,' he murmured, kissing her again.

When he broke off the kiss, tears had pooled in the corners of her eyes, but she reached for him, and nothing in the world would keep him from giving her a woman's pleasure.

He entered her, mindful now that this part of lovemaking she'd never experienced before. She was moist and more than ready for him, but he moved with easy strokes, slowly, until she met his rhythm, the eternal rhythm between man and woman.

Suddenly his own need took over and his pace quickened. She met him stroke for stroke until he felt her climax quiver against him and he exploded inside her.

She cried out, as did he, in a blast of pleasure that sent him to heights he'd never imagined. While he crashed back to his senses, she still grasped him to her, still in the throes of her own ecstasy.

When her body went limp, he collapsed on top of her, feeling triumphantly male for having pleased her so well. He slid off, gazing upon her face, flushed and glistening and beautiful.

Her eyelids fluttered and she opened them to gaze back at him.

'I'll not be forgetting that, Rose,' he murmured.

'Nor I,' she responded breathlessly.

She nestled against him, her graceful hand resting on his chest. 'Did I please you, Flynn?'

He gave a rumbling laugh. 'You pleased me very well.' He kissed the top of her head.

She gave a satisfied sigh. 'I was expecting something good, but I'm thinking that this was even better.'

'Are you feeling any pain?' He was mindful that he'd not gone easy on her at the end.

'No pain,' she said.

They lay there and Flynn thought he had never been more comfortable, more satisfied than at that moment. It reminded him of home, a place so familiar it inhabited the very pores of your skin, a place you knew you belonged. He felt as if his bones had left his body, his limbs were so relaxed, and he smiled, because he knew this time would not be the last.

As if she read his mind, she stirred beside him, moving on top of him, straddling him. She leaned down to kiss him as he had kissed her before. He grew hard again.

She noticed.

Regarding him shyly, she said, 'Harriette Wilson talked about the woman sitting on top.'

He was half-embarrassed by her frankness, half-tantalized. 'Did she now?'

'She did.' Her silken hair tickled his chest.

He gave her a twisted smile. 'And I suppose you'd be wanting to practise such a thing?'

She grinned at the return of his brogue. 'I would, if you'd not be minding too much.'

He kissed her, a hungry, demanding kiss. 'I'd not be minding.'

Rose lay in the bed, stretching luxuriously as she thought of what had transpired between her and Flynn. She'd imagined it would feel wonderful making love to him, but she'd never guessed it could be so magnificent, nor how it could change her. She rolled over, thinking of his touch, feeling her body come alive with the mere memory.

'Here we are.' Flynn appeared in the doorway, carrying a tray with the bread and cheese on it. The wine bottle was tucked under his arm and the stemmed glasses were between his fingers.

She sat up. 'I'm hungry.'

He set the tray on the bed and kissed her. 'I am hungry, too.'

She grinned against his lips. 'Perhaps there will be dessert.'

He moved back, smiling ruefully. 'Too much will leave you sore.'

Rose was not certain she cared. She wished to feast the day through and worry later about whatever was to come after. She placed her palm on her belly, daring to hope a baby might come from this coupling with him.

Tannerton would think the child his, she supposed. That thought disturbed her. If she bore Flynn's baby she would want to shout it from the rooftops, not pretend it to be another man's.

She could use the skills Madame Bisou taught to prevent a child from Flynn, but she could not bear the thought of preventing something so wonderful. Prevent another man's child, yes, but not Flynn's.

He poured the wine, and she glanced at him through her lashes. He might not realise it at the moment, but there would be more lovemaking before the day was done. She was hungry for him again, hungry for more memories to treasure in the desolation of future days. She loved what their love-making had done to him, making him relaxed and easy with her, even loosening his tongue into its brogue.

They supped like lovers and talked as if the day would never end. At times Rose glanced at the window, seeing the changing sunlight, the reminder that time was passing, but she quickly turned away.

She begged him for one more time of lovemaking, but he resisted her, insisting it would make her sore, vowing he would not give her pain. It occurred to her that he might be worried about Tannerton. Perhaps if she were sore, Tannerton would wonder why. Flynn would not want the marquess to guess at the events of this day, would he?

She chastised herself. Flynn's concern was for her, not worry over what the marquess would discover.

They spent the afternoon in each other's arms, and fell asleep in the warmth of each other's bodies.

Rose woke, noticing the light in the window had changed some more. She looked into his face and saw he was watching her with a contented expression.

'How long did I sleep?' she murmured.

'An hour or more,' he responded.

She hated losing that much time with him.

He toyed with a strand of her hair. 'We must leave soon.'

Her insides twisted. 'Not yet.'

He ran a finger down her cheek. 'The hour is late.'

'I do not care.' She rolled over and began to stroke his chest with her fingers. She kissed his neck and let her fingers trail down his body.

'Rose,' he warned.

'I do not care,' she repeated.

He made no effort to stop her.

She was now glad of the lessons that had taught her how to please a man, because they had instructed her how to touch him, how to convince him that one more time of lovemaking would not, indeed, hurt.

She let herself become very bold, touching the most male part of him, glorying in her power to arouse him.

He gave no further argument, allowing her to explore him as wantonly as she wished, until suddenly he grabbed her and turned her on her back. He kissed her fiercely this time, as if their hunger for each other had not been slaked earlier that day—twice. This hunger came from it being their last time. She felt it, too, ached with the knowledge.

She did not choose to hurry, but their urgency was borne of despair. She felt the need to grab all of him at once, to hold on to him and never let go.

His touches were equally as driven, but so filled with passion that her senses were quickly roused to a fever pitch. This was frenzied lovemaking, ungovernable, unstoppable. She heard her own panting mingled with his, felt the dampness of his sweat against her own, smelled the musky scent they created. Even so he tried for restraint as he entered her. Even in this maelstrom, he sought not to hurt her.

He need not worry. Her body was more than prepared for him, moist and slick with her need of him. Their coupling was as blazing as her feelings for him. It was fast and hard and rough.

She'd thought he'd already shown her what passion could be, but she'd been wrong. This was different, something wild but freeing.

He drove her higher and higher, until she called out his name, and her pleasure broke free, sparkling like the illuminations at Vauxhall, lighting the dark spaces of her loneliness, searing the memory on her soul.

He spilled his seed inside her at the same moment,

holding her even tighter as his pleasure rocked him, carrying her along as well.

But, as it must, the ecstasy ceased, plummeting them back to reality. When they collapsed beside each other, Rose felt bereft. This was goodbye. This was the end. This was final.

He gazed at her with an aching expression of love, one she tried to etch on her memory for ever.

'We ought to get dressed,' he said.

She nodded.

He got off the bed and walked over to the pitcher, wetting a cloth for her. She cleansed herself and stood, surveying the rumpled bed linens, stained with her blood and with other signs of what they had shared together.

'What shall we do about the bed linens?' she asked.

He was donning his trousers and shirt. 'I will take care of it, never fear.'

She found her shift and slipped it on. He came to assist her with her corset. She blinked away tears as he helped her fasten it. He picked up her dress and held it so she could put it on.

As he was tying the laces of her dress, she murmured, 'I do not want this to end.'

He turned her around and kissed her with exquisite gentleness. 'It will not end.'

'Oh, do not tease me.' She stifled a sob, determined to be strong.

'I do not tease you, Rose.' He wiped a tear from her cheek with his thumb. 'I, too, do not wish this to end. You must marry me so that we will have the rest of our lives for this.'

She went still as a stone statue, unsure of what she heard. 'Marry you?'

He smiled. 'I do not know why I did not think of it before. It is the only way—'

She pulled away from him. 'But you cannot mean it!'

'Of course, I mean it,' he said, reaching for her. 'I love you, Rose.'

She took a step back, shaking her head. 'Is it because I was a virgin, Flynn? That is foolish.'

'Not that.' He watched her with wary eyes, his voice less certain.

'But what of Tannerton?' she asked.

He shrugged. 'He will fire me, I am certain, but that is of no consequence.'

She wrinkled her brow and turned away from him, her mind whirling. She did not for once believe her virginity was not the cause. He was just the sort of man who would feel some foolish obligation for that reason. She ought to have realised he would experience some misguided sense of duty, but she'd thought the virtue of a woman on the stage meant little to any man. All she'd wanted was for him to be the first.

She could not allow him to throw away everything for which he'd toiled. Not for her sake. She could not allow him to give up a prince for her. He did not yet know what he would give up, but she did.

She girded her resolve. 'I was not meaning what Tannerton would do to you, Flynn. I was meaning what the consequence would be for me.'

He grew silent.

Finally he spoke, his words as Irish as his birth. 'I'm not understanding.'

She set the expression on her face before turning to him and speaking in the same hardened tone used by Harriette Wilson. 'Well, I would lose this house, would I not? And all the money Tannerton's going to give me? I can live well on that, even when he tires of me, can I not? He would even pay so I can work at King's Theatre, perhaps even something better.'

A muscle flexed in his cheek. 'Is that your worry, then?'

She made herself laugh. 'But of course, Flynn. Marriage to you—to any man—would be madness, would it not? We were taught that a courtesan has the best life. Her property is her own and no man can tell her what to do.'

'A courtesan…' His voice trailed off.

She walked over to him, taking the risk of touching him, running her hand through his hair. She'd never precisely told him she loved him, as he had done while they made love. She'd held back, thinking it would protect her own heart when she was forced to say goodbye to him. Now she was glad she'd not told him she loved him, because it would make it better for him. She must convince him that it was not love she shared with him, but something more carnal.

'I'm not saying I do not fancy you, Flynn. I do not care that you have no money, if you've a mind to visit me now and then. Lord Tannerton need never know.'

He twisted away. 'I'll finish getting dressed and take you back to Madame Bisou's.'

Her heart was breaking into a thousand pieces. She pressed on, giving a loud sigh. 'If you must. Though I would not mind it at all if we undressed again and returned to the bed.'

She made herself want to cry, but her goal now was to convince him he must not give up his dreams for her.

He turned to her with anger in his eyes, the anger of a lover scorned. She almost wished he would unleash that rage at her.

She deserved to be punished for hurting him. He would never strike back at her. Never. And she loved him for that, even while she hated herself.

When the prince returned from Brighton and called for his employment, he would be grateful she'd refused his guilty proposal of marriage.

While he dressed silently, she twisted her hair into a hasty knot, fastening it with the pins he'd removed earlier. Without seeming to take notice if she was ready, he left the room and descended the stairs to the hall. By the time she joined him, he was already in hat and gloves, waiting by the door for her. She hurried into her bonnet and gloves and he opened the door.

'We can walk, I believe.' He spoke stiffly. 'Greythorne will not know from where we came.'

She had forgotten about Greythorne. After he closed and locked the door, she glanced back at it, the place she'd felt such joy, such desolation. Outside its door nothing remained but the horror of Greythorne, the loss of her father, and the sordid prospect of becoming Tannerton's kept woman. Even worse, she would have to face all, knowing she'd lost Flynn totally.

She soon was out of breath trying to keep up with Flynn's stride. In too short a time they were at Madame Bisou's door.

'I leave you here, Rose,' he said. 'I suggest you remain indoors tomorrow. Tannerton will send word to you.' He turned to leave.

She grabbed his arm. 'Flynn!' she cried, forgetting everything but loving him. 'Will I see you again?'

The eyes that regarded her were like ice. 'If the marquess requires it, I shall comply.'

He turned away as Cummings opened the door, but she did not enter until he rounded the corner and she could no longer see him walking away from her.

Chapter Nineteen

Flynn walked immediately back to the rooms, dreading a return to the bedchamber, the place of loving her.

Inside, he took the steps two at a time, figuring it best to discharge the task quickly. He entered the room and strode directly to the rumpled bed, tearing off the linens and cramming them into a bundle he intended to throw away. Then he set about erasing all evidence of what they had shared in the room. It ought to have felt cathartic to do so. Instead it felt wretched.

How big a fool could he have been? She had completely misguided him. Even now he could not tell the exact nature of her character. Was she the virgin who schemed to be a courtesan, as she'd insisted? Or an innocent caught up in her own desires, and he the man who had awakened them?

No more than an hour later Flynn left the house as if he had never entered it with Rose. He walked back to Audley Street, telling himself he had no need to understand Rose. She would go to Tanner, and that would be the end of it.

As he walked, Flynn laboured to rebuild the wall that

hardened his heart. But then he'd catch a memory of her scent, the flash of her smile, or her face flushed with passion, and the wall would crumble, leaving him with no shelter at all.

He was startled by a man who emerged from the shadows, a man who turned and walked in the other direction. Flynn's heart went cold.

He'd almost forgotten there was a man out there who had killed over her, who might be stalking her at this very moment. No matter his tattered emotions, she still needed to be protected.

He entered Tannerton's town house at the same moment Tanner strolled out of the library and saw him.

'Where the devil have you been all day?' The question was a typical one for Tanner to ask when Flynn had been busy performing one task after another on his behalf. Today, however, his employer's voice grated on Flynn's shredded nerves.

'Errands,' Flynn replied, keen to get away.

It was no use. 'Come here a moment,' Tanner said. 'I have news.'

Resigned, Flynn turned and followed Tanner into the library.

'What news?' He tried to sound interested.

Tanner leaned casually against the desk, crossing his legs at the ankles. 'I heard from the Bow Street Runner I sent to Brighton yesterday. He returned not an hour ago.'

Flynn came alert. 'And?'

'No one has seen Greythorne for several days.'

Flynn's fingers curled into a fist. 'This is no surprise.'

'Indeed.' Tanner lifted his finger in the air. 'But it foxed me that the Duke did not send a message alerting me to that fact. It seems Greythorne arrived with his Royal Highness, but quickly shut himself in his rooms with reports he was suffering from some sort of contagious blight. Only his own servants attended him.'

'Clever of him. He appears to be in Brighton, but is not. And when he has finished his treachery towards…Miss O'Keefe…' Flynn's voice faltered. He had difficulty even speaking her name.

Tanner did not seem to notice. Rather, he finished Flynn's sentence. 'He will return to Brighton and show himself miraculously recovered.' Tanner pushed away from the desk. 'The Runner who went to Greythorne's town house is convinced he did not return there; however, in the part of town where the bodies were discovered, there had been talk that a gentleman had paid someone to dump them in place where they would be easily found.'

Tanner had spared no expense with these Bow Street Runners. How many had he hired?

'Thing is,' Tanner continued, his expression stricken, 'I didn't outwit Greythorne, Flynn. I merely made him more dangerous. Some game I engaged in.' He gave a frustrated sound and rubbed his brow. 'Where the devil is he?'

Greythorne disdained the plain black coat pulling across his shoulders. Its cut was common, as was its fit. But if he were going to pretend to be a merchant, he had better dress like one.

He looked down his nose at the creature standing before him, common to the core, but useful. 'Like I said, the gent and the girl left in a coach. I was able to follow it a ways. Heading into Westminster, it was, I'd wager on it.' The man wiped his nose on his sleeve.

Greythorne cringed.

The man continued, 'Couldn't keep up, I couldn't. So I

waited for 'em to return and, let me tell you, they took their time. Took all day, it did.'

Greythorne stifled a yawn. 'If you have information of value, I beg you would get on with it.'

The man grinned, showing the gap of a missing tooth. 'Most sure it is of value, sir. Worth a pound or two, I expect, but I'll let you decide, sir.'

'Get on with it,' Greythorne repeated. Paying well was the best guarantee of loyalty, he could agree, but this man was trying his patience.

'Well.' The man took a breath. 'Finally, after I waited all day—and let me tell you how hard it is to wait all day—'

'Do not.' Greythorne glared at the man.

'Anyways, when they finally arrive back at Madame Bisou's gaming-house, they are walkin', y'see. And seeing as how the gent left and didn't take a coach, I followed him.'

This account was tedious in the extreme. Greythorne amused himself by imagining what this creature's face would look like if a leather strap were twisted around his neck, cutting off the air—

'Interestingly enough,' the man went on, 'the gent didn't go in the direction of that fancy town house. He went the other way into a building on Great Ryder Street.'

Greythorne sat up. 'Is that so?'

'Stayed a few minutes, then come out with a bundle. Tossed the bundle and then walked all the way back to Audley Street.'

This was curious. 'What was in the bundle?'

The man rubbed his neck. 'Don't know, sir, some rascally boys grabbed it afore I could get to it, so I hurried off to see where the gent was going.'

Greythorne grimaced. If this business meant Tannerton got

to the O'Keefe chit before he did, he would be very unhappy. 'Tell me, what did the gentleman look like?'

'Dark-haired fellow. Looked Irish, if you ask me.'

Greythorne gave a silent laugh. The secretary, Flynn. Excellent. Greythorne had already discovered that Flynn had procured a set of rooms and hired servants. This must have been the girl's inspection of her new home.

Greythorne stood. 'Show me this place, and the two pounds will be yours.'

Rose sat at the window, watching gentlemen walk in and out of Madame Bisou's house, but none was Flynn. There was no use to hope for him to return. She had ensured he would not.

A knock sounded at the door, and Katy came in. 'Why don't you come downstairs, Rose? You could sit in the supper room. Those footmen Lord Tannerton sent over could sit nearby.'

Rose shook her head. 'I'll stay here. I'm thinking I'm in need of an evening to myself.' She didn't sing at Vauxhall this night.

Katy plopped on the bed. 'Don't sit here alone all that time. You'll think of your father or something.'

Her father. The grief of losing her father only made losing Flynn worse.

'I'll not think of my father, I promise,' she told her friend.

Katy swung her legs as she sat, looking like a little girl eager to play. 'Where were you all day, by the way? Cummings said you went out early, when I was still sleeping.'

'It was not that early.' She and Flynn had picked a time anyone might go out.

Katy's eyes lit up with understanding. 'You were with *Flynnnnn.*' She emphasised Flynn's name, drawing it out. 'Where did you go? I hope not to the magistrate again.'

'Not the magistrate,' Rose replied.

Katy waited for more.

Rose took a breath. 'Flynn showed me the rooms he found for me.'

Katy leaned forward. 'The ones Tannerton purchased?' She sighed. 'It is just like Harriette Wilson told us! You get property of your own. Tell me. Are they grand?'

Rose tried to sound as excited as Katy. 'They are pretty rooms, really. There is a kitchen and a drawing room, a dining room, and abovestairs, a sitting room, and…a bedchamber.'

Katy looked rapturous. But Rose turned away.

'There is something you are not telling me,' Katy said.

Rose felt tears spring to her eyes. 'There is nothing.'

Katy got off the bed and stepped in front of her. 'What is it, Rose?'

Rose turned away again.

Katy turned her back. 'Rose?'

Rose clamped her mouth shut.

'Oh, Rose! You were with Flynn!' Katy held her shoulders. 'Ack! I do not know whether to congratulate you or to shake you!'

'I am not saying I was with Flynn,' Rose retorted. 'I am not.'

Katy gave her a hug. 'Foolish, Rose. What are you going to do?'

'I am doing nothing,' Rose insisted. 'Nothing at all.'

'Tell me what happened,' Katy said.

Rose backed away. 'Katy, there is nothing I can tell you.'

'Well, did you take care of yourself?' Katy asked. 'You know, like Madame Bisou taught us.'

Rose did not answer her.

There was another knock on the door, and Katy hurried over to answer it.

The footman Wiggins stood there. 'Beg pardon, miss,' he said to Rose, 'Mr Flynn sent word we were to stay right outside your door.'

Her stomach did a flip-flop at hearing Flynn's name. 'Why, Mr Wiggins?'

'He said Lord Greythorne was about, and it would be best to guard you close. Me and Smythe will take turns.'

Katy turned pale.

'Thank you, Mr Wiggins,' Rose replied, walking over to the door. 'I shall feel very safe with you there.' She closed it behind him.

Katy trembled. 'He is near?'

It was Rose's turn to comfort. 'We are very safe, Katy. You are safe. He does not know you reside here, does he?'

She shook her head. 'I never told him.' She gave Rose a very intent look. 'Wait here.'

Katy returned a few minutes later. She lifted Rose's hand and placed a small sheathed knife in her palm. 'Take this, just in case. Wear it on you somewhere.'

Rose looked at the small weapon. 'I should not know what to do with it.'

Katy's eyes turned fierce. 'Jab it into his throat.'

The next afternoon, Cummings sent word that Rose had a visitor waiting in the parlor. The hope that it was Flynn swelled inside her. Wiggins and Smythe accompanied her, telling her to stay back while they entered the parlor first. They immediately emerged with grins on their faces. 'You can go in, miss.'

Nearly giddy with anticipation, Rose stepped into the room.

Tannerton stood there, smiling in greeting.

Her spirits plunged. 'Good day, sir,' she managed.

'And to you, Miss O'Keefe.' He crossed the room and blew a kiss over her hand. 'I thought to call on you to see how you were faring.'

'I am well, sir.' As always, she did not know what to say to this man. 'And you?'

He waved his hand dismissively. 'I am always well.' He gestured for her to sit on the room's sofa.

She hesitated, thinking he would sit beside her, fearing he would touch her. She was not ready for that. But she must become accustomed to doing what he wanted. She would be his mistress in one day's time.

She sat on the sofa.

To her surprise he flung himself in the adjacent chair. 'Flynn is over at your rooms, seeing all is in order. He told me he showed them to you. Are they to your liking?'

Hearing Flynn's name was painful, and it was painful to think of him in those rooms where she had been so briefly happy. 'They were very pretty. I'm thinking anyone would say so.'

'Excellent!' He seemed genuinely pleased. 'Tell me, are Wiggins and Smythe keeping watch over you?'

She nodded. 'They follow me everywhere.'

'Like spaniels!' He grinned. 'They are good fellows.'

She had no response and the awkward silence made her face grow hot with shame. Why could she not converse with him? He always behaved very well toward her. Even his kisses did not ask more of her than she could give.

'By the way—' he gave no indication that he had noticed the lapse in their conversation '—I can release you from your promise.'

Her heart pounded. 'My promise?'

He winked. 'To keep the secret I told you about. Flynn's new employment.'

She gaped at him. 'Flynn will work for the prince?'

'As soon as his Highness has returned from Brighton, assuming this Greythorne business does not change matters. I told Flynn yesterday.'

Her throat felt suddenly raw. She was happy for Flynn, she told herself. He would get his greatest desire. 'He must have been very pleased.'

He tilted his head. 'Well, not as much as I thought he would be, but you can never tell with Flynn. Let me warn you. Never play cards with the man. He gives away nothing of what he feels.'

She could disagree. He'd shown her all too well. Briefly.

'Flynn will go to the Prince after he returns from Ireland.'

'Ireland?' She sat up straighter. 'He is going to Ireland?'

'Wants to visit his family, I believe,' he said. 'Cannot fathom why he did not ask to do so before. Deuced long time to be away. I was beginning to surmise he had no family.'

Rose was suddenly homesick for Ireland herself, for its green hills and fresh air. For the lilting speech she'd sought to rid herself of, the kind of speech she and Flynn so gaily shared.

Tanner tapped his lips, looking thoughtful. 'I wonder what the prince will think when he finds out Greythorne deceived him.' He regarded her. 'The Bow Street Runner discovered that Greythorne gave his Royal Highness the slip. But, then, we knew he was back in London.'

Not knowing how else to respond, she merely nodded.

His mouth fell open. 'I do beg your pardon. I never offered my sympathy for the death of your father and his lady friend. Such a shock for you.'

'Yes,' was all she could say.

He took her hand, and it was all she could do to keep from pulling away. 'I promise you, we shall find Greythorne and bring him to justice for this. You have my solemn word on it.' He squeezed her hand in reassurance, nothing more.

'Thank you, my lord,' she said.

He stood and gazed down at her. 'I underestimated Greythorne, Miss O'Keefe.' He looked genuinely regretful. 'I am profoundly sorry for it.'

She rose, touched by his sincerity. 'I am not blaming you, sir,' she told him. 'It was Greythorne who…who killed them.'

His eyes did not lose their hint of pain, and she realised that this was indeed a good man. She wished she could rejoice in his interest in her and return the affection he deserved.

He averted his gaze and made to look at his timepiece. 'I had best be on my way.' He started for the door, but turned back to her. 'Flynn made all the arrangements for you to occupy the rooms tomorrow. I shall send my carriage in the afternoon, if that is to your liking.'

No, it was not to her liking, but what else could she do?

'I shall be ready.'

He smiled. 'Good! About three o'clock, perhaps? You will have time to get settled, then I will escort you to Vauxhall, if you like.'

She merely nodded.

He started off again, but again turned back, walking over to her. He gave her a quick kiss on the lips. 'Until then, Miss O'Keefe.'

The servants lined up in the small hallway for Flynn's final inspection of the preparations for Rose's arrival.

Wiggins and Smythe would also join the household as Rose's constant guards, with Bow Street Runners to relieve them.

Flynn questioned the house servants in turn, and each declared that they were ready to serve Miss O'Keefe. And ready to serve Lord Tannerton, as well.

Before turning to leave, Flynn glanced one last time up the stairway towards the bedchamber.

It was doubtful he would ever return to these rooms, now that Lord Tannerton had arranged his employment with the Duke of Clarence. Flynn could not have expected a better situation. The Prince was third in line for the throne, though the Princess Charlotte might knock her uncle down a peg when her baby was born. Still, the Duke of Clarence was much higher than Flynn had dared hope.

He ought to have whooped with excitement and clasped Tanner's hand in a vigorous handshake when he'd heard the news. Instead, he had coolly clarified his intention to travel to Ireland first.

If the joy of this advancement had been leached from his emotions, Flynn was at least satisfied with the honour of it.

He left Rose's new apartments and walked towards St James's Street. Crossing Piccadilly into Mayfair, Flynn told himself not to think of Rose or of Tanner, who would accompany her back to Great Ryder Street from Vauxhall.

Flynn returned to Tanner's house and almost feared encountering his employer on the stairway again. He entered the library and pulled out papers from the drawers, determined to work. Tanner's affairs would be in order before he left for Ireland, he vowed.

He began making a list from the papers he'd taken out of the drawer. They were bills he'd not yet paid, correspondence he'd not yet returned. Proceeding methodically through the stack, Flynn began to feel more settled. The mundane task kept his mind occupied, and he so much wished to keep his mind occupied.

He came across the bill of the Bow Street Runner who had travelled to Brighton, tallying his charges and expenses. Flynn placed the pen back into its holder and dropped his head into his hands. He could not leave Tanner's employ until he knew Rose was safe from Greythorne.

He tried to tell himself he could trust Tanner to see to her safety. It was the sort of challenge Tanner might skilfully meet, but Flynn would not rest while Greythorne still lurked about, waiting for his chance to capture Rose.

An image of her tied up and at Greythorne's mercy came to his mind. It would never happen.

Never.

Flynn rose from his seat, too restless to work. He stacked the papers again and returned them to the drawer.

Rose would be most vulnerable at Vauxhall, Flynn surmised, no matter how many men Tanner had hired to guard her. Flynn must go to Vauxhall, no matter how painful it would be to see her and know she would never be his. He must watch for danger. She would not have to know he was there, but he would ensure she made it to her new bed in safety.

Greythorne reviewed the plan one more time. It was a masterpiece of logistics, if he did say so himself, an elegant means of wreaking vengeance on Tannerton for presuming Greythorne could be disposed of so easily.

He looked at the men standing before him, an unkempt, unsavoury lot, but the sort you could pay to do whatever you wanted of them.

'You know your tasks?' he asked.

'That we do, sir,' one said.

The others nodded or mumbled agreement.

'You shall capture them, not harm them,' Greythorne reminded them.

The pleasure of harming them would be his alone.

Chapter Twenty

F lynn came to Vauxhall in a mask, ordinary garb in the place where nothing was as it seemed. What he'd once disdained he had grown to fancy over these summer weeks, now finding delight in the magic of the pleasure gardens. This, after all, had been the place he'd heard her sing, danced with her in his arms, and stolen kisses under the flickering lamps.

He stood in the Grove, off to the side where he could peruse the crowd, but still easily view the balcony. He fancied every unaccompanied man to be a danger to Rose, every masked one to be Greythorne. He spied Wiggins and Smythe easily enough and two of the Bow Street Runners who earlier had reported to Tanner their failure to find Greythorne. Flynn spied Tanner, too, also scanning for danger.

The orchestra sounded her introduction, and Rose appeared on the balcony. Flynn forgot everything else but the elegant tilt of her head, the graceful poise of her posture.

She began with 'Eileen Aroon,' and he was transported to the time he'd first set eyes on her. She was more beautiful now, if such a thing were possible. Her voice was richer, stronger, more suffused with sensuality. He let her voice envelop him as once her arms had done.

Her eyes searched the crowd as she sang. He longed to have her eyes find him, as they'd done before. He'd seen the awareness in her face that night, an awareness he shared. The magic connection they made that night was one his grandfather would have blamed on the fairies, the ancients, on Cupid.

She sang song after song of love, its joys, its loss. Never had her voice so plucked the strings of emotion, enough to crack the hardest heart. Flynn heard sniffles in the crowd, saw more than one person dab their eyes with a handkerchief. It was he who ought to weep, he thought. It was he who had lost her.

Ironically, though, her voice consoled him. Healed him. By the time she began her last song, he felt whole again, instead of a man torn into pieces.

She sang:

> Young I am and yet unskilled,
> How to make a lover yield…

He recognised the words, although he'd not heard her perform this song before. Its lyrics were from a Dryden poem about a girl who knew no love would be as pure or as true as her first love. Any men who came after would receive only a pretense of love.

'He that has me first, is blest,' she sang with undisguised honesty. It was as if a lightning bolt came from the dark night sky, striking him, filling him with its light.

She'd lied to him when she'd refused his proposal, Flynn realised. For some unfathomable reason, she'd lied about wanting Tanner's money, about wanting to be a mistress instead of a wife.

He was filled with energy, with excitement. He could hardly wait to find her, to tell her he knew the truth.

The truth was in her song.

It no longer mattered that he would make an enemy of a marquess and dash his dreams of serving royalty. The truth was, he coveted Rose more than that dream. He would marry her. Take her to Ireland with him. Show her off to his family and receive their blessing. Somewhere they would find a new life, a fine life, a life worth singing about.

> Take me, take me, some of you,
> While I yet am young and true.

Yes, Rose, he vowed. *I will.*

Her song ended, and the applause thundered like never before. Shouts of 'hurrah' and 'bravo' filled the air, over and over. She looked stunned, but dropped into a graceful curtsy before turning away and fleeing. The crowd surged forward, shouting, 'Encore!'

Flynn tried to push his way through the still-cheering audience to reach the gazebo door. When he finally got near, more admirers than ever crowded the area. Through the throng of men, he glimpsed Tanner, arm protectively around Rose, leading her away, flanked by Wiggins and Smythe. Flynn struggled to reach them, but the crowd forced him farther and farther behind.

He finally broke free on to the Grand Walk, but lost sight of them. Hurrying to the gate where Tanner's carriage would be waiting, he reached it in time to see Tanner help Rose inside the coach and Wiggins and Smythe climb on top. As the carriage sped away, Flynn caught a glimpse of a man crouched down and hanging on the back.

The hairs rose on the back of his neck.

Greythorne was making his move.

Flynn ran to the nearest hackney coach and shouted, 'Follow that carriage, and I'll triple your fare.' He climbed up next to the jarvey, who looked stunned.

It took some time for the hackney coach to manoeuvre on to the road, but Flynn could still see Tanner's carriage in the distance. The hackney coach's old nag was no match for Tanner's team, and soon all that was visible of Tanner's vehicle was the faint glow of the carriage's lamp.

'Sorry, guv'nor,' the jarvey said.

Flynn pulled the mask off and rubbed his face. 'Try to keep the lamplight in view.'

But that, too, quickly faded from sight.

Rose shivered, even though she wore her cape and the inside of the carriage was warm.

'That crowd was quite unexpected,' said Tannerton. 'But you are safe now.'

'Safe,' she repeated.

She had not been thinking of her safety from the crowds nor even from Greythorne. She'd been thinking about Flynn. Somehow, singing made her feel closer to him, as if he were with her still and would always be with her. As she'd sung the words of the love songs, the emotion behind them filled her soul, and it was as if a bright light illuminated their meaning. The songs, the music, the emotion, all were entwined with Flynn. She still shook inside from the power of it, the power of her love for him.

She glanced at Tannerton, who had leaned his head against the fine upholstery of the carriage seat and closed his eyes.

It would be wrong to pretend at loving with this man, she

suddenly realised. Had she never met Flynn, never fallen in love with him, never made love with him, she might have formed some true affection for Tannerton, but, as it was, she would always resent him for not being Flynn.

She felt bereft, but at the same time liberated. It no longer mattered to her that she sing at King's Theatre or Vauxhall or any other place. Nothing would replace what she'd so briefly had with Flynn. Nothing mattered as much.

She blinked away tears. She wanted to go home. To Ireland, even though she had no home there, no family left anywhere. Perhaps she would return to the school at Killyleagh and beg for work there, any work.

She pressed her palm to her belly, hoping that she might be with child. Bearing Flynn's child would be a joy. She would find some way to rear the babe, to bestow on Flynn's child the lessons of love.

She remembered suddenly that her mother had never spoken of leaving the London stage with regret. She never lamented the choice she had made, the choice of being with the man she loved and bearing his child.

Rose stared at Tannerton again. His face was softer than Flynn's, unlined, untroubled. He was a handsome man, the sort Katy would say made a girl's head turn, and a kind man. Whether he knew it or not, he deserved more than a pretence of love.

'Lord Tannerton?' She spoke quietly, not certain if he slept.

His eyes opened. 'Yes?'

'I have something to ask you. To tell you, really.'

'Then tell, Miss O'Keefe.' He smiled. 'Or shall I call you Rose, since we are about to begin our association?'

Their association. 'If you wish.'

'What is it, then, Rose?' His expression conveyed only mild curiosity, as if whatever she said would be easily forgotten. He did not realise how important her decision would be for him.

She drew in a long breath. 'About tonight, sir—'

Before she could speak another word, shouts sounded from the outside and the carriage came to a lurching halt.

Tannerton was instantly on the alert. 'Stay in here.'

He was halfway out of the carriage when a shadowy figure on the outside brought a club down hard upon his head.

Rose screamed.

Tannerton was shoved back into the carriage and fell into a crumpled heap beside her. She grabbed his coat and tried to set him upright to see if he were still alive.

A man climbed in. 'Good evening, Rose.'

Greythorne.

She lunged towards the door, but he shoved her back in her seat and was quickly on top of her. Rose tried to push him off, but he was too heavy. He pulled her cloak off her and tossed it upon Tannerton's body. Rose clawed at Greythorne's face and nearly succeeded in opening the carriage door so she could jump out. No matter it was now moving fast, she preferred jumping into the darkness to being Greythorne's captive.

But he seized the back of her dress and hauled her back in the seat. His hand closed around her neck like a vice as he straddled her again. His lips crushed against hers as his fingers cut off all air. Feeling herself blacking out, she prayed not to die with that man's lips on her.

Laughing, he suddenly released her. She gulped in as much air as her lungs could hold.

'I am stronger, Rose. Remember that.'

While she could do nothing but gasp and cough, he pulled out a cord from his pocket and tied her hands and her feet. She tried to scream for help, but only a rasping sound came out. He produced a piece of cloth and tied it around her mouth so even that pitiful sound was muffled.

'You are at my mercy,' he went on in a menacing voice. 'And I intend to show you precisely who your master is. You will do my bidding, if you want to live.'

He pulled more cord from his pockets and bound Tannerton's hands behind his back and tied his ankles. The marquess remained senseless. Rose prayed he was alive.

As if in answer to her prayer, Tannerton moaned.

'This man thought he could thwart me, fool that he is. Your father and that cow of a woman also thought they could thwart me.' He lifted Rose's chin, forcing her to look at him. 'I assume you know what happened to them.'

Perhaps she ought to have prayed instead that Tannerton had escaped the fate that awaited them.

Greythorne rubbed his hand on her neck, pretending he was going to squeeze it again, and laughed when she recoiled. He slid his hand down to her chest, pushing his fingers under her dress to roughly fondle her breast.

Bile rose in her throat, and she swallowed it, fearful she'd choke.

'Has he touched you like this?' he asked, his eyes boring into her.

For a moment she thought the 'he' Greythorne referred to was Flynn, but his glance slid to Tannerton.

She shook her head.

'Then I am not too late.' He squeezed her, watching her face as she tried to cry out in pain, the sound impeded by the gag in her mouth. He laughed again.

His eyes glittered in the scant light from the carriage's outside lanterns. He looked like an engraving she'd once seen of the devil.

She had the distinct feeling she was about to descend into hell.

Flynn peered into the night, hoping to catch sight of the carriage again. He was tempted to urge for more speed, but the hack's horses were already pushed to the limit and travelling faster on the dark road was too risky. There was only one way the carriage might go, at least for several miles, across the Vauxhall Bridge and on the road along the river. Flynn tried to remain calm.

Suddenly two men appeared at the side of the road, waving frantically for the hackney to stop. The jarvey did not rein in his horses.

'Wait!' cried Flynn. 'Stop the coach.'

'Could be thieves,' the man said.

'No, stop the coach.'

They had gone past the men by this time, but, as the coachman pulled the horse to a stop, one of the men ran toward them.

'Your assistance, sir!' the man cried. 'We have an injured man here.'

Flynn recognised him. 'Wiggins!' He jumped down.

'Mr Flynn, sir!' Wiggins said with some emotion. 'Wait for us. Smythe is hurt.'

He ran back to where another man he recognised as Tanner's coachman John stood next to Smythe, seated on the ground. The two men hoisted Smythe to his feet and carried him to the hack.

'Put him inside,' Flynn said. 'John, climb above and watch for Tannerton's coach.'

He helped Wiggins get Smythe into the carriage.

'It's my leg,' groaned Smythe. 'Broke it, I think.'

Flynn spared no time for sympathy. 'Tell me what happened.'

Wiggins's hand was bloody and limp. 'Two men on horseback stopped the carriage. They grabbed the horses, and one of them came alongside and pulled John Coachman off—'

'We tried to stop him,' Smythe broke in.

Wiggins nodded. 'Then, while we were pulling on him one way and the blackguard the other way, some fellow comes from behind and pushes us off.' He winced. 'I saw his lordship get hit on the head. With a club. It was that Lord Greythorne, I'd wager a year's pay on it. He got into the carriage and it drove off with the lot of them, before we could even get to our feet.'

Flynn frowned. Where were they headed? The Bow Street Runners had discovered nothing about where Greythorne had gone after sneaking out of Brighton. Was he even in London? 'We'll take you both to Audley Street and send for the physician.'

Never had the trip back from Vauxhall seemed so slow. It gave Flynn too much time to think. Too much time to remember the marks of torture on O'Keefe's and Miss Dean's bodies. Too much time to fear finding a shrouded Rose carelessly laid out on a wooden table.

He forced himself not to turn his mind in that direction, but something kept drawing him back. Something nagging.

By the time the hackney coach pulled up to the Audley Street town house, Flynn had the answer. He helped the injured men out of the coach and dug in his pocket for the promised triple fare. The jarvey stuck his whip in its holder and Flynn froze.

He turned to Wiggins. 'Get the physician and send a message to Bow Street. I need some men to help. Tell them to go to Madame Bisou's. I will leave the direction there.' He put the money in the jarvey's hand. 'I require more of you. To Bennet Street.' He climbed inside the hack.

When he reached Bennet Street, he hurried to the door. When Cummings answered it, Flynn said, 'Where is Madame Bisou? I need her.'

'Game room,' Cummings replied.

Several men and one or two women looked up from their play when he rushed in. He went directly to Madame Bisou.

'I would speak with you a moment,' he said, taking her arm.

Katy was standing nearby at the hazard table. 'What is it, Flynn?' She followed them out.

He took them aside in the hallway. 'Greythorne has captured Rose and Tannerton. I need to know who told Rose he used whips.'

Madame Bisou glanced towards Katy. Flynn swung around. Katy's face was white and she backed away.

He stopped her. 'Was it you, Katy?'

She shook her head and tried to get away. 'It was Iris. Ask Iris.'

'Iris is not here tonight,' Madame Bisou said in an alarmed voice.

Flynn grabbed Katy's arms. 'I must know, Katy. Tell me what you know.'

She trembled all over, and he thought she might sink to the floor. He put his arms around her. 'Katy.' He spoke kindly but firmly. 'I need you to help me find Rose. I am afraid he will kill her, and Tanner, too.'

'Tell him, Katy,' the *madame* cried, but Katy merely buried her face in Flynn's chest. 'He whipped her skin raw,' Madame Bisou said. 'But she escaped from him.'

Flynn made Katy look at him. 'Then you know the place. You must show me where it is.'

Her eyes were panicked, but she finally pursed her lips and nodded.

'Make haste!' Flynn pulled her towards the door.

'Take Cummings with you!' called Madame Bisou.

Rose pulled against the leather bindings on her wrists, but they held her securely to iron rings imbedded in the wall. Similar bindings held her feet. Katy had loosened her bindings when she'd been his captive, and Rose was determined to do the same.

Greythorne had carried her inside a town house, down a narrow set of stone steps, deep into a basement, to this room with its thick wooden door and long table with metal rings attached to it. The table frightened her. Would he bind her to it next? Another man had hauled Tannerton, dumping him on the floor like a sack of potatoes. Tannerton still lay on the stone floor. He moaned every so often, so at least he was alive, but for how long? Greythorne certainly intended to kill him.

Rose made her hand as narrow as she could and tried to slip the binding off, but it cut into her skin. She tried again, until her wrist bled.

Greythorne had warned he would be back when Tannerton regained his senses. Greythorne wanted the marquess to watch whatever he planned to do to her. She shuddered, knowing from Katy that he would strip off her soiled and ripped clothing and strike her with one of several whips that hung on one wall as orderly as teacups in a cupboard.

Tannerton moaned again, but this time he jerked against his restraints. 'Deuce!' he mumbled. 'Where the devil?'

'You are in a house in London. He didn't take us very far.'

He glanced over at her and struggled more, then shut his eyes and moaned. 'Greythorne.'

'He hit you on the head,' she told him.

He rocked himself into a sitting position. 'I feel it. Where is he?'

'Abovestairs.' She tried to speak calmly, but her voice shook. 'He said he wanted you to be awake. While he waited, he said he would change his clothes and have some supper.'

'Damned inhospitable of him not to offer us supper.' He leaned his head against the stone of the wall and closed his eyes again. 'I am sorry, Rose. Ought to have left the whole matter to Flynn. He'd not have made a muddle of it.'

She had been trying not to think of Flynn. Her dear Flynn, who would undoubtedly be called upon to view their bodies and tell the magistrate who they were.

'Did the bastard hurt you, Rose?' he asked.

She decided not to tell him about Greythorne strangling her. 'Not as yet. I'm thinking that comes later.'

'Deuce.'

She had been a prisoner once before. Miss Hart had freed her with cunning and bravery. She must be brave this time. And cunning. When dressing for Vauxhall, she'd stuck Katy's knife under her corset. She had no hope of reaching it, but Tannerton was less fettered than she.

'Lord Tannerton, can you get over here and stand?' she asked.

He opened his eyes in narrow slits. 'I have no idea. Why?'

'I have a small knife under my corset.'

He laughed, then winced in pain. 'Damned good place for it.'

'I didn't know where else to put it.' she said. 'If you can move over here, I think you will be able to get it out.'

He used his legs to push himself over to her. His head lolled back and forth as he moved, showing how dizzy he must be.

When he got to her, he said, 'I must grab on to you to pull myself up. It will put a strain on your arms.'

'No matter,' she said firmly. 'Just do it.'

It was difficult for him to pull himself up with his hands behind his back. It took him several tries before he stood. She thought her arms would come out of their sockets with his weight.

She tried to ignore the pain. 'Pull up my skirts. It is right at my waist under my right arm.'

He swayed as he lifted her skirt, and she knew he would not be able to keep his balance for long. She finally felt his fingers on her bare skin. She stretched her torso as best she could to give his fingers room to pull out the knife.

'Got it!' He tugged on it and it clattered to the floor. He swayed, and his eyes rolled back.

'Hold on to me,' she ordered. 'Lower yourself slowly.'

Somehow he did as she asked, finding the little knife and hiding it between his hands.

He sat very still. 'Dizzy.'

She feared Greythorne would find him next to her and become suspicious, but after a minute or two, he moved back to his place by the wall.

'Katy told me to carry the knife,' she said, still trying to battle panic.

'Good girl, Katy,' he mumbled.

She watched him awkwardly work the knife against the cord tying his hands. 'You were about to tell me something in the carriage.' He spoke as if they were sitting in some elegant drawing room.

'It does not matter now.'

'No, tell me,' he insisted. 'We must talk of something.'

'I will tell you if we escape.' She could not tell him she did not love him, not when he might die this night.

He did not persist. After a pause he said, 'De Sade. Wrote these books. Forbidden books. Passed around everywhere, naturally. Read them at Oxford. In French. *Les Prospérités du Vice. Justine.*'

She tried twisting her hands in their bindings. 'I am not understanding you, my lord.'

He opened his eyes and gave her an urgent stare. 'Listen, Rose. When he starts in on you, grovel, cower, beg for his mercy. Promise him you will do whatever he wants.'

She glared back. 'I never will.'

'Do it,' he ordered. 'He will enjoy your fear. It is the only way to outwit him.' He swallowed. 'Give him your fear, and he might release you from your bonds.'

If she could get free like Katy had done, she could fight him off. They would have a chance.

There was the scraping of a key in a lock. They both swivelled their heads to the door.

Greythorne entered, dressed in a brown banyan of figured silk, slippers and night cap.

He turned to Tannerton. 'You are awake. How splendid.'

'You have hurt him badly.' Rose turned her voice into a whine. 'He doesn't stay awake.'

Tannerton let his head droop. Had he caught her cue, or was he really passing out again? Greythorne marched over and pulled his head up by the hair. 'Stay awake if you know what is good for you.'

Tannerton's eyes rolled.

Greythorne approached Rose more slowly. She had never seen a snake, but she thought a snake must move the same.

'Don't hurt me, sir.' She tried to sound weak and frightened. It was surprisingly easy because it was so close to the truth. 'Don't hurt me. I'll do anything you ask, just don't hurt me!'

His eyes glittered with pleasure. He slithered up to her and took the pins from her hair. Flynn had done the same, she remembered, but out of love. Her hair tumbled down on her shoulders. He examined one of the pins, grinned, and made as if to poke her with it.

She shrank back.

He laughed. 'You think this pain?' He put his face an inch from hers and pushed the point of the hairpin into the flesh of her arm. 'You do not know what real pain can be.'

'I will do anything. Anything.' She looked around wildly. 'Do…do you want me to undress for you? I will undress for you, my lord.'

His eyes widened with interest.

'You will like it, my lord,' she said.

He glared at her. 'Have you ever undressed for Tannerton?'

She shook her head. 'I've never been with him, sir. Tonight was the night. I…I think I can please you, if you give me a chance.'

He walked over to the wall and selected one of the whips and cracked it next to her ear, so that she felt the wind it produced against her cheek. 'You have to be punished, you know.'

She nodded.

He undid her bindings and she fell to the floor, pretending to be afraid. When he stepped closer, his banyan fell open and she saw her chance.

She grabbed where he was most sensitive and squeezed with all her might, like Katy had done. He cried out, dropping the whip and doubling over. Tannerton had freed himself and was struggling to get to his feet. He dropped the knife, which clattered to the floor. He tried to reach for it, but she grabbed his arm.

'Come!' She pulled him out of the door, slamming it behind her.

He stumbled towards the stairs, but could only crawl up.

Rose followed behind, pushing him. 'Make haste.'

Suddenly Greythorne caught her and dragged her back to his room of torture. He threw her with such force she rolled on the floor and hit the wall with a painful thud.

He hauled her upright again, but she twisted away from him.

'Stay away!' she cried, grabbing one of the whips and driving him back with it, until he wrested it out of her hand.

'Bitch!' With eyes red and bulging, he slapped her across the face so that she fell to the ground. This time her fingers closed around Katy's knife. She silently swore she would use it.

When he pulled her to her feet, she came at his throat with the knife, jabbing it into his skin until he bled.

He staggered backwards and she ran out of the room once again.

Tannerton was trying to come down the stairs.

'Hurry.' She pushed him ahead of her. 'I've stabbed him.'

They stumbled out into a hallway, just as the door of the town house crashed open, and Flynn and Cummings rushed in.

'Flynn!' Rose fell into his arms. 'I think I've killed him.'

He held her. 'Rose.'

Tannerton leaned against the wall. 'Get her out, Flynn.' He slumped to the floor, and Cummings ran to assist him.

Flynn released Rose. 'I'll see to Greythorne. Then we'll summon the watch.' She did not want to leave his side.

As she led Flynn to the basement stairs, Greythorne burst through the doorway. He lunged at Rose, but Flynn knocked him aside. The two men grappled, pounding each other with fists.

'Flynn!' Rose cried in alarm, more fearful for Flynn than she'd been for herself.

Greythorne was wild with rage, swinging recklessly as Flynn hit him again and again. Greythorne crashed into a table and it shattered beneath him, but he jumped to his feet, brandishing the jagged end of one of the table's broken legs.

'Stay back, Rose.' Flynn pushed her behind him and backed away from the newly made weapon.

Suddenly Katy appeared behind Greythorne.

She hit him on the head with a bottle, shattering it, sending wine and glass flying.

'See how you like it,' she shrieked. 'See how you like pain!'

Greythorne stumbled towards the stairs to the basement, his foot slipping on a piece of wood from the broken table, then let out a cry as he tumbled down the hard stone steps, hitting the floor below with a sickening thud.

Rose followed Flynn to peek down at the crumpled, contorted form. 'Is he—?'

Flynn descended the stairs slowly, lest Greythorne rise up once more. When he reached the body, he pressed his fingers to Greythorne's neck.

'He's dead.'

Chapter Twenty-One

Flynn dispatched Cummings to summon the watch, and by the time Cummings returned to this Fleet Street residence where Greythorne was known as Mr Black, the Bow Street Runners had also arrived. Any servants who might have been in the house had run off, and Flynn suspected none would dare return. He also doubted the other ruffians who had assisted Greythorne would ever be found.

The Bow Street Runners and the watchman took charge of the situation, saying there was no need for anyone else to remain. Flynn was glad to get Rose away from there, but before leaving, he penned a letter for one of the Runners to carry to the magistrate asking him to call upon the marquess the next day.

Flynn decided they all must go to Audley Street, where Tanner could be tended to in his own bed. He sent Katy, Cummings and Tanner in one hackney carriage. He and Rose rode in another.

Alone with Rose at last, Flynn put his arm around her and held her close. 'How are you faring, Rose?'

She snuggled against him. 'I am faring very well now, Flynn.'

They did not speak. After the horror and danger she'd been through, he wanted only to give her peace. In their silence the closeness between them returned, as if their thoughts were one and there was no need to speak aloud. Flynn was content to have her in his arms. He had come so close to losing her, he doubted he would ever take a moment like this for granted.

He'd thought her asleep, but she murmured, 'I have something to tell you, Flynn.'

Flynn kissed the top of her head. 'I have many things to tell you, Rose.'

'Will you give me time to talk with you after we arrive at Lord Tannerton's?'

He gave a soft laugh. 'Indeed, I will.' Brushing her hair from her forehead, he asked, 'You do not mind I'm taking you there?'

She sighed. 'I'll mind nothing if it means being with you.'

They reached the town house right behind the other hack, and Flynn left her side to help with Tanner, who was only half in his wits. He could not walk without assistance, so Cummings and Flynn assisted him to the door and other servants took over once inside. The physician had not left from tending to Smythe's leg and Wiggin's hand, so he was present to take charge of Tanner's care. Flynn told the housekeeper and butler to give their guests, Rose, Katy and Cummings, some food and whatever else they needed.

'Wait for me in the dining parlour,' he whispered to Rose.

When Flynn finally reached the parlour, Rose was there alone.

She poured him some wine and fixed a plate of food for

him. 'Cummings went off to share sleeping quarters with one of your footmen, and your housekeeper set up one of the bed-chambers for me and Katy. Katy should be sleeping now.'

When she set the plate down in front of him, he grasped her hand and pressed her palm against his lips. He sat her on his lap while he ate.

'Will Lord Tannerton recover?' she asked him.

Flynn nodded, swallowing some wine. 'The physician believes so, after a rest.'

'You ought to rest, too, Flynn,' she said.

He smiled at her. 'I intend to go to bed directly.'

Rose leaned down and kissed his lips. 'As do I.'

She knew without asking him that she would be sharing a bed with him, not with Katy. With fingers entwined, he led her to his bedchamber, a room so neat and plain, she wanted to weep for its starkness.

Once the door was closed, Rose helped him off with his coat and boots. She unbuttoned his waistcoat.

He touched her neck and pain filled his eyes. 'You are bruised.'

She did not wish to bring the memory of Greythorne into this room. 'Do not talk of that. It is over.'

He stroked the skin of her neck and she fancied his touch erased the marks of Greythorne's cruelty.

He shrugged out of his waistcoat and reached around her to untie the laces of the dress that had been found for her. It was an easy matter for him to pull the dress over her head and to undo her corset. That done, she unbuttoned his trousers.

Their undressing felt like a dance to her, she taking one step, he taking another until all the barriers fell away. He lifted her on to the bed, not as grand as the one they had shared before, but tinged with his scent.

Their dance continued, though his hand faltered with each mark he found on her. He kissed the bruises on her neck, the scrapes and cuts on her wrists, the mark of Greythorne's hand on her cheek. Nothing could have felt more healing.

She traced the contours of his muscles, the roughness of his stubble. She let her fingers play in his dark, silken locks. Reverently they traded touch for touch, until soon he was above her and it was time to dance in unison.

When he entered her, she almost wept with joy. Only the day before she'd believed she would never feel the glory of him moving inside her again. Her back arched and she pressed her fingers into his skin as he set the pace.

As if following his lead in a waltz, she joined her movements to his. They had become one person, moving together, thinking as one person, feeling as one. She gazed into his eyes, and even their souls became one.

Together the excitement grew, the pleasure intensified, and their fevered panting melded like the voices of the King's Theatre chorus. She would savour this unexpected moment for the rest of her days.

Suddenly they reached the peak together, their pleasure intensified by its being shared by the other. Together they cried out as the waves of ecstasy washed over them.

Together they collapsed when the ecstasy waned, but as Flynn slid off her their connection held fast.

He kissed her. 'Now, what was it you were wanting to tell me, Rose?' Still holding her against him, he stroked her arm with his thumb.

She took a deep breath and released it slowly. 'I made a decision tonight to refuse Tannerton. To not go to bed with him, Flynn. I started to tell him when…when everything happened.' She pushed away that memory. 'I can never repay the money he spent on me—or repay you for doing so much for me in his name—but I cannot be his mistress.'

She expected him to be surprised by this pronouncement, but even the rhythm of his thumb against her skin was unchanged.

'Why, Rose?' he asked as if the question were expected of him.

She knew she must tell him what she had not said to him before. 'I love you, Flynn. I do not wish to bed another man.'

'You do not wish to be a courtesan?' His tone was almost teasing.

'I was not truthful when I said that.' She quickly added, 'I'm not expecting this to change anything for you, Flynn. You must take your employment with the Duke of Clarence. It is what you dreamed of.'

He leaned on one elbow to look at her. 'You knew of that?'

She nodded. 'Lord Tannerton told me a long time ago.'

The hard planes of his face seemed to soften. 'Working for a prince is no longer my dream, Rose. My dream is you.'

She was afraid to believe him. 'You don't need to be worrying about me.' She took another breath. 'I was thinking I could sell my pianoforte. It would give me a little money, enough to go home. To Ireland. I'm thinking my old school might still want me to teach music.' Or scrub the floors or work in the scullery, it did not matter.

He leaned down and kissed her so tenderly she ached with longing again. 'Come to Ireland with me.'

She wrinkled her brow.

He smiled. 'I want to marry you, Rose.'

She opened her mouth to speak, but he put his fingertips on her lips.

'Do not pretend you do not wish to marry me, Rose. I was at Vauxhall. I heard the truth in your song.'

Her heart beat faster. He'd learned the truth in the songs, just as she had.

His eyes filled with pain. 'I almost lost you, Rose. I'll not chance losing you again.'

She flung her arms around him. 'You'll not be losing me, Jameson Flynn.'

Tanner's head still hurt like the devil, but he'd risen early, dressed—or rather his valet dressed him—and had been reasonably coherent when the magistrate had come with his interminable questions.

To Tanner's surprise, everyone who had been involved in the previous night's fracas were gathered in his drawing room for the magistrate's visit. Rose, Katy, the Bow Street Runners— even Cummings was there. Flynn explained that Rose, Katy and Cummings had stayed the night, which certainly must have given the servants plenty to gossip about. Tanner wondered how long it would be until the whole of Audley Street knew he'd housed not one, but two ladies of questionable virtue.

When the magistrate came, Flynn and the others had done most of the talking. Fortunate, because Tanner could barely string two words together, let alone remember the events as anything more than a jumble.

Now they had all left and the drawing room was blessedly quiet. Tanner lifted a cup of tea to his lips, tea being the only beverage he could tolerate with his headache, which was a pity.

He put the cup down and rested his eyes, flashes of memory still coming to him. He'd thwarted Greythorne in the end, all right, but at what cost?

He forced his eyes open. It was not in his nature to dwell on such unpleasantness, especially his role in it. Besides, his head pained him more when he tried to think.

There was a knock on the door, and Flynn poked his head in. 'May I speak with you?'

Deuce. More talking. 'Of course.'

Flynn entered, followed by Rose, who held on to his arm. Tanner tried to rise.

'Do not stand, Lord Tannerton,' she said solicitously.

He gratefully sank back into his chair. 'Then please sit, both of you. Have some tea.'

They declined the tea and sat down next to each other on the settee.

'There's something I must be telling you, my lord,' she began, her expression serious.

Lord, he was not in the mood to hear more unpleasantness. Then a memory returned. She'd started to tell him something in the carriage. 'Oh, yes.' He took another sip.

Flynn turned to her, placing his hand on hers. 'You should allow me to say it.'

She looked back at Flynn, setting her chin firmly. 'No. I must do it, Flynn.'

Tanner would be delighted if one of them said it so they could go on their way.

Rose turned her gaze to him. 'It is only that I…I wish to back out of our arrangement.'

'What arrangement?' he asked, then it dawned on him. 'Oh, our *arrangement*. I'd quite forgotten about that.'

She continued, 'I know you spent a lot of money on me—'

He was having difficulty following the thread of her words. What had money to do with it? He'd been engaged in a contest, had he not? He always spent money to win a contest. 'What the devil are you talking about?'

Flynn broke in. 'It is my doing, Tanner. Mine alone. I have a confession of my own—'

Tanner groaned. Now he must listen to Flynn bare his soul? Could they not get to the point?

He released an exasperated breath. 'One of you. Explain.' His head hurt too much to make sense of their nonsense. He lifted his teacup to his lips.

Flynn leaned forward. 'Rose does not wish to become your mistress, Tanner, because she is to become my wife.'

Tanner almost dropped his cup. 'What?'

'It is something that happened between us from the first. And then we were in each other's company so often, it just grew stronger,' Rose explained. 'But I was most at fault. I wanted Flynn, you see. He resisted. He was always loyal to you.' She glanced away as if considering. 'Well, loyal except the one time, but I had insisted on being with him. Twice if you count last night.'

Tanner just stared at her.

Flynn spoke up. 'I wanted her just as much as she wanted me. Rose cannot take all the blame on to herself.'

Tanner held up his hand, comprehension reluctantly dawning. 'You mean to tell me you two were in bed together behind my back?'

They glanced at each other, but said nothing.

Tanner stared back at them. 'You carried on this affair the whole time?' He shook his head.

And burst out laughing.

'Lord Tannerton?' Flynn looked at him as if he were crazy.

He tried to sober himself. Laughing created havoc with his headache. 'I'll be damned. I had no idea. No suspicion whatsoever. Right under my nose.' He pressed his hand on his chest.

Rose and Flynn began speaking all at once about falling in love at first sight at Vauxhall. About Flynn asking her to marry him and her refusing at first. About how he would write to the Duke of Clarence, refusing the position. Rose apologized for taking his money for the voice lessons and for the ghastly King's Theatre opera, and Flynn said he would repay Tanner for everything, which was quite illogical. Flynn did not have that kind of money.

Rose looked at him with sympathy. 'It is for the best for you, too, Lord Tannerton. Like the song said, lovemaking should be be "full of love and full of truth." Otherwise it is not love.'

He congratulated himself at asserting some self-control. He refrained from rolling his eyes.

'We have no desire to embarrass you in this, Tanner,' Flynn went on after a tender look at Rose. 'We will go to Ireland—'

'Wait a moment!' Tanner broke in. 'You mean you are not coming back?'

They both looked stunned.

'You would want me back?' Flynn asked.

Tanner pressed his fingers to his temple. 'Well, I do not know. A married secretary would not entirely suit, but surely you will return to London.'

'I had assumed my presence in London would not be desired.' Flynn said.

'What of Miss O'Keefe's singing? There is no theatre to speak of in Ireland, is there?' Tanner had never known Flynn to speak such drivel.

'Surely you will tell everyone not to hire me,' Rose said.

'Why the devil would I do that?'

These two must be in love, Tanner thought. Their brains were more addled than his was.

'I cannot think with this headache.' He pressed his hands

to the top of his head. 'Go off and get a special licence or something, but leave me now. We can determine your future at a…a future time.'

Flynn gaped at him. 'You are not angry?'

Flynn's words stopped him. He considered this. No, he was not angry, Tanner realised, although he ought to be.

'I am persuaded you deserve each other.' He made a shooing gesture. 'Go.'

Rose and Flynn stood up, regarding him with so fond a look he felt like a favoured uncle or something as ghastly. Then Rose walked up to him and placed a warm kiss on his cheek.

'Thank you, my lord,' she whispered.

He glanced into her eyes, so filled with happiness and love that a sharp pang of envy shot through him.

His head hurt worse. 'Go,' he said again, more gently. 'We'll sort the rest out later.'

Flynn stepped forward and clasped Tanner's hand. The expression of gratitude on Flynn's face actually stirred Tanner's emotions.

Flynn put an arm around the coveted Rose and the two walked toward the door, Rose turned back, and Tanner smiled at her.

When the door shut behind them, Tanner lowered his head into his hands, his eyes stinging.

It was not that he'd wanted her, because he knew now that it had been winning that had mattered, not winning Rose. It was just that he…envied them.

He glanced at the brandy decanter, but lifted the teacup to his lips instead. He supposed he'd have to tell Pomroy. He imagined relating all this to his friend. The dramatic confession. The tender love scene. He could just see Pomroy's amused face. Tanner would never hear the end of it. A secretary cuckolding a marquess.

Tanner blinked away the stinging in his eyes and began to laugh.

Wait until he told Pomroy.

Epilogue

Dublin—October 1818

Flynn stood backstage, his heart still racing, as it had done unceasingly from the moment Rose stepped out on stage. The Dublin theatre was packed, although he suspected half the seats were taken up by Flynns and relatives of Flynns.

Ever since he and Rose had stepped off the ship at Belfast, husband and wife, they had been enveloped by a swarm of Flynns. His brother Aidan and sister Siobhan had met the ship that day, although Flynn had written that they would be travelling straight to Donnanew House, the home where he'd spent his boyhood, the home where his parents, Aidan and oldest brother Colman lived. Siobhan and her husband, with Aidan and his wife, escorted them to Donnanew House, to the welcoming arms of his mother and father, grey haired now and frailer than he'd like to admit.

Still, his mother and father made the trip to Dublin this day, to this new theatre for its opening night.

There were even a few O'Keefes in the audience. After they had arrived in Ireland, Flynn had searched out Rose's

family to inform them of her father's death. It turned out
Rose was not as bereft of family as she'd thought. Mr
O'Keefe's brother was still living. Miraculously, he and a
number of cousins had welcomed her like a prodigal child.

It had been a year of miracles—this theatre itself one of
them. Flynn still pinched himself to see if he really did own
it, was really manager of its first production. Until he'd
viewed the theatre, abandoned but needing little repair, he'd
not realised this was the challenge for which his soul had
yearned. He and Rose had brought it back to glorious life.

For the opening night, they'd staged a Sheridan classic,
The Rivals, knowing its Mrs Malaprop would guarantee
laughter and delight. Rose played Lydia and a more beautiful Lydia there never could be. They had just made it through
the play, but still Flynn's heart would not rest. Rose had
stepped out on stage to sing a selection of songs.

The musicians began playing and Rose stole one glance
to her husband before raising her voice:

> *When, like the dawning day*
> *Eileen Aroon*
> *Love sends his early ray...*

Flynn laughed softly, remembering the night at Vauxhall
when he'd first heard her sing this very song. How much had
changed since that night.

Rose had transformed his life. She'd given him what he
had not even known he'd lost. Happiness.

At the end of 'Eileen Aroon,' there was silence and Flynn's
stomach wrenched for Rose. The next moment, however,
brought a shout of 'Bravo!' and waves and waves of applause.

Rose went on to sing other Irish songs, and he could feel

the theatre-goers embrace her, more lovingly with each verse. At the final song, she needed to beg her audience to quieten down so they could hear her.

'This is the last,' she told them, and they groaned in disappointment. 'You must sing along with me!'

Flynn's brow furrowed. They had not planned such a thing. Rose gave him another glance, then hurried to where he stood in the wings. She pulled him back with her to the centre of the stage, hanging on to his arm as if fearing he'd run off. She was flushed with excitement.

Extending her free hand to the audience, she began to sing:

> *His hair was black, his eye was blue*
> *His arm was stout, his word was true...*

It seemed as if the whole body of the theatre gave a collective sigh. By the refrain, their voices—including Flynn's own—were thundering:

> *Shule, shule, shule agra...*

When the song came to the end, the audience rose to their feet. Flynn thought they might never cease their clapping, their 'Bravos' and 'Well dones.' Flowers cascaded on to the stage.

The other performers came out for final bows, but Rose did not release Flynn. It seemed an eternity before the audience settled down and rumbled their way to the exit doors.

Rose and Flynn had no more left the stage when Flynn's parents and brothers and sisters met them and showered them with hugs and kisses. Flynn was grateful his family had accepted his new ambition, a somewhat unusual one for a landowner's son. He doubted any English lord would have understood his choosing a poor Irish theatre over service to a Royal Duke. But none of that mattered any more.

Rose was being embraced by her uncle when she said, 'I must hurry to the dressing room.'

Flynn began herding the relatives away. 'Yes, we will see you all for supper at the hotel. It is all arranged.' He found his father for another hug. 'Thank you for it, Dad.'

He rescued Rose and put his arm around her as they walked to her dressing room.

'I'm thinking it was wonderful, Flynn. I sang with my heart.'

He kissed her on the cheek. 'You were wonderful, Rose.'

She laughed. 'Mr Hook would be proud of me.'

Flynn squeezed her tighter. 'He would indeed.'

Her voice softened. 'And my father, too.'

Flynn stopped to caress her cheek and look into her eyes. 'I fancy your mother and your father are looking down at you this very moment and are feeling proud.'

She smiled and gave him a quick peck on his lips. 'What would I be doing without you, Jameson Flynn.'

He did not answer, but he knew her life would have been quite different if the Marquess of Tannerton's secretary had not been an overly ambitious Irishman who'd fallen deeply for her from first sight.

They hurried through the labyrinth of backstage until they reached her dressing room.

A young maid stood as they entered, an infant in her arms. 'The babe just started her wailing,' she said.

Rose reached for their daughter. 'Oh, she's hungry, poor dear.' She held the baby for a moment, trying to quieten her, but the scent of her mother only escalated her cries. Rose handed her to Flynn. 'Hold her for a moment. Dierdre, help me out of these clothes.'

Flynn gazed at the biggest miracle in his life, his daughter, only three months old, still needing her mother's breast. 'Now, hush, little rosebud,' he murmured.

Soon Rose changed into a white gauze dinner dress, and her face was scrubbed clean of stage make-up. She looked more beautiful than ever. Her maid carried the costume out to be brushed and readied for tomorrow's performance, and Rose settled in a chair to nurse the baby, whose suckling sounds were the only noise in the suddenly peaceful room.

Flynn gazed down at them. 'Do you know how much I'm loving you, Rose, and my little rosebud, as well?'

Her beautiful green eyes glittered up at him. 'I know,' she whispered.

A knock sounded at the door and Flynn opened it a crack to see who it was. His assistant manager peeked in.

'A gentleman to see you, Mr Flynn.' He lowered his voice significantly. 'A real gentleman.'

Flynn glanced over to Rose, who grabbed a shawl to cover herself and the baby, and he opened the door.

Lord Tannerton ambled in. 'Thought I'd offer my congratulations,' he said as if he'd just wandered away from his billiard table.

'Tanner!' Flynn exclaimed. 'My lord.' He was too dumbstruck to say more. Never had he anticipated that the Marquess of Tannerton would make the trip to Dublin.

'Lord Tannerton!' Rose cried happily. 'We never expected you! How lovely of you.'

He gave Flynn a wink and crossed the room to Rose. 'Are you hiding something?'

She moved the shawl away so he could see.

He gazed at the baby for a long moment. 'She is just as Flynn described.' He gave Rose a wistful smile. 'As beautiful as her mother.'

Rose reached for his hand and squeezed it.

Flynn finally roused himself to walk over and shake Tanner's hand. 'I am speechless. Delighted you have come.'

Tanner found a chair and dropped himself into it. 'Well, I had to see to my investment, did I not? There's all manner of things I must attend to myself since I lost my secretary—my efficient secretary, I should say. This new one requires significant effort on my part.'

Flynn searched the room, finding the bottle of Irish whiskey he kept there. He poured Tanner a glass and handed it to him. 'Investment is hardly an accurate word.'

When Flynn had written to Tanner to ask if the marquess would vouch for him for a loan, Tanner instead sent enough money to buy the theatre and to renovate it. He'd written it was a wedding gift, adding that Flynn could repay the amount if he wished, but there was no obligation.

'I consider it an investment,' Tanner said. 'An investment in your future.'

Rose interrupted, perhaps sensing Flynn had again been rendered speechless. 'Lord Tannerton, you must come to supper with us and meet the relatives.'

Rolling his eyes, he responded, 'I have already encountered more Flynns and O'Keefes than I could have imagined in existence.' He grinned. 'They are a jolly lot. I would be happy to join you.'

The marquess left a few minutes later, after finishing his whiskey and again promising to come to the hotel for supper.

When Flynn closed the door behind him, he turned to Rose. 'I am astounded.'

The baby had finished nursing and Rose lay her over her shoulder, patting her back. 'You always told me he was the best of men.'

'Indeed. The very best of men.'

She stood, still holding their daughter against her shoulder. She walked over to her husband and he very gently put his arms around her, embracing them both. He leaned his forehead against hers and they stood there together like that, swaying slightly.

'I always disagreed with you, you know,' she murmured.

'You did?' He was lulled by the feel of her, the warmth of their infant, the scent of mother's milk.

'You are the very best of men, Jameson Flynn.' Her voice cracked with emotion. '*You,* my husband.'

* * * * *

The Vanishing
Viscountess

To Mallory Pickerloy, a lovely reader whose
name is worthy of a heroine.

Chapter One

October, 1818

The gale roared like a wild beast. Under its savage attack, the ship creaked and moaned and begged for mercy. Shouts of the crew echoed the ship's distress as men struggled to work the pumps and save the rigging.

Adam Vickery, the Marquess of Tannerton, or Tanner, as he was known to his friends, sat with the other passengers in the packet ship's cuddy, awaiting his demise. He remained still, arms crossed over his chest, eyes closed, reviewing his life.

He found it wanting. He'd left no mark on the world, no son to inherit his title and lands, no child to carry on his bloodline. All he had done was maintain what his father, grandfather, great-grandfather, and all the Marquesses of Tannerton had built. If he were truly honest with himself, he would say he'd not even done the maintaining. Other men did that work for him: his estate managers, men of business and secretaries. They toiled while Tanner enjoyed his gaming, his sport, his women.

A loud crack sounded and a thud on the deck shook the

whole ship. A woman wailed. Tanner opened his eyes to see the woman clutching an infant and a small boy to her breast. The cabin was filled with many women like her, shaking in fear, and men, like Tanner himself, cursing their helplessness. There was no way to stop the storm, no way to calm the sea, no way to hold the timbers of the ship together.

His gaze fell on one woman who neither wailed nor cowered from the storm. With an expression of defiance rather than fear, she stood next to a Bow Street Runner, leather shackles on her wrists, obviously his prisoner. Only a few hours ago, at the beginning of this voyage from Dublin to Holyhead, Tanner's gaze had been drawn to her, so dignified in her plight. What crime had she committed to warrant her escort from Ireland? He'd been too blue-devilled to bother inquiring about her, however. Now he wished he'd spoken to her, or at least smiled at her. She seemed every bit as alone as he.

When the winds began their fierce assault, the first mate had gathered all the passengers into this cabin. He'd told them they were close to the Anglesey coast. Of course, the Anglesey coast could be rocky and treacherous, although the man neglected to mention that part.

What could be worse? Tanner wondered. Plunging into the cold depths of the Irish Sea? Or being dashed upon some craggy rocks?

Either would mean death.

The first mate popped in a second time when the storm intensified. "All will be well," he reassured them. None of the passengers believed him. Tanner could see it in their eyes. He felt it in his own soul. Tanner watched a man remove a miniature from his pocket and stare at it, a portrait of a loved one he would never see again, of someone who would soon be grieving.

Who would grieve for the Marquess of Tannerton? His

friend Pomroy would likely drink a toast to his memory now and then. A mistress or two might consider him a fond memory. Perhaps the Duke of Clarence or even the Regent himself might recall him after the space of a year or two, but more likely not. Algernon, his fribble of a cousin, would be terrified at the prospect of inheriting the lofty title and its responsibilities. Tanner rubbed his face, regretting he'd never taken Algernon in tow and taught him how easy it all was. Algernon could busy himself with purchasing new coats or the latest fashion in boots or all the watch fobs and stick pins he fancied.

The Bow Street Runner began pacing, Tanner noticed, and the prisoner flashed the man an undisguised look of contempt.

Would she have anyone to mourn her?

She stood with her chin high and her startling blue eyes vigilant. He disliked thinking of what the sea would do to her, turning her body all bloated and white.

He glanced away, shaking that horrible image from his mind, but no matter where he looked, his eyes were drawn back to her.

She was tall and slender, with the same dark hair and piercing blue eyes of the woman who'd briefly captivated him a year ago. That was where the resemblance ended, however. Rose O'Keefe had made the right choice when she'd chosen Tanner's former secretary, Jameson Flynn, over Tanner himself. Flynn had offered the Vauxhall singer marriage, something Tanner would never have done. Flynn had also loved her.

Tanner laughed inwardly at the irony of it all. The secretary preferred over the marquess. He could not muster any resentment, however. Rose had picked the better man.

He frowned and bowed his head. Tanner's zeal had not

been to love Rose, but to outwit another rival for her favours. Three people had died as a result. Three lives on his conscience because of his heedless selfishness.

Purchasing the Dublin theatre for Flynn and Rose did not make amends for the destruction Tanner had set in motion, but it did give the married couple the means to a new life. That was the very least Tanner could do. He'd travelled to Dublin for their opening performance, and now he was crossing the Irish Sea again, heading back to England on this Holyhead packet.

The ship had been scheduled to land hours ago, but the storm stalled them and now the day was late. He pulled his timepiece from his pocket. It was near nine p.m.

Another shuddering crash came from above. Tanner stuffed his watch back into his pocket and glanced at the prisoner. Her eyes flashed with alarm. Tanner could not blame her. Her life— and his own empty one—appeared to be edging towards the end.

The cabin door sprang open and the first mate, drenched and dripping on to the wooden floor, yelled, "Everyone on deck! To the boats. Women and children first."

The death knell. The captain no longer expected the ship to remain intact. It was time to risk the lives of the women and children in the small boats.

There were quick anguished embraces as goodbyes were tearfully said. Panicked men tried to push in front of mothers clasping the hands of terrified children. Tanner rushed forward and pulled the men back. He used his stature and strength to keep the way clear. The prisoner was the last woman out of the door, her Bow Street Runner pushing her on, his hand firmly clamped around her arm. The man could have at least untied her shackles. What could it matter now? At least allow her to die free.

Tanner was the last person to come up on deck. As he stepped out into the air, the rain sliced him like knife blades, the wind whipping in all directions. The ship's masts no longer stood tall and proud, but lay like snapped twigs on the deck.

The sails, now in tatters, resembled nothing more than rags flapping haphazardly in the tempest. Tanner stepped over pieces of wood, remnants of sails and other debris. A loose barrel rolled towards him. He jumped aside, nearly losing his footing on the slick surface of the deck. More than once he had to grab hold of whatever was near to keep from falling.

Tanner pushed his way through to where the women and children were being loaded into boats. Although he feared the effort futile, Tanner pitched in, helping lift women and children over the side of the ship to crewmen waiting in the boats. Lightning flashed, illuminating the shadow of the shore, so distant when the sea churned like a cauldron, violently pitching the ship. The boat's fragile passengers would have a treacherous ride.

Let these people survive, he prayed.

He lifted a child into waiting arms and her mother after her. This was the last boat, and the crewmen manning it were already starting to lower it to the sea. Tanner reached for the woman prisoner, who, outwardly calm and patient, had held back so the others could go before her. Tanner scooped her into his arms to lift her over the side, but, at that same moment, the Bow Street Runner shoved them both, knocking them to the deck, jumping into the boat in her place. Tanner scrambled to his feet, but it was too late. The boat had hit the water, the crewmen rowing fast to get it away.

"Bastard!" Tanner cried. In the howling wind, he could barely hear his own words.

The prisoner's eyes blazed with fury and fear. She struggled to stand. Tanner grabbed her arm and pulled her to her feet.

"The ship's going to break apart!" the first mate cried, running by them.

Tanner glanced wildly around. Some of the crew were lashing themselves to pieces of mast.

"Come on," he shouted to the woman, pulling her along with him.

Tanner grabbed rope from the rigging and tied her to a piece of broken mast. He would be damned if that scoundrel Bow Street Runner survived and she did not. He lashed himself next to her, wrapping one arm around her and the other around the mast. The ship slammed into rocks, sending them, mast and all, skittering across the deck.

The vessel groaned, then broke apart in a cacophony of cracks and crashes and splintering wood. Their piece of mast flew into the air like a shuttlecock, the wind suspending them for several moments before plunging them into the churning water.

The impact stunned Tanner, but the shock of the needle-sharp cold roused him again. The howling of the wind, the hissing of the rain, the screams of their shipmates suddenly dulled to a muffled growl. The water was inky black and Tanner had no idea which way was up, but his arm was still around the woman. He had not lost her.

Their wooden mast began rising as if it, too, fought to reach the surface. Tanner kicked with all his strength, his lungs burning with the urge to take a breath.

When they broke the surface of the water, it was almost as great a shock as plunging into its depths. Tanner gulped for air. To his relief, he heard the woman do the same. She had survived.

Then a wave crashed over them and drove them forward.

Tanner sucked in a quick gulp of air before they went under. Again they resurfaced and were pushed forward and under once more.

When they popped to the surface, Tanner had time to yell, "Are you hurt?"

"No," she cried.

He tightened his grip on her as another wave hit. If the sea did not swallow them, the cold would surely kill them.

Or the rocks.

This wave thrust them further. Through the sheen of rain and sea, Tanner glimpsed the coast, but jagged rocks lay between, jutting up from the water like pointed teeth. Another wave pelted them, then another. The ropes loosened and were washed away. The woman's grip slipped from the mast. Tanner could hold on to the mast or the woman. He held on to the woman.

Her skirts were dragging them down and her bound wrists made it hard for her to swim. Tanner kicked hard to keep them above the water, only to see the rocks coming closer. He swivelled around to see if other survivors were near them, but not a soul was visible. No one to help them. No one to see. Perhaps no one to survive.

The next wave drove them into one of the rocks. She cried out as they hit. Another wave dashed them into another rock. Tanner tried to take the blows instead of her, but the water stirred them too fast. He lost feeling in his arms and legs and he feared he would lose his grip on her.

Not another death on his conscience. Tanner could not bear it. *God, help me save her,* he prayed. *Help me do something worthwhile. One last bloody something worthwhile.*

He slammed into a jagged rock and everything went black.

When Tanner opened his eyes, he felt cold wet sand against his cheek. He could see the water lapping the shoreline inches from his face. Its waves sounded in his ears, and whitecaps seemed to wink at him. There was hard ground beneath him, however. Hard solid ground.

The woman! He'd lost her. Let go of her, damn him. Despair engulfed him as surely as had the Irish Sea. His limbs felt heavy as iron and his soul ached with guilt. He'd let go of her.

A light glowed around him, bobbing, then coming to a stop. Suddenly someone's hands were upon him, rough hands digging into his clothes, searching his pockets.

He seized one of the groping hands, and his attacker pulled him upright, trying to break free. Tanner's grip slipped and he fell back onto the sand. The man advanced on him, kicking him in the ribs. Tanner rolled away, trying to escape the blows, but the man kicked him again.

"Your money," the man snarled as he kicked him once more. "I want your money."

Every English coast abounded with wreckers, people who flocked to the shore eager to see a ship founder, so they could seize whatever bounty that washed ashore. Tanner had never thought to meet one.

He curled himself against the onslaught of the man's boot, as he struck again and again. A loud thwack sounded and the man collapsed on top of him. Tanner shoved him off and sat up.

The woman stood above them, a long piece of wood, part of the ship, no doubt, in her trembling, still-shackled hands.

Marlena Parronley stared at the prone figure, the brute who had so violently attacked her rescuer, the Marquess of Tannerton. She'd hit the villain with all her remaining strength.

Perhaps this time she really *had* killed a man.

Tannerton struggled painfully to his knees, staring at her, holding his sides, breathing hard.

Marlena had recognised Tannerton immediately when she'd first seen him on board ship, but he'd shown no signs of remembering her.

Thank goodness.

That first Season in London—her only Season—he'd attended many of the entertainments, but he was already a marquess and she was a mere baron's daughter, a Scottish baron at that. He'd provided her and Eliza with some excitement in those heady days, however. They'd called him Tanner, as if they had been admitted to that close circle of friends he always had around him. They'd peeked at the handsome marquess from behind their fans, he so tall, his brown hair always tousled. And his eyes! They'd been in raptures about his mossy green eyes. She and Eliza had devised all manner of ways they might meet him, none of which they'd dared to carry out.

Too bad they had not thought of being caught in a gale on a ship that broke apart and tossed them in the sea.

We forgot that one, Eliza, Marlena silently said.

"Have I killed him, do you think?" she asked the marquess.

Tanner reached down to place his fingers on the man's neck. "He's alive."

Marlena released a breath she'd not realised she'd been holding.

Tanner rose to his feet.

"Are you injured?" he asked, his breathing ragged.

She shook her head, sending a shiver down her body. He still showed no signs of recognising her. He pulled off his wet gloves and reached for her hands to work on the leather bindings. When she'd been on the ship they had chafed her wrists, but she was too numb to feel them now. Her teeth chattered and she started trembling all over, making his task even more difficult. He leaned down to loosen them with his teeth.

Finally the bindings fell to the sand and she was free. Marlena rubbed her wrists, but she could not feel her hands.

"We need to find shelter. Dry clothing." He glanced around.

They were in a small cove, dotted with jutting rocks and a small patch of sand. Steep black cliffs imprisoned them as certainly as the walls of Newgate Prison.

Tanner touched her arm. "If that fellow managed to get in here, we can get out."

She nodded, but suddenly any strength she'd possessed seemed to ebb. It was difficult to think. The cold had seeped into her very bones.

He rubbed her arms, then pressed a hand on his ribs and winced. "Come now. We'll be warm and dry very soon."

He picked up the man's lantern and circled their prison walls. She could do nothing but watch. A huge wave tumbled ashore, soaking her feet again, but she could only stare at it swirling around her ankles. He crossed over and took her arm, pulling her away from the water.

He'd once danced with her, she remembered, although he never knew it. Lady Erstine had held a masquerade ball, a respectable one, and she and Eliza attended, having spent many agonising hours deciding what costume to wear. Tanner had danced one dance with Marlena without knowing who she was. Eliza had been green with envy.

"Stay with me," he said, holding her firmly.

What looked like one massive black rock was really two, with a narrow corridor between them. He held her hand and pulled her through. They climbed up smaller rocks that formed a natural stone staircase. When they finally reached the top, they found flat and grassy farmland. The storm had passed at last, but in its wake blew a cool wind that made Marlena's clothes feel like ice.

In the distance they spied one light. "A farmhouse," he said. "Make haste."

Marlena had difficulty making sense of his words. She liked his arm wrapped around her, but disliked him making her walk, especially so briskly. He made sounds with each breath, as if every step brought pain. Pain would be preferable to feeling nothing, Marlena thought. She was no longer aware of her arms or her legs.

The light grew nearer, but Marlena forgot what it signified. Her mind felt full of wool and all she wanted was to sleep.

She tried to pull away from him. "Rest," she managed to say. "Sleep."

"No." He lifted her over his shoulder and carried her.

They came to a cottage with a lone candle burning in the window. Tanner pounded on the door. "Help us! Open the door."

Soon a grizzled man in a white nightcap and gown opened the door a crack.

"Quick. I must get her warm," Tanner told him.

"Dod i mewn," the man said. "Come in, come in."

Tanner carried her inside and made her stand in front of a fireplace. The dying embers on the hearth gave heat, but the heat felt painful after the numbing cold.

"Bring some blankets," Tanner ordered. "I must warm her."

The man tottered into another room, and Tanner began stripping her of her clothing, which seemed a very odd thing for him to do, but nice, because her wet clothes were so very heavy, and she wanted to feel light again.

Suddenly dry cloth covered her shoulders and Tanner made her sit in a chair close to the fire.

The old man threw more lumps of coal into the fireplace,

and poked at it with the poker, which only made it hotter and more painful.

"M'wife and son are at the wreck," the man explained.

Oh, yes, Marlena dimly remembered, as shivers seized her. She had been on a ship that had broken apart. She remembered the shock of the cold water.

A cat ambled by, rubbing its fur against her legs. "Cat," she said to no one in particular, as her eyelids grew very heavy.

Marlena woke to find herself nestled in a nice warm bed with heavy bedcovers over her. She did not seem to have on any clothing at all, not even a shift. Next to her, also naked and holding her close, lay the Marquess of Tannerton.

Chapter Two

The woman felt warm against him, warm at last, when Tanner had thought never to be warm again. He slipped his hand down her smooth back, savouring the feel of her silky skin under his fingertips. He could still smell the sea on her, but they were both blessedly dry. And warm. He had saved her from the sea, thank God.

Thank God.

A shuffle sounded in the room and a murmur, and the woman pushed away from him with a cry.

He sat up like a shot.

The woman slid away to a corner of the bed, clutching the blanket up to her chin. Morning light shone through the small window and three pairs of eyes stared at them both, the wrinkled old man who had opened the door to them the night before, a wrinkled old woman and a younger, thick-chested man.

"What the devil?" Tanner growled.

The spectators jumped back. The old man gave a servile smile. "M'wife and son are back."

Tanner glared at them. "You disturb our privacy."

In actuality, he and the woman were the intruders. Tanner had given the old man little choice but to relinquish what was surely the bed he shared with the old woman. The night before all Tanner could think of was to cover the woman in blankets and warm her with his own body—and be warmed by hers. He'd left their clothing in a pile in the front room and carried her to the little bedchamber behind the fireplace, ordering the poor man to bring as many blankets as he owned.

The younger man—the farmer's son, obviously—rubbed his head and winced, and the hairs on the back of Tanner's neck stood on end. The son, he would swear, had been his seaside attacker. Tanner frowned. Their place of refuge suddenly seemed more like a lion's den.

He quickly regained his composure. "What are you doing in this room?" he demanded again, checking his finger for his gold signet ring and feeling under the bedcovers for the purse he'd had sense enough to remove from his coat. He held it up. "Were you looking for the purse?"

The younger man backed away to where clothing hung by pegs on the plastered walls above two wooden chests.

"We merely came to see if you required anything, that is all." The old woman simpered.

Tanner scoffed. "All three of you at once?"

The young man gave a chagrined expression and inclined his head.

Tanner glanced at his companion, still huddled under the blanket. He turned to the others. "Leave us," he commanded.

The old man and woman scurried towards the door. Their son moved more slowly, his hand returning to his head.

"We require our clothing." Tanner added.

The woman paused in the doorway. "Your things are still damp, m'lord." She tipped her head in a servile pose. "I've hung them out in the sun and the wind. 'Twill take no time at all to dry."

"Good." Tanner's tone turned a shade more conciliatory. "Treat us well and you will be rewarded." He lifted the purse.

The son smiled. "What else do you require, m'lord?"

"Some nourishment, if you please."

The man bowed and closed the door behind him.

"They thought they could nick my purse," Tanner muttered, rubbing the stubble on his chin. He did not have the heart to worry her with his suspicions about the farmer's son. "How do you fare, miss? Are you all right?"

She moved beneath the blanket as if testing to see if all parts of her still worked. "A little bruised, but unharmed, I think."

Her eyes flicked over him and quickly glanced away. Tanner realised he was quite bare from the waist up. From the waist down, as well, but the covers concealed that part of him. He reached for a blanket and winced, pressing a hand to his ribs.

"You are bruised," she cried, reaching towards him, but immediately withdrawing her hand.

He looked down at himself, purple bruises staining his torso like spilled ink. "Nothing to signify," he said, although his breath caught on another pang of pain.

He glanced at her again and the humour of the situation struck him. It was not every day he woke up in a naked embrace with a woman whose name he did not know.

He gave her a wry smile. "I do not believe we have been introduced."

Her eyelids fluttered, reminding him of shy misses one encountered at Almack's. "No, we have not."

He made a formal bow, or a semblance of one there in the bed only half-covered by a blanket. "I am Tannerton. The

Marquess of Tannerton. Tanner to my friends, which, I dare say—" he grinned "—I had best include you among."

The blue of her eyes sparkled in the morning light. "Marquess—" She quickly cast her eyes downward. "My lord."

"Tanner," he corrected in a friendly voice. "And you are…?"

He had the feeling her mind was crafting an answer.

"I am Miss Brown, sir."

It was a common name, and not her real one, he'd wager.

"Miss Brown," he repeated.

She fussed with the blanket, as if making sure it still covered her. "Do you know of the others from the ship? Did anyone else survive?"

He gave her a steady look. "The Bow Street Runner, do you mean?"

She glanced away and nodded.

He made a derisive sound. "I hope he went to the devil."

She glanced back at him. "Did any survive?"

"I know nothing of any of them," he went on, trying not to think of those poor women, those helpless little children, the raging sea. "We were alone on the beach, except for the man who tried to rob me." The man who had just left this room, he suspected. "We made it to this cottage, and all I could think was to get you warm. I took over the farmer's bed and must have fallen asleep."

She was silent for a moment, but Tanner could see her breath quicken. He suspected she remembered the terror of it all.

"I believe I owe you my life, sir," she whispered.

Her blue eyes met his and seemed to pierce into him, touching off something tender and vulnerable. He glanced away and tugged on the covers, pulling off a faded brown blanket. He wrapped it around his waist and rose from the bed. "Let me see about getting you some clothes. And food." He turned towards the door.

"A moment, sir," she said, her voice breathless. "Do—do you know where we are? Who these people are?"

"Only that we are in a farmer's cottage," he replied, not entirely truthfully. "There was a lamp in the window. I walked towards its light."

She nodded, considering this. "What do they know of us?"

His gaze was steady. "I did not tell them you were a prisoner, if that is your concern."

She released a relieved breath. "Did you tell them who you are?"

He tried to make light of it all. "Last night I only saw the old man. I fear I failed to introduce myself. My manners have gone begging."

"Good," she said.

"Good?" His brows rose.

"Do not tell them who you are."

He cocked his head.

"A marquess is a valuable commodity. They might wish to ransom you."

She was sharp, he must admit. Her mistrust gave even more credence to his suspicions. He had thought to bully these people with his title, but he now saw the wisdom of withholding who he was—as well as who she might be.

He twisted his signet ring to the inside of his palm and put his hand on the door latch. "I will not say a word." Her lovely face relaxed. "Let me see about our clothing and some food and a way out of here."

She smiled and he walked out of the room, still holding the blanket around his waist.

It took Marlena a moment to adjust when he left the room. The marquess's essence seemed to linger, as well as the image of him naked. She and Eliza had been too naïve to speculate on how the Marquess of Tannerton would look without clothing, but she could now attest that he looked spectacular. Wide shoulders, sculpted chest peppered with dark hair that formed a line directing the eye to his manly parts. She'd only glimpsed them upon first awakening, but now she could not forget the sight. He was like a Greek statue come to life, but warm, friendly and flirtatious.

He might not recognise her as the notorious Vanishing Viscountess, subject of countless Rowlandson prints and sensational newspaper stories, but he did know she'd been a prisoner. He would, of course, have no memory of the very naïve and forgettable Miss Parronley from Almack's.

She hugged her knees. As long as he did not recognise her, she was free. And she intended to keep it that way.

She had no idea what piece of shore they'd washed up on, but it must be closer to Scotland than she'd ever dared hope to be again. She longed to be in Scotland, to lose herself there and never be discovered. A city, perhaps, with so many people, no one would take note of a newcomer. She would go to Edinburgh, a place of poetry and learning. Who would look for the Vanishing Viscountess in Edinburgh? They would think her dead at the bottom of the sea.

She'd once believed she'd be safe in Ireland, in the ruse she and Eliza devised, governess to Eliza's children. Not even Eliza's husband had suspected. Marlena had been safe for three years, until Eliza's brother came to visit. Debtors nipping at his heels, Geoffrey had come to beg his sister for money.

Marlena would have hidden from him, or fled entirely, but Eliza and the children had been gravely ill from the fever and she could not bear to leave. Geoffrey discovered her tending to them. He'd recognised her instantly and suddenly realised he could raise his needed funds by selling the whereabouts of the Vanishing Viscountess.

Geoffrey had long returned to London the day Marlena stood over Eliza's newly dug grave in the parish churchyard, the day the magistrate's men and the Bow Street Runner came to arrest her.

She swiped at her eyes. *At least we nursed the children back to health, Eliza.*

She rose from the bed and wrapped the blanket around her like a toga. The room was tiny and sparse, but clean. There was no mirror, so she tried to look at herself in the window glass, but the sun was too bright. She felt her hair, all tangles and smelling of sea water. It was still damp underneath. She sat back on the bed.

She must look a fright, she thought, working at her tangled locks with her fingers, still vain enough to wish she appeared pretty for the handsome Marquess of Tannerton.

Except for the bruises on his chest, he had looked wonderful after their ordeal—his unshaven face only enhancing his appearance, making him look rakish. She inhaled, her fingers stilling for a moment with the memory of how his naked skin had felt, warm and hard with muscle.

Her whole body filled with heat. It had been a long time since she'd seen a naked man and a long time since a man had held her. She tried to remember if she had ever woken naked in her husband's arms. Perhaps she never had. He usually had fled her bed when he finished with her.

So long ago.

The door opened and the old woman entered, the scent of boiling oats wafting in behind her.

"Your gentleman says to find you some clothes, ma'am. Yours are ripped and would take too long to mend." She handed Marlena her stockings, which had somehow remained intact. "I told your gentleman I've just the thing for you in here." The woman rummaged through one of the wooden chests. "I've put the kettle on as well, and there is some nice porridge boiling."

Marlena slipped on her stockings. Porridge sounded as heavenly as ambrosia at the moment. Until she'd smelled it, she'd not known she was ravenous.

"That is very kind," she said to the woman. "What is your name?"

"I'm Mrs Davies, ma'am." The woman leaned over the chest, still looking through it.

Marlena made her voice sound friendly. "Thank you, Mrs Davies. Where are we, might I ask?"

"At our farm, ma'am." The woman looked at her as if she were daft. Her mouth opened, then, and she finally understood the question. "About a mile or so from Llanfairynghornwy."

Marlena blinked. She had no idea where that was, nor did she think she could repeat its name. "Is there a coaching inn there?"

"There is a coaching inn at Cemaes."

"How far is that?" Marlena asked.

"About five miles, ma'am."

Marlena could walk five miles.

The old woman twisted around, leaning on the edge of the chest. "But if I think of it, you'll want to reach Holyhead, not Cemaes."

Holyhead was the port where the ship had been bound. "How far is Holyhead?"

"Ten miles or so the opposite way, to reach the ferry, that is. You'll need a ferry to take you to Holyhead, ma'am."

Marlena nodded. Holyhead would likely be where other survivors would be bound, making it the last place she'd wish to be.

The woman turned back to her rummaging, finally pulling

out a shift and tossing it to Marlena, who quickly slipped it on. Next the woman pulled out a faded blue dress.

"Perhaps this will do." She handed it to Marlena.

The dress was made of wool in a fine, soft weave that seemed nothing like a farm wife's dress. Marlena stood up and held it against herself. The dress was long enough for her, although she was taller than most women and certainly a good foot taller than Mrs Davies. The dress would totally engulf the farm woman and would be big on Marlena as well.

Some other woman from some other shipwreck had once worn this dress. Marlena whispered a prayer for that woman's poor soul.

"It will do very nicely," she said.

The woman straightened and thrust something else at Marlena. "Here's a corset for you."

"Thank you." Marlena smiled. "I am so very grateful to you."

The woman started towards the door.

Marlena stopped her with another request. "I would like very much to wash. Would it be too much trouble to bring me some water?"

The woman looked heavenwards, as if she'd been asked for the moon, but she nodded and hurried out of the door.

Marlena inspected the corset. Its laces looked as if they could be tightened to fit her. She lifted the dress to her nose and was grateful that it smelled clean. She was eager to be clean herself, eager to wash the salt from her skin. What she would not give for a nice long soak in warm bathwater, but she would content herself with a quick wash from a basin. She paced the room, thinking, planning. She could easily walk to Cemaes this very day, but what would she do then? She had no money.

She must beg money from Tanner, she decided. It was her only choice. She was uncertain of him, although it was a good sign he'd not betrayed her to this farm family. If he discovered she was the Vanishing Viscountess, however, he would certainly want to turn her over to the local magistrate. It was best to slip away as soon as she could do so.

A knock sounded, and Tanner walked in with her basin of water, a towel over his arm like a valet. She grabbed the blanket and wrapped it around the shift. He was dressed in what looked like his own shirt and trousers. His hair was damp. Marlena touched her still-tangled hair, envious that he had been able to wash out the salt and the memory of the sea.

"Your clothes are dry?" she asked.

"Dry enough." He placed the basin on a small table in the corner of the room. "I thought you might like this." He pulled a comb from the band of his trousers. "I've washed it, although these people seem clean enough."

She took it from him. "Oh, thank you!" She immediately sat back on the bed and attacked her locks. "Have they told you anything of the shipwreck?"

He shook his head. "These people are a close-mouthed lot. The son left, but I hope it was merely to return to the beach. I gather these people are wreckers."

Like the man who attacked Tanner. The man she hit on the head. She remembered that suddenly, but it was like a murky dream.

"The mother and son were out there during the storm last night." He walked towards the door. "Is there anything else you need?"

"My shoes," she replied. "But do not leave yet."

He waited.

She took a breath. "I need to ask you—to beg you—to let me go."

His brows rose.

She went on quickly, "Mrs Davies—the wife—says there

is a town five miles from here with a coaching inn. You may go on to Holyhead, but let them all think me dead. Please. I want only to go home. That is all I desire." Not all she desired. She needed money, but she'd make that request only if he gave his permission to flee.

He leaned against the door. "Where is home?"

"Scotland," she said truthfully and an image of her Scottish home jumped into her mind. *Parronley,* home of her ancestors and her carefree childhood.

He peered at her. "You do not sound Scottish."

"I was sent to school in England." This was true, as well. At lovely Belvedere House in Bath, where she'd met Eliza. She'd been very keen to rid herself of any traces of a Scottish burr in those days, so eager for the other girls to like her.

He pressed a hand against his ribs. "Tell me why the Bow Street Runner was bringing you back to England."

Marlena flinched, feeling his pain. Her mind raced to think of a story he would believe. She borrowed one from a Minerva Press novel she and Eliza once read. "I was a lady's companion to a very nice elderly lady. I was accused of stealing her jewellery."

His mouth twitched. "And you did not do it."

"I did not!" She was not guilty of stealing jewellery or any other crime. "I was wrongly accused, but there was no way to prove it. Her son placed the jewels in my room."

How she wished she had been accused of the theft of jewels. Far better that than standing over the bloody body of her husband and being accused of his murder.

She made herself face him with a steady gaze. "I ran away to Ireland, but they sent the Bow Street Runner after me."

His eyes probed her. They were still that lovely shade of mossy green she remembered from those giddy assemblies at Almack's. "They went to a great deal of trouble to capture you."

She gave a wan smile, but her mind was racing to recall the details of the novel. "Not all the jewellery was recovered. My lady's son sold the rest. He made it look as if he was trying to recover it all, going so far as having me tracked down in Ireland for it." She glanced away from Tanner, and her voice came from deep in her throat. "He placed the blame on me."

In truth, it had been her own cousin who contrived to have her blamed for Corland's murder, and her cousin Wexin had once been a member of the Marquess of Tannerton's set. That had been seven years ago, when Marlena and Eliza had had their first Season, but for all Marlena knew Tanner could still count Wexin among his friends.

In that lovely Season, when she and Eliza had been so full of hope, she'd begged Wexin to present them to the handsome marquess. Wexin refused, although she and Eliza had been undaunted.

"Who were these people who employed you?" he asked.

"I cannot tell you," she replied truthfully again. "For all I know, the son may be one of your close companions." Like Wexin had been. "You would believe them and not me." She fixed her gaze on him again. "Let me go, I implore you. Let me disappear. Let them think I am dead."

He stared back at her, not speaking, not moving. Panic spread inside her like a wild weed.

"You have no money. How will you get on?" he asked.

She took a breath. "I would beg a little money from you."

He gave her a long look before speaking. "First wash and dress and eat. We shall both leave this place, then we will decide what to do next." He opened the door and walked out.

Her nerves still jangled. He had not precisely agreed to help her, but he had not sounded as if he would turn her in, either. She had no choice but to wait to see what he would do.

Marlena washed and dressed and managed to get her hair into a plait down her back. When she walked out of the bedchamber in her stockinged feet, the smell of the porridge drove all other thought and emotion away. She sat in a plain wooden chair across from Tanner at a small table. The old woman set a bowl of porridge in front of her. Marlena's hand shook when she dipped her spoon into the steaming bowl. The first mouthful was too hot. She blew on the next spoonful and the next and ate as quickly as she could. Tanner ate as hungrily as she.

The old farmer and his wife watched their every move.

When they finished, Tanner turned to them. "Bring the rest of my clothing, my boots and the lady's shoes. The lady also needs a cloak. You will undoubtedly have a cart. I should like you to take us to the nearest town."

"Holyhead?" the farmer asked. "You'll need a ferry to reach it."

Tanner reached into the sleeve of his shirt where he had tucked his purse. He opened it and took out a sovereign. "Very well."

The farmer's eyes grew wide at the sight of the coin. Both he and his wife sprang into action, leaving Tanner and Marlena alone.

Marlena gave him an anxious look. "I will not go to Holyhead. Just leave me, I beg you. I will not even ask you for money."

He shook his head. "I'll not leave you." He leaned closer to her. "But I have no intention of going to Holyhead either. Let them think that is where we are bound."

Warmth spread through her, and she did not think it was from the porridge. She wanted to throw her arms around him in gratitude. Instead she composed her emotions. "Mrs Davies told me Cemaes is five miles from here in the opposite direction from Holyhead."

"Then we shall go to Cemaes." He smiled.

Mrs Davies brought Tanner's coat, waistcoat, boots and Marlena's half-boots. She rose and took her shoes from the woman's hands. They were still damp and the leather tight, but she did not care. Tanner was going to help her to get to Cemaes.

Arlan Rapp sat in front of the fire in the inn at Llanfwrog, sipping hot cider, waiting for his clothes to dry through and through. He puzzled what he should do next.

All he really wanted was to return to London and get paid for his work, but he'd better not do that until he discovered if the Viscountess Corland had been lost with most of the other passengers and crew, or if she had by some miracle survived.

The Vanishing Viscountess had vanished again. That would make a good story for the newspapers, he'd wager, but he'd rather it not be widely known he'd been the one to lose her.

He stared into the fire and pondered the choices he'd made. He refused to feel guilty about taking her place in the last boat. She'd been as good as dead from the moment he first put her in shackles. He would have taken her back to a hangman's noose, nothing less. The Vanishing Viscountess had killed her husband in a jealous rage. Everybody knew her husband rutted with any female he could find. The Viscountess had been caught red-handed. Her cousin had discovered her standing over Viscount Corland's dead body, bloody scissors in hand. There was no doubt that she'd committed the murder.

She had escaped, however. The guilty always ran away if you gave them half a chance.

She'd escaped again, Rapp thought, rubbing his face. He hoped drowning was an easier death than hanging by the neck.

He took another gulp of cider. A log sizzled in the fireplace. He glanced around for the serving girl, who seemed to have disappeared. Rapp's stomach growled, ravenous for breakfast. He was also bone weary from being up all night, pulled out of the sea by local folk and sent to this inn in a wagon with the handful of other survivors.

Rapp bowed his head, thinking of the women and children in his boat. They had not been strong enough to hang on when the wave washed over them.

Rapp suddenly wanted to hurry home to his wife and children. He wanted to kiss his wife, hug his two sons, hold his baby girl. It was only right that he'd seized the chance to survive. His wife and children needed him.

Only eight passengers survived, as far as he knew, and a few more crewmen. The Vanishing Viscountess was not among them. If her body lay at the bottom of the sea, it might never wash up on shore. Rapp cursed the storm. Wexin would not pay him without proof that the Viscountess had perished.

He'd have to investigate, make absolutely certain she was among the dead. He was a Bow Street Runner. It should be a simple matter for him to discover who survived the shipwreck.

The serving girl finally set down a plate with bread and butter and thick pieces of ham.

He nodded his thanks. "Bring me paper, pen and ink," he asked her.

He'd pen a letter to Wexin, reporting the shipwreck, and one to his wife, as well, telling her he loved her, but that he must delay his return to London until he had searched up and down the Anglesey coast.

Chapter Three

By the time Mr Davies's old horse pulled the cart to the front of the cottage, Tanner was more than ready to leave this place. He had no wish to tarry until the son returned.

Tanner pressed a hand to his still-aching ribs, remembering the strength of the man's boot. He had no wish to meet young Davies again.

He stepped aside for Miss Brown to walk out ahead of him. The red cloak the old lady had found for her was threadbare, but Tanner supposed it would keep her warm enough. His lack of a top coat did not worry him overmuch. The temperature was not that harsh and would keep him alert.

Mrs Davies trailed behind him. "You promised us payment, sir."

He turned to her. "I will pay when your husband delivers us where we wish to go." He strode on.

She skipped after him. "How do we know you will pay? Your lady is walking away wearing my clothes. We can't afford to give our possessions away. Times are hard."

He stopped again and the old woman nearly ran into him. "You will have to trust my word as a gentleman, will you not?" He walked over to where Miss Brown waited next to the cart.

He did not know how much of her story to believe, but he'd be damned if he'd turn her over to a magistrate. No matter what she had done, she'd paid for it by what that deuced Bow Street Runner made her endure, leaving her to die while he saved himself. As far as Tanner was concerned, that alone should give her freedom.

Saving her life absolved him, in part, for the other deaths that weighed on his conscience. He would see her safe to help repay that debt.

He touched her arm. "I will climb up first, then assist you."

His ribs only hurt mildly as he got up next to the old man. He reached for Miss Brown's hand and pulled her up. As she settled next to him, he wanted to put his arm around her. He wanted to touch her, to keep fresh the memory of their naked embrace. He remembered the feel of her in his arms as he lay between sleep and waking. Her skin, soft and smooth and warm. Her curves, fitting against him as if tailored to him.

"Let us go," he told the farmer.

Mr Davies snapped the ribbons and the old horse started moving.

"You make him pay, husband!" Mrs Davies shouted after them.

The old horse pulled the cart past the vegetable garden, colourful with cabbages and kale. Wheat was already planted for the winter crop and a rook swept down and disappeared into the field of swaying stalks. The cart rolled at a slow speed finally reaching a road, leaving the cottage some distance behind.

At the road, Tanner turned to Mr Davies. "Take us to Cemaes."

The old man's head jerked in surprise. "Cemaes is north. You'll be wanting to go south to the ferry to Holyhead."

"We wish to go north. To Cemaes," Tanner said.

Mr Davies shook his head. "You want to go to Holyhead, I tell you."

Tanner felt a shiver crawl up his back. He'd wager the old man had some mishap planned on the road to the ferry. He held up the sovereign, which glittered in the sunlight. "If you wish to earn this coin, you will take us to Cemaes." He returned the coin to his pocket. "If not, we will walk from here." Tanner began to stand.

The farmer gestured for him to sit. "I'll take you to Cemaes," he grumbled and turned the horse and cart north.

The road, still muddy from the rains, wound past more farmland and other small cottages like the Davies's. Sometimes Tanner could glimpse the sea, looking calm this day, like a slumbering monster that had devoured its fill. The old man kept the frown on his face and did not speak. Miss Brown gripped the seat to steady herself as the cart rumbled along, but she, too, was silent. The cart jostled her against him, from time to time, keeping Tanner physically aware of her.

Her face was obscured by the hood of the cloak, and Tanner missed watching the play of emotions on her face. He'd seen her angry, earnest, frightened and relieved. He would enjoy hearing her laugh, or seeing passion light her face.

He also wished to discover her real name and the names of the people from whom she had supposedly stolen jewels. If she confided in him, he could help her. Even if she was guilty of the theft, he could make her troubles disappear. Money, power and influence overcame justice most of the time. If he repaid the son for the jewels, he'd wager the theft would be totally forgiven.

Tanner could not gaze at her without being obvious, so he

settled for the warmth of the sun on his face, the scent of the fresh sea air and fragrant fields, and the sight of the peaceful countryside. It was not precisely an Arcadian paradise, not with men toiling in the fields and cottages too small for comfort, but it was solid and timeless and vastly preferable to the cold, fickle sea.

As the sun grew higher in the sky, they passed a windmill spinning in the breeze, and a standing stone placed there by Celtic people long erased from history. Tanner guessed the time to be about noon. He dug his fingers into his pocket for his timepiece. It was no longer there.

His head whipped around to the old farmer driving the cart. The old man had gone through his pockets, he'd wager. "I wonder what time it is," he said.

The old man's jaw flexed.

Tanner coughed and winced as the pain in his ribs kicked at him again. Miss Brown looked over at him with concern in her eyes. He returned a reassuring smile, before glancing back to the old farmer.

He ought to deprive the man of the sovereign he'd promised, glad he'd had the presence of mind to hang on to his purse after he'd peeled every piece of wet clothing off his body, making a sopping pile on the cottage floor. Miss Brown had been shivering so violently, Tanner had been desperate to make her warm.

Mr Davies flicked the ribbons and glanced at Tanner nervously, fearful, no doubt, that Tanner would challenge him on the theft of his timepiece.

Tanner glanced back to the road. Let the man keep the watch, he said to himself. As payment for his bed. Tanner would have given the man anything for that warm bed. For *her.* To save her from the killing cold as he had saved her from the killing sea.

* * *

Two slow hours passed and Tanner suspected they could have walked faster than the old horse moved on the muddy road. Finally rooftops and a church bell tower came into view.

"Cemaes," said the old man, lifting his chin towards the town.

Miss Brown leaned forward. What was she thinking? Tanner wondered. What plan was she making for herself?

They came to the first houses, gleaming white, edged with chrysanthemums and marigolds. Up ahead the buildings became thicker and Tanner could see people walking about.

Miss Brown put her hand on Tanner's arm. "May we stop here?" She gave him that earnest look again.

He drank it in for a moment, then turned to the old man. "Mr Davies, you may leave us off here."

The old man's bushy brows shot up. "It is no distance to the inn."

"Good!" Tanner responded in a jovial voice. "Then it shall be only a short walk for us. Stop, if you please."

The farmer shrugged and pulled on the ribbons, halting his horse. Tanner climbed down and reached up for Miss Brown. Putting his hands on her waist, he lifted her down to the road and was reluctant to let go of her. He fished in his pocket for the sovereign and handed it up to Mr Davies, who grabbed it quickly, as if fearing Tanner would change his mind. Without a word of farewell, the man flicked the ribbons again, and the old horse clopped its way into town, to the inn and some refreshment for them both, Tanner suspected.

"You gave him a sovereign." Miss Brown said in a disapproving tone.

Tanner kicked a pebble into the street. "Yes."

She rolled her eyes.

"Too much?"

"I dare say," she responded. "Half that amount would have been generous."

He tilted his head, somewhat chagrined. "Especially since the man also stole my watch and I highly suspect his son was the man you hit over the head."

Her jaw dropped. "Tell me it is not so." Outrage filled her face. "How shabby of them to take such advantage."

This was an odd reaction for a supposed thief, Tanner thought. "Well, it is done…" He glanced around him, at the cobblestones in the street, at the tidy houses. "Why did you wish to be let off here?"

The sun illuminated her features and made her eyes sparkle like sapphires. He felt momentarily deprived of breath.

"I wanted a chance to talk with you." She gazed at him intently. "To prepare."

It took a moment for him to respond. "Prepare for what?"

She frowned in concentration. "I cannot enter that inn saying I am Miss Brown off the shipwrecked packet from Dublin, the prisoner escorted by a Bow Street Runner. I must think of some fiction to tell them."

Tanner nodded. He'd not thought much beyond being rid of Mr Davies and finding an inn with good food and a comfortable bed, but, then, he was not much accustomed to thinking ahead while travelling. The next meal, the next bed and the final destination were all he considered, and half the time they were arranged by his valet or his secretary.

She went on. "And I cannot walk in as the companion of the Marquess of Tannerton."

He felt a bit like a rejected suitor. "Would that be too scandalous?"

"It would be too foolish." Her expression turned patient,

as if speaking to a dull child. "The Marquess of Tannerton is sure to create a great deal of interest, especially if the marquess almost drowned. If I am seen with you, I will become an object of curiosity as well, and that I cannot have. I must slip away without anyone noticing me."

This woman must never look at herself in a mirror, Tanner thought. Surely she could not go anywhere and not be noticed.

"I see." He nodded, trying not to be distracted by his vision of her. "What do you propose?"

Her expression gave the impression of a mind turning like the intricate gears of his stolen watch. The road forked a few paces away and led to a stone bridge over a stream. She gestured for him to walk with her. They strolled to the bridge, where they stood side by side, leaning on the wall, gazing into the stream, swollen and brown from the previous day's storm.

She turned to him. "I—I must be on my way. The sooner I leave Anglesey, the sooner I will be forgotten. I want it thought that I drowned in the shipwreck. If they think me dead, no one will search for me."

Tanner disliked hearing her speak of being "on her way."

"Where will you go?" he asked. "Scotland is a big place."

She searched his face for a moment before turning her gaze away. "It is best for me not to say."

He frowned, unused to anyone refusing an answer to his question. Her mistrust wounded him when she so clearly needed a friend.

She turned back to him, her voice low and desperate. "I need some of your money."

He stared at her.

Nothing would be easier for him than to hand over the entire contents of his purse. He could get more money for himself later, on the mere strength of his name. Even in this remote place someone would extend the Marquess of Tannerton credit, enough to arrange for a post-chaise to carry him back to London. He could return to his townhouse in a matter of days.

He usually solved his difficulties by handing over money and letting someone else take care of it. Ironically, one of the rare times he'd taken it upon himself to solve a problem, three people died.

Perhaps he ought to leave her here in Cemaes.

Suddenly some of the colour drained from her face and her breathing accelerated. "Forgive my foolish request," she whispered. "You have done more than enough for me. I do not need your money."

She spun away from him and started to walk away.

He seized her arm. "Wait."

His conscience could not let her go, even with his purse in her hand. He knew he could help her. His name and influence—and his money as well—could save her from the hangman's noose or transportation or whatever fate might befall her if she was caught again.

"I have another proposal." He spoke in a low voice. "Come to London with me. Let me use my influence to help you. Whoever has caused you this trouble is not likely to have friends as highly connected as my friends, nor as much money as I possess. I am certain I can settle this matter for you. My power and influence are considerable."

She stepped away from him. "No!" She took a deep breath. "No," she said more quietly. "I thank you, but—but—you are mistaken. My trouble is—" She clamped her mouth shut on whatever it was she had been about to say.

He kept his gaze steady. "No matter what your trouble is, I assure you, I can help."

She shook her head. "You cannot know—" Again she

stopped herself from speaking. "It is safer for me to run. No one will look for me, because they will think me dead. They will forget me, and I may start my life anew."

She gazed at him with such intensity Tanner felt the impact resonate deep inside him. He moved towards her. What made her think *he* could forget her? What made her think he could let her be dead to him now when he'd refused to let her die in the sea?

"Surely you cannot travel alone," he tried.

"Of course I can." She glanced away, and he could sense her mind at work again. "I might be a governess travelling to a new place of employment. Who would question that?"

He did not like this idea. Some men would consider an unescorted governess fair game. "Someone would ask who employed you, for one thing. They would ask where you were bound."

"Then I would fashion answers."

She was slipping away. He remembered that horrible moment when he'd woken up on shore and thought she had slipped from his grasp. He did not want to let go of her now any more than he had wanted to then. True, he might easily return to his comforts, the diversions of London, the hunting parties he and Pomroy planned to attend, but how could he be content now if he thought her adrift, alone?

He glanced away, his mind whirling, as he'd fancied hers had done. All he could think to do was delay.

He gripped her arm, holding on to her like he had done in the sea. "I'll give you the money." He made her look into his face. "There is no obligation to pay it back. It is a trifling amount to me, I assure you, but listen to me. I am afraid our taciturn Mr Davies is at the inn this very moment loosening his tongue with a large tankard of ale." He glanced in the direction of the inn. "He will tell everyone we are husband and wife—that is what he and his wife concluded about us and I did not correct their impression. Did you?"

She shook her head. "I did not."

He went on, "Davies will tell them we are from the shipwreck, a husband and wife from the shipwreck. If we act as strangers now, we will increase suspicion about you, not reduce it."

She considered this. "Yes, that would be true."

His spirits rose. He held on to her still. He took a breath. "In this town we must also be husband and wife."

"Husband and wife?" She stared at him, a worry line forming between her brows.

Acting as husband and wife meant sharing a room. Tanner longed to hold her again, longed to again wake with her in his arms, to know he had kept her safe.

He looked into her face, suffused with reluctance, and realised she might not be as thrilled at the prospect of sharing a bed with him as he was with her.

"I will not take advantage of you," he said in as earnest a tone as he could muster, although his body pulsed with desire for her.

She glanced away, and again turned her eyes back to him, eyes as blue as the sky behind her. "Very well. Tonight we are husband and wife."

He heard the unspoken end to her sentence. Tomorrow they would part. Still, his spirits soared. He would have this brief time with her and maybe wherever they were bound on the morrow would reassure him she'd be safe.

He offered her his arm. "Shall we prepare? We must concoct a story for ourselves, must we not? Names. We need to have names, and, to own the truth, I do not think Brown is a good choice."

"Why?" she asked.

"It is the sort of name a gentleman gives to an innkeeper when he does not wish his identity known." He winked.

She gave a light laugh. "Is that so?"

"It is." He smiled. "Select another name."

"Smith?" A corner of her mouth lifted.

He rolled his eyes, playing along with her jest. "You are not good at this, are you?" He put his mind to the task, but the only names he could think of were ones too connected to him. Adam. Vick. Tanner. "I am hopeless as well."

"I have an idea," she said. "How about the name *Lir? Lir* is the god of the sea in Irish mythology."

He peered at her. "You know Irish mythology?"

"I lived in Ireland." She cast her eyes down. "I read about it in a book there."

"How do you spell it? Like Shakespeare's King Lear?" he asked. "Because I know how to spell that Lear. The Irish always use—well—Irish spellings."

She gave him a look that mocked the one he'd given her. "You know Shakespeare?"

He laughed.

Her eyes twinkled. "We can spell it like King Lear."

He smiled back at her, his heart gladdened at her mirth. Their first night together had been full of terror. This one ought to be peaceful and happy. He vowed he would make it so.

"I shall be Adam Lear, then. Adam is my given name." He waited for her to tell him her given name—hoped she would say it, so he might have that small piece of her to keep for himself.

She said nothing.

He took a deep, disappointed breath. "I believe I need an occupation as well."

Marlena enjoyed their short walk to the inn, and their creation of a story to tell about themselves. The Marquess of

Tannerton became Mr Adam Lear, stable manager for Viscount Cavanley, Adrian Pomroy's father, although they agreed it would be best to avoid mentioning Pomroy if at all possible.

Pomroy was another name from Marlena's past, from that one London Season. She had not thought of Pomroy in her four years of exile in Ireland or really even three years before that, not since her Season. She remembered him as a most ram-shackle young man. She and Eliza thought Pomroy was a re-lentless flirt, devoid of even one serious bone in his body. They'd laughed at his antics behind their fans, but neither she nor Eliza mooned over him the way they mooned over his good friend, Tanner. Even though they had been very green girls then, they knew an attachment to Pomroy would be a foolish one.

It was unfortunate that Marlena's judgement of character had not been that astute when it came to Corland, but then, her husband had disguised his true nature. Pomroy had been as clear as glass.

As Marlena walked at Tanner's side, she almost again felt like that carefree girl who'd enjoyed every moment of her Season. Tanner made her laugh again, something she'd not done since Eliza took ill. Marlena feared she was much too glad she would be spending another night with Tanner.

Imagine it, Eliza! she said silently. *I will be married to the Marquess of Tannerton. Very briefly, however. In name only, and a false name at that.*

She remembered then how warm his skin had felt, how firm his hand on her body. Her skin flushed with the memory.

She spied Mr Davies's horse drinking water from a trough at the inn, and the truth of her situation hit her once more. She was the Vanishing Viscountess, trying desperately to vanish once more. She was not the wife of the Marquess of Tannerton nor plain Mrs Lear. She was not even Miss Brown. She was a fugitive, and if Tanner was caught aiding her, he would face the same punishment as she faced, the hangman's noose.

She and Eliza had not known that fact when Marlena had fled to Ireland with her friend and became her children's governess. Once in Ireland, they had read a newspaper that described the penalty for aiding the Vanishing Viscountess, but Eliza had refused to allow Marlena to leave.

Tanner squeezed her hand as they walked in the door of the inn. "How are you faring, Mrs Lear?"

"A bit nervous, Mr Lear," she replied. At the moment, more nervous for him than for her. She stood to earn life from this masquerade. He risked death.

"We shall do very nicely," he said.

She pulled him back, "Tanner," she whispered.

He gave her a warning look. "It is Adam."

She bit her lip. She must not make such a mistake again. "Do not act like the marquess."

He gave her a puzzled look.

"Do not order people about," she explained.

He tilted his head, appearing very boyish. "Do I order people about?"

She nodded.

The innkeeper approached them. "Good day to you! Are you the lady and gentleman from the shipwreck?"

Mr Davies had indeed been talking of them.

"We are," said Tanner, his affability a bit strained. "And we are in need of a room for the night."

"If we may," added Marlena.

"If we may," repeated Tanner.

The innkeeper smiled. "We will make you comfortable, never fear. If you are hungry, we are serving dinner in the taproom. We have some nice pollack frying. You must let it be our gift to you for your ordeal."

Marlena was touched by this kindness.

"We thank you," said Tanner. He laughed. "I confess, a tall tankard of ale would be very welcome."

The innkeeper walked over and clapped him on the shoulder. "Ale it is. For you, m'lady—?"

"Lear." She cleared her throat. "Mrs Lear. I should like a glass of cider, if you have it."

"We do indeed," said the innkeeper.

Soon they were seated, drinks set in front of them. Marlena glimpsed Mr Davies, who gave them a sidelong look before slipping off his chair and walking to the door.

A woman wearing a bright white apron and cap walked over. "I am Mrs Gwynne. Welcome to our inn. My husband said you had arrived. From the shipwreck, are you?"

"We are." Tanner extended his hand. "It is a pleasure to meet you, Mrs. Gwynne."

"You poor lambs." She clasped his hand.

"Have you heard of any other survivors?" Marlena asked.

The woman clasped Marlena's hand next. "Not a one, but if you made it, others may have as well, God willing. Now, what can we do for you? Besides giving you a nice room and some food, that is. What do you need?"

Tanner rubbed his chin, even darker with beard than it had been that morning. Marlena suppressed a sudden urge to touch it.

"All we have is what you see," he told Mrs Gwynne. "Is there a shop where we might purchase necessities?"

She patted his arm. "There certainly is a shop; if you tell me what you want, I will purchase it for you."

"That will not be necessary. I will visit the shop." Tanner glanced at Marlena and back to Mrs Gwynne. "I have thought of something else you might do, however."

"Say what it is, Mr Lear. I'll see it done."

His gaze rested softly on Marlena. "A bath for my wife."

Marlena's mouth parted. There was nothing she could more desire.

Mrs Gwynne smiled again. "I will tell the maids to start heating the water."

She bustled away and soon they were brought a generous and tasty dinner of fish, potatoes and peas. After they ate, Mrs Gwynne showed them to their room, a chamber dominated by a large, comfortable-looking bed. There was also a fire in the fireplace and a nice window looking out at the back of the inn. The best part, however, was the large copper tub half-filled with water.

"There are towels next to the tub, and a cake of soap. The maids are still bringing the water, and one will assist you if you like." Mrs Gwynne folded her arms over her considerable chest.

"Thank you," Marlena rasped, her gaze slipping to Tanner.

"I'll leave you now," the older woman said. "Mr Lear, when you wish to go to the shop, either my husband or I can direct you."

"I will be down very soon," he said.

After the innkeeper's wife left, Marlena walked over to the tub and dipped her fingers into the warm water.

"Am I sounding like a marquess?" Tanner asked.

She smiled at him. "You are doing very well."

He blew out a breath and walked towards her. "That is good. I confess, I am uncertain how not to sound like a marquess, but if I am accomplishing it, I am content." His eyes rested on her. "I should leave, so you can have your bath."

She lifted her hand and touched him lightly on the arm. "Thank you for this, Lord Tannerton."

"Adam," he reminded her, his name sounding like a caress.

"Adam," she whispered.

His eyes darkened and he seemed to breathe more deeply. He glanced away from her. "What ought I to purchase for you?"

She thought the bath more than enough. "A comb, perhaps? A brush? Hairpins?"

He smiled. "I shall pretend I am an old married man who often is sent to the shop for hairpins. Anything else?"

She ought not to ask him for another thing. "Gloves?"

"Gloves." He nodded.

There was a knock on the door and he crossed the room to open it. It was the maid bringing more water.

She poured it into the tub. "I'll bring more." She curtsied and left.

"I will leave now, as well." Tanner opened the door and turned back to her. "Save me the water."

Marlena crossed the room to him. "Forgive me. I did not think. You must have the water first. I will wait."

He reached up and touched her cheek. "You first, Mrs Lear."

By the time she could breathe again, he was gone.

Arlan Rapp trudged down the Llanfwrog road to the blacksmith shop. A huge barrel-chested man, twice the Bow Street Runner's size and weight, hammered an ingot against his anvil. The clang of the hammer only added to the pain throbbing in Rapp's ears. He'd walked from one side of Llanfwrog to the other, but few villagers were even willing to admit to knowing of the shipwreck. He'd recognised plenty of them from when what was left of his boat washed up to shore. The villagers had grabbed crates and barrels. A few had been good enough to aid the survivors. He'd been whisked off to the inn, he and the others who had washed up with him.

He waited to speak until the smithy plunged the piece of metal into water. "Good day to you, smithy," Rapp said.

The man looked up. "Do you require something?"

Rapp smiled, although his fatigue made him feel anything but cordial. "Only a bit of information."

The blacksmith just stared at him.

Rapp cleared his throat. "I am from the packet ship that was wrecked last night."

No understanding showed on the smithy's face, but Rapp doubted anyone in Llanfwrog was ignorant of the previous night's bounty.

He went on. "I am searching for survivors, specifically a woman who had been my companion."

"I know nothing of it," the man said.

"Perhaps you have heard talk," he persisted. "Perhaps someone told you of survivors. I am most eager to learn her fate."

The blacksmith shook his head. He took another piece of glowing metal from the fire.

"I would pay for information," Rapp added, although he much preferred not to part with his still-damp money.

The smith placed the hot metal on the anvil and picked up his hammer. "Bodies wash ashore sometimes."

That was a grisly thought, but if the Viscountess's body washed up on shore, he could cease his search and go home to his wife.

"Where would bodies be taken?" Rapp asked, but the smithy's hammer started again and its din drowned out his words. He gave up.

No sooner had he walked out of the blacksmith shop than a smudged-face boy tugged on his coat. "I can show you bodies, if you want to see 'em."

Rapp squatted down to eye level with the little eavesdropper. "Can you now?"

The boy nodded energetically. "About ten or so."

Rapp took a breath and stood, squaring his shoulders. "Excellent, my good fellow. Take me there now." A few minutes of unpleasantness might mean he could be in London within a few days and still receive his reward.

"It'll cost you tuppence," the boy said.

Smart little cur, Rapp thought sourly. He fished the coin from his pocket and showed it to the boy. "Take me to the bodies and a tuppence you shall have."

Chapter Four

Tanner's shopping expedition proved to be a novel experience. He'd never shopped for ladies' hairpins before, nor any of his own necessities, for that matter. He typically sent his valet to procure things like razors and shaving brushes and polish for shoes and combs and toothbrushes. He dawdled in the shop for as long as he could to give Miss Brown time for her bath. The shopkeepers and two other customers were full of questions about the shipwreck, unknown to this village before Davies brought news of it. He practised being Mr Lear, although he could answer few questions about how much salvage had washed ashore.

When he left the shop and stopped for another tankard of ale in the taproom, the patrons there had more questions. The extra alcohol made him mellow and, while he talked, a part of his mind wandered to how Miss Brown might appear in the bath, how slick her skin would be, how scented with soap.

Because he had little information about the shipwreck, interest in him waned quickly. He drank more ale in solitude, if not peace. There was nothing peaceful about imagining Miss Brown in the bath. When he eventually carried the packages up the flight of stairs to the room he would share with her, his eagerness to see her made it difficult for him to keep from taking the steps two at a time. He walked down the hall to the door and, balancing the packages in one arm, knocked.

"Come in," she said.

He paused, took a breath, and opened the door.

She was dressed and seated in a chair by the fireplace, pressing a white towel to her long mahogany brown hair. He inhaled the scent of soap and wanted nothing more than to embrace her, soft and warm and clean.

"You are back," she said in a breathless voice.

He felt equally as robbed of air. "I tried to give you ample time."

She twisted the towel around her hair. "I fear you have waited too long. The water has gone quite cold."

He smiled at her. "It cannot be as cold as what we've already experienced."

She shuddered. "No, it cannot." Her eyes lifted to his and held him there.

He mentally shook himself loose from her. It was either do that or do something foolish. "The packages," he said, carrying them over to the table in the corner. He unwrapped one and brought it to her. "I suspect you would like these now." He handed her the brush and comb he had purchased.

They were crafted from simple tortoiseshell. Tanner thought of how many sets of silver brushes and combs he'd had his former secretary, Flynn, purchase for his mistresses. There was nothing so fine in the Cemaes shop, but Miss Brown's eyes glowed with excitement when she took the items from his hands.

"Oh, how wonderful," she cried. "I can comb out the tangles and brush my hair dry."

No gift he ever gave a mistress had been so gratefully

received. He grinned, pleased he had pleased her. She was too busy working the comb through her hair to see.

Tanner strolled over to the tub and felt the water, now on the very cold side of tepid. At home, his valet would be hovering with pots of hot water to add, making certain his bath remained warm from start to finish.

She rose from her chair, still holding the comb. "I could ask Mrs Gwynne for more hot water."

They faced each other over the tub and it took Tanner a moment to remember to speak. "You cannot go out with your hair wet."

"I shall put it in a quick plait," she assured him. "I will need to go out anyway so that you can bathe."

He could not help gazing at her. It took time for him to compose another thought, that thought being he did not wish her to leave. "Will not the Gwynnes think it odd that Mrs Lear walks to the public rooms with wet hair?" He reached over and fingered a lock, marvelling at how it already shaped itself in a curl. "They would not expect you to leave your husband merely because he bathes."

She held his gaze, and he fancied her mind working again, mulling over this latest puzzle.

"I believe you are correct." Her eyes were large and round. "I shall position my chair so that my back is to you, and I will comb my hair with the lovely comb you have purchased for me."

With resolution, she marched back to her chair and set it to face the fireplace. Tanner watched her pull the comb through her hair, wishing it was his fingers doing the task.

He shrugged out of his coat and waistcoat and laid them on the bed. Sitting next to them, he removed his boots and stockings. As he pulled his shirt from his trousers, he watched Miss Brown totally absorbed in combing her hair.

He laughed.

Her comb stilled. "What amuses you?"

He had not realised he'd laughed aloud. "Oh, I was merely thinking that when I'm in the company of a woman, undressing is usually a quite different prospect."

She paused for a moment and then began combing again. "Have you been in the company of so many women, Tanner?"

He faced her, naked and aroused and wishing she would turn and see the evidence of his desire for her. He wished she would come to him and let him make love to her right at this moment, to the devil with bathing.

Such thoughts were dangerous. He'd promised her he would not touch her. "I have known enough women, I suppose," he mumbled instead, padding over to the tub, cringing as he tested the water again.

Again she hesitated before speaking. "I suppose you have lots of mistresses."

He frowned at her assumption of him. "I assure you I am quite a success." His attempt at a joke fell flat to his ears. Truth was, he tended to be involved with only one woman at a time, and none but the briefest of encounters in this last year. At the moment he was wondering what the appeal had been in any of them.

She cleared her throat. "Are there towels folded nearby? And the soap?"

He walked around the tub to see them. "I've found them."

Bracing himself, he put one leg in the water, which was as cold as he expected. He forced himself to put the other leg in and began lowering the rest of him, making the water splash loudly in the room.

"Ye gods!" He shot up again when the water hit the part of him most sensitive to temperature. "Ah!" he cried again as he lowered himself a second time, but now it was because his ribs hurt from jumping up so fast.

"It is too cold," Miss Brown said. "I knew I ought to have sought hot water."

"It is tolerable," he managed through the pain and the chill.

He picked up the soap and lathered himself as quickly as he could, grateful for having had the foresight to do a fairly decent job of washing his hair that morning. In his rush, the soap slipped out of his hand and fell into the water. He fished around for it, making a lot of noise doing so. When he finally caught it and lifted it out of the water, it slipped from his hand again, this time clattering to the floor and sliding too far away to reach.

"Deuce," he muttered.

"You've dropped the soap?" she asked from her seat facing the fireplace.

"Yes." This was a damned odd conversation to have when naked with a woman. "It is of no consequence. I believe I am clean enough."

She stood. "I will fetch it for you."

"It is not necessary, I assure you." he told her.

"I do not mind."

Before he could stop her, she turned to face him. Their gazes caught, but she lowered her lashes and searched for the soap, picking it up and bringing it to him. He quickly glanced down to see how much of himself he was revealing at this moment. The water was too cloudy to see anything.

"There you are." She placed the bar of soap in his hand as calmly as if she'd been handing him his hat and gloves. After wiping her hand on a nearby towel, she returned to her chair and resumed combing her hair.

Tanner guessed he was as claret-faced as she'd been un-flappable. "You are not missish, are you, Miss Brown?"

"Mrs Lear," she corrected. "And you are correct. I am too old to be missish."

"Old," he repeated. "How old are you exactly?"

She chose another lock of hair to work the comb through. "Now that is a question no woman wishes to answer."

He shot back. "As old as all that, then?"

She turned her head to him and smiled. "I am twenty-five."

"Good God," he cried in an exaggerated voice. "You are in your dotage!"

She laughed. "And you, sir, are teasing."

He liked the sound of her laughter. He also liked that she was not prone to blushes and foolishness like that. He never could abide the young misses who flocked to London during the Season, looking for husbands when they'd barely been let off leading strings. Miss Brown was ever so much more interesting.

He turned back to his bathing, frowning at what it might mean that she was not missish. What was her experience of men, then?

He realised he was merely sitting in the water, which was turning him into gooseflesh.

"I warn you, I am about to rise from this bath and stand up in all my glory." He started to rise, but stopped. "You may wish to look, seeing as you are not missish."

He tried to make it sound like a jest, although he wanted her to look at him with a desire matching his own of her.

Because of the cold water, however, a part of him was not showing to its greatest advantage. In fact, it had no glory at all.

"I'll look away," She kept her back to him while he dried himself and donned his shirt and trousers.

"It feels glorious to be clean, does it not?" she said.

"Indeed," he agreed, pressing his hand to his ribs. "But I would be happier if I had a clean shirt." He picked up one of the packages and walked over to the bureau upon which sat a mirror, a pitcher and a bowl.

She switched to the hairbrush and turned around again. "It must be wretched wearing the same shirt."

He smiled at her. "It is not that bad. It merely smells like the devil." He rubbed his chin. "I suppose I shall have to shave myself. Now that is a wretched prospect."

He unwrapped the package and took out a shaving cup, brush and razor. She picked up the soap and brought it to him, her long dark hair falling about her shoulders in soft waves. He wanted to touch it again. In fact, he wanted to grab a fistful of it.

Their gazes caught for a second when she handed him the soap. She lowered her eyes and walked back to her chair.

He took a deep breath and started to lather his face. "It is a fortunate thing my valet developed a toothache on the day we were to leave for Dublin."

"I meant to ask you if anyone accompanied you," she said in a sober voice.

"No one." Thank God, because he did not wish to have more lives on his conscience. Chin and cheeks lathered, he turned away from the mirror to look at her.

"I am glad of it," she murmured.

"I am as well," he responded.

He turned back to the mirror and scraped at his beard. "Pomroy and I once went two weeks without shaving." He made another stroke with the razor. "We went to one of my hunting lodges, but it rained like the devil. There was nothing to do so we drank great quantities of brandy and grew beards."

She giggled. "I wonder you had the energy for it."

"We wagered to see who could grow the longest beard in two weeks." He smiled. "I won it."

"Who was charged with measuring?"

"Our poor valets." He laughed. "We made them switch."

He twirled his finger for emphasis. "Pomroy's valet measured my beard and my valet measured Pomroy's. It made the two men very nervous."

He scraped at his cheek some more until his face was nearly clean of soap, except for tiny lines here and there. He rinsed off with the clean water and dried his face.

He presented himself to her. "How did I do?"

To his surprise, she reached up to stroke his face. "You did well," she murmured.

The part of him that had retreated during his bath retreated no more. He leaned closer to her, so close he saw the lines of light and dark blue in her eyes. Her hand stilled, but her fingers still touched his cheek.

He wanted to breathe her name into the decreasing space between them, if only he knew it.

There was a loud knock on the door.

"Deuce," he murmured instead.

He walked to the door. "Who is it?"

"It is Mrs Gwynne, lamb. If you are finished with your bathing, we've come to fetch the tub."

He glanced over to Miss Brown. She nodded.

"You may fetch the tub." He opened the door.

Removing the bath was almost as laborious as filling it had been. The maids had to make several trips. The towels were gathered up for laundering and, when all this was accomplished, Mr Gwynne appeared to carry the copper tub out of the room. Mrs Gwynne remained the whole time, chatting in her friendly way, pleased, Tanner suspected, that she had made her guests so happy.

"Now," the innkeeper's wife went on. "If you would care to come to the taproom, we have a nice supper. We also could give you a private parlour for dining. Or, if you prefer, we'll bring the food to you here."

"It shall be as my wife desires." Hc turned to Miss Brown.

As his wife desires, Marlena repeated to herself, her heart pounding at the way his voice dipped low when he spoke the word *wife*. He spoke the word softly, intimately, as if he had indeed kissed her as he had been about to do. Her whole body tingled with excitement.

"I should like to stay here," Marlena responded.

She did not want to break this spell, this camaraderie between them, this atmosphere that had almost led to a kiss.

"We are commanded, Mrs Gwynne." Tanner smiled at the woman.

Marlena enjoyed Tanner's teasing manner. She and Eliza had not known of his good humour all those years ago, something that would undoubtedly have given them more to sigh over. Now his light-heartedness made her forget she was running for her life.

Mrs Gwynne said, "We shall be back directly."

After she left, Marlena asked, "Did you truly agree, Tanner? With having supper here in the room?"

He walked back to her, and lowered himself in the chair adjacent to the one she had been sitting in. He winced as he stretched out his long legs. "I wanted to do what you wanted."

She did not miss that his sides still pained him.

"It is just that my hair is not yet dry," she rattled on. "And I do not wish to put it up yet." And also that she liked being alone with him in this temporary haven.

"You do not have to convince me. Your desire of it is sufficient." His eyes rested softly upon her.

Her desires had never been sufficient for her husband to do what she asked. Early in her marriage she'd learned that Corland's desires took precedence and that she must do what he wanted or he would be in a foul mood. Later in their three-year marriage, she had not cared enough to attempt to please him.

It occurred to her that she had been on the run for as long as she had been married. In a way, Corland still directed her life. It was a mystery to her why Wexin had killed Corland, but because of it, she was on the run.

Marlena fiddled with the brush in her hands, disliking the intrusion of Corland and Wexin in her time with Tanner.

How would it have felt if Tanner had, indeed, kissed her?

It had been so long since a man had kissed her. Corland's ardour for her, mild at best, had cooled after the first year of their marriage, after her money had dwindled and his debts increased. After she discovered his many peccadilloes. Actresses, ballet dancers, their housemaid.

Her last sight of her husband flashed into her mind, lying face up on the bed, eyes gaping sightlessly, naked body covered in blood.

She shuddered and glanced at Tanner, so gloriously alive, so masculine even as he slouched in his chair.

His expression had sobered. "What is it?"

She blinked. "I do not understand what you mean."

He gestured towards her. "You were thinking of something. Something disturbing, I'd wager."

She averted her gaze. "Nothing, I assure you."

When she glanced back at him, he frowned, and the peaceful, intimate feelings she'd had a moment before fled.

All she need do was think of Corland and clouds thickened.

There had been a time when she blamed all her woes on her husband. He was to blame for many things—his gambling, his debts, his affairs—but he would never have done to her what her own cousin had done. Who could have guessed Wexin was capable of such treachery?

Was Wexin still among Tanner's friends? she wondered. If she had so difficult a time believing what her cousin had done, surely Tanner would not believe it.

"Do not be angry with me, Tanner," she murmured.

His brows rose in surprise. "I am not angry." He gave her a very intent look. "I merely wish you would tell me what cloud came over you. Tell me your secrets. Trust me. I know I will be able to fix whatever is wrong."

She shook her head.

"Then at least tell me your name," he persisted, putting that teasing tone back into his voice, but still looking at her with serious eyes. "Tell me your given name. I gave you mine. Adam. When we are private together, let me address you with one name that belongs to you."

She stared back at him.

Would he know the Vanishing Viscountess by her given name? Would her name be enough to identify her as Wexin's cousin, Corland's widow, the young girl who'd had such a *tendre* for him at age eighteen that she blushed whenever he walked past her?

Marlena had been named for a distant French relative who'd died on the guillotine in the year of her birth. She had been Miss Parronley to everyone, save childhood friends and family and Eliza. And Wexin, of course. Even the newspapers after Corland's death and her flight had never printed her given name. She could not think of a single instance when Tanner would have heard of the name Marlena and, if he had, would never associate it with the Vanishing Viscountess. She opened her mouth to speak.

Tanner stood, blowing out a frustrated breath. "Never mind." He ambled over to the window. "Forgive me for pressing you."

The moment to tell him had passed. Her body relaxed, but she grieved the loss of the easy banter between them.

"I asked Mr Gwynne about coaches," he said, still looking out of the window. "I told him we were travelling north." He turned to her.

"Yes, I wish to travel north," she said.

"To Scotland, correct?"

She nodded.

"Well, Mr Gwynne's recommendation was to take a packet to Liverpool." He looked at her intently. "Where in Scotland?"

She bit her lip.

He made a frustrated sound and turned away.

"Edinburgh," she said quickly. "I wish to go to Edinburgh."

He turned back, lifting a brow. "Is Edinburgh your home?"

She hesitated again.

He waved a dismissive hand. "I ought to have known not to ask."

She turned away, her muscles tensing. "A ship."

"Could you bear it?" His voice turned soft.

She faced him again and saw sympathy in his eyes. "If I must."

"It sails in the morning."

"I will be ready." She would get on the packet, in any event, no matter if her courage accompanied her or not. She stood, but was hesitant to approach him. "What will you do?"

His brows rose. "Why, accompany you, of course. It would look odd otherwise."

She released her breath. The ship would be a little less terrifying with Tanner at her side.

Liverpool would certainly be big enough a town for her to pass through unnoticed. From there she could catch a coach, perhaps to Glasgow first, then on to Edinburgh.

So close to Parronley. Her estate. Her people. One place for which she yearned, but dared not go.

She was Baroness Parronley, a baroness in her own right.

The Parronley barony was one of the few that included daughters in the line of succession, but Marlena would have preferred not to inherit. It meant losing her dear brother Niall and his two little sons. Her brother and nephews perished of typhoid fever. So unexpected. So tragic.

Marlena had been with Eliza in Ireland when they read the account in a London newspaper that Eliza's husband had had sent to him. Marlena could not even mourn them, her closest family. She could not wear black for them, could not lay flowers on their graves.

With the shipwreck she would eventually be pronounced dead, the end of a baroness who had never had the chance to claim her title, the end of the Parronleys. Wexin would inherit. Her people, the people of Parronley, would be in the hands of a murderer.

Another knock on the door sounded, and Mrs Gwynne herself brought in their supper on a big tray. Two steaming meat pies, a pot of tea, and a tall tankard of ale.

Tanner took the tray from the woman's hands and set it on the table. "Ah, thank you, Mrs Gwynne. You even remembered ale."

She beamed and rubbed her hands on her apron. "After all these years, I ought to know what a man wants."

He smiled at her. "You knew what this man wants." He lifted the tankard to his lips and took a long swallow.

After the woman left, Marlena picked at her food. The camaraderie she'd shared with Tanner had disappeared. They ate in silence.

As she watched him finish the last of the crumbs of the meat pie's crust, she blurted out, "You do not have to travel to Liverpool with me, if you do not wish it."

He looked up at her with a mild expression. "I do not mind the trip."

She sipped her cup of tea. "If it were not for me, you would probably be headed for London tomorrow."

"Probably," he responded.

She regarded him. "I do not even know if there is someone in London awaiting your return."

His eyes clouded. "The usual people, I suppose."

She flushed, embarrassed that she had not considered what his life might be like now. He had been the marquess of her memory, dashing and carefree and unmarried. "Forgive me, but I do not know if you are married. If you are—"

"I am not married," he replied, his voice catching as he pressed his hand to his side. "A delay in my return should not inconvenience anyone overmuch. My affairs are well managed and rarely require my attention."

She felt a disquieting sense of sadness from him. Still, that once innocent, hopeful débutante brightened.

He was not married.

Their meal struggled on with even fewer words spoken until Mrs Gwynne again knocked. Tanner rose stiffly.

"I've come for your dishes, lamb," she said as he opened the door. "But first I have something for you." She placed folded white garments into his hands. "Nightclothes for you."

"Thank you," Marlena exclaimed, surprised again at the woman's kindness. She placed their dishes on the tray.

"That is good of you, Mrs Gwynne." Tanner took the garments and placed them on the bed. "Might we purchase them from you?"

The woman waved a hand at him. "Oh, I hate to ask you for money after all you have been through."

"I insist," he said.

Mrs Gwynne gave him a motherly pat on the cheek. "Then we will settle up tomorrow, Mr Lear. Is there anything else you might require?"

"I can think of nothing." He turned to Marlena.

She shook her head and handed Mrs Gwynne the tray full of dishes. She walked over to open the door for the woman.

Marlena stopped her before she crossed the threshold. "Wait." She glanced over to Tanner. "Would it be possible for someone to launder my—my husband's shirt? He would so like it to be clean."

Mrs. Gwynne brightened. "It would indeed be possible. I'll see to it myself and dry it in front of the fire." She stepped over to Tanner again. "Give it over, lamb."

Tanner glanced at Marlena before pulling the shirt over his head and draping it over Mrs Gwynne's arm. "Thank you again."

The innkeeper's wife smiled and bustled out of the room.

Tanner turned to Marlena. "That was thoughtful of you."

His skin glowed gold in the light from the oil lamp and the fireplace, but he was no less magnificent than he'd appeared that morning or as he bathed. Just as one is tempted to touch a statue, Marlena was tempted to run her fingers down his chest, to feel his sculpted muscles for herself.

She resisted. "No more thoughtful than you asking for my bath. I would say we are even now, except for the matter of you saving my life."

His mouth curved into a half-smile. "We are even on that score, as well. Do you not recall hitting Mr Davies-the-Younger over the head?"

"I am appalled at that family, the lot of them." She shook her head.

He smiled. "You'll get no argument from me on that score."

He picked up one of the garments Mrs Gwynne had brought them and put it on, covering his spectacular chest. "I'll walk down with you to the necessary, before we go to bed."

Go to bed repeated itself in her mind.

The sky was dark when they stepped outside to the area behind the inn where the necessary was located. Marlena was glad Tanner was with her. The darkness disquieted her, as if it harboured danger in its shadows.

When they returned to the room, he said, "Spare me a blanket and pillow and I will sleep on the floor."

"No, you will not," she retorted, her voice firm. There was no way she would allow the man who had rescued her to suffer through such discomfort. "Not with those sore ribs of yours. You must sleep in the bed."

He seized her arm and made her look at him. "I'll not allow you to sleep on the floor."

Her heart pounded as she looked directly into his eyes. "Then we must share the bed."

Chapter Five

M arlena's heart pounded as Tanner stared at her. He said nothing.

She must have made a terrible mistake, must have mistaken the meaning of his almost-kiss. Surely he would give her some sign of wanting to make love to her after her brazen invitation. Not this silence.

She felt the rebuff as keenly as she'd once felt those of her husband. Corland, however, had voiced his disgust at her wantonness. She'd believed him, too, thinking herself some unnatural sort of wife to desire the lovemaking, until she discovered that Corland had no such disgust of other women bedding him.

Tanner's reaction confused her all the more.

Perhaps she was not a temptation to any man. She'd not really had the opportunity to find out while playing governess to Eliza's children.

"I—I ought to speak more plainly," she prevaricated. "I meant we ought to share the bed, which is big enough. I was not suggesting more."

He swung away from her, so she could not tell how this idea—outrageous all on its own—had struck him.

He finally turned back to her. "You wish only to share the bed."

She nodded, wishing she had merely insisted upon sleeping on the floor and been done with it.

"I will turn my back while you undress, then." He faced the chest where the water and bowl were.

Marlena undressed as quickly as she could, although her fingers fumbled with the laces of her corset. She slipped the nightdress over her head and noticed the comforting smell of lavender lingering in the fabric. She laid her clothing over one of the chairs so that it would not wrinkle.

She crawled beneath the covers. "I am done."

He'd been so still as she undressed, adding to her discomfort, but he moved now, removing his boots and the coat he'd donned over his nightshirt when they'd gone below stairs. She peeked through her lashes at him, watching him unfasten the fall of his trousers and step out of them, the nightshirt preserving his modesty.

He walked towards the bed and climbed in beside her. The bed shifted with his weight. When he faced away from her, she wished it could have been as it had been that morning, his arms around her, bare skin touching bare skin. She was certain she would never sleep a wink the whole night, but soon after his breathing became even and rhythmic, she drifted off.

The dream came. She'd not had the dream in ever so long, but now, with all the fear and danger, she dreamt it like it was happening all over again.

She'd been restless, unable to sleep that terrible night. Corland and Wexin made plenty of noise when they returned from their night of debauchery. Wexin often slept off the effects of their entertainment in one of the bedchambers, so it did not surprise her that he stayed the night.

When she finally dozed, a woman's cry woke her. Earlier in the day the housekeeper had warned her that her husband had his eye on Fia Small, the new maid, a girl Marlena had hired mostly because she came from near Parronley and was so very young and desperate for employment. A light shone from beneath the door connecting her husband's bedchamber to hers.

Again in her dream, Marlena rose from her bed and walked to the door. She turned the key and opened it.

A man who looked as if he were dressed in women's clothes grappled with someone, something in his hand, trying to strike with it. Marlena ran and grabbed his arm. The weapon was a large pair of scissors and the person with whom he struggled was the new maid. He swung around to Marlena, slashing the weapon towards her.

"No!" the girl cried, trying to pull him off Marlena.

He flung the girl away.

Marlena fought him, both her hands grasping his arm, holding off the lethal scissors. She finally saw the man's face.

In her dream the face loomed very large and menacing.

It was Wexin. *Her cousin.*

"Wexin, my God," she cried. The dream turned him into the image of a demon. He drove her towards the bed and she fell against it, losing her grip on his arm. He brought the scissors down, but Marlena twisted away.

She collided with her husband, her face almost ramming into his. Corland's eyes were open and lifeless, blood spattered his face, pooling at the wound in his neck.

Before she could scream, Wexin called out, "Help! Someone, help!" He tore off the woman's robe and threw it at Marlena. He thrust the scissors into her hand.

Footsteps sounded in the hallway.

Wexin swung around to the maid. "I'll see you dead, girl,

if you speak a word of this. There will be nowhere you can hide. Your lady here has killed her husband. Do you understand?"

Marlena threw aside the robe—her robe, she realised. The scissors in her hand was sticky with blood. Her nightdress was stained with it. Wexin pulled off his gloves and stuffed them in a pocket. He was clean while she was bloody.

The maid glanced from Marlena to Wexin and back again. With a cry, she ran, scampering through the hidden door that led from Corland's room to the servants' staircase.

Wexin laughed at the girl's escape. "There goes your witness, cousin," he sneered. "You have killed Corland and there is no one to say you have not."

Marlena jolted awake, her heart pounding.

The nightmare had not ended, however. A man leaned over the bed and slammed his hand over her mouth.

Tanner woke with a start.

A man, no more than a black figure, had his hands on Miss Brown. Tanner grabbed for the man's coat, knocking him off balance.

The man released Miss Brown and pulled out of Tanner's grip. Tanner sprang from the bed and lunged at him before he could reach her again. They both fell to the floor, rolling and grappling, until slamming against the mantel, the coals on the hearth hot on Tanner's back. They illuminated the man's face.

Davies, the son come back to finish what he'd started on the beach.

"No!" Miss Brown ran towards them, pulling the back of Davies's collar.

"Stay back!" Tanner yelled, although he was perilously close to having his nightshirt catch fire.

Davies released him and scrambled to his feet. Miss Brown backed away from him, but he came at her, clamping one big beefy hand around her neck. Tanner stood and advanced on him.

"Keep away or I'll kill her," Davies warned, squeezing her throat for emphasis, and dragging her towards the door.

"Leave her," Tanner commanded. "The purse you want is in the bed."

The man glanced to the bed, but shook his head, squeezing Miss Brown's neck tighter. "She'll be worth more, I'll wager." The man swallowed. "I saw your ring. Only a rich man wears a ring with pictures on it. You'll pay me more than what's in that purse for her."

Tanner suddenly felt the weight of the signet ring on his finger, the ring that was so much a part of him. He'd tried to disguise it, but Davis had obviously seen it for what it was.

"I'll have you arrested and hanged," Tanner growled.

"I'll kill her first," the man replied.

A choking sound came from Miss Brown's lips. Tanner had no doubt Davies would make good his threat.

"I'll not pay for her if she is dead," Tanner said, playing for time.

Tanner kept his distance as Davies neared the door. He could barely see in the darkness, but he knew one thing. He would never let that man take her out of the inn.

The intruder reached the door, and Tanner could hear him fumbling with the key to unlock it. "Do not raise a din," Davies warned, "or I'll snap her neck and run for it."

He lifted the latch and swung the door open. At that same moment, Miss Brown brought her heel down hard on his foot.

Smart girl!

Davies cried out in pain and she twisted away from him.

Tanner came at him, landing his fist square on Davies's jaw and spinning him around into the hall towards the stairway. The man's hand groped for the banister, but slipped, and he tumbled down the stairs.

Tanner rushed after him. By the time he reached the stairs, Davies was back on his feet and out of the building. Heedless of his bare feet, Tanner ran down the stairway and into the inn's yard, the nightshirt tangling between his legs and hampering his progress. Davies disappeared into the darkness.

"Hell," he yelled, stamping his foot and lodging a stone painfully between his toes.

Breathing hard, Tanner limped back to the inn where Miss Brown stood framed in the doorway.

He hurried to her, touching his hand to her neck. "Did he hurt you?"

She placed her palms on his ribs. "No, but what of you? Has he injured you more?"

He had forgotten that his ribs still pained him. He put his hand over hers and pressed his side. "Nothing of consequence."

He wrapped his arms around her, holding her close with only the thin fabric of their nightclothes between them.

A commotion sounded behind them. The innkeeper and his wife appeared, along with several curious lodgers.

"What is this?" asked Mr Gwynne, in his nightshirt, robe, and cap.

Tanner reluctantly released Miss Brown. "A man broke into our room and tried to rob us."

"Oh, dear!" Mrs Gwynne's hand went to her mouth. "Who would do such a thing? And you with so little. Did he take anything of value?"

Tanner put his arm around his pretend wife. "My purse almost, but we stopped him." He glanced towards the yard. "He ran off."

"Shall I alert the magistrate?" the innkeeper asked.

"No!" cried Miss Brown.

Tanner tightened his arm around her to let her know he understood she would not wish to speak to a magistrate. "It is no use. The man is gone, and it was dark. I'd not know him in the light."

"You poor lambs!" Mrs Gwynne ushered them inside and closed the door. "What can we do for you?"

"We need only to return to sleep. I am certain he will not come back." Tanner blew out a breath and reconsidered her offer. "I might appreciate a glass of port, come to think of it."

"I'll fetch you a whole bottle," said Mr Gwynne.

The other lodgers crowded around them with questions, sympathy and speculation. Tanner suppressed his natural inclination to merely order them away. He was not precisely sure how Mr Lear the stable manager might act in such a situation, so he merely answered what he could and thanked them for their concern.

Acting as a husband came easier. Tanner kept a protective arm around Miss Brown and walked her through the entrance hall to the staircase. He only released her when Mr Gwynne handed him a bottle of port and two glasses. She hurried up the stairs and Tanner followed.

When they reached their room, the door was ajar and a breeze blew through from the open window, undoubtedly how Davies had gained entry.

As soon as Tanner closed the door behind them, he faced her. "Are you certain he did not hurt you?"

She gazed up at him. "Very certain."

He wanted to touch her, to examine her all over, to reassure himself she was unharmed, but his hands were full and he was fairly certain his touch would not be welcome.

For a fleeting moment earlier that night he'd believed

she'd invited him to do more than share the bed. Thank God he had not acted on that belief. A second later he realised he'd presumed too much.

"Would you like some port?" He placed the glasses on the table and pulled out the bottle's cork. "I am in great need of it."

"Yes." She put her hand over his, and his desire for her flared anew. "But I will pour for you."

She took the bottle, and Tanner paced. The encounter with Davies had set his blood to boiling and he had not yet calmed down. He still burned to pummel his fists into the bastard's fleshy face and beat it to a pulp.

All that unspent energy was in grave danger of being misdirected. Not in violence, but in passion. He surged with desire for this woman who again had been in danger. Tanner felt the need to have her. Now.

He shuddered. He must force himself to remain civilised.

He walked over to the window, closing it and taking a taper from the fireplace to light the lamp on the table. Anything to keep his hands off her.

"The money!" he cried, nearly dropping the taper.

She looked up, holding a glass in midair.

Tanner rushed over to the bed and groped under the pillow. The door of the room had been open for several minutes. Anyone might have walked in. He exhaled in relief as he pulled out the purse.

Her arm relaxed. "Thank goodness." She held out the glass to him. "Was it the money he was after—or—or me?"

He returned the purse to its place under the pillow and took the drink from her. "I would not have let him take you," he murmured, brushing a lock of hair off her forehead.

She looked up into his eyes, and he felt the surge of passion return.

She poured port into the other glass. "Do you think Davies knows who I am?"

Tanner took a sip, the sweet, woody wine warming his throat, but not cooling his ardour. "*I* do not know who you are."

She averted her face. "I mean, he still seemed to think me your wife, did he not?"

"My wife," he murmured.

He took a gulp of the port. The light of the fireplace behind her revealed the outline of her body beneath the thin white fabric of her nightdress. A vision of her naked filled his mind, full high breasts, narrow waist, flat stomach, long silken legs.

Lust surged through him. Curse him, she'd already made it clear that sharing a bed meant only sharing a bed.

He glanced away from her, but looked back again to see her lips touching the glass, her pink tongue darting out to lick off a stray droplet of port. He downed the contents of his own glass and walked over to the table to pour another one.

With his back to her, it was easier to speak. "Davies saw my ring when we were at the farmhouse, evidently. I doubt he could identify the crest, although someone more knowledgeable might do so. I've since turned it around on my finger."

"So he thought me your wife?" she asked again.

"I believe he did." It fitted with what Davies had said about wanting Tanner to pay for her.

She finished her port. "What time does the packet ship sail?"

He turned around to answer her, but a sharp pain pierced his ribs. He leaned on the table until the worst of it had passed. "Mid-morning," he answered in a tight voice. "And another one later in the day. Mr Gwynne said we should be at the docks by ten o'clock for the morning departure."

She put down her glass, and crossed over to him. "You are hurt." She gently touched his ribs. "Is it where he kicked you? You must go back to bed."

She put his arm over her shoulder to help him over to the bed. Instead, he turned and wrapped his arms around her, taking pleasure in merely holding her.

"Let us both go back to bed."

She looked up at him, a question in her eyes.

He garnered more strength than he'd used to battle Davies. "To sleep?"

She stared at him. "To sleep."

She doused the lamp, and helped him to the bed, sweeping the covers back and waiting for him to climb in. She moved to the other side and climbed in next to him, covering them both with the blankets.

This time, rather than turn away, Tanner faced her. He put his arm around her and drew her close. The pain protected him from doing more and finally exhaustion brought him sleep.

Lew Davies stumbled into the cottage as dawn peeked over the horizon. He did not trouble himself to be quiet, still too angry at this latest failure. The other wreckers had found all sorts of treasure. Crates of cargo and bits of jewellery, coin, clothing from the dead. Why did he have to find a fellow who was alive? The only thing his family had to show for the best shipwreck in years was a bloody timepiece with that same picture on it that had been on the man's ring. Davies did not even know where they might sell such a thing.

He shrugged out of his coat and let it fall to the floor. His foot pained him like the very dickens from where the woman had stomped on it, his jaw ached from the man's fist, and his muscles were sore from the tumble down the stairs. He'd been lucky to escape.

He was sick of being foiled by these two fancy people. First on the shore, then on the road to the ferry when his father's cart never showed up for him to ambush, and finally in Cemaes. He flopped down into a chair and pulled off his boots, tossing them into a corner.

He'd been stupid to decide to take the woman instead of the purse. The idea just came to him suddenly when he'd grabbed her. He should have left as soon as the man saw his face. If he was lucky the gentleman wouldn't go to the magistrate about him.

From now on, he'd stick to wrecking and hope for another storm off shore very soon.

The bedchamber door opened and his mother tottered out. "Well, did you nab the purse?"

He rubbed his jaw. "No, they woke up. I was lucky to get away in one piece."

She clucked her tongue. "We need that money."

"I know, Mam." He dragged a hand though his hair.

She crossed the room and picked up his coat, hanging it on the peg on the wall. "Well, I want you to try again, but this time take the woman."

He gaped at her. "Take the woman?"

"You heard me." She stood with her fists on her hips. "A man came asking questions after you'd gone. Looking for the woman, he was." She pumped some water into the kettle and placed it on the fire. "He bought her clothes from me, if you can imagine it. More like rags they were, but I'd not have got a half-crown for 'em elsewhere."

He sat up. "He gave you half a crown for them?"

"Well, yes, he did." She opened the tin box where she kept the chicory and took out a piece of the root.

"Half a crown." Davies still could not believe it.

"That fellow told me she was running from the law and that he is supposed to bring her to London. I'll wager there is a big reward or else this fellow would not pay half a crown for her rags."

"A reward?" Davies's foot started paining him and he lifted it on to his knee to rub it. "What about the gentleman she was with?"

"I told the fellow about the gentleman, but he didn't have anything to say about him." His mother shrugged as she plopped the chicory into a tea pot. "I did not tell we had the man's timepiece."

Davies put his foot back down and sank his head into his hands. He could have earned a big reward if only he had not let go of her.

"So this is what you have to do," his mother went on. "You go back to Cemaes and get the woman. If she's gone, follow her until you find her and bring her back. We will take her to London for the reward."

He looked up at her. "You'll have to give me money."

She checked the kettle, which was starting to hiss. "I'll give you the sovereign the gentleman gave us, but you must find her before that man does."

"Did you tell him they went to Cemaes?"

She glared at him. "I'd not do anything so daft, but I reckon he'll find out before the day is through."

Young Davies reached for his boots. "I'll do it, Mam. I'm going back to Cemaes right now."

His mother waved a dampening hand at him. "First you have some chicory tea and some bread and cheese. I'll not send you out again without something in your stomach."

He leaned back in the chair. "Yes, Mam."

He'd obey his mother, but as soon as he'd eaten, he'd walk back to Cemaes and wait for the perfect time to nab the woman. He did not think he could get in her room again, but he could follow her and the gentleman wherever they went. He didn't care how long or how far it might be.

With a big reward at stake, he'd nab her, all right.

Chapter Six

Marlena gripped the ship's railing as land came into view, a welcome sight indeed. She'd felt the whole trip as if she had been running, rather than merely scanning the sky for storm clouds and the sea for surging waves. Tanner remained next to her the entire time, unwavering and as solid as land beneath her feet.

She supposed it was good to board a ship so soon after another one broke to pieces around them, like remounting a horse after being thrown off its back. When she'd first seen the ship, her fear had tasted like bitter metal in her mouth, but she'd forced one foot in front of the other, gripping Tanner's arm all the way, and she'd made it onboard.

"We should be close to landing," he said, gazing out at the land, still just a line of green and grey on the horizon. For the last hour they had seen more and more sails in the distance, other ships traversing to and from the busy port of Liverpool.

"Yes," she responded. Words had not come easily to her during the voyage, but he did not seem to mind, making comments here and there that demanded no more of her than monosyllables in return.

She felt him flinch and knew another pain had seized him. It was no use for her to beg him to go below and sit; he would not leave her side, and she could not leave the deck where she would at least not be surprised if danger descended upon them again.

He remained beside her while the day waned and the land came closer and closer. The nearer they came to the port, the easier it became to breathe, but, at the same time, Marlena felt like weeping. Setting foot on the solid ground that was Liverpool also meant parting from Tanner and continuing her journey alone.

She glanced at him. The plain felt hat Mr Gwynne had given him looked incongruous with his expertly tailored coat and trousers.

He must be cold, she thought. Why did he not leave her and go below?

He turned his head and caught her watching him. He smiled. "What is it? Do I have a smudge on my nose?"

She looked away. "No." She decided against asking him one more time to leave her and seek somewhere warm. "I was merely thinking that the hats you have in London must be so much finer than this one."

He cocked his head. "Perhaps, but, I tell you, this hat is quite comfortable. I may not give it up."

"The Gwynnes were dear people," she said.

Both Mr and Mrs Gwynne insisted they keep their money and send payment for the room when they reached their destination. "You'll have many expenses," the innkeeper had said. "We can wait for payment." The Gwynnes had also insisted they take the nightclothes with them and a small satchel in which to carry their meagre belongings. And the hat.

Tannerton's eyes, now the colour of the sea, turned soft.

"Never fear. I shall see the Gwynnes are well rewarded for their kindness."

If things had happened differently, she could have done the same. Baroness Parronley ought to have been a wealthy woman. The last she knew, her brother had well managed the family's estate and fortune.

There was no use repining what could never be.

"I wish I could repay them," she murmured.

How would Parronley fare under Wexin? Would he gamble its fortune away as he seemed bent to do when he and Corland went out together night after night? Wexin had never liked Parronley. He used to tease Marlena and her brother Niall that they lived in a savage land.

Who was the savage in the end? Wexin's face flashed before her once more, and Corland's bloody body.

"You've gone off once more."

Tanner's voice startled her. She glanced back at him, feeling as if she'd just awoken from the dream.

One corner of his mouth lifted. "I surmise you will not tell me what you were thinking."

She turned back to stare out at the land, very close now, the mouth of the Mersey River in plain view. "I was thinking of nothing at all."

She felt his position shift and his arm brushed against hers. "I dare say it was not nothing." He paused. "Do not fear. I will not press you." He tilted his head, looking boyish in the floppy hat. "I do wish you would tell me your name. I dislike calling you Miss Brown."

She made herself smile and tried to make the topic into a joke. "You ought to be calling me Mrs Lear, at least for a little while longer."

The expression he gave her was impossible to decipher, something resembling disappointment or, perhaps, wounding.

She turned away from him again. Soon she would part from him and she would not see his face again. She blinked away tears. It was for the best. Perhaps he would never discover he had aided and abetted the Vanishing Viscountess.

A shout went up from the first mate and soon the deck was teeming with crewmen, all busy at their stations as the ship sailed into the mouth of the Mersey River towards the docks. It suddenly seemed as if a multitude of ships dotted the water, like a swarm of insects all flying towards a lamp.

The activity freed her from having to talk with him further as they sailed up the river. Liverpool's buildings came into sight, a town swollen with brick warehouses and a sprawl of lodgings for the people whose lives depended on this busy port.

"Oh, my!" She swivelled around in alarm as a large ship loomed up on the opposite side of the packet, dwarfing their vessel and looking as if it would collide with them.

"Do not fear." Tanner touched her arm. "I am certain these captains have navigated this port many times without mishap."

She found it hard to breathe again, nonetheless. Even so, there was so much to see, so much going on, that time passed more swiftly than it had on the open sea. Soon the packet ship reached its dock and soon after that, they were among the first of the passengers to disembark.

The docks were bustling with activity, even as the daylight waned. Cargo was unloaded and carried into the warehouses. Raucous shouts came from nearby taverns, where seamen tottered from the doorways, swaying on their feet. Marlena was one of but a handful of women on the dock, and it seemed to her that all the men stared at her. Some of them looked like the pirates of storybooks, dark and dangerous and, above all, dirty.

She felt a *frisson* of fear travel up her back at the prospect of facing men such as these without Tanner at her side, but soon they must come to more civilised streets. At least she felt quite anonymous in this motley crowd. If Tanner left her at this moment, no one would notice.

Tanner stopped and looked around. "We need to discover where to go."

Marlena tried to breathe, but not enough air reached her lungs. "Perhaps we should part here. Say goodbye."

He scowled at her. "The devil we should. I should feel as if I am leaving a lamb to be slaughtered."

As if to prove his point, a huge sailor stumbled towards them, but Tanner was quick enough to step out of the man's way.

"See?" He pulled her to safety. "I'm not abandoning you to the mercy of such miscreants."

The man paused a moment, glancing back at them before weaving his way in the direction of another one of the passengers on the packet.

A pickpocket, she realised. "Take care for your purse," she warned Tanner.

"I have it well concealed," he reassured her. 'Come." He increased their pace.

Leaving the warehouses behind, they found the road where a line of hackney coaches waited.

Tanner approached one of the jarveys, who was leaning against his vehicle. "Take us to an inn, man. A respectable one for the lady."

The jarvey gave Marlena an assessing look. "A respectable inn, eh?" he said lazily.

Marlena knew she must present an odd picture in her ill-fitting dress and shabby cloak. Tanner was not much better for all his once-elegant coat and trousers had endured.

"Looks more like Paradise Street, if you ask me." The man chuckled.

Marlena guessed this Paradise Street housed less-than-respectable ladies. She pulled at the hood of her cloak to disguise her face.

"A respectable inn, sir," Tanner repeated in a firm voice.

"Aye." The man roused himself to open the door of the coach.

Tanner helped Marlena inside and climbed in beside her. She straightened her skirts and glanced out of the window of the coach as it started to move. "When we arrive at the inn, perhaps you can wait a bit and we will walk inside at different times."

"I think not," Tanner said.

Marlena's head jerked back to look at him. "Very well. We can say we merely shared the coach."

He gave her a level stare. "We will remain together."

Her heart beat faster, although she did not know if his words were the cause or the intensity of his eyes. "I do not understand."

He shifted his gaze to look around him. "After last night, do you think that I would allow you to make your journey alone?"

"But that was merely the Davies's son. I daresay such a thing could not happen again." She tried to make her voice sound nonchalant.

"The Davies's son is not the only man who might endanger you." He caught her in his gaze again. "Did you not see how the sailors looked at you on the docks?"

She blinked. "But we are not at the docks."

He gestured to the front of the coach. "Neither is the jarvey who is driving us. You recall his impertinence, do you not?"

She indeed recalled it. Her fingers fiddled with her skirt. "I shall be all right. I can look after myself. I did so with Davies, did I not?"

He shook his head. "I'll brook no argument. I am staying with you until you reach a place where I might safely let you go. I could not look myself in the mirror if I did not."

She clutched his sleeve and pleaded with her eyes. "You do not understand. If I am caught again and you have been found to have assisted me, you could suffer the same punishment." She shook his arm. "Think of it. What would be my punishment for stealing a wealth of jewellery? Never mind that I really did not do it."

He turned to her, placing his hands on her shoulders. "I have no fear of that. My position and my money will be enough protection. Let me take you back to London. I have told you, I can make the whole matter disappear."

She turned away. Perhaps a marquess could make a theft disappear by paying back the amount lost, but there was no way to pay back the murder of a peer.

Three years before, the newspapers that reached her and Eliza in Ireland had for weeks detailed everything about the murder. The bloody robe, the scissors from her sewing basket, her bloody hands. Wexin's eyewitness account. No one would believe anything except that she was the murderer.

Even if she could find Fia Small, the maid who'd shared her husband's bed that night, who would believe a maid over an earl?

Fia had run that night, the same as Marlena, and Marlena could not blame her. She hoped the girl had escaped, because, if not, Wexin had probably killed her, too.

She turned back to Tanner. "Do not risk yourself for me, Tanner, I beg you."

He reached up to caress her cheek. "I will finish what began on the ship from Dublin, Mrs Lear," he murmured. "How could I do any less?"

Fia Small hoisted four tankards of ale at once in her two hands and carried them to the table where men she'd known her whole life sat for a bit of rest after a hard day's work.

"We thank you, Fia," said Lyall, giving her a long and significant look.

"Ay, we thank you," echoed his twin, Erroll.

She knew who was who only because Erroll had a scar across his forehead, but as a child it had taken her years to remember which name went with which boy.

"Well, aren't you two talking like honey's pouring from your lips?" Mr Wood, one of the nearby crofters, shoved Lyall and laughed.

The Reverend Bell grinned from his seat on the other side of the table.

"You know they are merely being polite," Fia retorted. "You might take a lesson or two from them, Mr Wood."

Errol and Lyall laughed, and Lyall shoved Mr Wood in return.

It was plain as a pikestaff that both Lyall and Erroll were sweet on her. Fia did not take their interest seriously. They were merely at an age when they wanted to be married. Almost any passably handsome and biddable girl would do. She'd turned down proposals of marriage from other men in the village these past three years and those men always found another girl to marry. True love did not last a long time.

At least that was what the songs said, old Scottish songs of love sung sometimes in the taproom, unhappy love that usually ended with somebody dying. Sometimes when Mr. McKenzie, a tutor to some of the local boys, had too much whiskey in him he recited the poems of Robert Burns:

O my Luve's like a red, red rose,
That's newly sprung in June.

Ha! She much preferred it when he recited "To A Louse On Seeing One On A Lady's Bonnet at Church." That poem made her laugh and had more truth in it.

There was no such thing as love, Fia knew. Men mistook lust for love, but it really was merely lust.

"Fia!" one of the men on the other side of the room called to her. "We're thirsty over here."

"I'm coming over." She walked towards the man, knowing Lyall and Erroll's eyes were on her back.

Once Fia had pined for the excitement of the city, travelling all the way to London and begging for work from Miss Parronley—Lady Corland—the Baroness, she meant. If only Fia had been content with her little part of Scotland.

She liked working in her uncle's tavern. It was hard work, and it kept her very busy most of the time. No time left over to think.

She trusted the twins would soon tire of making moon eyes at her and they'd turn their two heads towards some girls who might believe in true love. Or in the need to have a husband.

Fia next served some strangers staying at the inn. There were never many travellers passing through Kilrosa, but sometimes the laird had people come to see him. Most people travelling in this area stopped at Peebles where the coaches came through. Even Parronley, five miles down the road, received more visitors than Kilrosa. She eyed the strangers carefully, but they did not seem to take any special notice of her.

A part of her would always fear that *he* would find her and silence her for good. Lord Wexin, an equal to the devil in her mind.

She scooped up empty tankards and walked into the kitchen, greeting her aunt, who was busy stirring the stew that would feed anyone asking for a meal.

She carried the tankards into the scullery, pausing when she saw the huge man standing there with his arms elbow-deep in water, his shirtsleeves rolled up so that she could see his muscles bunch as he scrubbed a pot.

She gritted her teeth and entered the room. "More for you."

Bram Gunn swung around and wiped his arms on his apron. He smiled at her. "I'd say thank you, but I would not mean it."

He took the tankards from her, and she gave an awkward nod of her head as she turned to leave.

"How is it out there this evening?" he asked her. "From the dishes that have come back to me, it is a busy one."

He always tried to engage her in talk, ever since he had come back from the Army. He'd come home from France only a week ago, leaving the 17th Regiment behind him, so he said. He planned to stay in Kilrosa and help with the inn now that her cousin Torrie was in Edinburgh becoming educated.

It shouldn't be so hard to talk to him. She'd grown up with Bram, after all, like he was her own kin. He was her uncle's son, born to her uncle's first wife who died birthing him. Fia's aunt, her mother's sister, raised him. It seemed to Fia that Bram had always been around when she was a wee one, until he left to be a soldier.

"'Tis busy enough," she said.

He grabbed a large tray. "Shall I clear tables for you?"

Bram was always trying to do nice things like that. Fia told herself he was being a good worker for his father, not being nice to her.

"If y'like," she said.

She started to leave again, but this time he stopped her with his huge hand upon her arm. "Wait, Fia. Have I done something to anger you?"

She stepped back. "Nay."

He shook his head. "Then did I do something to frighten you, because you always seem in a hurry to be away when I'm near?"

"Don't be foolish," she retorted.

But there was too much truth in what he'd noticed. She felt

both afraid of him and angry, though she could not explain it, not even to herself. He did not look on her with that same sort of wanting that Lyall and Erroll had on their faces, but those lads did not make her think about being a woman like Bram did. She could feel her breasts when Bram was near. She felt her hips sway when she walked. And she ached sometimes, down *there*, and the remembering would come. Lord Corland. And Lord Wexin.

Bram walked close behind her through the kitchen. Even with the scent of the stew cooking, she fancied she could smell him, the fine scent of a man.

"If something troubles you about me—or anything else— you can tell me, y'know." His voice was low pitched, rumbling so deep Fia felt it as well as heard it.

"Nothin' troubles me but getting the work done," she told him, entering the taproom and walking to the bar. "Nothin' troubles me at all."

The hackney coach pulled into a coaching inn whose sign depicted a black man in exotic garb.

"It is not too late for us to enter separately," Miss Brown said.

"Say it no more." Tanner placed the strap of the satchel over his shoulder. "I will stay with you until you have reached safety in Scotland, if that is the only help you will allow me to give you. We can hide behind being Mr and Mrs Lear or any fiction you wish to create. It matters not to me, but I'm not leaving your side."

The intensity of her frown dismayed him, but he was determined. If he parted from her, he would always fear harm had come to her. He refused to have her life on his conscience adding to the tally.

He climbed out of the coach first and turned to assist her. The coach driver called down from the box, "This is the

Moor's Head, a place respectable enough, with all the coaches coming and going."

Tanner handed the man some coins. The inn looked adequate. He took Miss Brown by the elbow and escorted her inside.

They registered as Mr and Mrs Lear again, but this time the innkeeper had little interest in them, except to ask for payment in advance. He called a maid to show them to the room.

When the maid left and shut the door behind her, Tanner put their satchel down on a chair. Miss Brown, a frown still on her face, removed her cloak and hung it on a peg.

He'd hoped for gratitude from her, at least.

A lie. He hoped for more than gratitude.

He wanted her. She fired his blood in a way totally new to him.

His interest in women typically burned very hot upon the first encounter, at which time he would do anything to make the conquest. Flynn had been excellent at assisting him at this stage, purchasing the correct gift, finding the correct housing if matters went that far, arranging perfect liaisons. Tanner's love life had not been quite the same since Flynn left, but, then, Tanner had not found a woman to interest him until now.

Tanner could not deny he burned hot for Miss Brown, whoever she really was, but the difference was, he cared more for saving her than winning her.

Typically, hesitancy on the woman's part served to increase his resolve to win her. Miss Brown's hesitancy merely brought back the loneliness he'd been wallowing in shortly before the shipwreck.

Tanner gave himself a mental shake. No matter that she affected him differently, the important thing was to preserve her life, the life he'd saved in the storm.

He glanced at her. "Are you not hungry? I'm famished.

Shall I have the innkeeper secure us a dining parlour and some food?"

She swivelled to face him, elbows akimbo, looking the tiniest bit resigned, but not liking it at all. "If you insist on making this journey with me, no matter how unnecessary— no, *foolish*—it is, then we ought to consider how much money you possess before eating in dining parlours."

Tanner almost smiled. That tirade seemed better than an I-wish-never-to-see-your-face-again one. In fact, it seemed quite sensible.

He fished out his purse and dumped the coins on the bed. She walked over to stand next to him to count the money.

"Thirty-one pounds!" she cried.

He frowned. "It is not much, is it?"

"It is a great deal to some people." She recounted it. "But we'd best save where we can."

That would be a novel experience. Tanner was unused to saving. In any event, he was made quite happy by her use of the word *we*. "What do you suggest?"

"For one thing, no private dining room. We should eat in the taproom."

"Very well." He scooped up the coins and returned them to his purse.

The taproom was crowded and noisy, which did not bother Tanner overmuch, except for it being unpleasant for her. It was not much different from White's on a crowded night, except the smells were different. Neither better nor worse, necessarily, merely different.

They could talk little during their meal, at least about how they were to go on, because they risked being overheard— if, that is, they could even hear each other above the din. Tanner bought a bottle of port to take with them above stairs. When they returned to their room, he lit the lamp, removed his boots and settled in a chair by the fire with the port. Miss Brown sat in a chair next to him.

He poured her a glass. "We should create a plan."

She took the glass. "If you insist on coming with me, perhaps you have considered how it may be done."

He had not, really, but he could be roused to do so. He took a sip of his port. "I believe I can discover a way to travel to Edinburgh."

Chapter Seven

It should be astonishingly simple to reach Edinburgh, Tanner thought. The only limitation would be the amount of money remaining in his purse, but he had no doubt he had enough to get her safely to Edinburgh.

He wished Miss Brown would be as pleased to extend their acquaintance as he was. The look she gave him before crawling between the covers made it clear she was still peeved with him for not leaving her.

He ought to be amused by the irony. Women usually had their hysterics because he *did* leave them. Those women were easily consoled when money was offered to them. This woman refused the help his wealth could offer.

It made for a fitful night's sleep. During the hours that he lay awake, acutely aware of her warm body so close to his, he puzzled over the best way to get her to Edinburgh, to a place where she could be forever buried in the identity of someone she wasn't. Forever Miss Brown, perhaps.

He could not even toss and turn for fear of waking her, so he slipped out of bed and walked to the window, which faced the street, quiet now in the dead of night.

They ought to sail to Glasgow, that was what they ought to do. It would be fast. They'd be in Edinburgh in under a week if travelling first by ship to Glasgow, then by coach.

He had not yet suggested sailing to Glasgow, however. She'd been terrified enough on the ship to Liverpool. He'd been afraid as well, if truth be told. If he never sailed again, it would not trouble him in the least.

He took a deep breath and set off a spasm of pain that encircled his chest. He stood still, waiting for the spasm to pass. Davies's boot had done proper damage to his ribs. Tanner did not know what disgusted him more, Davies kicking a man who'd barely survived a shipwreck or Davies putting his hand around Miss Brown's throat.

Yes, he did know. His blood still boiled whenever he thought about Davies touching her, hurting her. Tanner's own hand curled into a fist with the memory.

The tensing of his muscles set off another spasm. He groaned and pressed both hands to his ribs and held them there until it subsided.

She stirred in the bed and he feared he'd wakened her. She murmured something and rolled on to her back. Dreaming, he realised.

"No," she cried suddenly. "No. Do not do it. Do not." She thrashed her head to and fro. "No!" she cried louder, her hands grasping at the air.

He rushed to her side and clasped her hands in his own, folding them against her chest. "Wake up, now," he said, trying to sound calm. "Wake up, now. It is a dream."

Her eyes flew open and she gasped, staring at him for a moment, still in the dream. Then she sat up and threw her arms around his neck. "This time he was going to kill you," she cried, burying her face into his neck.

He let his arms encircle her and he held her close, holding

her as if she were a small child. "See, I'm all in one piece. It was only a dream."

Curse Davies, he thought. Frightening her into nightmares like that.

"It always seems so real," she said, clinging to him.

The notion she was like a small child vanished like smoke through an open flue. She felt all woman to him, all soft, warm woman. How the devil was he to control his response to her trusting embrace?

"Just a dream." He carefully pulled away from her. "Lie down now and try to go back to sleep."

She grabbed his hand. "You will not leave me?"

He smiled at the irony of her speaking the same words they'd argued over half the evening. "I'll not leave you."

Thinking it would be wiser to go in search of some frigid bath water, he nonetheless crawled into bed beside her.

She moved over to him, lying like a nesting spoon against him. "Hold me, Tanner. Do not leave."

He took a bracing breath at the exquisite pleasure of it and made his ribs hurt all the more. It was not only his ribs that tortured him, however, but another much sweeter torture.

Her body trembled in his arms, and, among other needs, the need to protect her surged through him. He waited to hear her fall asleep before he placed his lips on her smooth, soft cheek.

"Mmm," she said, snuggling closer.

His last waking thought was a renewal of his vow to get her safe to her destination, to make certain the life he'd saved remained saved.

Marlena had a vague memory of waking during the night and asking Tanner to hold her, but she was not certain of it and dared not ask him if she'd done so. Instead she slipped from the bed and dressed and was pinning up her hair when he woke, stretching and giving her that lazy smile of his.

"Good morning." His voice was rough with sleep.

He rubbed his face, shaded again with his dark beard, and she wished she could rub it, too, to feel it scratch her fingertips.

He sat up and winced.

She frowned. "You are still in pain."

The corner of his mouth turned up again. "Only when it hurts." His eyes glittered with amusement at his joke. He stood. "I merely have to start moving again."

He walked over to the satchel and removed his shaving things, carrying them to the bureau upon which sat the water pitcher and bowl. She could not help but watch him. He glanced in the mirror after soaping his face, catching her at it.

She quickly turned away and busied herself with straightening the bed covers.

After he was dressed they went below stairs for breakfast. Tanner told the serving girl their belongings had been stolen rather than lost in a shipwreck. He asked where they might purchase clothing.

"You are fortunate," the girl responded. "It is not far." She gave them the direction.

The taproom was nearly empty at this hour, so after the serving girl walked off to fetch their food they were free to talk as they wished.

"I have been thinking about the trip to Edinburgh," Tanner said. "I dare say the fastest way would be by ship to Glasgow."

Marlena's heart seemed to rise into her throat. "Indeed." She swallowed. "How long on board?"

He tilted his head. "More than one day, for certain."

"Oh, my," she whispered. She picked up her teacup, but held it in two hands because she was shaking. She mentally scolded herself for her cowardice.

Setting her chin, she gave him a direct look. "If we must go by ship, we must."

His eyes seemed to shine in the low light of the taproom. "We do not have to travel by ship. Perhaps public coaches would not be more than a day or two longer."

She glanced away. "It must be your pleasure, since you insist upon being my escort." And, of course, his money would pay for the trip.

He took another sip of tea. "If you are not in too great a hurry, public coaches will do."

Two more days with him would be heavenly.

She glanced around, but no one seemed within earshot. "You must need to return to London as soon as possible. They will think you dead."

His brows knitted. "I have thought on this. Flynn, the man I visited in Dublin, was the only one to know I was on that ship. I dare say he won't learn of the wreck for two days or more, and then it will take a few days for a letter from him to reach London. I suspect no one will worry overmuch even then. I should have more than a week before I need to send word of my survival. My presence is not required. I may stay away as long as I wish." A bleakness flashed through his eyes, but so fleetingly she thought she must have imagined it. "We may travel by coach."

Marlena's muscles relaxed. No sea journey and two extra days with him. She ought to chastise herself for being selfish.

She met his gaze again. "Thank you, Tanner," she whispered.

His expression softened. "We are decided, then."

They finished their meal and left the inn in search of the clothes market where the serving girl had directed them.

"I need only a shirt or two and other underclothes," Tanner said. "And a top coat."

She glanced over at him. "You need a coat and trousers as well, if you wish to look the part of a stable manager."

He paused on the pavement to look down at himself. "Is my coat too shabby now?"

She examined him as well. "On the contrary, your clothes are too fine. Your coat fits you as perfectly as if it was made by Weston, and your trousers by Meyer."

He grinned. "They were."

After walking several minutes they found the street with its clothing traders, one stall after another, all calling to passers-by to come to examine their wares. Marlena found two dresses almost right away, and she picked through a box until she found two shifts that would fit her that looked tolerably clean. At another stall, she discovered corsets of all shapes and sizes and selected one that she could put on without assistance.

He walked away briefly, but soon returned to her side carrying a portmanteau. "I purchased this. We can pack as we go along."

She placed her purchases inside.

At other stalls Marlena picked up small items: a proper hat to shield her face from the sun, a sturdier pair of gloves, a spencer so she would not always have to wear the cloak. When they turned their attention to men's clothing, Tanner took the task in his stride, though he must never in his life have worn clothing that had once belonged to another. They found him a good brown coat and a pair of wool trousers, as well as a caped top coat, all that had seen better days. When he slipped on the coat to check its fit, she realised that it was the man who made the clothes, in his case, not the reverse. He looked every bit as handsome in a plain brown wool coat as he did in the one that came from Bond Street.

It was afternoon by the time their battered portmanteau was filled with clothes. Marlena could not remember when she had so enjoyed a shopping expedition, even though neither of them could have ever imagined making such purchases a short time ago. They dropped the portmanteau off at their room in the Moor's Head and ate dinner in the taproom before venturing out again to discover the schedule of public coaches.

Lew Davies left his dark corner of the taproom and hurried through to the outside door. He'd not yet found the right opportunity to snatch the woman. This time he'd be smarter and catch her alone and unawares, rather than break into their room at night.

In Cemaes, he'd followed them to the docks and boarded the same ship to Liverpool as they'd boarded. On the ship he'd watched them as best he could without them seeing him. He'd followed them off the ship in Liverpool and caught a hackney coach to follow behind the one they had got in. He even took a room at this same inn and had been following them all day, but everywhere they went, too many people were around, especially at that clothing market.

Davies watched the man drop some coins on the table as he and the woman rose to leave the taproom. Davies waited a moment before following them into the street, but he'd waited too long. They were no longer in sight. Not to worry. They would return to the inn eventually, and he'd already scouted out a good place to catch her unawares.

He returned to the taproom to have one more tankard of ale.

By the time he and Miss Brown had returned to their room in the inn, Tanner felt a pleasant sort of weariness. He lounged in a chair, the pain in his ribs settling into a tolerable ache.

He'd enjoyed this afternoon's adventure. Haggling with vendors had been much more enjoyable than he could have imagined, and he did not know when he had been required to figure out the best coaching route to anywhere.

Tanner watched her unfold their nightclothes and other thoughts filled his mind, infinitely more carnal. He'd have a few more days with her, a few more days to burn with wanting her. It occurred to him to merely ask her for what he craved from her with his body and his soul, but how was she, so indebted to him, to refuse him?

She stood in front of the mirror and removed the pins from her hair. Tanner watched her dark, touchable curls tumble down to her shoulders. If that were not enough, she drew her fingers through her locks and shook her head so that her curls bobbed a quick dance before settling again.

Dear God.

He blew out a breath. "Let me know when you wish to walk down to the necessary."

She turned around, now brushing her hair.

He shifted in the chair.

"In a little while." Her voice was soft. Caressing. "Unless you wish to go now."

At least the topic of the conversation was sufficiently dampening. He did note, however, that she gave the decision back to him. Even in this matter she would acquiesce to his wishes. It would be no different if he asked for a kiss. Or more.

"No need for haste on my part," he said.

A few minutes later he followed her down the stairs, through the corridor to the back of the inn and through the door to the yard where the necessary was located. Adjacent to the stables, it was convenient for those whose carriages and coaches merely stopped for a quick change of horses, as well as those staying at the inn. She'd donned her newly purchased spencer against the crisp chill of the night. The horses in the stables nickered as a door slammed in the distance.

She entered first and, as he waited for her, he kicked at pebbles in the cobbled yard and listened to the muffled voices coming from the taproom. He laughed to himself that this was yet another example of the intimacy he shared with the secretive Miss Brown. Except for the obvious ultimate intimacy about which he could not stop thinking, he'd never been closer to a woman. And he did not even know her blasted name.

She came out and he smiled at her. "I'll be only a minute."

When he finished, he heard muffled sounds from outside and rushed out.

She was gone.

Another sound came from a dark, narrow passageway next to the building. He hurried in that direction and, in the darkness, could barely make out a man walking at a fast clip, carrying a bundle over his shoulder.

Tanner charged after the man, who broke into a run, reaching the alley behind the buildings. Tanner caught up with him and seized him from behind. The bundle slipped from the man's shoulder, a blanket wrapped haphazardly with rope. The bundle's contents were struggling to get free.

Tanner swung the man around. There was just enough light to see it was Davies.

"You!" Tanner growled, pushing him back against a wall. "If you have hurt her—"

Davies seized a wooden box stacked up next to him and slammed it into Tanner's already injured ribs. The jolt of pain loosened Tanner's grip, and Davies squirmed out of his grasp and ran down the alley.

Tanner turned to the bundle. "It is me," he reassured her, pulling at the ropes.

They loosened easily and she threw off the blanket and pulled out the cloth Davies had jammed in her mouth.

"Ah," she cried, taking deep breaths. "Who was it? Who was it?"

He pulled her to her feet. "Davies." He felt her neck, her arms. "Are you hurt?"

She shook her head, still breathing hard, eyes flashing in alarm.

He clutched her to him. "I thought I'd lost you." But this was not the time to panic. "Come. We must leave here."

He retraced his steps back to the inn and they hurried inside and up the stairs to the room.

"Pack up everything. We are leaving now," he said.

"Now?" she cried.

He scooped up his razor, soap and shaving cup and shoved them into the portmanteau. "Now."

She picked up her hairpins while he rolled up their nightclothes. They stuffed everything into the portmanteau and hurried down the stairs. They crossed the empty entrance and went out into the street.

"We'll go to another inn. I noticed one on the way to the clothes market." He held her arm, and they walked along at a brisk pace, trying at the same time not to call attention to themselves.

Tanner watched for Davies, but it was impossible to tell if he was following them or not. There were too many dark places for a man to hide.

They finally reached the inn and entered the taproom to ask for the innkeeper. His brows rose in surprise at the request for a room at such a late hour, but he took their money and showed them a room two flights up.

It had little more than a bed and a table and two wooden chairs, but Tanner did not care as long as it kept her safe. He dropped the portmanteau on the floor and waited while the innkeeper laboured at lighting a fire. When the innkeeper left and closed the door, Tanner brought one of the chairs to it and wedged the back of the chair under the door latch. Then he crossed over to the window and looked out. A man would need a ladder to climb up to it.

Tanner turned back to her. "I think this is safe."

"Tanner…" Her voice cracked and she stared at him with pleading eyes.

He stepped towards her and took her in his arms. "You are safe now, I promise you. I promise you." He held her as close as he could and she moulded herself to him, clinging as if they were one person.

God forgive him, he'd lose his battle with his carnal desires if she did not break away from him.

When she did pull away, he threw his head back in frustration and relief, his breath ragged. He closed his eyes, trying to compose himself.

Her hands, fingertips soft and warm, closed on the back of his neck and pulled him down to her, down to her waiting lips.

The floodgates of his desire were nearly unleashed with the touch of her mouth against his. He forced himself to kiss lightly, trying with all his strength not to take more than she offered. Perhaps all she wanted to give was a mere kiss of thanks for thwarting Davies again.

They separated, and into the breach she breathed his name again. "Tanner." She closed the distance between them and this time pressed her mouth against his, opening her lips, taking his breath inside her.

He groaned and spread his legs, his hands reaching around her to press her against him. Her tongue touched his teeth, like a tapping on a door. He flung the door wide and invited her inside, letting her tongue dance with his. Her fingers dug into his hair, massaging his scalp, sending shafts of need to his loins already so on fire he might torch them both.

She made small noises as she kissed him, the sound rousing him even more.

"Make love to me," she murmured against his lips.

He broke away to stare at her, uncertain if he had heard her correctly or if his own desire merely rang in his ears.

She grabbed fistfuls of his hair and found his lips again. "Make love to me," she repeated.

He tilted his head, trying to see into her eyes. "Do you mean this?"

"Yes. Yes," she said, pulling him by his hands to the bed. "Now, Tanner. I want you to."

"You are certain?" he asked again.

She laughed. "Yes."

Now that the invitation was clear, he could barely move. Irony, again. "Have—have you done this before, Miss Brown?"

She backed into the bed and still pulled him towards her. "Yes, I have done it before."

His mind started whirling. She'd said she was a lady's companion. Since when was a lady's companion experienced in lovemaking?

"Oh, very well," she cried, suddenly pushing him away. "I did not mean to offend you."

"Offend me?" He was totally confused now.

"By throwing myself at you." She looked as if she would cry. "Forgive me."

"Forgive you?"

"Stop repeating what I say!" She whirled around and pressed her forehead against the window frame.

"Repeating—" he started, but caught himself.

He had mucked up something, but he was uncertain what. All he knew was, he'd been on fire for her—was still on fire for her—and he had somehow sent her skittering across the room.

"What the devil is going on?" His voice came out harsher than he intended.

Her fingers fiddled with the curtain. "I forgot myself." She took a shuddering breath and turned, hiding half her face with the curtain. "It has been a long time."

"A long ti—" He shook his head. "Talk plain, Miss Brown, or I may be echoing you into the next decade."

A small giggle escaped her lips.

Now he was really confused.

"I am sorry, Tanner." She gave him a wan smile. "I—I was so upset about Davies and having to run here. I did not mean to be so forward. I know you do not…think of me in that carnal way. I think I must have just needed—"

"Not think of you in that carnal way?" he repeated, then shook his head again. "What makes you think I do not think of you in a—carnal way?" Good Lord, he could hardly think any other way when he was with her.

"You looked at me so."

"Looked at you so?" He lifted his hand when he realised he'd repeated again.

She laughed.

He smiled. "I seem to have some affliction."

She waved a dismissive hand and walked back to the bed. "Perhaps we ought to go to sleep. It has been a long day."

When she passed close to him, he grasped her arm. "Let me clarify one thing," he murmured. "I think of you in a carnal way, Miss Brown." He made her face him and he rubbed his hands down her arms. "And I would very much like to know you in a carnal way, if you would wish it."

"If I would wish it," she repeated. She smiled. "I would wish it very much."

Chapter Eight

Marlena waited, her heart pounding, hoping. She longed to let her fingers explore where her eyes once wandered, to feel the muscles of his chest, the ripples of his abdomen, the roughness of his cheek, shadowed now with beard. She dared not act the hoyden again. He might change his mind; if he did, she might shatter like glass.

His eyes looked dark and soft in the dim light of the room. He gently lifted her chin with his fingertips and lowered his face to hers. With soft, gentle lips, he brushed her mouth, and, though her heart pounded, she remained still while he sampled, wishing he would instead take more of what she yearned to give.

The emotions of the night still stormed inside her: Terror at being captured, rage at being bound, frenzy at their impulsive flight. Marlena burned with the need to release all the passion her emotions ignited. If she stayed quiet and still much longer, she would surely combust.

Tanner broke off the kiss. She drew in a breath and held it. If she pulled him back to her, she feared he would withdraw altogether. To her great delight and relief, he, instead, slid his hands to her shoulders and gently turned her around. He untied the laces of her ill-fitting dress and pulled it over her head, tossing it aside. Next his fingers lightly brushed her as he loosened the laces of her corset. When freed, she grasped his hands and held them against her ribs, relishing the warmth of them, the strength of his fingers. She longed to move his hands to her breasts, but she feared showing so much wantonness.

She turned back to face him. "Shall I help you now?" she asked. She could not resist placing her hands upon his broad shoulders, sliding them down to his chest and underneath his coat.

One corner of his mouth lifted in a half-smile, but his words were breathless. "Recall, my coat fits well. You must peel it off."

She looked into his eyes. "I shall be delighted to do so."

She slid the coat off his shoulders and then pulled on first one sleeve, then the other. Reluctant to stop touching him for even an instant, she flung the coat over a chair. Tanner's half-smile was replaced by eyes that seared her with smouldering fire. She could not look away as she unbuttoned his waistcoat.

He stood very still while she removed it, and again she feared appearing too eager for him, wanting just to rip it off.

"Do you make your valet do all this work?" she asked, trying to slow herself.

He looked down at her with his half-smile. "My man would be shocked if I did not. A marquess must not undress himself, after all."

She undid the Dorset buttons at his neck and pulled his shirt from the waistband of his trousers. As she lifted it, the white cloth of the shirt billowed out to form a canopy that enclosed them both.

From inside the canopy, while the blood was racing through her veins, she laughed softly. "You are Mr Adam Lear now, are you not?"

His half-smile fled. "But who are you?"

It seemed as if the blood in her veins turned to ice. She continued to pull his shirt over his head, but she turned away to place it on the chair with his coat, and to retrieve his waistcoat from the floor.

She heard him move away, the ropes of the bed creaking as he sat upon it.

She turned back towards him and saw him pulling off his boot.

"I will do it." She crossed over to him and tugged at the heel of his right boot. It reluctantly parted from his foot. The left boot did the same.

"They are in sad need of polish, are they not?" he remarked, but the warmth had gone out of his voice.

Marlena suddenly felt as if thousands of tiny doors had quietly closed on all the impassioned emotions of a few moments before. She'd heard the doors latch the second he asked, *But who are you?*

With her head bowed, she turned and set the boots next to the chair. She dearly wished she could tell him who she was, laugh with him about her silly infatuation with him when she and Eliza first spied him at Almack's, describe to him how she and Eliza had decided he'd become much more handsome after they discovered he was a marquess. He'd enjoy a folly like that.

She could never be that girl again, however. She'd become the Vanishing Viscountess, the woman who, hiding in Ireland, had been hunted all through England, the woman who still had a price on her head, a reward her cousin Wexin offered for anyone who could prove she was dead or else bring her back to face her fate.

She walked to the portmanteau and took out their nightclothes, draping them over her arm.

"Will you not come back?" he asked, his voice low.

She glanced at him in surprise. "Come back?"

The corner of his mouth turned up again. "You've caught the affliction."

Her brows knitted. "Affliction?"

He grinned. "The Repeating Blight."

She smiled.

He offered his hand.

She raced forward to take it, dropping the nightclothes on the floor. His fingers closed around her hand and drew her back to where he sat.

"Now where did we leave off?" he whispered, his voice warm again. He brought his gaze to hers.

"I removed your boots," she said in a tone a little too clipped, a little too loud.

"Ah, yes." He placed his hands at her waist.

She stood between his legs. His fingers pressed into her flesh and suddenly those thousand doors blew open in a brisk, hot breeze. She closed her eyes, relishing the sensation again.

He gathered the fabric of her shift in his fingers, inching it up her legs before pulling it off altogether. A moan escaped his lips. She opened her eyes, suddenly nervous.

Corland said she was too tall, too thin, and she feared she would see disappointment on Tanner's face. Instead, his eyes caressed her. He touched her neck and his hand slid down to her collarbone, to her breast. He stroked her as lightly as he had kissed her. Sweet, sweet torture.

He moved over on the bed to make room for her, and she climbed up next to him, reaching for the buttons of his trousers, but he stopped her, holding up a finger that he twirled around and pointed to her legs.

He smiled at her. "Your stockings."

She reached down to remove them, but he held his finger up again. With more sweet torture, he pushed her stockings down her legs, his hands touching her bare skin. She gripped the bed covers to keep from writhing under his touch. When her stockings, too, were tossed aside, his gaze seemed to feast on her.

"You are lovely, Miss—" He started to use the name she'd given him, but cut himself off, and his expression hardened for a moment.

Not wishing to again lose what was building between them, she shifted positions, getting up on her knees. "Now you recline and I will roll your stockings off."

He lay back, but his eyes remained on her. Never before had she been so aware of her nakedness, and never before so relished it.

She removed his stockings and began to unbutton his trousers. His arousal pressed against the fabric. A thrill flashed through her and she daringly let her hand brush against it, wondering if she'd be brazen enough to touch it without the barrier of clothing. His muscles tensed and his breath was ragged.

Marlena had never removed a man's stockings before, certainly not a man's trousers. Corland came to her already undressed, covering himself in only a banyan. Sometimes he had not even troubled himself to remove her nightdress. In those first months of their marriage, though, when she'd been in love with being married, she had not known any better. The belief that Corland loved her had been sufficient to make lovemaking a thrill. She'd relished being touched, being kissed, feeling close to another person. Her body had responded.

Later Corland had used her eager response like a weapon against her, saying it gave him a disgust of her. Of course, he had no such disgust for the many other women he coupled with. She'd refused him her bed after that discovery, but it mattered little to him.

At this moment, however, she no longer cared if she acted unnaturally wanton. She was consumed with wanting the pleasure a man could give, and she wanted it with Tanner. Perhaps she had always wanted that pleasure from Tanner. Perhaps that had been what her once-girlish infatuation had been all about.

Do you think so, Eliza? she asked silently.

With a surge of energy, she pulled off his trousers.

As she moved from him, he grabbed her arm. "If you leave this bed to fold that garment neatly on to the chair, I vow I will start repeating everything you say."

She glanced back at him, the bubble of laughter tickling her chest. "I was about to do so."

With a flourish, she tossed his trousers into the air, letting them fall to the floor wherever they might.

He smiled. "Come."

She slid closer to him, and in a swift movement he was above her. His legs, rough with hair, pressed against hers. The male part of him also pressed against her. She was seized with an urge to look at it, like he had looked upon her, but he covered her with his body, and she soon forgot anything but the contour of the muscles that rippled beneath his skin, the weight of him, the heat of him.

Tanner raised himself up on his arms, enough for her to breathe and for him to kiss her. There was no gentleness in this kiss, no restraint.

She could not hold back now either, not even if he required it of her. She abandoned herself to kissing him back, taking his tongue inside her mouth, wanting more of him inside her.

She writhed beneath him, and he broke off the kiss. She burned with impatience. He must take her now! *Now.*

He did not. Instead he engaged in the exquisite torture of nibbling on her neck and sliding his lips to her breast. He took her nipple into his mouth, warm and wet and sending shafts of aching need throughout her.

She moaned, arching her back for more. He obliged her, tasting her other breast, tracing her nipple with his tongue, sliding his hand down her body to touch her in her most intimate place.

She gasped with surprise that he would touch like this. Corland had never done so—but soon she moaned at the delicious sensations Tanner's touch created. Suddenly, he slipped a finger inside her, another shock. Another delight. Her release came, rocking her with pleasure, and she clutched at him until the sensations eased.

She'd finished before they'd even started. Disappointment mingled with her satisfaction. "Oh, Tanner," she cried.

He removed his fingers and again held himself over her. "I wish I knew your—" He cut himself off, shaking his head.

He lowered his lips to hers instead, and, to her surprise, her body flared to life again. She ran her hands over his shoulders, his back, his buttocks, as firm as the rest of him. With his knee he urged her legs apart and she trembled with anticipation. In a moment he would enter her. In a moment they would be joined. They would become one.

She held him back, splaying her hands on his chest. He gazed down at her with puzzled eyes.

"Marlena," she rasped, barely able to make the word leave her lips. "My given name is Marlena."

He flashed a smile and kissed her again. "Marlena," he whispered low and deep.

He entered her, and Marlena abandoned thought and

embraced sensation. The air was filled with the scent of him and of their lovemaking. The only sound was their breathing and the caress of their skin as they moved in rhythm. His skin was hot and damp with sweat, and inside her he created feelings more intense than anything she could ever have imagined.

She did not want this to end and yet she rushed with him to its climax, building, building, until from beneath her closed eyes she saw flashes of dancing light. As her pleasure exploded within her with even more intensity than before, she felt him spill his seed inside her, his muscles bunching underneath her fingers.

She felt his muscles relax, felt the weight of him envelop her before he slid off and lay at her side.

"Marlena," he repeated, wrapping his arms around her, clasping her against him.

She melted into him like candle wax under a flame, warm from the passion they shared and from the heat of his body. Tomorrow she would think of how glorious it had been to make love with him, but now she was content to think of nothing but the comforting rhythm of his heartbeat.

When Tanner opened his eyes, she was still asleep next to him, his arm encircling her. He could feel her breath on the skin of his chest: warm, then cool, warm then cool. She felt soft and sweet. Her hair tickled his hand. He grasped a strand between his fingers and toyed with it.

Light shone through the window. They should rise and leave Liverpool as soon as possible. Once Davies realised they were no longer at the Moor's Head where he had last seen them, he would begin to check other inns nearby. They needed to be gone before he reached this one.

It seemed damned odd of Davies to pursue them this far.

For a farmer's son to travel to a city like Liverpool seemed nonsensical all on its own, but it seemed clear his intent was not to steal money, but to abduct Marlena.

Marlena.

She'd given him her name at last, while they made love, a gift that made his emotions surge when he joined with her. It must be her real name, as well, because the name was too unusual to be invented. Something else unique about her.

His ribs began to ache. A change of position would alleviate the discomfort, but he was loathe to wake her, so peaceful in sleep.

He distracted himself from the pain by setting his mind on the problem of Davies's pursuit. It would be foolish to assume Davies would give up now if he had not yet done so and it would be an easy matter for him to discover their direction if they travelled by coach. He could easily catch up to them by hiring a horse—

Tanner almost sat up, but stopped himself lest he woke her. *Hiring a horse.*

A horse might travel all manner of routes, but a public coach had a predictable schedule. If he and Marlena—he enjoyed even thinking her name—*rode* on horseback to Edinburgh, they could stray from the coaching roads. It would be nearly impossible to find them. They could change identities whenever they wished, stay at inns in smaller villages.

He grew more excited the more he thought of this. If they owned rather than hired horses, they would be even more difficult to discover.

Tanner frowned. Purchasing a horse cost more money than he could afford. There must be a way…

His arm fell asleep beneath her and his ribs felt like someone was drumming on them from the inside. He tried very gingerly to shift her body, just a mite.

She stirred. "Mmm." Her eyes fluttered open and she looked into his face. And smiled.

He smiled back and suddenly his aches and pains vanished.

She stretched and propped herself up on one arm, glancing towards the window. "It is morning."

"Well into morning," he responded.

"I suppose we should get up." She made no move to do so, however.

He gazed at her, her creamy skin, the swell of her breasts, the deep pink of her nipple. He caressed her neck. "In a moment."

Her eyes darkened. He leaned down and touched his lips to hers. This time she did not restrain herself as she had initially the night before. This time she kissed him back, twining her arms around his neck, pulling him down to her.

His blood raced again and he was instantly hard for her. "Marlena," he murmured against her lips.

She laughed from deep inside her, and found his lips again. He relished this eagerness of hers, a match to his own. She'd surprised him the night before, and pleased him. He was more than ready to be pleased by her again.

Davies waited in a dark corner of the taproom of the Moor's Head, waiting to see the man and woman who called themselves Mr and Mrs Lear come down to breakfast as they'd done the previous morning. The hour was growing later and later and he was beginning to worry.

He'd bungled another attempt to capture her. It was that gentleman's fault. The gentleman always interfered. Davies vowed he would not stop him the next time he had a chance to grab her.

He rose and strolled to the entrance hall where he found

the innkeeper talking with a man Davies had not seen at the inn before. The man was dressed in what Davies would call city clothes and he spoke like a city man, too.

"I have a message for Mr Lear," the man told the inn- keeper. "Very important. Where can I find him?"

Davies's ears pricked up at the name Lear.

"I have not seen Mr Lear come below stairs this morning, sir." The innkeeper held out his hand. "I will see he gets the message, if you like."

The man shook his head. "I have to give Mr Lear the message myself. It is not written down. Just tell me what room he is in."

The innkeeper seemed to consider this. With a shrug, he said, "One flight up, three doors on your left."

The man bowed and quickly took the stairs. Davies waited only a moment and then followed him. As Davies reached the top of the stairs, he saw the man trying the doorknob. He had not knocked.

The man opened the door and entered the room. Davies quickened his step. If this man had come for the woman, Davies figured he knew who the man was—the man who had bought the woman's clothes from his mother.

Davies reached the room, and the man came out, almost colliding with him. He appeared furious.

Davies peeked inside the room. It was empty. "They are gone?"

The man looked at him in surprise. "Who are you?"

"Lew Davies."

"Davies…" Recognition dawned on his face. He gave Davies an assessing gaze. "What do you know of them?"

Davies frowned, unsure how much he should say. "I've been watching them. I followed them here from the ship and I know this is their room." Davies decided not to tell the man about his failed attempt to capture the woman. Or that he'd failed twice. "They were here last night."

"Well, they are not here now." The man peered at him. "Why do you follow them?"

"My mam figures there is a reward or you would not pay money for the woman's rags." Davies shrugged.

In a swift movement, the man grabbed his collar and pulled him down so that their faces were an inch apart. "Now you listen here, Davies. I'll brook no interference in this matter. If you value your health, you will stop this and go home to Anglesey to your miserable little farm."

Davies tried to pull away, but this man's grip was too strong. "I'll not go home empty-handed."

The man released him. "I dislike competition. I'm a reasonable man, however. If you give me any useful information to assist me, I'll pay you ten pounds. You must agree to give up this chase, however, or I promise you, if I see you again, you will never return to that farm of yours."

Davies considered this. Ten pounds was pretty good money and he was heartily sick of this chase. "The gentleman with her wore a gold ring with pictures on it."

"What pictures?" the man asked.

Davies rubbed his face. "A stag and an eagle." He thrust out his hand. "Now give me the ten pounds and you'll see no more of me."

The man reached inside his coat and withdrew his purse.

Marlena donned one of her new dresses. Her newly purchased dress, she should say. Although not even as fashionable as the clothing she wore as a governess, the dress was a pleasure to put on after the ill-fitting gown Mrs Davies had begrudgingly given her. And for which Tanner had paid.

She glanced at him standing by the mirror in a shirt not

nearly as fine as the one now packed in the portmanteau with his finely tailored coat. For her sake Tanner was willing to wear baggy trousers and an ill-fitting coat.

She watched him carefully draw the razor down his cheek. Marlena pressed her fingers to her own cheek, remembering how rough his beard had felt against her skin. She sighed, and the mere memory of their lovemaking brought all her senses to life again.

After all the dangers they had endured together, perhaps their lovemaking had been inevitable. Whatever the reason, she would treasure the memory when she reached Edinburgh and must say goodbye to him.

Tanner wiped his face with a towel and turned to her. "I am—unused to making love with ladies' companions." His expression was troubled. "Do—do you know how to care for yourself?"

She did not know what he meant. "Care for myself?"

He averted his eyes. "You know. Prevent a baby."

She had become accustomed to not thinking about this. She waved a dismissive hand. "Do not fear. I am unable to conceive."

She expected him to look relieved. Instead, he looked sympathetic.

Corland had not been sympathetic. After a year of frequent visits to her bedchamber, he'd forced her to have a painful and humiliating examination by a London physician. Afterwards the man put a hand on Corland's shoulder and solemnly pronounced Marlena unable to have children.

Corland had wheeled on her, eyes blazing. "And how am I supposed to beget an heir?" he'd shouted at her, as if the physician's horrible news had not broken her heart.

Tanner dropped the towel on the bureau and walked over to where she stood. He said nothing to her, but lightly touched her arm before crossing to the bed where she had laid out his new-but-old waistcoat and coat, both brown in colour. She took his place at the mirror to pin up her hair.

He was stomping his boots on when he said, "I'll go below and see if they can give me pen and ink and sealing wax." He crossed the room to her and placed a kiss on her neck. "If you can spare me a moment."

She turned and put her arms around him. "Perhaps not."

He leaned down and kissed her, pressing her against him, urging her mouth open with his tongue. She regretted all the clothing they wore, the late hour, the need to hurry out of that inn. All she wanted was to tumble into the bed with him once more.

She managed to release him and draw away. "I will survive your absence if you are not gone too long." He tried to steal another kiss, but she playfully pushed him away. "Go."

Flashing a grin, he walked to the door and removed the chair wedged against it. "Put the chair back." His tone was stern. "And do not answer the door to anyone but me."

She nodded and walked over to him. He gave her another swift kiss before leaving.

After they had made love that morning and she lay in his arms, he told her his new idea of how to safely reach Edinburgh.

On horseback.

They would continue to pretend to be a stable master and his wife, but say they were on a working holiday to discover what horses were bred in whatever part of the country they happened to be at any given moment. He explained that she would have to ride astride, as a stable manager's wife would do, not as a lady in a side saddle.

Marlena had ridden enough in Ireland with Eliza, but she had not ridden astride since a child, climbing on ponies in the paddock, trying hard to keep up with her brother, Niall, and Wexin. Tanner suggested they purchase a pair of trousers for her to wear under her skirts to protect her legs. That idea amused her. She'd often envied her brother and cousin their breeches, when she'd been confined by her skirts.

Tanner's plan to purchase the horses was even more amusing—and daring. He planned to write a note, signed and sealed by the Marquess of Tannerton's signet ring. The letter would authorise his stable manager, the bearer of the letter— Tanner himself—to purchase horses on the marquess's behalf. The money would be transferred from the Liverpool bank. Tanner wrote another letter of reference for "Mr Lear" to show, also signed and sealed by the marquess. With any luck, someone in the horse market of Liverpool would accept the documents. When the letters reached London, his men of business would certainly be puzzled, but they would honour them.

And it would be proof that Tanner had survived the ship-wreck and had been in Liverpool. By that time, however, he would likely be on his way back to London.

Within an hour Tanner and Marlena were riding in a hackney coach on their way to a horse market, with no one in the inn wise to their destination. Within three hours, Tanner stood haggling with a horse trader, while Marlena stroked the snout of a sweet bay mare with whom she had fallen in love.

Even though their pace would be slower than if changing horses frequently, the horses needed to have stamina and strength for a cross-country ride. It meant adding more days to the trip than a coach would have taken, but Marlena could not help but look forward to more days—and nights—with Tanner.

As if reading her thoughts, Tanner glanced over at her. She did not dare show how much her heart was set on this horse lest the dealer raise the price. The same dealer also had a strong brown gelding that suited Tanner.

Tanner winked, and she knew the horse would be hers to ride. He followed the man into a room off the stable and Marlena hugged the neck of the horse.

"Dulcea," she whispered the horse's name, "I do believe you will be mine. For a while at least."

A few minutes later Tanner joined her. "It is done." He smiled. "Though my guess is each horse is a good four years older than he told me. No matter, they should do us nicely." Dulcea nudged him with her nose and he patted her neck. "Two forgettable horses." He turned back to Marlena. "Now to the saddle maker. With any luck we should leave Liverpool and our pursuer this very day."

He offered her his hand and she grasped it. Marlena had given up on happiness when Mr Rapp, the Bow Street Runner, arrived at Eliza's graveside, but this trip, alone with Tanner, through the beautiful countryside, swelled her heart with joy.

Chapter Nine

Fia made slow work of gathering the wash from the lines behind the inn. The sun had bleached the bed linens a dazzling white and they flapped in the breeze like an army of flags. It was too fine a day to hurry at her task, a day that almost cheered her.

She pulled one of the bedsheets off the rope strung from one post to another and did battle with a wind determined to prevent her from folding it. The sheet blew over her face for the third time, its scent as fresh as the air around her.

"Would you like some help with that, lass?"

She knew who spoke without seeing him, would have probably sensed his presence even if he'd not spoken. She'd been all too aware of Bram Gunn since his return to Kilrosa.

He caught the end of the sheet and uncovered her face, starting to help her fold the cloth even before she'd answered.

"I can manage this if you have other chores to do." She tried not to look at him, the sun lighting his face and giving reddish glints to his dark hair.

He smiled at her. His two front teeth still overlapped a bit, she noticed. They'd been a distraction every time he'd spoken to her. "If you need help, I've nothin' else to do."

He took the corners of the sheet and walked them over to her, so she could hold them against the corners already in her hands. He was a large man and she felt dwarfed by his size when he came so close. She wondered if the French soldiers he'd fought in the war found him an awesome sight when he charged at them.

Fia shook her head and took the folded ends he offered her. They repeated the process until the sheet was too small for two people. She placed it in the basket and he took the next sheet off the line for her. Somehow the silence between them made Fia too aware of his thick-muscled arms and the lingering scent of the lye soap used to wash the dishes.

"This must seem tame work after the Army," she said.

He smiled, handing her the ends of the sheet. "I prefer it tame. I was fair sick of fighting."

"Uncle Gunn used to say you liked soldiering. He thought you would never come home." She took the ends.

A shadow crossed his face. "Och, I'd had my fill by Waterloo, but the Army took several years t'let me go."

Everyone knew the Scottish regiments saw very hard fighting at Waterloo. Several families around Kilrosa and Parronley lost sons and husbands and brothers to the great battle. It upset her to think Bram, too, might easily have been killed.

He smiled again as they brought the ends of the next sheet together. "And Da thought you would stay in London and marry some fancy footman or shopkeeper."

She glanced away. "London was not what I thought it would be."

They met again and his warm brown eyes were filled with sympathy. "Da also wrote about the business with Miss Parronley. Lady Corland, I mean. It must have been a nasty place for you to be, when she killed him."

She kept her eyes averted. "As they say."

When she looked his way again, his expression was puzzled. She placed the second piece of folded bed linen in the basket and he was ready with another one, the breeze giving him a struggle with it. She grabbed the flapping ends.

He went on, "I must admit, I was glad to hear you'd come home where you have family to look out for you. I thought one of the village boys would have married you by now, though."

She peered at him, thinking he might be fishing for an explanation. Or perhaps Uncle Gunn had already told him she had refused offers of marriage. "Well, I'm not married."

Of all people, she would not wish to tell him why she was not married, that she'd sinned so greatly, sharing Lord Corland's bed, even though it was for fear of being tossed out on the street. Or about how she'd stolen some coins from Lord Corland after he'd finished with her and had fallen asleep. How she'd been putting on her clothes when Lord Wexin came in, dressed so funny. From the dressing room she watched Lord Wexin stab Corland in the neck with a pair of scissors and she'd cried out. Lord Wexin had then tried to stab her with the scissors.

She'd be dead next to Corland if Lady Corland had not come in and fought Lord Wexin off so bravely. Fia had been a terrible coward. She had run away after Wexin threatened to kill her. She'd packed her things and used the coins she'd stolen to travel home to Kilrosa. When the news of the event reached Scotland, Fia learned that everybody thought Lady Corland had killed her husband and Lady Corland had also run away.

Fia had been glad that Lady Corland had escaped, because Fia was still afraid Lord Wexin would kill her if she told anybody what she had seen that night. She did not know if she would have had the courage to tell, even if Lady Corland had not escaped.

Fia did feel a terrible guilt that Lady Corland could not become Baroness Parronley, like she should be. They said that Lord Wexin would inherit Parronley if Lady Corland died. If Wexin came to Parronley, Fia would run away again, but this time she would have no place to go.

"Fia?" Bram stood waiting for her to take the ends of the sheet he held for her.

She snatched the sheet from his hands. "I don't have time for all this talking. I can fold faster on my own. Go to your own chores, Bram."

She expected him to look cross, but his eyes were only tinged with wounding. "Ah, lass," he murmured.

He helped her finish folding the sheet, but turned away when it was done and walked back towards the kitchen door.

Marlena woke in the Carter's Arms, an inn in the lovely Lancashire town they'd reached the previous afternoon. Her muscles felt a bit sore after the ten-mile ride through the countryside, but they did not hurt too badly. She rolled to her side and watched the man lying next to her.

They'd made love again the night before, to her great delight. It had been a languid, leisurely kind of lovemaking, bringing her a night's sleep uninterrupted by nightmares. She smiled, feeling truly rested for the first time since Eliza and the children had taken ill.

Marlena let her gaze fall on Tanner's face, so boyish in repose. She felt a swelling of emotion for this man, so good, so strong, so clever—clever enough to find a way to take her to Edinburgh that no one would think to follow.

He'd purchased a road book and set them on paths where coaches did not travel. The coach from Liverpool went to Ormskirk, so they journeyed on roads west of Ormskirk, ending up a little closer to Scotland, in this lovely little village of Kirkby, with its redbrick buildings and white stucco inn. They'd had a lovely afternoon of sunshine and crisp breezes, setting a comfortable pace for the horses, all of them becoming more acquainted. She smiled just to think of it.

"Thank you, Tanner," she whispered.

His eyes moved beneath his lids, and she examined the fine lines visible at their corners. The lines deepened when he smiled. He had a strong nose, she thought, but soft cheeks. The beard that shadowed his chin was a bit lighter in colour than his hair, his thick, curly hair, so wayward, its flecks of grey barely visible at his temples. His hair always looked as if someone had just run their fingers through it.

Marlena took a finger and lightly touched one of his curls. *If you could only see him now, Eliza,* she said to herself.

To her surprise, tears stung her eyes. She knew it was because she'd need to say goodbye to him in Edinburgh. He had been so good to her. Would he have been so willing to help her—to make love to her—if he knew she was accused of murder?

He opened his eyes and smiled at her, the lines around his eyes creasing. "Good morning." The lines deepened. "What troubles you?"

She blinked and returned his smile. "Nothing troubles me."

He looked sceptical.

She took a breath. "I suppose I am finding it difficult to believe Davies will not charge into the room or ambush us on the road."

He took a strand of her hair and twirled it around his fingers. "How can he know where we are headed when I do not even know myself?"

She laughed. She loved how he made her laugh when she thought she would never laugh again.

He stretched his muscles, then winced and pressed his side.

She covered his hand with her own. "It still pains you?"

He reached across himself and put his other hand over hers. "Not so much when you touch me."

She slipped her hand from his and stroked his chest, letting her fingers explore the hair peppered there. She returned to the part of his ribcage where there remained a purplish bruise. "Does it hurt still?"

His eyes turned dark. "I would not care if it did."

He pulled her on top of him and kissed her, a long lazy kind of kiss. When it ended she stayed on top of him, liking how his skin felt against hers. She touched his face, tracing where his beard grew.

"Does it hurt to shave?" she asked.

He gave her his appealing half-smile. "Only when I cut myself."

"You could grow a beard like old men sometimes do." She rubbed her finger on his chin.

He pulled her face down to his, scraping his scratchy chin against her. "I could do that. Would you like me to grow a beard?"

She rested her elbows on the mattress next to his ears and fingered his curly hair. "I am certain I cannot tell a marquess what to do."

He laughed. "But you might tell Mr—" He stopped himself. "Who the devil am I today?"

"Adam Timon." She gave him a stern look. "You must remember it."

As they'd ridden through the peaceful countryside the previous day they had discussed using different names each place they went. Tanner suggested using names from Shakespeare. "So I'll have a chance of remembering them," he'd said. He'd made her laugh then, proposing names like Yorik and Coriolanus and Florizel. At least she'd heard of those names. She had never heard of Shakespeare's *Timon of Athens*.

"Adam Timon," he repeated, flashing a smile. He swiftly kissed her, scraping her face with his beard. "May I make love with Mrs Timon, do you suppose?"

"If you promise to remember her name," she retorted.

His lips caressed hers more gently. "I'll remember." He kissed her again and whispered against her mouth, "Marlena."

She felt a flutter inside, glad she'd given him her name, something of her true self. She started to slide off him, to share more of herself with him.

He stopped her. "Stay with me," he murmured.

Her brow wrinkled in confusion, but he soon showed her the purpose of his request, positioning her and entering her this new way. She gasped and quickly realised she must set the rhythm of their lovemaking. She would be responsible for their pleasure this time.

Feeling giddy with the power of it, she moved against him, watching his face.

He pressed his fingers into the flesh of her waist. "Marlena," he groaned.

She watched his passion grow in the changing expressions on his face and felt it in the pressure of his hands and the flexing of his muscles. She was giving him pleasure, giving him herself, as she so ardently wished to do. There was so much she could not share with him, but she could share this pleasure. She could totally share this part of herself.

The need built inside her, as well, and she moved faster and faster until their pleasure erupted in unison, rocking them both. Marlena abandoned herself to the pulsing release, crying aloud as it reached the peak of intensity.

After the sensation ebbed, she rested on top him, as if she were his blanket. His hand lazily stroked her back.

"We should get up," she murmured.

"We should," he agreed, but he continued to stroke her. "In a minute."

She fully savoured that minute of languor, hating the moment of parting when she finally slid off him. To her delight, he pulled her back, rising over her and delaying their departure a little while longer.

Two hours later they were on the road again, with extra food packed in case they became hungry and a plan to continue north, on any road except the way the public coach would travel. The coach from Liverpool passed through Preston and ended its day at Kendal. Tanner plotted an alternative route, choosing half that distance to see how the horses fared at the end of the day.

Leaving Kirkby, they passed carts and riders and people walking to and from the village. Tanner greeted those who looked at them with curiosity. He was doing quite well at not acting like a marquess. Even so, Marlena could not see how people could not take note of him and remember him, he rode with such confidence and made such an impressive sight.

Marlena feared one of the faces of the people they passed would be Davies, but he could not know where they were bound. He could not know she was the Vanishing Viscountess, although each day passing made it more possible that a newspaper would reach here, reporting that the Vanishing Viscountess had been in a shipwreck and was missing. She was reasonably certain Davies could not read, but he would certainly hear others talking about her being lost at sea.

How many others had died? she wondered. Had Rapp died? She almost dreaded to know.

As they followed a dirt path through the moors, she relaxed. Here it felt as if she and Tanner were the only people in a beautiful world of undulating fields, brown and green and purple from the heather. The air was fragrant with heather and peat and the day was as fine as God could have created.

"It is so lovely," she said, overcome by the beauty of the place.

He smiled at her. "Indeed."

His eyes reflected the green of the hills. She would remember that when their journey was done.

He glanced at her again and began to sing, "Oh the summer time is coming, and the trees are sweetly blooming..."

When he finished the stanza, she laughed. "How is it you know that song?"

He rolled his eyes. "It has been sung at many a *musicale* at which I've had the misfortune to be trapped." He grinned at her and sang the second verse.

A breeze swept through the fields, rippling the colours. Marlena joined him in the chorus. "...all around the blooming heather, Will ye go, Lassie, go..."

This is happiness, she thought. *Look at me, Eliza. I am happy.*

Howard Wexin sat in a comfortable chair in the library of his London townhouse, sipping an excellent brandy he'd managed to procure and gazing absently at the leather-bound volumes filling the mahogany bookshelves that lined the wall. He'd managed quite a nice collection of books, he thought.

The room was elegantly but comfortably furnished. The large black lacquered desk at one end of the room made the tedious business of sorting his papers and reading correspondence almost a pleasure. The comfortable chair in which he sat was upholstered in Chinese brocade, as was the nearby *chaise longue.* The very best of Chinese porcelain and the occasional marble bust of learned men completed the decoration.

Wexin smiled.

His lovely wife, Lydia, was a marvel at choosing the best in décor. Every room of this London townhouse, which her father had purchased for them as a wedding gift, bore the mark of Lydia's excellent taste.

Wexin was grateful, oh so grateful that the Earl of Strathfield had permitted his daughter to marry him. Wexin had possessed equal rank with Strathfield, but Wexin had had no fortune. His father and grandfather had nearly spent the family into ruin. He had not married Lydia three years ago for the extravagant dowry her father offered and he'd fight a duel with any man who said he had. He had married Lydia because he adored her. Nothing could have stopped him from marrying her.

Nothing except her father.

Wexin stared into his brandy glass, remembering how close he had come to incurring Lord Strathfield's disapproval, to losing his lovely Lydia.

He smiled.

The Earl of Strathfield had, in fact, been of great emotional support to Wexin in those difficult days searching for his cousin Marlena to bring her to justice. The earl had even put up some of the money for the reward of her capture—or proof of her death.

That whole sordid affair would soon be over and justice finally served. After three years Marlena had been found in Ireland. She ought to be on her way to London at this very moment. Ironically, when justice was finally served and dear cousin Marlena hanged, Wexin would become the prosperous new Baron Parronley. Wexin had never expected this good fortune. He'd been way too far down the line of succession.

When, several months ago, news arrived of Niall's death and the death of his sons, Wexin could not believe it. As soon as Marlena was disposed of, Wexin would have both his Lydia and wealth. Life was very, very good.

He took a generous sip of the brandy, relishing its fine taste and comforting warmth as he swallowed.

A knock sounded at the door, and one of the footmen entered. "The mail has come, sir."

Wexin waved his hand. "Place it on the desk, if you will."

The footman bowed and left the room.

Carrying his glass, Wexin rose from his chair and settled in the leather desk chair. He might as well sort the mail now and see if there was anything important, such as a letter from the Bow Street Runner confirming arrival at Holyhead.

On top were two letters for his wife, one from her mother, one from her sister. He smiled at those, knowing they would bring her pleasure. Next was marked Llanfwrog. Odd. He broke the seal and scanned to the signature, his excitement growing. *Arlan Rapp,* the Bow Street Runner.

As Wexin read, however, he shot to his feet. A shipwreck? It was only a bloody short voyage from Dublin. How could there be a shipwreck? She was missing. He looked for the date of the letter. Four days ago.

This was not good news, although, if the Vanishing Viscountess were at the bottom of the Irish Sea, it would save the nasty attention and expense of a trial. He would have to wait longer for the Parronley fortune, in that event, and he greatly needed the funds.

Wexin took a larger gulp of his brandy.

The door opened and his wife, the beautiful Lydia, Countess Wexin, swept in. Her blonde curls were a confection of artful disorder and her morning dress showed enough creamy décolletage for him to feel hungry for her.

"The mail has arrived?" She breezed over to him and planted a kiss on his head. "Is there anything for me, my darling?"

He lifted his face for a proper kiss and pulled her into his lap, pressing his hand against her belly. He hoped she was with child this time. She'd miscarried twice, but perhaps this time the baby would take. He deserved an heir.

He held up the two letters. "Would these be for you, I wonder?"

She snatched them from his hand. "My mother! And my sister!" She slipped off his lap and hurried to the *chaise*. "I must read them straight away."

Her sister remained in Wiltshire at the country home of her wealthy baronet husband. Her mother and father were in Venice, halfway on a Grand Tour.

Wexin gazed fondly at her. "What is the news?"

She waved a quelling hand at him. "Do let me finish, then I will tell you."

He refolded Rapp's letter and placed it in one of the drawers. There was one more letter. He glanced at it and saw that it, too, was from Llanfwrog in Anglesey. He broke the seal. This letter was dated three days ago. There must be news if Rapp wrote again after only one day.

Wexin took a deep breath and read.

"Dash it!" he exclaimed. She was alive. Worse, she had vanished once more.

"What is it, Howard?" Lydia asked.

He looked up. "Nothing. A business matter. Read your mail and do not heed me."

He read the letter again. Rapp had discovered her clothing. She was in the company of a man who'd worn a gold ring and who spoke like a gentleman, and it was known she was travelling north. Rapp said he would follow her and made assurances that he would find her, seize her, and return her to London, but Wexin could not merely sit still and wait. The man had lost her once—who was to say he would not do so again?

Curse her! Damned chit. Marlena had always been an annoyance, even when they were children. She always wanted to do whatever her brother, Niall, did. Niall, like as not, would indulge her and ruin their games.

This whole matter was Corland's fault anyway. The cursed man had not been able to win at cards even when luck stood at his shoulder. It had not been Wexin's fault that Corland resorted to moneylenders who'd been breathing down his neck. It had not been gentlemanly of Corland to call in his vowels, however, money he knew Wexin could not pay, then to threaten to tell the Earl of Strathfield and all the gentlemen of White's Club that Wexin refused to pay his gambling debts.

The Earl of Strathfield might have forgiven Wexin for being the cousin of a murderer, but he would never have forgiven him for not paying debts of honour. If Corland had made good his threat, Strathfield would have refused for his daughter to marry Wexin.

And nothing could have stopped him from marrying Lydia. Nothing.

He just wished he could finish mopping up the mess Corland had created for him. Hang Marlena and be done with the matter.

Wexin covered his mouth with his fist as he rested his elbows on the desk and pondered what to do about his dear cousin Marlena, the Vanishing Viscountess, who ought to vanish for good. He doubted she would go back to Ireland.

She was friendless there now. There was only one place he could think of where she would go.

To Parronley. Perhaps she would rally supporters to her cause, and prevent her return to justice here in England. Or perhaps she knew the whereabouts of the maid, the girl who nearly foiled his whole scheme and could foil it still. Unless Wexin found her first.

He glanced over at his wife, her lips moving slightly as she read, breaking into a smile or a frown at whatever the words said on the page. He would still do anything to keep her.

She put down the letter and glanced over at him. "Shall I read them aloud to you?"

He rose and walked over to her, joining her on the *chaise*. After she read her letters he would tell her that important business would take him away from her for a time, though he hated even a day not in her company. If he used a fast coach and changed horses often, it would take four days, five at the most, to reach Parronley. He could not fathom how long it would take to find Marlena.

When he returned to London and the matter was resolved, nothing would ever again threaten to destroy his happiness.

"Read to me, my dearest," he said. "I am all yours."

Chapter Ten

One eventuality for which Tanner had not prepared in his brilliantly conceived plan was for rain. A grave error.

The moors, so serene and beautiful, now were dismal, cold, and wet. The horses, real workers the last three days, were slogging through, but too many of the side roads were like bogs. They'd been forced to stay on the main route, the route the coaches took.

He swivelled around in the saddle to check on Marlena, who followed a little behind him, looking forlorn in her cloak, rain dripping from its hem.

"Let me give you my top coat," he called to her.

She shouted back, "I've said no."

True. She'd refused his top coat at least three times.

"It is as soaked through as my cloak, is it not?" she added. "It would not help."

That was the closest she came to complaining, admitting that help of some sort would be desirable.

They ought to have stopped at the inn in the village they'd just passed, at least longer than the time it took to give the horses some oats and a rest, and themselves something hot to drink next to a warm fire. It had been a coaching inn, however. Some coaches were still on the roads. Even though it was unlikely Davies would find them after so many days and so many miles, Tanner had not been willing to take the chance.

They came to a fork in the road with a signpost bearing the name Pooley Bridge.

Good God. Pooley Bridge.

He had no idea they were near Pooley Bridge.

He turned around to Marlena again. "We'll stop near here."

She followed him unquestioningly as he followed the sign to Pooley Bridge. They soon entered the town, its narrow streets and stone houses familiar. He'd visited only the year before. Then he'd travelled to the area from Northumbria, which was perhaps why he had not realised how near they were. A year ago, after Flynn left him to marry Rose O'Keefe, Tanner had dragged Pomroy along on a tour of all his properties. They'd been gone for weeks.

Had it been only a year? It seemed a lifetime ago that he and Pomroy rode through this town and drank whisky and ale with the farmers and fishermen at the local pub. It even seemed a lifetime ago that Tanner had visited Flynn and Rose in Dublin. A lifetime since he'd stood in the cuddy of the packet ship home, lamenting his useless existence, diverting himself only by watching the woman who now shared his bed.

Sometimes it seemed to Tanner that time began when he and Marlena plunged into the bone-chilling sea. He had been reborn in a manner of speaking, with a new identity and new names each time the sun rose in the sky. Dash it. What was his name today? He had totally forgotten. Lennox, perhaps.

It did not matter.

"That was an inn," Marlena called to him, her tone a tad irritable.

He turned to her. "I saw it. We'll not be stopping there."

She scowled from beneath the drooping hood of her cloak.

"Soon we'll stop," he assured her. "Soon."

The streets were nearly empty of people, and, as he hoped, those caught outside in the rain appeared not to notice that the marquess again rode through their town.

Tanner and Marlena crossed the bridge over River Eamont and were soon in a tree-lined lane. The bright reds, yellows and oranges of the autumn Lake District foliage were muted by the grey curtain of rain.

"Have you made a wrong turn, Tanner?" she called to him.

He brought his horse to a stop and waited for her to come alongside. "Losing faith in me, are you, Marlena?"

She frowned. "I have lost faith in everything these last few hours. Ever since the rain soaked through to my skin."

His brows knitted. "I told you. I will give you my top coat—"

She held up her hand. "Do not even say it. I might snap your head off for it."

He laughed. "Miserable, are we? Do not fret. I promise we shall be warm and dry before you know it."

"We are headed into wilderness, Tanner."

Soon, however, the wilderness opened up, revealing a great expanse of lawn at the end of which was a large stone house, three storeys high.

"Tanner?" Marlena said.

He trotted ahead.

"Tanner," she called again. "This is somebody's house."

He trotted all the way to the front entrance and dismounted.

She followed him. "Tanner, this is somebody's house."

"I know." He extended his hand to help her from her horse.

They climbed the stone steps, and Tanner sounded the knocker on the door, striking it as loudly as he could.

"I greatly dislike this idea," Marlena grumbled. "It was not in our plan to visit houses."

He pounded the knocker again. "Neither was rain."

The two horses drooped their heads and nuzzled the grass, not even bothering to nibble. Tanner knew precisely how they felt. Too weary of being wet and cold to even think of eating.

He sounded the knocker again.

"There is nobody at home." Marlena pulled at his arm. "Let us go back to the village."

"There must be someone home." He pointed towards the roof. "I saw smoke from a chimney."

Finally the door opened a crack.

"Kenney, is that you?" Tanner asked.

The man opened the door wider. "My lord?"

Tanner laughed. "It is indeed. Let us in, man, and have our poor horses tended to. They are as weather-worn as we are."

The man nodded and stepped aside so they could enter.

"Whose house is this?" Marlena whispered as Tanner put his hand on her back and escorted her inside.

He leaned down to her ear. "Mine."

"Oh, dear," said Kenney, looking down at his plain brown breeches and brushing off a coat patched at the sleeves. "Let me assist you. Or should I see to the horses?"

Poor man. This was the shock of his life, the marquess visiting without notice, catching him in his comfortable old clothes instead of livery. "Tell us which room has a fire burning and we shall tend to ourselves. I should like the horses cared for immediately."

Kenney's face creased with wrinkles. "The kitchen has a fire, but that is the only one, my lord."

Tanner took Marlena's arm. "Then we will head for the kitchen, if you will alert the stable. Have them bring the baggage we carried on our saddles as well."

Kenney bowed. "Very good, sir."

Tanner led Marlena through the hall, down a corridor and some stone steps to reach the kitchen. As they came near, he heard the sound of pots rattling.

"Mrs Kenney! Ho there. You have visitors," Tanner called a warning. He did not wish to give her too bad of a fright.

"Oh!" she exclaimed as she turned towards the doorway. "My stars, it is you, my lord. Such a surprise." She eyed Marlena with blatant curiosity. "Good gracious me."

Tanner brought Marlena forward. "Mrs Brown." He put strong emphasis on the *Mrs,* hoping both Mrs Kenney and Marlena would heed his saying of it. A married woman could be excused behaviour for which an unmarried woman would be condemned. "This is Mrs Kenney, wife to Mr Kenney whom you have already met. The Kenneys are the caretakers of the house."

Mrs Kenney curtsied. "Welcome to Dutwood House, Mrs Brown."

Mrs Kenney's curiosity about the unaccompanied woman her employer had brought to his Lake District house was almost palpable. Tanner had no doubt Mr and Mrs Kenney would gossip with the villagers about Marlena after they left, but he'd brook no ill treatment of her while she was here. He trusted the Kenneys were wise enough to realise that.

"Mrs Kenney," he went on. "Mrs Brown is chilled to the bone. May I depend upon you to keep her by the fire and find some dry clothes for her? I will run above stairs and change out of my wet things. I believe I left some clothing here."

Mrs Kenney sprang into action. "Oh, my poor dear. Come here at once."

Mrs Kenney was so genuinely sympathetic, Tanner decided he had nothing to worry about from her. She would treat Marlena well.

The older woman ushered Marlena to the hearth of the large kitchen fireplace and helped her remove her soaking wet cloak. Tanner shrugged out of his top coat and draped it over a chair near the fire. He gave a quick squeeze to Marlena's arm and hurried out, hoping his memory had not failed him and he'd left some clothing in the bedchamber there.

Fia had nothing to do but look out of the window of the inn and watch the rain pouring down. Visitors were few, scattered at tables, merely passing time until the rain stopped.

She did not much relish being idle. It was so much better to be busy. Being busy gave her no time to think.

Someone walked up behind her. She could feel who it was.

Bram.

"It is a nasty day." He stood next to her.

She had hardly spoken to Bram these last few days, ever since he'd helped her bring in the washing and made her think on things she'd rather not think on. Worse than that, he had hardly spoken to her.

"Yes," she managed to reply.

It was a puzzle to her why she could feel the heat of him, even though he merely stood next to her. She could feel his breathing and sometimes she even fancied she could hear the beating of his heart. Fia worked around numbers of men every day. The taproom was a favourite place for men to gather, but she never felt the presence of any of those men this acutely.

With everything so quiet, she was even more sensitive to Bram, whose presence seemed big enough to fill the whole room, rather than just the space by her side.

He rocked on his heels, holding his hands behind his back. "The only thing rain is good for is to give us a rest."

She turned to him. "Surely rain is good for crops."

He smiled. "That is true."

She wished he would not smile. His smile made things flutter inside her. She turned back to the window. "I'd rather be working than standing here doin' nothing."

"Bram!" her uncle called from across the room. He was sitting with his feet up on a chair, passing the rainy interlude in conversation with Reverend Bell. "If you've a mind, the glasses could use a bit of wiping."

"Enough restin', I gather." Bram nodded to his father and smiled at Fia. "Come help me, lass."

What could she say? She'd already told him she did not like to be idle.

Bram smiled down at her with his warm brown eyes. "It will give you something to do."

She lifted one shoulder and moved a chair aside so she could go to the bar without walking next to him.

He stepped behind the wooden counter over which his father served the drinks and handed her a cloth, then a glass. She wiped it and gave it back to him to put back on the shelf.

"I have been troubled by something." Bram handed her another glass.

He expected a response. Since he was not looking at her, it was easier for her to oblige. "By what?" She wiped another glass and gave it back to him.

He took it from her hand. "I must apologise to you. The other day when we were out of doors in the fine weather folding sheets, you might have thought I was prying into your troubles."

Her heart raced. "I have no troubles." She reached for a glass and made the mistake of looking into his eyes.

"As you say, lass." He gazed back at her, and she felt something melt inside her. "All the same, I am sorry. I did not mean to distress you."

She snatched the glass from his hand. "I was not distressed."

She wiped with extra vigour and thrust it back at him. He accepted it with annoying calmness. In silence they finished all the glasses on one shelf and started on those on the next.

He finally spoke again. "It is said Lyall and Erroll are vying for your hand."

She handed another wiped glass to him. "Losh, they are mere lads. I do not heed them."

"They are not much younger than you are, surely," he went on. "You are twenty-one, if I'm doing the sums correctly."

She did not miss that he remembered her age. "And they are eighteen. It is a big difference."

"So a man and a woman must be the same age? To marry, that is."

"I did not say that."

"Och, but I think you did say that. You said—"

She interrupted him. "I meant only that a lad of eighteen is too young, when the lass is three years older."

"What if the lass is younger than the man? Is that different to you?" He took a glass from her hand and gave her another one.

"It would be different, aye." She wiped.

He inclined his head towards the vicar. "So if Reverend Bell sought your hand, that would be all right, then?"

She handed the glass back to him. "I'll not be marrying Reverend Bell and he's not wanting me, anyway."

He winked at her. "I was talking about age. Making a point, you might say."

She turned away from him. "My marrying or not marrying is not a matter for you to concern yourself over."

He touched her shoulder. "Come," he said in a soft voice. "I was merely talkin'. I did not mean to poke at you."

"I was just talkin', as well," she mumbled. She took another glass from his hand.

They continued their work again, but this odd awareness of him was worse when they were silent. She smelled the soap of the scullery on him, as well as the smoke of the kitchen fire. She felt each shift of his feet, each move of his muscles. He did not seem a man to be inside a house, even on a rainy day. She could easily imagine him in shirtsleeves, striding through the fields, rain plastering the cloth to his chest, parting his hair into wet curls—

She frowned and wiped twice as hard. She hated being at leisure to think.

"You—you are so much talkin' of marrying," she said, her voice accusing, even though the problem was inside her own head. "Maybe you are thinking of marrying. Maybe you have your eye on some lass here in Kilrosa or in Parronley, now you are done with soldiering."

His expression sobered and his fingers brushed hers as she handed him the glass. "The time is not quite right. I must wait a wee bit more."

She blinked up at him in confusion, not catching any sense to his words. His expression unsettled her so much it felt like her insides had coiled into knots. She wanted to be at peace, not to feel, but just to work and forget.

Ever since Bram had returned home, her peace had fled and she'd started thinking again about Lady Corland and Lord Corland and that horrible night. She again felt that same sick fear she'd felt for months after she ran away from London. It was as if Bram somehow made her numbness go away and now she must feel everything inside her.

"What is it, Fia?" He stepped towards her and put a concerned hand upon her arm. "You look so distressed."

She pulled away. "It is nothing, Bram. Give me another

glass. Let us finish this task. I've—I've decided to mop the floor after this."

His eyes continued to gaze upon her with concern, but they continued through the shelves until all the glassware was clean.

At the coaching inn in Penrith, Arlan Rapp sat nursing his ale, talking across the table from a local man. He'd asked the man if he'd seen a gentleman and lady passing through.

The man rubbed his chin. "A well-looking woman?"

Rapp nodded.

"Saw a fellow in Clifton travelling on horseback with a well-looking woman." He took a gulp of ale. "The man was no gentleman, though. Tall fellow. Just a man and wife travelling, seemed like."

"On horseback, you say?" Rapp lifted his eyebrows.

"That is so."

Rapp drummed his fingers on the table.

Several towns before someone had spoken of a tall man and a pretty woman. No horses had been mentioned, however. Horses explained a great deal.

In Liverpool Rapp had discovered that the elusive Mr and Mrs Lear had fled the Moor's Head and stayed at a different inn. They had made enquiries about ships to Glasgow, but had not booked passage. Even though the Viscountess and her companion had purchased seats on the public coach to Kendal, they had not used them.

Rapp knew deep in his gut that the Viscountess was headed to Scotland. He had to follow that belief. Trust that he would find her.

He lifted his tankard to his lips.

They were on horseback.

He'd assumed they had hired a private coach. He'd been wrong, but now at least he was on their trail. If he did not find the Viscountess on the road, he would certainly locate her in Parronley. He would pen another letter to Wexin, appraising him of his progress. He'd sent a letter from Liverpool, but this time he could be even more confident he would apprehend her.

He gazed out of the window where the rain continued unabated. Wherever they were at the moment, they would not travel further this night. Suddenly the bed in the room he'd let at the inn sounded very appealing.

He stood and threw some coins on the table. "I thank you for your information and bid you goodnight. Have more refreshment on me."

Chapter Eleven

Mrs Kenney brought Marlena a nice linen shift and the very softest wool dress her fingers had ever touched. The kitchen fire had warmed her enough that she could step into the scullery for a good wash before donning the dry clothing. She simply went without her corset, which was still too wet, but that was not so awful a thing.

Tanner returned to the kitchen, dressed in plain, comfortable clothes that Marlena imagined were intended for hunting.

"What have you that we might eat, Mrs Kenney?" Tanner asked.

"Some soup is all, m'lord." Her forehead wrinkled in worry.

Tanner smiled at the woman. "Soup sounds splendid." He turned to Marlena. "Does soup not sound splendid to you, Mrs Brown?"

"I should like nothing better," Marlena responded truthfully.

During their meal he entertained her and Mrs Kenney with tales of his visit last year with Pomroy, including a more detailed telling of the beard-growing competition. Marlena was full of admiration for him. He eased Mrs Kenney's distress at being totally unprepared for the arrival of her employer, by showing her that everything she did pleased him. And he eased Marlena's own discomfort, for surely the Kenneys thought her to be Tanner's mistress.

Marlena and Tanner left the kitchen when Mr Kenney reported that fires were built in other rooms prepared for their use. Tanner showed Marlena to a wainscoted drawing room with furniture built for comfort rather than fashion.

She settled herself on a large sofa facing the fire and wrapped a blanket around her for added warmth. Mrs Kenney brought them tea.

Tanner gave her an uncertain look. "Do you mind if I leave you for a moment? There must be a bottle of brandy in this house somewhere that Pomroy and I overlooked."

"Go," she said. "I shall be very happy by this fire with my cup of tea."

While he was gone she sipped her tea and allowed herself the luxury of thinking of nothing at all but the glow of the peat fire, the hiss of moisture escaping it, and the lovely scent that hearkened her back to childhood.

He strode into the room. "Found a bottle!" He lifted it into the air.

"Do you plan to drink your way through this rainstorm the way you and Pomroy did the last time you were here?"

He sighed in mock dismay. "I fear not. There is just this one bottle of brandy and no more than three bottles of wine. I shall save those for our dinners."

He opened the bottle, poured a glass and lifted it to his lips. His eyes closed in satisfaction. "Ah. I have missed this."

He never requested brandy at the small village inns where they'd stayed. To even inquire about brandy would have signalled him a gentleman in disguise.

"Are you not enjoying our trip, Lord Tannerton?"

"Not enjoying it?" He rolled his eyes. "Sleeping at inns that have been the very essence of mediocrity, eating the blandest food England has to offer, being required to recall which blasted name I possess each day—not to mention getting soaked through to the skin—what was there not to enjoy?"

She laughed, but then sobered at the honesty in his words. "Do you regret your insistence on accompanying me?"

He strolled over to the sofa, brandy glass still in hand. Brushing a curl off her forehead, he murmured, "There have been some compensations."

The mere tips of his fingers aroused her senses. Until the rain, their days on the road had been filled with breathtaking vistas and picturesque little villages. Their nights had been filled with lovemaking even more remarkable, more than adequate compensation for the discomfort they endured.

She moved over on the sofa and patted its cushioned seat. "Sit with me."

He lowered himself into the seat and wrapped an arm around her shoulders. Marlena nestled against him, savouring the scent of him mingling with the scent of burning peat.

"You must have had a more enjoyable time with your friend Pomroy," she murmured. "Staying at the finest inns, drinking the best brandy, and eating fine food."

He kissed the top of her head. "Good God, no!" He shuddered. "Pomroy and I were heartily sick of each other by the time our stay was complete." He tapped her on the nose. "Some advice for you. Do not embark on a long journey in the sole company of another person, no matter how great a friend."

She sat up and stared at him. "Is that not what you and I are about?"

He gave a chagrined smile. "Forgive me. I must have sounded gravely insulting."

She settled back against his chest. "You may indeed become heartily sick of me by the time we part."

He did not respond for a while, but tightened his arm around her. "I think not."

She knew she could never tire of his company. He made the morning worth waking for and filled the nights with exquisite pleasure. When she was forced to part from him, her world would turn as grey and dismal as this relentless rain.

Marlena wanted him to think of her as she was now, although she supposed he would eventually read accounts of the Vanishing Viscountess, who drowned in the Irish Sea. He would learn her true identity then. Would he believe she was a murderess? She would never have the chance to know.

Edinburgh should be no more than two or three days' ride now. In two or three days Marlena would vanish for good. She nestled closer to him, wishing the rain would never stop and they would never have to leave this place.

"How many houses do you have?" she asked him, just wanting to hear him talk, to feel his voice rumble in his chest as her ear rested against it.

"Let me see." He took a sip of brandy and she heard him swallow. "Six, I believe. Seven if you count the townhouse in London. I have my properties written down somewhere."

"Seven houses," she whispered. "Did you live in one of them over the others?"

"At Tannerton Hall, almost exclusively."

She and Eliza had managed to get their hands on *The Berkshire Guide: An Account of Its Ancient and Present State* from the lending library and they had all but memorised the entry describing Tannerton Hall as one of the largest and most magnificent houses in the county, the house and gardens designed by William Kent. She was certain she could still recite the description of its ponds and cascades and its sham ruins.

"Until I was sent away to school," he added. "Where I met Pomroy."

Marlena remembered her brother Niall leaving for school at age nine, looking very brave and, at the same time, as if he might cry. Tanner might have even known Niall from Eton, but she could never ask.

"You and Pomroy are indeed friends of longstanding." Like she and Eliza had been.

"We are," he agreed, taking another sip of his brandy. "Pomroy and I are too much of a kind."

That was not how she remembered it. Pomroy had always been full of outrageous mischief, frivolous beyond measure. Tanner, she and Eliza realised even then, had been made of something more solid and dependable.

"Useless creatures, Pomroy and I." He finished the contents of his glass.

"Useless?" she asked.

He shrugged. "When you have an elevated title, the people you employ are the ones who have the knowledge and skill to do the work. Not me." The clock sounded the nine o'clock hour. He inclined his head towards it. "Like the clock. The hands are what you see, but it is all those tiny wheels and things inside that truly keep the time."

She felt sad for him, that he could so belittle himself. "So what do you do with your time?"

He stared at his glass. "Play cards, attend the races, show up at country-house parties." He looked over at her and smiled. "I've even been known to attend the opera." Even his smile seemed sad.

He gently eased her away and walked over to the table where he'd left the bottle. He carried it back to the sofa and poured himself another glass. Marlena reached for her tea and finished the last of it.

He lifted the bottle to her. "Do you desire a glass? I am quite willing to share."

She shook her head. The wine from their dinner had been enough to make her eyelids heavy. She did not desire to fall asleep when she could spend her time with him.

He sat down next to her and she snuggled beside him again, taking his free hand into her own. "I think your hands are very nice."

He gave a low laugh and squeezed her fingers. "When they are against your skin, they do seem to be of some use."

She sat up and faced him. "Do not speak of yourself as useless when you have done so much for me."

He drew her back against him. "My finest moment, perhaps. Dashing from the privy to rescue you. Devising a means of escape that neglects to take into account the likelihood of rain—"

She put her fingers on his lips. "Stop this. I will have no more of it."

He grasped her hand and placed a kiss on her palm. "Very well, if you do not wish to hear me enumerate my many faults, there is no recourse but to talk about you."

The very last topic of conversation she would have chosen.

He went on, "For a start, where did you live as a child?"

She leaned against him again, not answering him. Her heart wanted him to know her, wanted them both to share all their experiences, their hopes, their dreams. She'd once wanted the same with Corland, but he used her girlish confidences to mock her later. Tanner was Tanner—he was not Corland and could never be, but there was little Marlena could tell Tanner without divulging herself to be the Vanishing Viscountess, pursued by a man Tanner once called a friend.

"I grew up in Scotland," she finally said. "And I, too, went off to school."

"Where in Scotland?" he asked.

She hesitated. "The Lowlands."

He shook his head in seeming exasperation. "Where did you attend school, then?"

"England."

He edged her away, placing his hands on her shoulders so she faced him. "Tell me more, Marlena."

She could not look at him. "It is enough."

He blew out a breath. "Tell me something. Anything. How did you get to be a lady's companion? How did you wind up in Ireland?"

She glanced away, trying to recall the details in the novel she and Eliza had read. "I—I was orphaned and had to make my own way. The school found me the position."

His eyes continued to watch her with scepticism. "Why Ireland?"

For this answer, she could only think of the truth. "When—when I ran away, I went to a friend who took me to Ireland to hide."

His eyes grew dark. "What sort of friend?"

She was puzzled. "I do not understand."

A muscle flexed in his cheek. "A gentleman friend? The man who…introduced you to lovemaking, perhaps?"

"Oh!" She realised why he might suppose this. The fiction she had told him about herself had not included a way to explain her experience in lovemaking. "No, it was not a gentleman. A school friend."

He nestled her against him again. "Then who was the man who—"

She told the truth. "A man who thought women in his employ must serve him in all ways." That described Corland very well.

"The son?" Tanner's arm flexed. "The man accusing you of theft?"

She did not say a word to counter the conclusion to which he'd leapt.

"That bloody bounder."

Yes, he had been. She hated allowing Tanner to believe something untrue.

Tanner must have known her husband. Gentlemen gathered at the same clubs and gaming hells in London. Marlena suspected Corland would have been very charming to a wealthy marquess. Her husband had been quite a charming man when he chose to be, to all appearances a fine fellow, in the same way everyone had thought Wexin to be a fine fellow. Tanner cared about her, she knew. He might believe in her innocence.

She still could not tell him the truth, however. If she told him the truth and he believed her, he might insist on clearing her name. She feared he would only earn the noose for himself if he admitted helping her, an accused murdercss.

He twisted around to face her again. "Tell me who this man is. I will avenge you for it. I will make certain you need never fear his despicable wrath another moment."

Yes, he would risk his life for her, she had no doubt.

She put her arms around his neck and snuggled into his lap. "There is no need to avenge me. Soon he shall think me dead and it will all be over."

He held her face in his palms. "It will not be over for me until I know this enemy."

"If I named names," she said truthfully, "no good would come of it."

He released her and rose to his feet. "Do you have so little faith in me?" He picked up his glass and finished his second brandy. "I do not care if you are a jewel thief or not. Let me help you. You do not need to go to Edinburgh—"

"No." She put her legs up on the sofa and hugged her knees. "No," she repeated.

Tanner rubbed a hand through his hair, staring at her. He turned and reached for the brandy bottle again. He could fix this for her. He longed to fix it for her. Pummel that bounder into a bloody pulp for what he'd done to her. That was a task he would perform with pleasure.

At least he could get rid of the charges against her. Why would she not allow him to do so?

He poured himself more of the brown liquid and took a gulp, hoping the brandy would burn some calmness into his chest.

It did not work.

He looked down at her. "Tell me enough for me to help you," he asked again. "Tell me the name of this man and I will make certain he is laid so low he'd dare not lift a finger against you. You would not need to hide. You could—" He cut himself short.

He'd been about to say that she could come back to London with him. She could marry him. He could see that she was protected and cosseted for ever.

It had not been clear to him until this moment. He wanted to marry her. *Her,* not one of the fine, unblemished girls at Almack's who circled him like vultures, waiting for the instant he decided to give up bachelorhood. This was the moment and this was the woman to whom he wanted to give his hand.

He lowered himself down in front of her, his hands on her knees. "Tell me all if it, Marlena. Do not keep secrets from me. Do not decide I cannot help you."

She turned her head away.

He stood again and reached for his brandy, resisting the impulse to smash the glass and the bottle into the fireplace, to flare into flames.

"It grows late." It wasn't long past nine. In London the entertainments would just be starting, but he was suddenly bone weary. "I believe I shall go to bed." He turned to her. "Do you wish me to escort you to your bedchamber, or do you stay here longer?" His voice, so devoid of expression, sounded as if it came from someone else's lips.

Her eyes were huge when she looked up at him. "I shall retire now."

She unfolded herself and stood in her stocking feet. He imagined her feet would be cold on the wooden floors until the riding boots he'd purchased for her and her own pair of half-boots dried. How long before their clothing dried and the rains stopped? How long before he must let her go?

Tanner imagined their clothing was laid out to dry somewhere in the house. He'd told Mr Kenney to open only the rooms they might use. He had readied the drawing room, a dining room and two bedchambers.

Tanner took a candle from the drawing room, its small flame lighting only a few feet around them. The dark wainscoting faded into black as they walked in silence up the stairway. At the top a sconce lit the hall leading to the bedchambers, set side by side. An ancestor and his wife must have slept in the rooms Kenney had chosen. There was a connecting doorway in between. Mr and Mrs Kenney had made the correct assumption about Tanner and his 'Mrs Brown.' They simply had chosen the wrong night.

He walked her to her door. "You have your own bed," he said, still in this voice that did not feel like his own.

"Yes." She went inside, closing the door behind her.

Tanner leaned his forehead against the doorjamb, his mind and stomach churning with emotion.

If she did not allow him to help her, he would have to let her go, to say goodbye, to lose her into whatever name and life she disappeared when he delivered her to Edinburgh. He might never be able to find her again.

He pushed himself away from the wall and walked to the next door, the bedchamber designated for the lord of the house. When he entered, he saw that a lamp burned on a table. Tanner blew out the candle he held in his hand and set it down, looking around the room. Mr and Mrs Kenney had done a fine job of making the house ready and comfortable for them. He'd see they were well rewarded.

He'd been keeping a tally of those people along the way who had helped them or even merely been kind. They'd all be rewarded.

His purse was on the bureau. He walked over to it and poured out the coins. Not too many remained.

Perhaps Mr Kenney would be willing to loan the marquess a little spending money.

Tanner dropped the purse, still damp from the rain. He removed his coat and waistcoat, and kicked off his shoes. After washing, he put on the silk banyon Kenney had unearthed from some trunk. The garment still smelled of cedar. He strode to the door connecting his room with Marlena's, the silk robe billowing as he moved.

She might turn him away, but that would be preferable to her feeling that he had turned her away. His time with her was too precious to squander on a selfish need to have matters his own way.

He opened the door.

She sat at the dressing table in a white nightdress, turning around at the sound of his entrance. As he walked slowly towards her, she turned back to the mirror and brushed her hair.

He took the brush from her hand and did the job himself. From the light of a lamp, her hair looked black as midnight, pouring over her shoulders like liquid night, falling in soft waves and feeling like silk beneath his fingers.

She stared at him in the mirror.

He gave a wan smile. "As a lady's maid, am I coming up to snuff?"

A ghost of a smile appeared on her lips. "I shall have to make do with you."

He leaned down and planted a kiss on the top of her head. "I perform other duties as well."

Her eyes darkened. "Such as?"

He squatted down, turning her chair towards him. "Such as apologising." He wrinkled his brow. "I am not precisely certain for what I am apologising. Not for wanting you to confide in me. Not for wanting to make things right for you." He stroked her neck with his thumb. "For making you think I did not want you, perhaps. That was dishonest of me."

She clasped his hand. "Tanner…" she began, her face pinched in distress.

He made her look into his eyes. "If you wish to sleep alone, I will return to my bed." He could not help but add, "My cold and lonely bed…"

She laughed and rose from the chair, pulling him up with her. "I am certain we both have had enough of being cold."

He lifted her into his arms, his banyan falling open as he did so. She slipped her hands up his bare chest to wrap around his neck. He placed her upon the bed linens and threw off the robe, letting it float to the carpeted floor.

She reached for him and he obliged her, climbing on the bed next to her and wrapping her in an embrace all at once. His kiss was hungry, needful, as if he'd already experienced what it would be like to lose her.

She pulled up her nightdress and he broke off the kiss only long enough to tug the garment over her head and toss it away. She was beneath him, warm and soft and already pressing against him, urging him to enter her, to take her fast.

He thrust himself into her as if he too felt the need to hurry. Gentleness was forgotten as he took her as fast as she demanded and as hard as he wanted. She met him with each stroke, nails digging into the flesh of his back, uttering sounds from deep in her throat. He, too, could not remain quiet, his growls melding with hers in a strange duet, a song they both seemed powerless to silence.

He drove her faster and faster—or was she driving him? He did not know. They were like one person, not separate, not alone, not lost to each other.

Sensation rose, higher and higher, more and more intense. Thought vanished and sheer need took over, and still he moved with her, feeling the same growing crescendo inside her.

He felt her release vibrate and pulse around him, her cry ringing in his ear as his own release came, his own cry, his own symphony of pleasure.

It took a while for the sensation to ebb enough for him to collapse beside her. Though no longer connected to her in the most intimate way, he still felt they were one.

He wanted to crow with masculine delight at it, this feeling of belonging to another person, being a part of her.

"Now that is better," he murmured into her ear, tasting it with his tongue.

"Better than what?" she asked, squirming under his lips, her hands exploring his flesh.

He rose on one elbow. "Than being a damned fool." He lowered his mouth to her lips and tasted them again with more leisure. She pressed herself against his leg. Her fingers played in his hair.

With some rationality restored, Tanner decided it was far preferable to enjoy the time they had together than to rage at its impending end. Besides, he still had a few days to change her mind. She would not be rid of him so easily.

If he accomplished nothing else in his life, he was determined to accomplish this: making Marlena his marchioness, his wife.

He settled next to her, holding her close. "Do you know what, Miss Brown?"

She wrapped a leg over his. "What, Lord Tannerton?"

"I am in a puzzle."

"A puzzle?" Her fingers were now twirling the hairs on his chest.

Dear God. It did not take much from her to arouse him again. He almost could not talk. "That bout of lovemaking was quite…pleasurable—"

"But?" Her hand was now splayed on his stomach.

"Mmm, uh, it has also been very nice to proceed at a leisurely pace." He rubbed his thumb on her arm, hardly parity with what she was doing to him.

"And?" Her hand slipped lower.

"I—mmm—was about to suggest we try it slowly and—ah—debate which we prefer later."

"Very well." She touched him, circled him with her hand.

Other women had touched him so, but the jolt of emotion that accompanied the sensations she created was totally unique.

He lay on his back and flung his arms over his head, savouring each daring touch.

Suddenly she stopped and rolled away from him. "You must think me terribly wanton."

He turned to her, touching her on the shoulder. She curled up in a ball.

"What is it, Marlena?" he whispered.

"I was being too—too bold, too dissolute, too trollopy."

A laugh escaped him. "Trollopy?"

She rolled over to face him. "Is that not a word?"

He pulled her into his arms, his face level with hers. "I like you trollopy," he murmured. "In fact, I did not think your wantonness terrible in the least."

She blinked. "You did not?"

He kissed her on the forehead. "I was rather enjoying how…trollopy you were behaving."

She laughed. "Are you ever serious? I do not know what to think."

He searched deep into her eyes. "I am entirely serious, Marlena. Your enjoyment, your boldness, is a delight."

She regarded him a long time. "Then I should like to delight you more."

It took Wexin two days before he had made all the arrangements to travel to Parronley. He hired three men to accompany him, men who could be trusted to do what he wanted if he paid them enough. He'd hired them before, when he'd first searched for Marlena and that maid. Even though the men had not found either of them, he'd paid them well and they were more than willing to work for him once more, even to perform his ultimate wish, if he desired them to. He had a fast postchaise ready to transport him and a coachman who thought they could reach Parronley in four days.

Perhaps he would find the deed done already. Perhaps the Bow Street Runner had already recaptured Marlena. All the better. One thing he knew, Marlena would never escape again.

His valet made a final tug on his neckcloth, brushed the fabric of his fine coat and declared him ready to attend the opera. He and Lydia were to go in the company of friends, including two gentlemen who wanted his support in a bill they would present in the Lords.

Soon, he thought with a rush of excitement. *Very soon my worries will be over.*

He nodded to his valet and crossed the room to his wife's door.

He knocked and opened it. "Are you ready, my dear?"

Her maid was fastening a garnet necklace around her neck. "One moment, Howard."

The maid stepped back. "There, ma'am."

Lydia fussed with the jewels. "Thank you, Nancy." She stood and turned to her admiring husband. "I am quite ready now."

"You look ravishing," he said.

The maid held out her velvet cloak. Wexin took it and draped it over his arm. "Let us go then, my dear."

She held his arm down the marble staircase. "I do wish you would not go off on business tomorrow, Howard. I shall miss you so."

He patted her hand. "And I shall miss you."

They reached the hall where the butler bowed and said, "The carriage is waiting, sir."

Wexin took his hat and gloves from the man and put them on.

"Then allow me to accompany you," Lydia persisted. "I should like to go with you.

He turned to assist her into her cloak. "I would not dream of putting you through something so tedious." He smiled. "I assure you, I will return very soon."

Her beautiful eyes were tinged with unhappiness.

He patted her on the hand again. "Do not look so sad. I shall bring you a gift."

She frowned. "I do not want a gift. I want to be with you."

"Ah. but it shall be a great gift." He smiled. If only she knew how great a gift he planned to give her. He planned, after all, to secure their future together.

Chapter Twelve

Marlena woke to the sound of rain pattering against the window glass. For a moment she thought it was still night, it was so dark in the room, but she could spy a very grey morning through a gap in the curtains.

Tanner was not next to her. She sat up and combed her fingers through her tangled hair.

"Good morning." Tanner stood in the doorway connecting his bedchamber to hers. He rested against the doorframe, dressed in the coat and trousers he'd worn the night before.

"You are dressed already," she said.

He smiled and crossed the room to her, leaning down to give her a warm kiss.

He murmured against her lips, "I could easily undress again."

She was tempted and laughed. "What time is it?"

"Eleven."

"Eleven!" She grabbed her nightdress and put it on. "I had no idea it was so late! Why did you not wake me?"

He sat on the bed. "To what purpose? It was my pleasure to let you sleep as long as you wished."

She slipped off the bed and padded over to the water pitcher and bowl to splash water on her face. "I am not used to staying in bed so long."

Marlena had not slept this late since Corland had been alive and she'd had so little to do.

He walked over to her and hugged her from behind. "Shall I act the lady's maid this morning?"

She reached up and stroked his hair. "I do not know a lady's maid who acts as you do."

He stilled. "Did you once have a lady's maid, Marlena?"

She wished she had not spoken. It was becoming more and more difficult to lie to him about herself, especially when Tanner knew her more intimately than anyone else ever had.

"I did have a lady's maid." She averted her gaze.

The muscles of his arms flexed as if he were surprised that she answered him. They stilled again as if he were thinking of asking her another question about herself.

She turned to him. "Perhaps you can sit on the bed? You make a particularly distracting lady's maid. I will tell you when I need you."

He nuzzled her neck before complying.

It was erotic in its own way to have him watch her wash up and dress. True to his promise, he assisted her in tying the laces on her dress, brushed the tangles from her hair, and, when she was ready, he escorted her below stairs for a simple breakfast of fresh bread, cheese and coddled eggs.

"What did you do while I was sleeping?" she asked as they ate.

His brows came together. "I wrote a letter to London. News of my being aboard the wrecked ship should be reaching my people by now, as well as the documents for the horse purchase." He pierced a piece of egg with his fork and smiled. "My cousin Algernon will be delighted I did not drown. He would have apoplexy if he thought he must become the marquess."

Marlena could not recall ever meeting Tanner's cousin, but she could too easily imagine how those close to Tanner would grieve his loss. "Of course you must let them know you are alive."

He became serious again. "By the time the letter reaches my secretary, you shall be...settled. You need not fear. No one will question my decision to visit one of my properties."

His concern for her brought an ache to her heart. No man had ever cared so much for her. No man had ever put her needs above all else.

For all her initial protests that she could make this journey alone, she knew now she could not have done it without him. She not only owed him her life—she owed him her freedom. The thought of parting from him became ever more unbearable.

He took a sip of tea. "Kenney will carry the letter into the village as soon as the rain clears."

Marlena could imagine Mr and Mrs Kenney telling their friends in the village that the marquess had brought a woman with him. She was confident they would never realize her true identity. Even if they read of the shipwreck, Tanner had said nothing to them about being on the ship. They would never know enough to connect Tanner with the Vanishing Viscountess.

Tanner would know, however. Marlena's appetite fled.

He cleaned his plate and leaned in his chair, balancing it on its two back legs. "What shall we do today?"

She half-expected the chair to slip out from under him, but he seemed heedless of the possibility. "Whatever you wish. I confess it will feel odd to be inside instead of travelling." To be at leisure instead of running.

He smiled. "Let us go on a treasure hunt."

"A treasure hunt?"

He lowered the chair again, to her relief. "We'll explore the house. My grandfather was fond of this house. I can recall visiting him here. Let us see what treasures he and my grandmother left behind. We may discover something useful for our trip."

By mid-afternoon they were in the attic, digging through big wooden chests. Tanner had discovered a lovely wool shawl, now draped around Marlena's shoulders. He also unearthed a gentleman's white wig and coat of bright green silk.

He put both on. "These might have been my grandfather's, although I can well remember my father in wig and lace." He posed for her. "How do I look?"

She giggled. "Quite foppish, actually."

He grinned and knelt down to rummage through the cedar-lined trunk.

"How old were you when your father died?" she asked.

He looked up. "Nineteen."

"So young?" She tried to imagine him that young having such an important title thrust upon him.

He shrugged. "He was thrown from his horse."

"And your mother?"

He pulled the wig off his head and busied himself with the contents of the trunk. "I was about ten. She died in childbirth."

She knew he did not have any brothers or sisters so he had lost his whole family, just as she had.

He sat back and fixed his gaze on her. "And your parents?"

She stared at him for a moment, then told the truth. "My— my mother died of childbirth fever. My father died much later. He was struck by lightning."

"Struck by lightning?"

She nodded. "I confess to having a fear of storms ever since."

His eyes filled with sympathy and he reached across the trunk to stroke her cheek. "And have you any family left?"

Tears stung her eyes as an image of her brother and her sweet little nephews formed in her mind. She shook her head.

"Then we are alike, you and I. Alone," he murmured.

The ache in Marlena's heart returned as their gazes held.

Tanner withdrew his hand and returned to the chest. Marlena peeked inside at more bright-coloured brocades that Tanner folded over as he searched deeper.

"I do not think pink silk is the thing to wear while travelling, do you?" He glanced up at her, his usual good humour returning—except for a remaining hint of emotion in his eyes.

She smiled. "Perhaps not."

He felt along the sides and the bottom and pulled out a flat wooden box. "Here's something."

He opened the hinged lid. Inside were lovely ladies' handkerchiefs of white linen and lace.

"You must have these." He said this in the most casual of voices.

She lifted one and unfolded it. "They are beautiful."

He gazed at her, one corner of his mouth lifting into a wistful smile.

He looked down at the box again. "There is something else." He unfolded one of the handkerchiefs to reveal a lady's ring.

He placed it in Marlena's hand.

"Oh, my!" She held it up to the light of their lamp.

It was a delicate sapphire ring, its glittering blue stone encircled in tiny gold leaves and flowers. "It is so lovely."

She handed it back to him, but he would not take it. "Try it on."

She slipped it on the ring finger of her right hand and it

fitted her as if made for her. She held her hand so he could see how pretty it was.

He smiled. "It must have been my grandmother's."

Marlena admired it a moment more before she began pulling it off.

He stopped her with his hand. "Wear it. I want you to have it."

"But it is a family piece," she protested.

He waved a quelling hand. "I want you to have it."

She gazed down it again. "I shall treasure it always."

They turned their attention back to the trunk and then to the next trunk and the next, eventually selecting two old top coats that might prove useful on the journey, as well as the lace handkerchief and Tanner's grandmother's sapphire ring. When they were finished it was nearly time for dinner.

That evening when they sat in the drawing room, Tanner read *Timon of Athens* from a copy of the Shakespeare play he'd discovered in the library. Marlena relaxed by the fire, listening to his deep, expressive voice, the woollen shawl wrapped around her shoulders, the sapphire ring sparkling in the firelight. She wished the rain would never end. She wished she could stay right where she was, with Tanner, for ever.

As she did every Sunday, Fia accompanied her Uncle Gunn and Aunt Priss to the old stone church that had stood between Parronley and Kilrosa for over two hundred years. Bram, of course, was also one of the party, and it was only natural that he walked next to Fia. Even though the sun shone, the roads were still muddy, and Bram took hold of Fia's arm when the ruts in the road made walking difficult.

Fia followed her aunt and uncle to their usual pew, filing

in after them. Bram sat next to Fia, looming over her like he always did. She picked up the prayer book and opened it.

Soon the service began, and Reverend Bell recited the Ten Commandments, the congregation responding in unison. When the reverend came to *Thou shalt not commit adultery,* Fia closed her eyes.

"Lord, have mercy upon us, and incline our hearts to keep this law," she answered along with the others. She hoped God knew how fervently she meant what she said.

Sometimes Fia felt as if she did not belong in the church with all these good people. Still, the sound of their collective voices in prayer, the light filtering through the coloured glass of the windows, the smell of wood and stone and people, all gave her comfort.

Reverend Bell began his sermon, speaking on the virtue of moderation. Fia had to stifle a smile at his choice of topic, this man who spent so much time drinking immoderately in the taproom of the Black Agnes. She made the mistake of glancing at Bram, whose twinkling eyes reflected her amusement.

When the last amens were spoken, the congregation filed out of the church and back into the sunshine. Most lingered to greet Reverend Bell and the elders, as well as to pass time with their neighbours. Fia drifted off to the edge of the group to wait for Uncle Gunn and Aunt Priss, who were as busy chatting as were the others. Pretty Jean Skinner waylaid Bram and now held him captive with her flirting and her silly talk.

Fia glanced away and took another step back. Lyall and Erroll gave her a friendly nod as they walked by, but, as she had predicted, their affections had been transferred elsewhere, to the Brookston sisters, who giggled at every word they said. For once, though, Fia wished they would pay her such attentions, so that perhaps she could be distracted from this odd pain in her chest from watching Bram with Jean.

To her shock Fia felt tears stinging her eyes. She blinked several times, but the tears kept forming anyway. She was also finding it hard to breathe without shuddering. If anyone noticed, what would she ever say? How could she explain?

"Aunt Priss," she called out, hoping she was too far away for her aunt to see anything amiss. "I'm startin' for home."

Her aunt nodded and waved and Fia spun on her heels, trying her best not to look like she was in a big hurry.

As soon as she reached the top of the hill, she turned off the road. Her aunt and uncle would visit with their friends for at least half an hour. She could take the time to collect herself before she walked back to the inn and began working. She did not want to start bawling while she was working. That would be nearly as bad as bawling outside church. Somebody would ask her what was wrong, and she didn't know the answer to that question.

She took the path that led up another hill, climbing to the top where a castle once stood. It was naught but a pile of old stones now, but she liked the place. She climbed up on one of the stones, warmed by the sun, and sat cross-legged, gazing down at Parronley House in the distance.

Seeing the fine house made her think of the lady who ought to be living there now. Everybody knew Lady Corland was now Baroness Parronley, since her brother and his little boys died. It was Fia's fault that the Baroness could not return to her house. If Fia had not sinned with Lord Corland, maybe all the awful things would not have happened.

If only Fia had not left Kilrosa. If only she'd stayed and waited and heeded the scriptures and remained a virtuous girl, she might be worthy to marry a good man.

She did not try to stop the tears. She had not cried for over two years now and she had thought all her tears were gone. But then Bram came home and now she felt like spilling tears every day. Seeing him with Jean had done it this time.

Some day Jean or some other good, decent girl would marry Bram in that very church where Fia sat next to him this day. Maybe if Fia cried out all her tears now, she would have no more to shed when Bram married.

Fia rocked back and forth, arms wrapped around herself, keening with grief. That day Lord Corland died, it was like she had died, too, and Lady Corland—Baroness Parronley. She and Baroness Parronley might as well be dead.

"What is this, lass? Why are you weeping?"

She jumped and snapped her head up to see Bram walking towards her. She turned away from him, but he soon was standing in front of her.

"Are you ailing?" he asked.

She took a shuddering breath and shook her head.

His hand touched her arm. "Fia lass, tell me what is wrong."

She wiped her eyes with her fingers. "I came here to be alone, Bram."

His hand fell away. "I saw you leave the church and somethin' told me to follow. You don't do weeping like this without reason. If something is so wrong, let me aid you."

She lifted her face to him and stared into his eyes. "You cannot help me." She glanced away. "There's nothing to help me."

He climbed up on the stone and sat beside her. She moved away, but could not go far or she'd fall off.

He stared out on to the valley below. "You were just a wee lass when I left for war, Fia. Twelve years old, but already the bonniest lass I knew. Bright-eyed and lively and full of wanting to know everything. You were the daughter Mam

Priss prayed for." He shifted his position. "What happened in London to change you?"

She tried to shrug him off. "You were gone, Bram. You do not know that anything changed me but time."

He lifted his hand, but dropped it again. "Mam Priss said you came back different. And you came back after Miss Parronley killed her husband."

She twisted away from him. "She'd be Baroness Parronley."

"Baroness, then." He peered at her. "Does it have to do with the murder, then?"

She jumped off the rock. "You all talk a great deal."

She started running down the hill but he caught her from behind and spun her around. She tried to swing a fist at him and to pull away, but he held her fast.

"Let me go, Bram," she cried, struggling, but unable to dislodge his large hand around her arm.

He pulled her against him and wrapped his arms around her, engulfing her with his huge warm body. "I will hold you 'til you tell me, lass. I promise to tell no other, but let me know what disturbs you and I'll not bother you over it again."

"Are you forcing me, Bram Gunn?" she mumbled into his chest.

"Ay, I am indeed." He murmured, holding her closer. "Now commence with talking."

"First you have to let me go," she said.

"Say something that is not blather and I'll think on it."

She could never tell him how her heart seemed to cleave in two pieces when he smiled at Jean Skinner. That would be too shaming, but, in the shelter of his strong arms and warm body, she thought it might be safe to tell him about that terrible night. She wanted to tell Bram, who seemed so strong he could carry anything, including this burden she had carried alone for so long.

"I'll do it. I'll do it," she said. "Give me room to breathe."

He loosened his hold on her only a bit.

"Lady Corland did not kill her husband," she began.

His brows rose.

"I was there, Bram." She felt herself turn cold as she remembered it. "I saw it all."

He took her hand and walked her back to sit upon the rock, settling next to her. "Tell me of it, lass."

She took a breath. "I was in the room—in—in Lord Corland's bedchamber."

Fia glanced at Bram, expecting to see his lips purse in disapproval. Instead, he merely nodded for her to go on.

"A man entered the room. He did not see me, but I saw him. He—he was dressed oddly. In Lady Corland's robe. I knew it because it had a lace trim." She swallowed. "The—the man walked over to the bed and leaned over. At first I thought he was going to kiss Lord Corland, but instead—instead…" She faltered.

"Who was the fellow?" he asked mildly.

She turned to face him. "Lord Wexin."

"Lord Wexin?" His eyes widened.

She nodded. "Lady Corland's cousin. The man who inherits Parronley if she is dead." She glanced away again. "He—he—pulled out scissors and—and stabbed Lord Corland in the throat." Her fingers flexed and her hand jabbed as if it were she holding the weapon.

He covered her hand with his own.

Her voice rose higher in pitch and the words poured out. "I guess I screamed, because he came after me then, but Lady Corland ran into the room and stopped him from stabbing me and I thought he would kill her, too. Instead he cried out for help, like it wasn't him doing the stabbing. He—he put the scissors in Lady Corland's hand and the robe, too—it was all full of blood—and then he told me he would kill me if I told anyone what I saw."

Bram's arm tightened across her shoulder.

She pulled away and looked him in the eye. "I ran away then, Bram. I ran and didn't stop until I reached Kilrosa."

"No one can blame you for running, Fia." His expression remained open and accepting.

She felt waves of guilt, however. "You don't understand, Bram. I—I left Lady Corland with him blaming it all on her. It is said she ran away—but what if he found her and killed her, too?"

He took her hand between his two strong ones. "Now, lass. That did not happen. If it did, he would come claiming Parronley, now, wouldn't he?"

His hands felt warm and rough with calluses, but so gentle and calming.

He made her look him in the eye. "Now, y'see, you have nothing to worry over."

Her breathing slowed. Her muscles relaxed, as if she'd indeed passed the weight on to his shoulders and off hers.

His eyes were warm and comforting. "Nothin' will hurt you, Fia. Nothin'. I'll see to it." He paused a moment. "I will take care of you, Fia. For always."

"What are you saying, Bram?" she whispered, feeling the blood drain from her face.

He averted his gaze and his cheeks turned pink. "I'm asking to court you, Fia."

She pulled her hand away. "No!"

The baffled and wounded expression on his face nearly broke her heart.

"You do not understand, Bram." She shook her head. He tried to turn his face away, but she held his chin and looked into his eyes. "Do you not wonder why I was in Lord Corland's room?"

He seemed to look at her very deeply. "You were in Lord Corland's bed."

Her jaw dropped. He spoke the truth like it was nothing.

He smiled wanly. "You were out in the world alone, lass, in a gentleman's house. The world is a treacherous place, I've learned, a place full of temptation—"

"Temptation? It wasn't temptation, Bram." She blew out a breath.

He responded in a quiet voice. "I meant only that I'd not judge you for whatever happened."

She slipped off the rock and stood before him. "I went willingly enough, Bram. I did not want to lose my employment, which he said I would and that no one would hire me again. I did not have any money. I'd seen enough of London to know what happened to girls with no money, and I didn't want that to happen to me. So I bedded him and stole his money so I could get home." She backed away, adding, "Reverend Bell's sermons say I'm not fit to be married, and I'll not pretend I am."

She spun around and started walking down the hill, but she did not make it far before Bram fell in beside her. They walked in silence.

When they were halfway back to Kilrosa he spoke. "War makes a man do terrible things, Fia."

She darted a glance at him, not knowing why he was speaking.

He went on. "A soldier's job is killin'. The commandment says, 'Thou shalt not kill.'"

Fia frowned, puzzled as to why he was telling her this.

He stopped walking and gazed into the distance. "Some of those Frenchies were no more than lads, but I killed them. I can still see their faces, some of them—" He bowed his head and fell silent. When he lifted it again, he looked directly at her. "So I'll not judge what another person does to stay alive, in either body or soul."

He reached for her hands and she allowed him to take them. She lifted her face to his, her breath stolen by the tenderness in his expression. He glanced around, but they were alone on that stretch of road. Very slowly, he leaned down to her and placed his lips on hers.

Chapter Thirteen

Tanner and Marlena spent three wonderful days in Dutwood House. The rain had ceased after their first full day there, but it took time for the land to dry enough for them to venture back on their journey.

Tanner had been delighted to provide her with a chance to rest, to heal her horse-weary legs and his sore ribs. She was able to sleep as late as she wished each morning. All that was required of them was to decide what card game to play, what book to read aloud to each other.

Their time together at Dutwood gave Tanner a taste of what life with her would offer. He was a man easily bored, but all their forced leisure had not brought him even a moment of tedium. Everything they had done had delighted him, mind and body.

Because he'd shared the time with her.

They had ventured out of doors the previous day, donning old boots and trudging through the woods to the lake and back again. The fresh crisp air had put roses in Marlena's cheeks and her blue eyes glittered as brightly as the sapphire in the ring she wore beneath her glove.

Now the idyll was over, but Tanner was resolved that it would not be over for ever.

Mrs Kenney sent them off with a hearty breakfast, knapsacks full of bread and cheese, and laundered, dry clothing. The clean air and bright sun made for an exhilarating morning and the horses at least seemed to relish the return to their journey.

Rather than backtrack to Penrith and the Pooley Bridge, Tanner decided they should travel north through Greystoke, threading their way along minor roads to return to the coaching road near Calthwaite.

Still on his property, their horses climbed a hill below which was the Greystoke road. The valley was alive with colour, the trees even more vibrant with yellow and gold than before the rain.

Tanner glanced at Marlena. She made a lovely picture on the bay mare, with all the bearing of a marchioness, even if riding astride like a farmer's daughter.

"It is lovely here." She gazed out over the fields ahead, lying before them like square patches on a peasant's quilt. Marlena swung around to look behind her where Dutwood House still peeked through the trees.

She sighed. "I shall miss this place."

As would Tanner. Dutwood House was perhaps the most humble and rustic of his properties, but it very lately had become his favourite, because he'd shared it with her.

"By God," he exclaimed suddenly, inadvertently pulling on his horse's reins. "I have an idea." The horse danced in confusion until Tanner got him back under control. "Why not live at Dutwood? You need not go to Edinburgh. You could wait here. You would be Mrs Brown, whom I allowed to live in my house—"

"No, Tanner." Her expression turned stony. "I could not."

"But you could," he insisted, the plan rising fully formed into his head. He would leave her here and return to London. He'd set about discovering her identity and the identity of the man who was her enemy—her seducer. It should not be too difficult. How many lady's companions were accused of theft? Whose father had died of a lightning strike? When he'd cleared her name, he would travel back to Dutwood and return with her as his wife.

"What better place to hide away?" he persisted.

She brought her horse nose to tail with his. "No, Tanner. I've involved you in my troubles enough. You already take too much of a risk merely escorting me to Edinburgh."

He waved a dismissive hand. "You take the risk too seriously."

"I assure you I do not." She spoke quietly.

He signalled his horse to start down the hill, not looking back, but hearing her following him.

When he reached the bottom of the hill, she called to him. "Tanner?"

He turned and waited for her to catch up.

She brought her horse alongside his and reached over to grasp his arm. She made him look into her pain-filled eyes.

"Being with you has been the happiest time in my life." She lowered her head. "But I must leave you in Edinburgh."

He leaned towards her, and with a small, desperate sound in her throat, she closed the distance to put her lips on his. He kissed her back, pouring his emotions into the touch of his lips, trying to show her he would not give her up so easily.

When they finally broke apart, he managed to smile at her. "I shall endeavour to make our last days together as pleasant as possible."

"Yes." Her smile was as forced as his. "It is a lovely day and there is so much beauty to see."

He gazed at her. "So much beauty."

He vowed he would not distress her further, that he would do his best to make her laugh, anything to keep the pain from her eyes.

But he would not give her up so easily.

"Shall we avoid the main coaching route again?" he asked. "These roads seem dry enough."

"It will be safer, will it not?" she responded. "And it will make our trip longer."

He smiled.

They rode at a leisurely pace, stopping by crystalline streams to refresh the horses while they ate Mrs Kenney's bread and cheese and drank the one last bottle of wine from the Dutwood House cellar. As the afternoon wore on, they approached a little village, not far from Carlisle and near the border to Scotland.

Tanner halted his horse and looked down at the village. "If there is a half-decent inn here, I suggest we stay."

"It looks large enough for an inn," Marlena said. "And as sweet a place as Cumberland could offer."

The houses were grey stone and white stucco, in neat rows on the main street and fanning off to the side. An old stone church stood at one end of the town. Thin wisps of smoke came from the chimneys.

As they rode in, Tanner turned to her. "Who are we today, by the way?"

She laughed. "Mr and Mrs Antony."

"Antony," he repeated. "Antony… I have lost the habit of being someone else."

They found the inn, a small but cosy place. Tanner dismounted and held his hand out to help Marlena from her horse. They found the innkeeper inside and arranged for a room.

"Would you care for refreshment?" the innkeeper asked. "We are serving a mutton stew."

"Excellent," Tanner replied. "I need to see to the horses. Is there somewhere my wife could sit undisturbed until I return?"

"There is a private room off the taproom. She is welcome to wait for you there."

Tanner raised his brows to Marlena.

"I think that sounds lovely," she said. "Especially if I might have some tea."

"Indeed, ma'am." The innkeeper led her to the taproom and Tanner walked outside.

He gathered their baggage and placed it right inside the inn's doorway. Then he led the horses to stables kept by the village's smithy.

From the entrance, he could see the smithy talking to another man with a horse. Tanner waited at the door.

"I am looking for someone," Tanner heard the man say to the smithy. "A man and woman."

Tanner stilled.

"They were on horseback. Have they passed through here?"

"Not my stable. You can ask at the inn," the smithy said. "What is the name, in case they show up here?"

The man cleared his throat. "That is the thing. They are not travelling under their own names. The woman is a fugitive. There is a reward for her capture. If you assist me—"

Tanner did not wait to hear more. He backed up the horses, who whinnied in protest at not getting their expected bag of oats. He pulled them back to the inn and ran inside finding the innkeeper in the hall.

"Where is my wife?" Tanner demanded.

The innkeeper looked alarmed. "This way." He led Tanner through the taproom to a small private parlour.

Tanner wasted no time. "We leave now." He threw some coins on the table.

Marlena's eyes grew large with fright, but she followed him, running ahead to the horses while Tanner grabbed their luggage.

She was already seated on her horse. Tanner tossed her one of their bags.

"Go," he said, mounting at the same time.

From behind him, Tanner heard a shout. "That is them! Stop them!"

They took off at a gallop, too fast to be stopped. When they were clear of the town, they slowed the horses, but not to the leisurely pace of that morning. Tanner kept them moving north, keeping an eye on the position of the sun. When the road bent too far in another direction, he led them off the road and over the countryside. He pushed the horses as much as he dared, aware that the animals were tiring and the day advancing. Already the sun was low in the sky and the foliage leeched of vibrant colour. They must stop soon.

Over the crest of a hill, Tanner spied a river wending its way through the valley. Its banks were thick with trees and foliage.

"We'll stop by the river," he called to Marlena.

They descended the hill and followed the river along its banks until Tanner found a sheltered spot where it would be easy for the horses to drink. Tanner's gelding dipped his muzzle in the water even before Tanner dismounted. Tanner helped Marlena from the mare, and, while the horses drank, he fetched the road book and the satchel containing the leftover cheese, bread, and wine. He led Marlena to the shelter of a nearby tree.

"Eat something," he said.

She nodded and pulled out a piece of bread, handing the satchel back to him. "Are we in Scotland now?"

"I believe so." He opened the road book, straining his eyes in the waning daylight. "This must be the River Esk. I think I know about where we are." He closed the book again. "I had better tend to the horses."

Once the horses had enough water, Tanner led them to a patch of grass. They immediately gnawed at the green blades. Taking a cloth from one of the bags, Tanner wiped the sweat off his horse.

Marlena joined him. "Is there another cloth?"

He pulled one from the bag and handed it to her. She tended to her horse, eyeing Tanner cautiously as she worked.

They had barely spoken during the hard ride from the village, but she must realise he was consumed with questions, questions that invaded his mind as he rode, blocked only by the more pressing need to see her to safety.

"We will not reach an inn tonight." Tanner would ask his questions later, after they had settled themselves. "We must stay here. Build a fire."

She made no complaint about spending the night outdoors. She did not grumble that she would be cold or whine that she was hungry and thirsty.

"I'll collect firewood," she said instead.

Tanner removed the bags from the horse's saddles and loosened their girths. Marlena cleared an area for the fire while Tanner walked upstream to a place where the water flowed swiftly. He filled the water skins he'd had the presence of mind to toss in their bags before leaving Dutwood. In a still part of the river he spied some large fish nibbling at the underwater plants, mere shadows in the waning light.

He walked back to Marlena, who had gathered some rocks from the river's edge and was placing them in a circle.

"Give me a hairpin."

She reached under her bonnet and pulled a pin from her hair. "What is it for?"

He picked ..p a stone and sharpened one end. "To hook a fish. I just need something colourful for bait."

"I'll find something." She rummaged through one of the bags and pulled out a tiny piece of ribbon. "Will this do?"

"It will."

He hated the loss of ease between them and feared he might never find it again.

Tanner walked back to the fish-filled pool and uncoiled a length of string. He tied the improvised hook on one end and stuck the piece of ribbon on it before dropping it into the water.

He used to fish like this when a boy wandering around Tannerton, bothering the gameskeeper enough times that the man eventually took him under his wing and taught him all manner of useful things. Tanner had nearly forgotten them.

At the small pool he and a big fat fellow of a fish sparred until the fish finally took the bait in its mouth. Tanner jerked up on the string and his fish threshed noisily in the water until he pulled him out.

When he returned to Marlena, she had stacked thick pieces of wood with plenty of tinder underneath.

"You've built outdoor fires before," he commented.

"Yes," she admitted.

He opened his tinderbox and struck a flame.

He roasted the fish, which they ate with their fingers, remaining silent. It was obvious to Tanner that Marlena had hidden something from him about herself, something so important a reward was on her head and a Bow Street Runner was pursuing her.

After he ate, Tanner rose to check on the horses, safely tethered nearby. When he returned, the sun was no more than a glow on the horizon, but the fire burned brightly. Marlena still sat by the fire, hugging her knees and wrapped in his grandmother's woollen shawl.

He sat near her.

She spoke, breaking their long silence. "It was Rapp, wasn't it?"

Tanner nodded.

She stared into the fire. "I thought Davies was pursuing us, but it was Rapp. Rapp knows I am alive."

He fixed his gaze on her. "There is a reward on your head, as well. I heard him speak of it. Do not tell me it is due to the theft of a few jewels."

Marlena lowered her head to her knees, then turned to gaze at him. The flames of the campfire illuminated his handsome face, filled with anger and confusion and pain. She took a deep, ragged breath, aching with the knowledge that everything had changed.

Rapp knew she was alive.

"Answer me," Tanner demanded.

She swallowed and averted her gaze, not knowing how much to tell him. She quickly glanced back. "Did Rapp see you? Did he see your face?"

He looked puzzled. "I do not think so, but—"

"That's good," she whispered, more to herself than to him.

"You did not answer me," he accused, his voice turning deeper, rougher.

There was only one way to convince him that matters had changed. She must tell him the truth. "I am an accused murderer."

His brows rose.

She fought for courage to continue. "I tell you this much only to impress upon you how serious this is. There is no fixing this, Tanner. They mean to see me hanged—you, too, if you are discovered helping me." She searched his face to see if he comprehended. "It is not too late for you. Rapp still does not know who you are."

He waved his hand. "Never mind that. Who are you supposed to have murdered?"

Marlena gave him a direct gaze. "My husband."

He gaped. "Husband!"

She turned her face away. "Yes."

He laughed drily. "So your tale of being a lady's companion accused of theft—that was a lie?" It was more a statement than a question.

She nodded.

"And this man who supposedly seduced you…" He glared at her.

It seemed too difficult to explain that she had partially told him the truth. She had described Corland. "A lie, Tanner. It was all a lie." She bowed her head.

His hand closed into a fist. "You were *married?*" He put a biting emphasis on the word *married.* "You were not some lady's companion at the mercy of her employer's son—" He broke off as if he was too angry to form words. Tanner rose to his feet and paced next to her.

She looked up at him. "Tanner, you must see I did not know you at first. I could not tell you I was an accused murderer. You were a marquess and, as such, how could I know you would not turn me in? The shipwreck gave me a chance to be free. I could not allow anything to jeopardise that chance."

He was too tall for the glow of the campfire to reach his face. She could not see his expression, but she could feel his emotion. "I was not always a stranger, Marlena, not after we shared a bed."

She glanced away.

He persisted, his voice low and pained. "A husband, Marlena. How can you justify not telling me you had been married? Married."

His words were like a sharp sword. "Tanner, I regret—" She covered her face with her hands, before lifting her head to him again. "I ought to have informed you of the danger I placed you in."

"The danger?" He scoffed.

"It was wrong of me."

He pulled off his hat and swept a hand through his hair. "Do you think I care of that?" He paced again, then leaned down to her, grabbing her chin in his hand. "When we made love, Marlena—you should have told me a husband preceded me. Who was he? Am I to know that?"

She pulled away from his grasp. "No."

He straightened, his face in shadow again. "No?"

Marlena rose to her knees. "I will not tell you. Not now. Not when Rapp knows I am alive."

"I fail to see what that has to do with it." He placed his hands on his hips.

"We must separate. Rapp will pursue me, do you not see that? If he or anyone discovers you have been seen with me—" She broke off again, sitting back on her legs. "Your ignorance of me may offer some protection. You shall be able to protest that I duped you—which I did—and you had no idea whom you assisted."

He stared down at her. "Do *you* not see that I am not speaking of Rapp, but of you and me and what I thought was real between us?"

She wrapped her arms around her waist. Wounding him so much cut her up inside like a thousand knife blades.

He folded his arms across his chest, almost a mirror image of her. "We are close to Edinburgh. Two, three days at the most. I will take you to Edinburgh and that will be the end of it."

He was mistaken. The end had already come.

He turned from her and strode over to where they had placed their bags. He returned to toss one of them at her.

She caught it and clutched it to her breast.

"It will be cold tonight," he said in a flat voice. "Cover up as much as possible."

He turned and walked away, the darkness covering him. Marlena fingered the sapphire ring he had given her before opening the bag to do as he'd bid.

After he returned to the campfire, Marlena feigned being asleep. She watched him through slitted eyelids as he settled by the fire, making a pillow of one of the bags and covering himself with a top coat.

She watched him thrash around in search of a comfortable position. When he settled the campfire illuminated his face. When the furrows in his brow eased and the rigidity of his jaw slackened, his features took on a boyish vulnerability. She knew he had finally fallen asleep.

Marlena had watched him until the fire dwindled to embers and dawn glowed through the trees. She now rose carefully, trying not to make a sound.

She rolled the extra top coat they'd brought with them from Dutwood House and stuffed it in the bag. With one last long look at him, she mouthed, "Goodbye." Forcing herself to turn away, she carried the bag to Dulcea.

The horse nickered in greeting.

"Shhhhh," she whispered.

She slung the bag on the horse's back and tightened the girth. Tanner's horse became interested in this project and nudged her with his muzzle. She turned and stroked the gelding's neck.

"Take good care of him," she whispered, rubbing her cheek against the horse's coarse hair.

The animal snorted and nodded as if understanding her command.

She untied the reins of the mare and led her away on foot, mounting only when she was at some distance. She followed the river, which led her north as she needed to travel, pushing the horse to walk as fast as possible over the uneven ground.

When the sun rose in the sky and melted the mist, she stopped to remove Tanner's grandmother's shawl from under her cloak, holding it against her for a moment, as if embracing Tanner again. She folded it and put it in the bag. Dulcea put her nose in the clear water of the river and drank. Marlena then led the horse to a little glade where she nibbled some grass.

The land around Marlena looked like the hills of home. The Scottish air even smelled like home. What she would give to see Parronley again, to have the comfort of familiar old faces, to feel home once more. Likely no one would remember her there; thirteen years had passed, and she had changed so much. She doubted anyone could find the young carefree girl she'd been at age twelve in her face now. She did not even speak the same as she once did. She'd lost her Scottish burr like she had lost everything else of her life in Scotland.

Marlena turned around in her saddle to gaze back from where she'd come, from where she had left Tanner. Was he awake now? Perhaps when he found her gone, he would curse her so much he would turn south and make his way back into the safe life of the Marquess of Tannerton.

She remounted her horse and threaded her way upriver. The River Esk flowed near Parronley, she remembered. All she need do was follow the river, then watch for signs pointing to Edinburgh to the east. She stayed on the natural terrain, although it slowed her pace. Sometimes she'd glimpse the road and be tempted to use it. Then a carriage or a cart or a rider would pass by, and she'd shrink back to the river bank again.

Try as she might to think only of the land ahead of her, Tanner invaded her thoughts. She tried not to imagine how he must despise her, not only for lying to him, but also for sneaking away while he slept.

When the sun grew high in the sky, she selected a spot for her and the horse to drink from the river. After they were refreshed, she walked the mare up a hill to get her bearings. The horse nibbled on the grass, but Marlena had brought with her only one small piece of bread and two smaller chunks of cheese, leaving the remainder for Tanner. She nibbled on one piece of cheese, careful to eat only half.

At the crest of the hill, Marlena saw that the river led into a town. Within the town the river broke into two branches. Which branch was the River Esk? The sun was now directly overhead, so she could not tell which way was north. Worst of all, it appeared she had no choice but to ride down and cross the bridge. She could not avoid being seen.

She sank to the ground, resting while Dulcea ate her fill. The town bustled with activity. Perhaps the number of people would protect her. She could attempt to merge with them unnoticed as she passed through.

She led the horse back down the hill and continued to follow the river bank until she found a good place to join the road when no horse or vehicle was in sight. Soon, however, she was among several other riders, carts and pedestrians. A sign indicated the town's name was Langholm, a name that only dimly rang in her memory, a market town, perhaps. Its stone-and-stucco buildings reminded her of

Parronley, as did the hills rising around it like the frame around a painting.

As she entered the town the smell of roasting meat and baking bread wafted from the shops and inns. Her hunger increased, but she was determined to save her meagre stash of food for the night. One establishment she passed smelled of cooking fish, reminding her of Tanner's fish dinner the night before.

Trying to look as if she belonged with the flow of traffic, she rode closer and closer to the bridge. The sun seemed to hover over her left shoulder now, and the bridge seemed to lead her north. Her nerves calmed, even though seeing children dashing through the streets, shopworkers standing in doorways, farmers driving their carts, all made her feel very alone.

I'll become used to it, won't I, Eliza? she said to herself. *I'll become used to being alone.* Used to being without Tanner.

She passed the parish church and prayed God would keep her safe. And keep Tanner safe. It comforted her somewhat that Eliza would be looking down in heaven watching out for her. *Watch over Tanner, too, Eliza,* she begged.

The bridge was very near now and Marlena's heart beat faster. Her ordeal was almost over and it had been astonishingly easy. When she reached the bridge, she breathed a sigh of relief. She crossed, already searching for a place where she might leave the road again.

Out of the corner of her eye she saw a horse come from behind her. The horse rode so close she felt it brush Dulcea. When the horse's muzzle came level with Dulcea's shoulder, Marlena spied a man's arm reaching towards her.

She signalled Dulcea to take off at a gallop, hearing a voice behind her. "Halt, my lady."

She did not look back. She galloped past a farm cart and

some pedestrians who jumped to the side at her sudden approach. She could hear horse's hooves behind her in pursuit.

He caught up to her at an empty dip in the road, a place where no one could see a man accosting a lone woman, no chance someone would come to her aid. Rapp tried to grab her horse's bridle. She jerked the horse's head away from him and Dulcea reared and gnashed her teeth.

Rapp backed his horse away. "Give it up," he demanded. "I have you now."

"No!" she cried.

Dulcea reared again.

Suddenly there was the pounding hooves of another horse. A lone horseman bore down on them.

Tanner!

He reached them in an instant, looking more like a bandit than a rescuer. His face was covered by a cloth and he advanced on Rapp, not slowing his pace, and knocked Rapp from his saddle with one swing of his arm. Rapp's horse skittered away.

"I'll get you," Rapp cried, jumping to his feet, his fist in the air.

Tanner turned to Marlena. "Come on," he cried, as Rapp went for his horse.

Marlena set Dulcea into a gallop again, Tanner riding at her side. They galloped away from Langholm. When the road rose high they looked behind and saw that Rapp was following, although his form was a mere speck in the distance. When the road dipped again, Tanner turned them off through a break in the trees.

"This way," he called.

They rode to a place where the trees and brush cloaked them, slowing their tiring horses to a walk. Soon they reached the banks of a narrow stream, shallow enough that the rocks beneath the water were clearly visible.

"The horses must rest." Tanner dismounted and only then pulled off the cloth that masked his face. "Let them drink here."

He walked over to her and held out his hands to assist her from her horse. She put hers on his shoulders, and he grabbed her waist, holding her until her feet reached the ground. He still did not release her.

Looking into her eyes, he said, "Stay here. I am going to obscure our trail."

She nodded and he moved off, grabbing a small branch to carry with him. She held the reins of the horses by the riverbank, pulling their heads away when it seemed as if they were drinking too fast.

Her emotions were in turmoil. Her heart had leapt into her throat when she had seen him coming to her rescue. She wanted only to touch him, hold him, taste his lips. At the same time she felt as if she had doomed him to a terrible fate.

For if Rapp knew she was alive and correctly guessed that she had been headed towards Scotland, Wexin also knew this and Wexin was twice the danger Rapp was.

Marlena's heart beat faster when she heard Tanner return, leaves swishing as he approached. He walked with his head down. The dear, rumpled hat the innkeeper in Cemaes had given him obscured his face. As he came close he lifted his head, his expression thunderous as if he were holding back a maelstorm of anger. After glaring at her, he walked upstream a little way, disappearing around a bend.

When he came back he walked over to her. "How are the horses?"

"They seem to be settling," she replied, almost unable to breathe. "I did not let them drink too much all at once."

He nodded in approval.

"Tanner—" she began.

He held up a hand, and could scarcely look at her. "How did you intend to find your way to Edinburgh without even a map?" he snapped.

"I was going to follow the river. The River Esk flows near Edinburgh."

He shook his head. "That is a different River Esk."

Her eyes widened in surprise. She had no idea there could be two River Esks in Scotland. She might have been wandering the countryside for days without food or money.

"Enough of this foolishness." He gave her a level look. "I'll see you to Edinburgh. I'll see you there safely, but you stay with me. I'll not have your life on my conscience as well."

She opened her mouth to ask him what he meant, but he turned away from her, looking upstream.

"We ride in the water," he said. "Even if Rapp finds where we left the road, there is a chance we can still throw him off."

He helped her to remount and she rode her horse into the stream. He mounted and did the same, but rode his horse across to the other bank and then he made the horse back up into the water.

A clever ploy. The sort of trick Niall would have played on Wexin when they were gambolling over Parronley as boys.

They stayed in the stream for as long as they could, but the rocks underneath were slippery and difficult for the horses to walk upon. Tanner led them to the far bank of the stream and in a moment they were back to a landscape of rolling, grassy hills.

Tanner dismounted. "The horses need to feed."

She slipped off her horse before he could assist her.

He walked up to the crest of the hill, his very stride conveying an aura of command, of power. She watched him, as hungry for his smile, his laughter, as she was for food. Her stomach hurt and she pressed her hand to it.

When he returned he said. "There is nothing to be seen to give me any bearings. I think we should stay off the roads and ride north as best we can."

"Tanner—"

He fixed his gaze on her. "I am remaining with you."

She nodded, her throat tight. His words had an axe-hard edge.

She had assumed the pain she caused him would drive him away. Instead he had come after her, rescuing her once again, saving her life one more time.

He'd done more than save her life, however; he had made her want to live again.

After Corland was killed, Marlena's way of life died, too, then her family died—Niall and his dear little sons. Then Eliza. Everything Marlena thought worth living for had gone. Seeing Tanner again on the ship from Ireland rekindled those days when life had been full of dancing, and dreams and happiness. She'd briefly found happiness again at Tanner's side.

He glanced over at the horses. "We'll let them eat as much as they want, then we'll start off again."

He avoided sitting with Marlena, but rather paced to and fro, looking out on the valley, perhaps expecting Rapp to appear below. When Tanner and Marlena mounted their horses and rode again, their pace was slow over the hilly terrain.

In spite of her worries, Marlena was awed by the Scottish landscape, so unexpected and yet familiar at the same time. The hills retained a hint of the vibrant green they wore in summer, but had donned browns and oranges and purples as well.

She had forgotten how much she loved this land.

"Oh, hell," Tanner muttered.

She glanced towards him.

He pointed to the horizon where black clouds formed a line, like an army ready to attack.

"Rain," he said. "We had better find some shelter."

There was not much shelter to discover in the wilderness, however. When they came to the crest of yet another hill, the ruins of a castle came into view. They headed for it as the first of the raindrops started to fall and the roll of thunder sounded in the distance.

"If we are fortunate, it will have a roof," Tanner said as they approached the huge crumbling building, its brownish-grey stone walls whispering of days long gone.

"There is thunder, Tanner."

The stone was the same colour as Parronley, Marlena noticed, trying to distract herself from the approaching thunderstorm.

There was, indeed, a room large enough for the horses, sheltered on three sides with enough of a roof to keep the rain away. One tower of the castle remained intact, its stone staircase circling up to the battlements from which arrows once flew and vats of hot oil were poured on invaders.

They took the bags and saddles and blankets off the horses and carried them to the staircase of the tower.

"No fire tonight," Tanner said as he dropped the bag on the stairs.

"No fish, either," Marlena responded, trying to disguise her fear of the building storm.

He turned to her with concern. "You must be hungry."

She opened her bag. "I have some cheese and bread saved. We can share it." She broke it apart and gave the larger piece to Tanner. He took out a skin that he'd filled with water and handed it to her. With old stone walls surrounding them, they ate and drank in silence while the heavens opened up and lightning flashed, followed seconds later by a loud clap of thunder.

"Put on as many clothes as you can," Tanner told her. "I will check on the horses." He was no more than a silhouette against the tower's threshold.

"Tanner—" Marlena began, wanting to ask him not to leave her alone with the thunder and lightning crashing around them.

He turned away and began to walk out.

"Wait!" She felt like she could not breathe.

He looked over his shoulder.

"The storm…" She took a breath.

"I'll return. Stay here." His eyes bore into her. "No more leaving, Marlena."

"No more leaving," she repeated.

Fia looked up when the door of the taproom opened, and Lyall and Erroll Gibb entered, in mid-conversation, hair dripping from the rain.

"Och, no harm will come to them," Lyall said to his brother. "You are worried for naught."

"You know how these Englishmen can be, Lyall." Erroll nodded to Reverend Bell who sat over in a corner, his hand wrapped around a glass. "You cannot trust them with your women."

Erroll tripped on the leg of a chair, grabbing it before it fell and making it look as if he'd chosen it to sit upon.

Lyall flopped down in the chair opposite him. "There's naught we can do about it."

Fia walked over to them. "I hope you both wiped your boots before tracking mud in here."

Lyall smiled up at her. "That we did, Fia, so hold your scold."

He gave her that besotted stare, and she worried that

perhaps his affections had not been attached to one of the Brookston girls, after all.

"What will you be having?" she asked them both.

"Ale," replied a disquieted Erroll.

"Ale," agreed his brother.

"Ale it is." She nodded, but Erroll blocked her way with his arm before she could be off to the tap.

"Tell us, Fia." His brows knitted together so tightly they looked as if they were only one jagged line across his forehead. "You worked in London, in a fancy house—"

She felt a knot grow in her stomach. "It was long ago."

"Ay, but—" Erroll swallowed as if he had difficulty bringing out the right words to speak. "We were wonderin' what it was like. What the English laird of the place was like."

She felt blood drain from her face.

He went on. "I mean, could ye trust the man?"

Fia struggled to find her voice. "What reason do you have for asking me the question?"

Lyall reached over and whacked his brother on the shoulder. "You idiot! You know what happened where Fia was. Miss Parronley-that-was and all that." He looked at her in apology for his brother. "Don't mind him, Fia. He's daft."

Her knees shook.

Errol tossed his brother a scathing look. He turned back to Fia. "I was just askin' because Mary and Sara Brookston went to work at Parronley and I was worried because—"

She stopped him. "Why did they go to work at Parronley?" The house had been shut up with minimal staff ever since Baron Parronley and his two boys had died, and his poor, grieving wife went home to her parents. Lady Corland was the Baroness, but, of course, no one knew where to find her.

Lyall answered, "Lord Wexin showed up, wantin' to stay

there; seeing as he will be the laird there some day, they opened the house and needed girls to help with the cleaning."

Lord Wexin.

The room went dark and the sounds of people talking became like echoes.

Fia had feared this day. She'd hoped it would never come. Parronley House was an old and draughty place that had been neglected for years. Before they died, the young baron and his children only came for summers. With Lady Corland gone and no one in charge, things were in even more disarray. The crofters continued to farm the land, but not much else happened there. Fia hoped Wexin would stay on his own English estate and leave Parronley alone.

"I'll fetch your ale," she mumbled, walking through the maze of tables and chairs by memory.

The only reason for Wexin to come to Parronley would be if he inherited, and if he inherited it meant that Lady Corland was dead.

This likelihood loomed over Fia like a shroud. If Lady Corland were dead, it was Fia's fault. No matter how, no matter where. Her fault for not telling what she saw.

Fia managed to reach the bar where Bram was drawing ale while his father took a rest.

Her vision cleared enough to see Bram look upon her with concern. "What is it, lass?"

She forced her voice to sound unaffected. "Two ales for the Gibb brothers."

He reached over the bar to her. "No, I meant, what is it with you? Are you ill?"

Though her heart was beating a rapid tattoo, she made herself look him in the eye. "I'm not ill. I merely want you to give me two ales."

He paused, still examining her like her sleeve had caught

fire or something. He eventually drew two ales from the tap and handed them to her.

She carried them to Lyall and Erroll and did not tarry a moment in case they would start talking again. She went straight to the kitchen and kept walking through to the outside door.

Her aunt was stirring a pot of soup. "Are you ill, Fia? You look pale."

Fia pasted a smile on her face. "I'm in need of air," she said. "The taproom is quiet enough. I'll be only a moment."

She stood in the shelter of the doorway, trying to will herself to stay put and not run into the rain and as far away from Kilrosa and Parronley as she could get. To run like that would only be foolhardy. She needed to pack. She needed her money. She needed a place to go.

Because if Wexin found her here, he would kill her.

Chapter Fourteen

The night was over, the patrons gone, and Fia had somehow made it through. It helped that the rain thinned the numbers in the taproom, and that she became numb, acting like one of those automatons she'd seen in shops in London. Her aunt and uncle were abed, due to rise early and fix the breakfast. Bram was in the kitchen. Fia was alone, wiping the tables. In the solitude, she could think.

Wexin visited Parronley, not Kilrosa. It would be odd of him to come to Kilrosa when Parronley was the closer village. He could have no business here. Kilrosa had no one more important than Laird Hay, whose lands bordered the village and were not nearly as vast as the Parronley lands. She could easily keep out of Wexin's path. He could not possibly stay long.

If Wexin came to live in the area, though, she would have to leave. There would be no other choice to make. Perhaps Erroll and Lyall could find out from the Brookston sisters, if she could think of a way of asking them without raising their curiosity.

Fia wiped the last table and set the chairs up on top of it, so she could mop where the mud had inevitably been tracked in. She turned to go and fetch the mop and bucket and nearly ran into Bram, standing with his arms folded.

She must have numbed herself so well she had not sensed him, but now her heart pounded in her chest and her blood raced through her veins.

"You startled me," she said, her voice too breathless. "I thought you were cleaning the kitchen."

"The kitchen can wait." He merely watched her, his brown eyes looking black in the dim light. "What happened to you tonight?"

She shook her head and started to march past him. "I have no time for your silly questions, Bram. Nothing happened. It was a dull night."

He seized her arm and bent down to her. "Somethin' frightened the blood from your face, lass, and you near to fainted. Tell me."

She tried to pull away. "Do you not have work to do?"

He held fast and stared into her eyes. "Nothin' is more important than you, lass."

She felt as if her knees would give out from under her, but Bram's hands kept her upright.

He flipped a chair off the table and sat her down in it. Then he grabbed another and sat facing her. "Now tell me of it."

"Oh, Bram…" her voice cracked and tears of fear filled her eyes "…Lord Wexin is at Parronley."

His eyes grew wide. "Lord Wexin!"

"Aye." Her body trembled. "I am afraid. He will kill me, Bram. I know he will kill me."

He took her by the hand and gently settled her on his lap, wrapping his strong arms around her. "There now," he murmured in a soothing voice. "No harm will come to you. I will see to it."

She pulled away from him. "You must not go near him,

Bram. Do you hear me? Don't get any foolish ideas. I won't stand for it. I won't."

He held her tight against his chest. "Och, if you keep actin' this way, I'll be thinking you care about me."

"I do care about you, Bram. I couldn't bear it if something happened to you because of me." Her words were spoken into his chest.

He held her and rocked her and she almost felt safe. "I'm afraid his comin' here means something bad. Like he's killed Lady Corland or something. He's never come before." She shuddered.

"What does he know of you, Fia? Would he guess you are here?" he asked.

She shook her head, rubbing her cheek against his apron, which smelled of hops and ferment and comfort. "I do not think he knows my name or anything about me. He would have come for me before if he knew. I thought about this a long time and I figured out that he could not very well ask about me, not without causing people to have questions he would not want to answer."

"Ay," Bram said, the sound rumbling in his chest. "He'd be revealing you were in the room."

"You have no idea how many months it took me to realise that." She sighed. "Bram, I'm worried about why he's here. He's found Lady Corland, is all I can guess. She must be dead."

He brushed the hair from her brow and tucked it back under her cap. "That may not be, lass. I'll invent an errand in Parronley and find out what I can." He gave her an intent look. "But if anyone comes here who frightens you, tell Da you are sick and hide yourself until I come back."

Rain dripped through the roof of the castle ruins, making puddles on the stone floor. Tanner rubbed down the horses and checked their tethers. The two animals seemed content enough in their makeshift stable, munching on the blades of grass that grew up through the cracks in the floor as if they were feasting on troughs of hay. By the time Tanner finished, the scant light had waned and the storm intensified, lighting his way back to the stairwell with flashes of lightning.

When he reached the doorway, he could not see Marlena on the stairs and, for a fleeting moment, feared she had run off again.

"I did what you said." Her tremulous voice floated down from above and he could just make out her shape sitting several stair steps up from the open doorway.

"What I said?" he repeated, remembering how when he'd repeated things before it had led to lovemaking.

"I put on as many clothes as I could," she said. "And I took out some clothes for you, as well." She lifted some dark garment to show him.

Lightning flashed and she gasped, clutching the garment to her as the thunder followed.

He hurried up the steps. "The storm will pass soon."

She handed him the coat. "I know."

He removed his top coat and put the coat she'd given him on top of the one he already wore.

"I moved everything up here. It is not so damp and is more sheltered from the wind." The shaking of her voice was unmistakable.

He sat beside her and covered them both with his top coat. She had placed their bags on higher steps to act as pillows, and the horse blankets beneath them as the cushions for their stone settee.

Lightning flashed again and she flinched.

He put his arm around her. "We're safe enough here."

She laughed softly. "It is silly of me to be afraid."

He drew her closer, needing her as much as she needed his comfort.

His anger had fled, but a knot of fear still lingered. She'd come so close to being captured, and he no longer knew if his fortune and influence could save her.

Tanner closed his eyes and again saw Marlena battling the Bow Street Runner, who nearly had her in his grasp. His blood still burned with the thought of that man's hands upon her.

When Tanner woke that morning to find her gone, he'd been frantic with worry and enraged at himself for not anticipating her flight. With luck, guesswork and prayer he had followed her trail and finally caught a glimpse of her in the crowded streets of Langholm. He'd seen Rapp as well and he'd feared they were too far ahead for him to catch them up in time.

The storm quieted, the lightning faded, and the thunder seemed to roll away. Tanner felt Marlena relax and she seemed to melt against him.

When he'd embarked on this adventure, his intention had always been to save her, to give back a life, to atone for those lives that were lost because of him. He had not expected to fall in love with her.

Tanner had pretty much despaired of falling in love. The respectable women he met never captured his interest, and his string of mistresses quickly bored him. Both sets of women were more enamoured of his money than of him.

Marlena, on the other hand, had refused the help his money could offer her.

"Are you warm enough?" she asked.

"Yes," he responded in a quiet voice. "Sleep if you can, Marlena. With luck we will reach Edinburgh tomorrow."

The darkness and the silence did not help him fall asleep, however. He felt her warmth, heard her breathing, smelled the scent that was uniquely hers. He couldn't shift his position for fear of disturbing her sleep.

"Tanner?" Her voice drifted through the darkness. "What did you mean when you said you did not want my life on your conscience *as well.*"

He paused before answering. "That I will see you safe to Edinburgh, is what I meant."

She shifted, moving even closer to him. "No, you said *as well.* What did you mean, *as well?* Do you have a person's life on your conscience?"

He paused again, considering how to answer. "I did not kill anyone, if that is what you mean, but I caused the deaths of three people."

"How did you do that?" She asked the question in a soft voice, an accepting voice.

"Arrogance," he replied. She might as well know the sort of man he was. "Let us say, I coveted a prize so much, and fancied myself so clever, that I never thought my adversary would kill to win."

She touched his leg. "Then was it not your adversary who caused the deaths?"

The sensation sent need flashing through him. "I do not hold the man blameless," he admitted. "But neither am I absolved. Had I not decided to rub his nose in my superiority, he might be alive and the two others as well." It was surprisingly difficult to admit this to her. "They died because I cared only about winning."

She threaded her arm around his and leaned her cheek on his shoulder. "If only we could know what was to happen, we could decide very well then, could we not?"

He could only think how good it felt having her so near again.

"You are the best man I have ever known," she rasped.

He held her tightly. *There is no fixing this,* she'd said the night before. They would part in Edinburgh, but in his heart she would always be his marchioness.

"When I bring you to safety, I might deserve a piece of that regard," he said.

She groped in the darkness until she found his face. Holding his head in her hands, she guided him to her, missing his lips at first.

When she found his mouth, he pulled her on top of him. Into the kiss he poured all his terror at almost seeing her captured and his grief at losing her for good.

Marlena contented herself with kissing him, being held by him, touching him. It was like a gift.

She wished this castle still had its old bedchambers with big, old beds made of dark wood. Parronley used to have musty unused rooms where Marlena had pretended she was a maiden sought after by knights in chain mail and armour.

She sighed. Tanner possessed more chivalry than all the knights gathered at King Arthur's Round Table. Tears stung her eyes. She squeezed them shut, determined to defer the grief of losing him until after she sent him away.

Marlena had awoken several times during the night, each time savouring anew the bittersweet joy of feeling engulfed by him, of relishing the scent of him, of being soothed by the even cadence of his breathing. When she opened her eyes and saw light peeking through the cracks in the wall, her spirits plummeted.

He must have heard her stir, because he woke, too. His eyes were even more intense in the growing light, tinged with the same sadness that tore her apart inside.

"We must rise. Be on our way," he said.

But he made no move to leave. Instead he held her in a

long, warm, sheltering embrace, and she wanted nothing more than to remain for ever in his strong arms, a place of safety, refuge. Love.

Inevitably they had to depart. After they shed their extra clothing, Marlena repacked the bags. Tanner saddled the horses. Their two stalwart steeds seemed none the worse for spending a damp night in the castle and were even eager to continue the journey. Too soon Marlena and Tanner left the castle behind and headed north once more.

The ground, still wet from the rain, made their progress difficult. Marlena ought to have rued the slow pace, but instead it raised her selfish hopes for one more night with Tanner.

Tanner turned to her. "We should chance stopping at a village. Give the horses something proper to eat and ourselves as well." He smiled at her. "Unless you are not hungry."

She smiled back. "I am famished." Her smile quickly fled. "But what of Rapp? Dare we stop?"

His brows knit. "If we stay in this remote area, the chance of Rapp coming to the same village at the same time seems unlikely. We need food." He patted his horse's neck. "All of us." He gave her a reassuring gaze. "Let us look for a road to follow."

They found a path that wound around a hill and followed it, hoping it led to a road. The morning wore on without them finding a village.

"Will we make Edinburgh today, do you think?" Marlena asked at one point.

"I believe so," he said in a flat voice.

They fell silent, plodding along to the next hill, still no road in sight. The path widened enough for them to ride side by side.

Tanner looked over at her. "What happens when we reach Edinbugh, Marlena?"

She darted a glance at him, but quickly looked away. "We must part."

After a pause, he spoke again. "Am I to simply leave you, or is there someone waiting for you, someone to help you?"

She could barely look at him. "There is an old teacher from my school…" It was, she hoped, the last falsehood she would tell him. She knew no one in Edinburgh, but, then, she was counting on no one in Edinburgh knowing her.

His pained expression told her that he'd recognised her lie.

She changed the subject. "What of you, Tanner? Will you have enough money to get back to London?"

He frowned. "When I become the Marquess again, I will be able to get funds easily enough."

She was relieved, not wishing him to endure any more hardship on her behalf.

He spoke again. "I have been thinking. Before we part, we must set up a way for me to send you money—"

She broke in. "No, Tanner. You must not be connected to me ever again."

"I will not leave you destitute and alone." His horse jumped forward at his sharp tone.

"I will get by, Tanner," she called after him.

He increased his pace and she fell far enough behind to make further discussion impossible. Soon the terrain required all their attention as they climbed higher and higher to the crest of a hill. Marlena felt a *frisson* of nerves travel up her spine as they climbed, but she knew of no reason why.

When they reached the crest, he stopped and waited for her. As she caught up to him, Marlena scanned the vista. Low clouds gave a dreamlike appearance to the valley below until a sudden breeze swept them away.

In the distance was the sea and before it sat a great house

built of brownish-grey stone complete with turrets and towers and pointed rooftops. The house, once hazy from her long absence, was now all too clear in her vision.

Parronley House.

Each room, each view, every walkway in the garden, every furrow in the parkland, every rock in the cliffs beyond the house, rushed into her mind. Again, she and Niall ran through the rooms, frolicked in the garden, jumped from the cliffs into the deep pools of water in the sea.

"No," she cried, backing her horse away from the sight.

Tanner looked around him. "What?"

She caught herself and shook her head. "Nothing, Tanner. The house looked like a place where ghosts might dwell."

There was truth to that. Too many ghosts would inhabit this place, if only in her memory—her parents, her brother, the life she had left behind…

The living demons were who she must fear the most, however. She and Tanner had come directly to the place Rapp would think to look for her. *Parronley.*

Marlena pointed to her left. "I—I thought I spied a road over that way. Just a glimpse."

She knew there was a road there, a road that led away from Parronley, a road that could lead them on to Edinburgh, only about ten miles away. They must reach Edinburgh now. She would push him on.

At the bottom of the hill, exactly where she said it would be, was the road. When they reached it, the sun was high, near noon for certain. They came upon a signpost Marlena knew would be there. Kilrosa one way; Parronley the other. While her nerves jangled so severely she thought he would notice, he stopped to consult the map.

He pointed to Kilrosa. "This way."

She breathed a sigh of relief.

"We must stop at this next village," he said. "The horses are tiring and we all need food."

She wanted to tell him she was not tired. She was not hungry. She wanted to beg him to go on to Edinburgh.

They no sooner rode past the road sign when Tanner's horse began to falter. "Deuce," he said. "My horse has thrown a shoe."

Marlena's panic escalated. More delay.

Tanner dismounted and lifted the horse's hoof. "He needs a new shoe for certain. I hope he has not injured his leg. The village should not be too far."

About five miles away, Marlena recalled.

Five excruciating miles. Tanner had to lead his horse on foot and their progress seemed snail-like. Marlena expected every minute that Rapp would descend upon them.

She hoped no one in Kilrosa would recognise her. Surely her appearance had changed dramatically, and no one would look for that little girl in this plainly dressed woman with dirt splattered on her skirt and mud caking her boots. None of them, she hoped, would be expecting the Baroness Parronley in this disguise.

They came upon the church, which was just as she remembered it, made of the same stone as Parronley House. The buildings of Kilrosa would be made of that stone as well, so different from the buildings of London. Or Bath. Or Kent, where Corland's estate was located. So many memories came flooding back, of riding with Niall over these same hills, walking these same roads to the church on fine-weather days.

The village was soon ahead and it too sparked memories of the handful of times she visited it as a child. Parronley had been closer to her father's estate than Kilrosa and there had been few reasons to travel the extra miles to visit it. Still, as they entered Kilrosa, its winding main road with shops and the inn and smithy were familiar.

"Let us first find a stable and a smithy," Tanner said.

Marlena could have taken him directly to the stable, suddenly remembering one of the rare times her father allowed her and Niall to ride with him on some errand in the village. The local laird's property was nearby, she recalled, and her father had met the man in the local inn.

At the stable, a man approached them. Marlena held her breath, but to her relief, he showed no sign of recognising her.

"Good day to you," Tanner said to the man. "Is this your stable?"

"It is," the man said.

Tanner offered the man a handshake. "We've been travelling and my horse has thrown a shoe."

"Let me have a look at the fellow." The stableman lifted the horse's leg and examined its hoof. He rubbed his hands over the leg. "He's strained it, but he's not lame. You are lucky. I'll fetch the smithy and we'll tend to him, but you'd better rest the horse a day or two."

Marlena turned her head away as she dismounted, feeling as if every drop of blood had drained from her face.

She heard Tanner ask, "Is there an inn here?"

The man pointed to it, but Marlena could have pointed to it as well. "The Black Agnes. Not many folks come to stay there." He shifted from one foot to another. "Folks more often stay at Parronley, over yonder." He inclined his head in that direction. "When folks had business with the baron when he was alive. Poor devil. Not so much now."

"The baron?" Tanner asked conversationally.

Marlena thought Tanner must have known Niall as Baron Parronley once, from school or in London.

"Died of fever some time back, his boys with him." The man patted Tanner's horse. "Aye. Parronley has seen its share of troubles. There's worse—"

Marlena broke in. "I do apologise for interrupting, but I should like to go to the inn now." She had no wish for the stableman to go on about the sad tale of the baroness who killed her husband.

Tanner gave her a sympathetic glance, and took the bags from their saddles. "We'll be at the inn if you need to reach us," he told the man. "I'll check with you later, in any event."

The man peered at him. "English, are ye?"

Tanner laughed. "Yes. We are."

Marlena started to walk away. "May we go, please?"

Tanner bid goodbye to the man and caught up to Marlena. "You must be hungry."

"As must you." She hurried towards the inn.

They entered, but found no one in the hallway. Tanner stepped into the taproom and returned with a smiling older gentleman who looked so perfectly like an innkeeper Marlena could not tell if she had seen him before. She kept her face averted just in case.

"Sorry for not seeing ye come in," the innkeeper said. "My name is Gunn."

"Pleased to meet you, Mr Gunn." Tanner shook his hand. "Are you filled with guests or do you have a room for us?"

Perhaps Tanner's question was his way to check if Rapp could be staying at the inn. Marlena knew that if Rapp were this close—and she greatly feared he would be—he would stay in Parronley.

Gunn laughed. "As it is, you are our only guests. I'll show you the room, but I'd be obliged if you would sign the book for me."

Marlena relaxed a little bit. The Black Agnes in Kilrosa seemed safe enough for the moment.

Mr Gunn dipped a pen in ink and handed it to Tanner. Marlena glanced over to see what named he signed, so she would know who they were this day. *Adam Henry and wife,* after all the Henries in Shakespeare's plays.

She stared at his signature. *Adam Henry and wife.*

Under Scottish law a couple only needed only to declare themselves as man and wife in front of a witness to be legally wed. She and Tanner would be considered married the same as if they had been two impetuous lovers eloping to Gretna Green.

She would never claim to be Tanner's wife, except in her own heart. She touched the sapphire ring he had given her at Dutwood House. She would think of it as her wedding ring.

Mr Gunn took them up the stairs. "You can put your bags in the room and I'll start a fire."

"Can we get a meal in the taproom?" Tanner asked. "We have been on the road since morning."

"You may indeed," Gunn replied.

"May I have water to wash with first?" Marlena asked.

"And we had better change our clothes." Tanner added. "Is there someone who can brush the dirt of the road off them?"

Mr Gunn smiled. "You do have a wee bit o' mud on you, haven't you? I'll bring water directly and we'll launder what can be washed and also tend to the rest."

As soon as Gunn left, Tanner turned to Marlena, putting his hands on her shoulders. "Is anything amiss, Marlena? You've not said much since my horse lost a shoe."

Since seeing Parronley House, she thought. "I am tired and sore and hungry, that is all."

He kneaded her shoulders and wrapped his arms around her. "We may be forced to rest here a day or so, if my horse requires it. Would you mind very much?"

She hoped he didn't feel her tremble. She feared Rapp was in Parronley, or would be shortly. He might take it into his head to look for them in Kilrosa. If he found Tanner with her, Tanner would lose his chance to escape.

"I cannot like you being seen with me, Tanner, not with Rapp about."

He put his arms around her and held her against his chest. "We will take care." He pulled away. "Let us change into clean clothes so they can launder these."

They changed out of their mud-spattered clothing and Marlena sat on the bed to wait for the water.

Tanner touched her face. "I will go down to the taproom and discreetly inquire if anyone has seen Rapp." He gave her a reassuring smile. "Do you wish for me to come back up to fetch you?"

She caught his hand and held it to her cheek. "I'll come down to the taproom. Have them bring you your food as soon as you are ready."

When he opened the door to leave, he turned to her. "I do not regret that we must stay together longer."

After he left, Marlena lay down on the bed, exhausted from the ride and the worry. She closed her eyes and even her hunger could not prevent her from falling half-asleep.

A knock came at the door. "Your water, ma'am."

"Come in." Marlena sat up and rubbed her eyes.

The girl carried the water pitcher and some towels to a small table near the fireplace.

"Thank you so much." Marlena stood.

At that same moment the girl turned towards her and Marlena saw her face.

Fia Small.

Marlena gasped.

The girl's face went white. "Lady Corland."

The last Marlena had seen of Fia Small had been when Corland lay dead in a pool of blood, and her cousin had thrust the murder weapon into her hand.

Chapter Fifteen

The ale felt cool on Tanner's throat and greatly welcome. Gunn had reassured him that no stranger had been in the town for days. He could relax with a pint while he waited for Marlena. He'd built up a powerful thirst on that stretch of road. How long had it been since he'd walked five miles? Since he'd walked anywhere, come to think of it? His feet had held up tolerably well. Thanks to his bootmaker, he suspected. Hoby's cobbling skills were unsurpassed.

Gunn brought him a plate of bread and cheese and Tanner tore off a piece of bread and chewed on it.

He thought of strolling past Hoby's boot shop on St James's Street, of popping into Locke's for a new hat, of spending the afternoon at White's with other bored aristocrats.

He lifted the tankard to his lips and washed down the bread. The time he'd spent with Marlena meant so much more to him, even with all its discomforts.

A large man in an apron walked out of the kitchen, stopped abruptly and looked around.

The man turned to Gunn. "Where's Fia?"

The innkeeper inclined his head in Tanner's direction. "We have guests. Fia's tending to the room."

The young man swung around and stared at Tanner, suspicion and challenge in his eyes.

"Well, go ask the man if he desires another ale." Gunn made a shooing gesture with his hands.

The large man approached Tanner with a less-than-friendly demeanour. "Do you want more?"

Tanner looked up at him. "I do." He handed the man the tankard.

The man reached for it, looking directly into Tanner's face. Both his hand and his jaw dropped. "M'lord, what are you doin' here?"

Tanner looked around to see if anyone heard, but there was only one other patron in the taproom and he was sitting off in a corner his hands wrapped around a glass. Mr Gunn was busy behind the bar.

"You've taken me for someone else," Tanner said quickly.

"Nay, I have not." The big man's voice was still full of wonder. "You are the Marquess of Tannerton. I'd know you anywhere."

This man couldn't be more than thirty years, was definitely Scots, by his accent. He looked as if he'd stepped out from that Morier painting Tanner had seen once, the painting of the Battle of Culloden, hardly England's finest hour. Where the devil would he have met the fellow?

Tanner peered at him. "How is it you think you know me?"

"I was there, m'lord," the man said with reverence. "In Brussels after the battle. I saw what you did for the lads. No man worked harder for them than you, sir." He bowed.

Tanner glanced around again. "For God's sake, sit down, and keep your voice low."

The man sat, but stiff as the ramrod he'd probably carried in the battle.

"You were a soldier?" Tanner remembered the wagons of men that poured into Brussels after the battle. Men bleeding, missing limbs or eyes or entire faces, some crying for their mothers, some stoically helping others.

"71st Infantry," the man said.

The 71st helped send Napoleon's Imperial Guard packing, Tanner recalled. "What is your name?"

"Bram Gunn. This is my father's inn." He stood up abruptly. "I'll fetch your ale."

Tanner watched him carefully to see if he'd tell his father the Marquess of Tannerton sat in their inn looking more like a crofter than a marquess, but young Gunn only asked his father to draw another tankard of ale. Tanner blew out a relieved breath.

When Gunn brought the ale, Tanner again gestured for him to sit. The man stared at Tanner, his eyes wide, sitting as stiffly as if he'd been in Wellington's presence.

Tanner took a sip. "You are perhaps wondering why I do not at the moment look like a marquess."

Gunn nodded.

Tanner decided to tell the truth—but not all of it. The elder Gunn sauntered into the kitchen and the other patron was nodding off. No one would overhear.

"I am with a lady," he told young Bram. "She is in some danger, and I am escorting her to a safe place. I do not wish to call attention to myself." He gazed at the former soldier, trying to gauge his reaction. "Hence the clothing."

Gunn's eyes narrowed and he tilted his head slightly. "My father said our guests were a man and his wife. Would that be you and the lady?"

Taken a bit aback by the man's reaction, Tanner took another sip. "That is our disguise, yes."

Gunn leaned forward. "You are in Scotland, m'lord. Did you not know that if you say you are man and wife in Scotland, you are married?"

Tanner took a huge gulp. He ought to have remembered that fact. "It is all part of the ploy," he managed.

Tanner had inadvertently been granted his wish—to make Marlena his marchioness. The irony was painful, but marriage to Marlena pleased Tanner very much.

"So long as you know it," Gunn said.

Tanner gave him a direct look. "It is very important to me that this whole matter, who I am, who I am with, is not spoken of to anyone. May I trust you to say nothing of it?"

Gunn met his eye with a serious and determined look. "I'd do anything you ask, m'lord. Some of the lads you helped were like my brothers."

Tanner smiled at him. "First thing is to call me Henry, not m'lord. I am Mr Henry here, accompanied by Mrs Henry."

Gumm grinned back. "I'll do my best, m'l—Henry."

The door opened with a bang, and both Tanner and Gunn looked over. A well-dressed man swept in.

"Is there no one in this village?" The man spun around.

Hell, thought Tanner. He knew this man.

Wexin.

Who would have thought there could be two people who knew him in this tiny village completely surrounded by Scottish hills?

In his younger days, Tanner and Pomroy made the rounds of London's gaming hells with Wexin and others, but Wexin and his cronies gambled too recklessly for Tanner and Pomroy's tastes and the association ended. Tanner knew Wexin had married Strathfield's daughter when Tanner had still been in Brussels. He'd seen them from time to time at London social events.

Gunn stood up and the man came closer.

"I need the direction to Laird Hay." His head jerked back when he saw Tanner. "Good God, what are you doing here, Tanner?"

Tanner stood and inclined his head towards Gunn. "Passing time with Bram here. We knew each other in Brussels." He extended his hand to Wexin. "I might ask the same of you, Wexin."

Bram stepped back suddenly and knocked over a chair.

Wexin gave the young man a look of disgust and turned back to Tanner. "Business. At Parronley, you know."

Tanner did not know, but he had the feeling he ought to have known.

Wexin went on. "I am invited to dine at Laird Hay's and I do not know the direction." He snapped his neck again and looked Tanner up and down. "Why do you dress like a ruffian?"

Bram spoke up. "His lordship is wearin' clothes I found for him, sir, until his are cleaned and dry."

Tanner smiled. "I was caught in the rain. Everything I owned got wet." He fingered the cloth of his coat. "These garments are remarkably comfortable."

Wexin gave a sniff of disgust.

Bram glared at him. "If ye be seeking the laird, you must ride the main road out of town, about one mile. Follow the first fork you come to in the road and it will lead you to Laird Hay."

Wexin's brows lifted. "About a mile, you say?"

Bram nodded.

Tanner pulled out a chair. "Have a drink with us. The ale is quite nice, I assure you. Bram was about to get us both another pint."

Wexin's nose rose in the air. "I am expected at the laird's. When do you leave this godforsaken village?"

"Early on the morrow," Tanner said. "Too bad you cannot stay. I wanted to hear all the London news. How is your lovely wife, by the way?"

"She is well. I am anxious to return to her." Wexin's voice softened.

"Then I shall see you back in London," Tanner said. "Or have you and Lady Wexin retired to the country?"

"We remain in London." Wexin looked impatiently towards the door. "I must beg your leave."

Tanner waved his hand. "By all means. I would be grateful if you would refrain from informing Laird Hay of my presence here. I should like to avoid the delay of a dinner invitation."

Wexin sighed. "As would I. But I must be on my way. Do forgive me."

"Indeed. Good to see you." Tanner sat down again as Wexin left.

Bram stared at the man's back until he was out the door.

"Thank you, Bram." Tanner blew out a breath. "You saved my hide."

Bram watched Wexin through the window as he mounted his horse and rode away. "Is he a friend of yours?" Bram asked.

Tanner shook his head. "Not a friend. Merely someone I know." He peered at Bram. "Why?"

"I do not like the man," Bram replied.

Marlena rushed over as the maid's eyes rolled back in her head. She caught the girl before she fell and eased her across to a chair.

Fia bent over, her head in her hands. "I thought you were dead, m'lady. I was sure of it, because—"

Marlena spoke at the same time. "I feared you were dead, too. I feared he'd found you." She touched the girl's shoulder.

Fia sat up, some colour returning to her face. "I've been here in Kilrosa. I was a year here before I stopped being afraid he'd come. And now—"

"I am so glad." Marlena crouched down so her face was even with Fia's. She took the girl's hands in her own. "I am so relieved. I wanted you to be safe and not try to tell anyone what happened."

Fia's eyes widened. "You do not mind I did not tell what I saw?"

Marlena squeezed her hands. "He would have killed you."

Fia shuddered. "You will not tell anyone about me. Please?"

"No," she reassured. "I promise."

Fia looked at her. "Where did you go, m'lady? They were searching for you everywhere."

"A friend took me to Ireland to be her children's governess. But her brother came and recognised me. I—I had to leave there."

"Oh, m'lady, you had to be a governess?" The girl looked horrified.

"It was a happy time," Marlena reassured her. "Really."

Fia's eyes were still wide. "Why did you come here? This is not a safe place for you."

"We did not mean to come here. We wound up too far east." Marlena clamped her mouth shut before she revealed too much. It was better not to speak of her final destination.

"M'lady, are ye married again?"

Yes, Marlena thought. *To Tanner.* "There is a man helping me."

"But if you stay the night with him—"

Marlena knew. The marriage would be consummated.

They heard a horse outside and someone shouting in the street below. Fia's chair was right next to the window. She opened the curtain and peered out.

With a gasp, Fia drew back, her fist in her mouth as if to keep from screaming.

"What is it, Fia?" Marlena opened the curtain, but all she saw was a man's figure entering the inn.

"It is him." The girl rose from the chair and backed away. "Him."

Marlena crossed over to her. "Who?"

"Lord Wexin!" Fia's voice cracked and she trembled all over.

Marlena froze.

She had expected Rapp, not Wexin. He must have come to find her. Marlena dashed to the fireplace and grabbed the poker for a weapon. She stood by the door and listened, fearing to hear his footsteps approaching.

The next sound they heard was not footsteps on the stairs, but horse's hooves again.

Fia ran to the window. "He's riding away!"

Marlena released the breath she'd been holding and leaned against the door.

Fia turned to her. "When I heard he had come to Parronley, I thought it meant you were dead."

"It means he is looking for me, I fear." Marlena's mind was racing. What should she say to Tanner? Wexin must never know Tanner was here with her, but what if he'd seen Tanner here?

"If he finds me—" Fia's voice broke.

A knock on the door made them both jump. "Fia! Are ye in there?"

"It is Bram," Fia said.

Tanner's voice also came through the door. "Marlena?"

She hurriedly put the poker back by the fireplace.

Tanner opened the door, and a large man pushed past him to rush to Fia's side. "I've something to tell you, lass."

"I know…" she glanced to the window "…we saw him,

but, Bram, you will never guess." She extended her arm towards Marlena. "This is Lady Corland!"

Fia's Bram bowed. "My lady."

"I do not wish it to be known—" Marlena began.

Tanner turned to her. "Lady Corland?"

His eyes scanned her and her heart thumped painfully in her chest. She could just feel him searching his mind for where the name fitted into the puzzle.

His glance slid to Fia and her Bram. "I would like to be alone with her."

Bram bowed. "Of course, m'lord."

Tanner's expression did not change. "Take care, Bram. Say no more than that we are Mr and Mrs Henry. To anyone."

Bram glanced to Fia and back to Tanner. "May I tell Fia, m'lord? The lass has a right to know."

Tanner's gaze turned to Fia. "She knows more than I do, I believe," he murmured. He nodded, looking back at Bram. "No one else, Bram. This lady's—" he shot a glance to Marlena "—*Lady Corland's* well-being depends upon it." He spoke the name with venom. "Corland," he repeated in a near-whisper.

"Ay, you have my word—Mr Henry." Bram took Fia by the arm and whisked her from the room.

Marlena braced herself as Tanner faced her, not speaking. His expression told her he had put the facts together.

He knew.

He walked over to the window and looked out. "What was it the newspapers called you?" His voice was flat, devoid of humour, devoid of any emotion.

She felt sick inside. "The Vanishing Viscountess."

"That was it. *The Vanishing Viscountess.*" He nodded, still gazing into the street where Wexin had ridden off. "I was in Belgium, I believe. We were busy with other matters at the time."

A few weeks after her story reached the newspapers, the battle of Waterloo took over everyone's attention. That horrible news had erased her from the printed page, and she'd been largely forgotten.

"But I do recall a newspaper reaching us." He turned back to her. "Lord Corland was murdered in his bed, as I recall."

She straightened her spine. "He was."

He turned away. "Corland was your husband."

A shaft of pain pierced her heart. "I did not kill him," she added helplessly. "But you must see why I did not tell you."

He spun around again. "I do not see that at all, Marlena. Did you think I would not believe you?"

She straightened her spine. "You would not have believed me at first. Corland. Wexin. You knew those men. You would not have believed me."

His brows came together and he stared towards the window. "What has Wexin to do with it?"

"Wexin killed Corland. He placed the blame on me."

"Wexin?" He glanced back at her in surprise.

"He is very dangerous, Tanner." She spoke in an even tone. "He would kill you if he knew you were with me."

His expression turned sceptical. "Wexin?"

She took a breath and released it. "I knew you would not believe me. I would not have believed it myself if I had not seen what he'd done. I still have no idea why he did it. Wexin and Corland were friends, but Wexin—my cousin—set it up to look as if I had killed my husband." She shivered. "He is searching for me, Tanner."

He continued to gaze at her. "Why would Wexin search here?"

She gave a wry smile. "He assumed I would flee to Parronley."

His brows came together again. "Why?"

"It is my home, Tanner." She glanced away from him, seeing the house and land once again in her mind. "I spent my childhood in Parronley. When…" her voice faltered "…when my brother—you knew Niall, I think—and my two little nephews died, I became the heir. The title was such it could pass to daughters as well as sons."

"You are the Baroness?"

She shrugged. "I could not claim the title, of course, but, yes, the Baroness Parronley."

He pressed his fingers to his temple. "I do remember your brother. I remember reading about his death." His eyes, however, were filled with anger, not sympathy. "You had better tell me the whole now, Marlena. I would be obliged if you would trust me with the truth."

She told him all of it. Of coming upon Wexin dressed in her robe, holding her scissors, wiping Corland's blood on her clothing. Of seeing Corland, eyes staring, throat cut.

She told him how Wexin called for help and how servants came running. How when they waited for a magistrate, she escaped and ran to Eliza, who gave her refuge.

She told him everything except about Fia, because she had promised the girl not to reveal her part in it.

Tanner listened, but she could not read his stony expression. He stood still, taking in all she said.

As she spoke, she heard how ludicrous her version of the story sounded. Who would believe it? She'd always known Wexin had set up a brilliant plot against her.

When she finished, Tanner said nothing and still did not move. She could not bear any longer to watch him and she turned to lean on the nearby table, where the jug of water waited for her.

"You do not believe me," she whispered into the tense silence.

He lifted a hand as if to silence her. "That is not it,

Marlena." He backed away from her. "I need to be alone. I'll send food up to you. Stay in the room. Do not leave."

Before she could say a word, he was gone.

Marlena sank on to the nearest chair. She buried her head in her hands.

Chapter Sixteen

"You must tell what you know, lass." Bram held Fia's hands in his big strong ones.

Fia looked away. She hated Bram knowing how weak and cowardly she was.

They stood in the yard behind the inn. It was chilly outside, but she'd hardly felt anything since they'd left Lady Corland's room.

Lady Corland had found a strong man to protect her. A Marquess must be a grand man indeed. She did not need Fia to help her. Bram was strong, too, and he said he'd protect Fia, but she was still afraid.

"Think on it," Bram went on. "She's been hiding all this time, and so have you. You can go to the laird and tell him the truth. You'd both be free then."

She shook her head. "You do not know what Wexin can do, Bram. We'd have to go to London, and Wexin would kill us before we got there."

"I'd go with you, Fia. Naught would happen to you." He brushed a hand through her hair.

She pulled away. "Then he would kill you, too, Bram, and that would be worse!"

The door opened and Fia's aunt appeared in the doorway. "What're you two doin' out here? There's people wanting food and drink inside."

"We'll come now, Mam," Bram said.

Aunt Priss went back inside, the door slamming behind her.

"Come, lass, we must work." Bram held out his hand.

Fia hung back. "I want to go to my sister's house tomorrow, Bram. Will you take me? He won't chance to find me there."

Her sister was married to one of the laird's crofters. If Fia hid there, Wexin would not happen upon her as he almost had today. Bram could come fetch her when Wexin went away again.

Bram frowned. "If I can't change your mind, lass…"

They walked inside, passing through the kitchen, where Aunt Priss handed Bram a tray. "Some food and tea for the guest upstairs, Bram. Will you take it to her?" She turned to Fia. "There's people waiting in the taproom. What's got into you, Fia?"

"I'm sorry, Aunt Priss," she replied. "I forgot the time."

Bram, carrying the tray, followed Fia as she hurried into the taproom.

As soon as they crossed that threshold, Lord Tannerton stopped them. "Is that food for her?" he asked.

Bram nodded. "Aye."

The marquess glanced around and leaned forward, a fierce look in his eyes. "Will you betray her? Will you tell the magistrate that she is here?"

"Tell the laird? No!" cried Fia. "Don't say such a thing, m'lord."

"Call him Mr Henry, Fia," Bram corrected. "You have our vow. We'll not betray Lady Parr—we'll not betray her."

Tannerton nodded, but he blocked their way again. "Why? Tell me why you won't betray her."

"She did not do it," said Fia.

"You believe her?" Tannerton looked from one to the other.

Fia had been certain Lady Corland would tell the marquess about her seeing the murder and now it seemed as if she hadn't.

Bram gave her a glance. He turned to the marquess. "We believe her, sir."

Fia felt tears well in her eyes. Bram could have told the marquess right then about her seeing what really happened. He didn't, even though he thought the marquess was a very great man because of what he'd done in Brussels.

"Do ye not believe her, sir?" Fia asked the marquess.

"Of course I do," he answered sharply. His voice softened. "I merely wondered if I was the only one."

He thanked them again for agreeing to keep Marlena's secret and he returned to a table where a tankard of ale waited for him.

Fia reached for the tray in Bram's hands. "Will you let me take this to her? Will you care for the patrons 'til I'm back?"

"If you like." He gave her the tray.

Fia carried it up the flight of stairs and knocked on the door to Lady Corland's room. "It is Fia, ma'am."

Lady Corland opened it.

"Some food for you, ma'am." She set the tray on the table.

The lady looked pale and upset, and Fia felt a wave of guilt for not wanting to try to help her by telling the laird what she'd seen so long ago. She could not do it. She was so afraid inside she thought she might break in pieces.

"You didn't tell the marquess about me," Fia said.

Lady Corland looked at her in surprise. "I promised you."

"I thank you." Fia hung her head. "I—I want to go away. Is it all right with you, m'lady? Is it all right I don't tell what I know?"

The lady gave her a soft look. "It would be very danger-ous to tell what you know, Fia. With my—my friend's help, I can go into hiding again. Then we both will be safe."

"Where will you be going, m'lady?" What place would be safe for her? Wexin was a rich man. He could go anywhere to find her.

Lady Corland's expression turned serious. "I'll not tell you, Fia. I don't want you to have the burden of knowing it, but you are not to worry. Eventually Lord Wexin will leave Parronley. You should be safe to live your life here with your young man."

Fia felt her face go hot. "Och, Bram is not my young man."

"Isn't he?" The lady smiled.

Fia was too embarrassed to answer. She glanced towards the door. "I'd best be seeing to the patrons."

"I understand."

"You can place the tray in the hall if you'd like it to be out of your way." Fia shuffled her feet. "I'll fetch it later."

"I will do that."

Fia walked to the door and opened it. "If I don't see you again, I wish you fare well."

"I wish you fare well, too."

Fia smiled because her ladyship spoke the words just like a Scotswoman. Fia hurried out of the room and down the stairs.

The first patrons Fia saw in the taproom were Erroll and Lyall Gibb. "Ho, you, Fia. We heard you had a guest in the inn. The man over there? Who is he?"

She remembered what the marquess asked of her. "He's somebody who got lost. What other reason has a stranger to come to Kilrosa?"

She glanced over at Bram who was working the tap at the moment. He had an approving look on his face.

"Now what do you want to drink?" she asked the Gibb brothers.

Tanner swayed a bit as he took the first step on the stairway. He grasped the banister to steady himself. Perhaps he should not have switched to whisky. Damned good drink, however.

He reached the room and entered with a clatter. Night had fallen. He'd intended not to wake her. He glanced to the bed, but it was empty.

Damnation. Had she run again?

He steadied himself on the edge of the bed, but he really wanted to pound his fist into the wall. Suddenly from the corner of his eye he saw something move.

She stood up from a chair near the fire.

Her hair was loose and flowed down to her shoulders. She wore the nightdress that the wife of that first innkeeper had given to her. After their nights together, he knew the feel of the cloth and the feel of her beneath it.

"You are still awake?" Idiotic thing for him to say. Of course she was.

"I rested some." Her voice floated across the room as if on the wings of angels.

He was waxing poetic. Must be jug-bitten.

"Sleeping is difficult," she added.

Her scent seemed to fill the room, the scent of soap and something indefinable, like a rare flower.

There he went again. Poetic. "Have you been in the room all this time?"

"I went below stairs to the necessary," she said.

He frowned. "All alone?"

"I was careful," she replied.

He winced with guilt. He should have checked on her; should have seen if she needed him. "I would have gone with you. Why did you not come to get me in the taproom?"

"I thought you did not want me there."

He wanted her wherever he was. Wanting her had consumed his thoughts while he'd been consuming multiple glasses of whisky. "I would not have minded."

He felt himself listing to the side, and grabbed hold of the bedpost. "Did you have enough to eat?"

"I did, thank you."

Blast it. He hated the caution in her voice. He desired hearing her voice filled with the same passion that burned inside him. That passion for her had remained constant even when faced with her unbelievable story.

No matter how preposterous her story, he believed her. He'd spent days with her. He'd lain with her. He *knew* her, knew the woman she was, no matter what name she went by, what story she told.

She should have trusted him. After that first time of love-making, she should have told him who she was—that she had been married. Blast the idea of protecting him.

"I knew Corland," he told her, as if she could follow the direction of his mind.

She lowered her head. "I presumed you knew him."

Tanner's throat went suddenly dry. "Did you love him, Marlena?"

She glanced up. "I thought I loved him at first. He was very charming."

"He was a damned fellow," Tanner said.

She met his gaze. "He—he was not unlike the man I invented in my tale for you."

Tanner gave a disgusted laugh. "The fictional jewel thief?"

She nodded.

"At least some of what you told me was true." He advanced towards her. "Corland was a bounder and debaucher. Did you not think I would understand—?" He stopped short of touching her.

She interrupted him. "Understand why I would kill him, do you mean?" She spun away from him.

He put his hands on her shoulders and turned her to face him. "You cannot think I do not believe you."

She avoided looking at him.

He lifted her chin with one hand. "I cannot abide thinking of you married to Corland, of your being in his bed—" He needed to brace himself on her shoulder.

"Tanner," she said breathlessly.

He shook his head. "You should have trusted me, Marlena. You've made me bring you to the place of greatest danger to you. Wexin is not five miles away."

She said nothing, merely looked into his eyes.

He released her, lifting both hands before placing one of them on the table for balance.

Did she think he would never discover she was the Vanishing Viscountess? During his stay in the taproom, he realised the crime made no difference to him. He could not leave her merely because it was not theft, but a murder charge on her head. He'd move all the mountains of Scotland to keep her from the hangman's noose. To protect her from Wexin.

"Wexin." He spat out the name. "The cursed villain! Why the devil did he wish to kill Corland in the first place? He gambled unwisely, but otherwise I would not have thought him capable of such tresh—treachery."

He swayed and lowered himself carefully into the chair next to him.

She sat on the opposite chair. "Are you drunk, Tanner?"

He tried to give her a composed look. "Merely a trifle disguised."

A smile teased at the corner of her mouth.

He smiled in return, but forced himself to at least look sober. "I was thinking we should go to France."

"France?" She sat up straighter.

He leaned on the table. "Instead of Edinburgh. Although we'll have to go to Edinburgh, I think, to get passage to France. The thing is, Wexin cannot get to you in France. You cannot be arrested in a different country. I should think Wexin would give it up with me protecting you."

"Wait." She touched his hand. "What do you mean *we* should go to France?"

His hand tingled at her touch, the sensation spreading through him. "I would not send you there alone," he managed to respond.

"Tanner—"

' His mind was clear, even if the alcohol made him a trifle unsteady. He knew what must be done, what he wanted above all things.

"I worked this out, Marlena." He met her gaze soberly. "I'm not needed here. There is nothing for me to do but pursue pleasure. Gambling. Hunting. Other sport." Words were failing him and he wanted to make her understand." He winced. "The last time I amused myself, three people wound up dead—"

"The responsibility for that was not yours," she protested.

He waved a hand. "It was. No escaping truth. Thing is, I can help you. Have helped you. Might as well keep helping you—"

"Tanner, traveling with me to Paris will take time. Weeks, maybe. The more time you spend with me, the more risk there is of being connected with me and accused of helping me escape."

He laughed softly. "You do not know what I am trying to say. I would take you to Paris and stay with you. Live with you."

"No." She rose from the chair. "You cannot mean this."

"Of course I mean it."

"Tanner, you are a marquess." She gaped at him.

He wanted to pull her on to his lap and show her he was a man first, before a marquess.

She stepped away from him. "You cannot leave your responsibilities."

He waved his hand again. "That is just it. I can. I have hired a legion of workers who do an excellent job running the whole lot. That is my point, Marlena. *I* am not needed. My affairs have been set up to run well. For two generations the set-up has worked to perfection. I am the least important person in keeping them running well." He stood. "Oh, perhaps I may be needed for a signature or two, but documents can be couriered to me. You would be safe. We could have a life together." He touched her face, gently. "What do you say, Marlena?"

"Oh, Tanner." She wrapped her arms around his neck.

He seized her in his arms and captured her lips, kissing her with more hunger than when they'd gone without food. She was all softness, all curves, and his hands glided over her body, relishing where he touched, longing to feel her bare skin.

She pushed his coat over his shoulders and pulled on the sleeves until the garment fell to the floor. He wanted to laugh for joy, because she wanted him, too. She had thought of undressing him at the same moment he had thought of undressing her.

They were like two sides of a coin, he realised. Parts of the same whole, making no sense unless they were together. He wanted to show her, make her understand that they belonged together.

That he could not live without her.

This revelation had come to him in the taproom. *He could not live without her.*

She unbuttoned his waistcoat, and he shrugged out of it, pulling the shirttails out of his trousers next. Her delicate hands worked the buttons on the fall of his trousers, tantalising him, making him yearn for her fingers to touch where he was now so powerfully aroused for her.

Her fingers skimmed that part of him and again he had the fancy that they thought with one mind.

"Your boots," she murmured, urgency in her voice.

Damn the boots, he thought, not wanting to stop for such practicality as removing his boots. She knelt before him to pull them off, and his trousers after them. Her hands stroked his thighs as if wanting to come closer.

"Marlena," he rasped, unable to wait.

He pulled her on top of him, his hands under her nightdress, finding her breasts, feeling her nipples harden for him.

She moaned. "Can we do it now, Tanner? Here."

One mind, he thought. One passion. Never had he been with a woman so attuned to him. Never had he felt so complete as when joining with her.

"You and I can do whatever we wish." He felt more powerful with her than with all the trappings his title afforded him.

He positioned her on to him, entering her there on the chair. The moment of joining accelerated his joy and his need of her. They even moved as one, in perfect rhythm, their need growing in unison. He closed his eyes and let himself be lost in her, to relish this belonging to one person. To feel that this, above all else, gave meaning to his life.

They were as one in their moment of satisfaction, as well. He felt the release of his seed, the culmination of his pleasure at the same moment he felt her pulse against him. Their voices cried out together, and their last writhing of ecstasy came as if they were one.

He'd long abandoned the idea of leaving her in some god-awful place in Edinburgh without the intention of freeing her and coming back to her. Now he realised he did not want to leave her at all. It would be like leaving all that gave his life meaning.

He held her quietly on his lap for a few minutes until the reality of cramped muscles set in.

"I'm taking you to bed," he murmured into her ear.

She slid off his lap and pulled him to her as soon as her feet touched the floor. A kiss joined them once more, a uniting kiss.

He picked her up into his arms and carried her to the bed where they quickly disposed of her nightdress and his shirt and joined each other, skin to skin, under the covers. To his delight their passion rapidly rose again.

Afterwards she lay in his arms, and he savoured the smoothness of her skin against his.

He turned his head and kissed her on the temple. "You know what this means, do you not?" he said to her, his voice tinged with the joy that permeated every part of him.

"Mmm, what?" she murmured sleepily.

"We are married." He grinned and turned to her for a quick taste of her mouth. "We are in Scotland, claiming to be husband and wife, and we have just consummated our union." He swept a hand through her now tangled hair. "We are married."

"Married." She sighed.

In spite of all his drink, he lay awake while she drifted to sleep, his mind spinning with plans to reach Edinburgh. They would have to hide there somehow until he was able to access his funds and get enough money to set themselves up in France. He'd like them to be married properly, by clergy, if possible, but he could not feel more married to her than he did at this moment.

Soon he would be able to shower her with everything his wealth could provide her. He fell asleep, thinking of jewels and dresses and shoes and trinkets, every luxury he wanted to buy her.

Lord Wexin returned to Parronley in the dark after a deadly tedious meal with Laird Hay. He did learn a bit about how landowners were increasing their profits here in Scotland, by forcing out the crofters so there would be more land for sheep. The wool industry seemed to be doing quite well.

He frowned as he left the horse to a stable boy and found his way up the dark path to the great mausoleum of a house that smelled of years of being closed up. He could do nothing here until he inherited, and, unless Rapp located Marlena, that might never happen. He needed her to be found. Needed even more for her to be dead. Why the devil could she not have drowned in that shipwreck and her body wash up on shore? Everything would have been so easy that way.

He entered the house and found the elderly butler napping in a chair in the hall.

"Here, man!" Wexin said loudly. "Take my things."

The man woke with a snort and struggled arthritically to his feet. "M'lord," he mumbled, taking his hat and gloves and catching the top coat that was thrown into his arms. "Begging you pardon, m'lord, but a man arrived while you were out."

"A man?" Wexin raised his brows.

"Ay, sir," the old man said. "He said you would wish to see him this night. A Mr Rapp, sir."

"Why did you not say it was Rapp in the first place?" Wexin snapped.

The butler shrugged. "He waits in an anteroom near the kitchen."

"Is the drawing room lit with candles and a fire as I instructed?" Wexin demanded.

The butler bowed. "Ay, m'lord."

"Then bring me some brandy and have Rapp attend me there."

Wexin made his way across the hall, his heels clicking on the stone floor. The drawing room had none of the elegance and fine taste that his lovely Lydia had brought to their London townhouse, but he supposed it would do for the likes of Rapp.

A few minutes later Wexin was settled with a tolerable bottle of brandy. The butler announced Rapp, who strode in.

Wexin waited for the butler to close the door and for the man's receding footsteps to be heard.

"How did you know I was here?" Wexin demanded.

Rapp responded, "Your arrival was spoken of in Parronley. I am staying at the inn there."

Wexin waved an impatient hand. "Well, what is your report?

Rapp straightened. "I have seen her travelling in the company of a man. I am convinced she is coming here."

"You saw her and did not capture her?" Wexin huffed.

Two spots of colour tinged Rapp's cheeks. "She managed to elude me. Once in Liverpool. Once on the road outside Langholm, but I am confident she will not elude me a third time."

Wexin gave a sardonic laugh. "One woman managed to elude you twice? Three times if we count your losing her in the shipwreck?" He should have hired a more ruthless man to escort his cousin back to London, one who would have seen that a shipwreck ended her life.

"The man in her company came to her aid," explained Rapp.

Wexin glared. "And who is this man?"

Rapp pressed his lips together before speaking. "I have not seen his face. They change names at every stop. He may wear a signet ring, however."

"A signet ring?" Wexin's excitement grew. "Do you know the seal?"

Rapp lifted his chin. "Only that it included a stag and an eagle."

Tannerton's seal!

Wexin took a sip of brandy to disguise a smile. How many other gentlemen with a stag and eagle on their crest would be rusticating in this god-forsaken part of Scotland? It had to be Tannerton, and Marlena was with him. Wexin's hand trembled. He had been so close to her this very day.

He retained his composure. "This is all you have for me? That she travels in this direction with a man wearing a ring? I could have guessed as much."

Well, he would not have guessed she'd have a man with her, let alone a marquess, but it did make sense that she could not have come this far all alone.

"They travelled on horseback," Rapp responded, an edge in his voice. "That made it more difficult to follow their progress. They have largely remained off the coaching and toll roads."

Wexin waved a hand. "Go. You are dismissed. I'll have no further need of your services. Return to Bow Street and wherever else the deuce you belong."

Rapp frowned. "What of my pay, sir?"

Wexin eyed him with disdain. "No prisoner. No pay." He waved a hand. "Be off with you. I cannot abide incompetence and failure. I dare say you can find your way to the village. Do not show your face in this house again."

Rapp took one threatening step towards Wexin, but then he seemed to think better of it. He turned around and walked out, slamming the door behind him.

Wexin released a grin. He'd wait long enough for Rapp to be gone and then he would send for the men he'd brought with him from London, men who would not let a woman and a pampered marquess defeat them so easily.

He raised his glass in a toast. "To you, cousin Marlena. Soon we see each other again. Then you will meet your fate."

Rapp stormed out of the house and back to the stable for his hired horse.

Damned Wexin. He released a whole string of epithets towards this man who had not only cheated him out of his pay, but also the sum of money he'd spent along the road. He would show the ruddy man. There was still a reward waiting in London for the return of the Vanishing Viscountess. Rapp intended to collect that reward and Lord Wexin could go to the devil for all he cared.

Chapter Seventeen

Marlena awoke in Tanner's arms, with the delicious knowledge that each morning from now on she would awaken in the same spot. She'd never dared hope for happiness again, but Tanner had delivered it to her as surely as he had rescued her from the Irish Sea, impossible tasks both.

She ignored the twinges of guilt that teased at her conscience. She'd not asked Tanner to give up his life in England for her. He'd offered it. He wanted it. She pushed away the nagging thought that he would some day regret leaving his duties, his country.

She could not help but worry about the people of Parronley. Perhaps she could assume her title as Baroness when she was in France. Perhaps she could care for her people *in absentia* as Tanner planned to do.

At least they would not be under Wexin's care.

Another fear tugged at her sleeve. Would Wexin come after her even in France? Would she and Tanner still have to constantly look over their shoulders?

His eyes opened and gazed warmly into hers. "Good morning, wife."

She smiled. They were married. Could she really allow herself to believe that dream had come true?

Eliza, she thought. *Am I married to the Marquess of Tannerton?*

"Good morning," she responded.

He gathered her in his arms and kissed her, her body answering with the flushed excitement and yearning he always elicited in her, even in those days when she and Eliza were mooning over him.

She laughed softly. "Did you know you danced with me once, Tanner?"

His face screwed up in disbelief. "I would have remembered."

She touched his mouth with her finger tracing the outline of his lips. "At Lady Erstine's masquerade ball. I was dressed as a maiden from the time of King Arthur with a pointed hat and a flowing veil. And a mask, of course. You never saw my face."

His lips formed into a rueful smile. "I would treasure the memory—if I remembered it."

She laughed again. "I would never expect you to remember me. I was a very forgettable girl in those days, but my friend Eliza and I kept an account of you. We were quite enamoured of you."

"You jest."

She stroked his chin, loving how scratchy his growth of beard felt on her fingertips. "It is true, but a long time ago. A marquess was reaching too high for us. At the end of the season, Corland became my suitor and my brother declared he would make me a good husband."

Tanner's smile disappeared. He took a strand of her hair and twirled it in his fingers. "Your brother ought to have known better."

"Oh, I suppose Corland charmed Niall as thoroughly as he did me."

Tanner's brow furrowed. "Did you have any happiness with Corland, Marlena?"

She stared into his eyes, seeing flecks of brown in their mossy green. "Briefly, when I was too starry-eyed to know better, and Corland still had my money to spend." She cupped her palm against his cheek. "It never felt like this."

His eyes darkened and he placed his lips on hers again, giving her more in one kiss than she'd ever imagined a man could give.

"Marlena," he murmured, tasting of her lips again and again. "Wife."

She was certain of what love meant now. It meant how she felt about this man, how his mere whispering of her name sent shafts of desire through her, how his touch aroused her senses, how his smile filled her with joy.

She rolled on to her back and he covered her, worshipping her with his gaze, soothing her with his hands, thrilling her with his coupling. When he entered her it was all that she could do not to cry out in joy. He was hers. She, a fugitive everywhere else, was at home with him.

He moved with exquisite gentleness, making their passion grow. Though lost to sensation as the pleasure built inside her, one thought remained. She would belong to him like this for ever.

Sparkles of light seemed to dance behind her eyelids as he brought her passion to its peak. She imagined the light passing through her skin, becoming a part of her, belonging to her in a way she would never have to give up.

When she lay again in his arms, sated and safe, her joy turned to contentment.

She must have fallen asleep again, because when she woke, he was at the basin shaving, wearing only his trousers.

"Why did you not wake me?" she asked. The room was bright with sunlight. The morning well advanced. "It must be late."

He turned. "No need to do so. We have only ten miles to go by the map. An easy ride. I thought I would dress first and let you sleep."

She rose from the bed and retrieved her nightdress from the floor. Slipping it on, she walked over to him and hugged him from behind.

He turned and kissed her, then wiped the soap he left on her face with his thumb. "I think it best you remain in the room while I check on the horses. With any luck my horse will be fit for the journey."

"I do not mind." She loved their simple room in this humble inn. It was the site of her wedding, after all, and it felt safe.

She washed and dressed, finishing just as he was ready to go out of the door. As she started to pin up her hair, he gave her another swift kiss. "I'll be back. Before I head for the stable, I'll arrange for some food to be sent up for us."

After he left, she hurried to the window to watch him walk out of the inn, so tall, so commanding in his masculine stride. She felt as giddy as the girl she'd once been, watching him saunter into a ballroom.

Dare I be so happy, Eliza?

When he was no longer in sight, she finished dressing her hair and covered it with a cap. She straightened the bedcovers, her hand smoothing the linens, remembering how they had become so twisted and tangled with their lovemaking.

She had just finished tidying the room when Fia's Bram brought her breakfast.

He set the tray on the table. Such a big bear of a man, she

thought and smiled to herself, remembering Fia's protest about him. They were so obviously besotted with each other.

"How is Fia today, Bram?" she asked.

"Och," replied the large man, "I walked her to her sister's early this morn. That cursed flesher has her in a great fright, y'know. Best she hide for a bit."

Flesher. She had not heard that Scottish term for *butcher* in many years. It was an apt name for Wexin, she thought with a shudder.

"Whatever keeps her safe." She caught Bram's eye. "Wexin is a very dangerous man, Bram. You must be very wary of him, for Fia's sake."

A hard, determined look came over his face. "Aye, I'll keep her safe."

"Good." She smiled.

"Lord Tannerton will see you safe, as well, m'lady. He is a fine man. He'll see you to your destination without that demon finding you." He nodded his head in emphasis.

Marlena regarded him with curiosity. "From where do you know Lord Tannerton, Bram?"

"From Brussels, m'lady."

"Brussels?"

"Ay." He nodded again. "It was after the great battle. I was in the 71st, ma'am, who fought in the battle. After that day I was walkin' into Brussels with the wounded." He pushed up his sleeve and showed her a jagged scar. "I was not bad hurt, but others were dyin'. His lordship carried the lads from the wagons. He found houses to take the lads and tend them and he paid with his own money for the caring of them. Did it all day, m'lady. And the next. And the next."

"Lord Tannerton did that?"

"Aye, ma'am, and there were plenty lords who ran back to England that day, but not his lordship." His chest puffed out in pride as he spoke. "And then a year later I heard my officers talking that his lordship spoke in Parliament, to help the lads that came back, maimed and unable to work."

Parliament. The House of Lords.

Tanner had neglected to tell her that he had taken his seat in the Lords, but of course he would have done so.

Bram concluded. "Lord Tannerton is a great man."

"Yes," she agreed, her voice suddenly cracking.

Bram glanced to the door. "I'd best be going back to my duties, ma'am, if you are no longer needing me."

"No," she said distractedly. "I do not need you, but I thank you, Bram."

He bowed and strode out of the room.

Marlena grabbed hold of the bedpost, pressing her cheek against the smooth wood. She squeezed her eyes shut.

A great man, Bram had said. Tanner was a great man, a man who organised the care of the wounded at Waterloo. A man who spoke for those men in the House of Lords. He had said nothing to Marlena of this part of his life.

Marlena sank into the chair, but had little appetite for the food in front of her. She absently nibbled on a piece of bread, picturing Tanner's strong arms carrying men from wagons, seeing Tanner heedless of blood staining his clothes, thinking only of what must be done. She thought of him standing in the Lords, among all those important, titled men, his deep masculine voice booming to the far recesses of the room.

He was an important man.

There was another quick knock at the door, and Tanner walked in, a line of worry between his brows.

He smiled at her, though, and crossed the room to her, kissing her upturned face. When he sat down across from her, the worry line remained. "The horse needs another day of rest, the stableman tells me."

"I see," she responded.

He tilted his head. "I tried to barter for another horse, but the man did not think he could procure one before the end of the day."

"Could we walk or take one horse?" she asked.

He shook his head. "It slows us considerably. Should Rapp or Wexin encounter us, we'd have little chance of escaping." He lifted his palm. "I also thought about a carriage, but Bram said this village does not have a coaching inn. We would have to go to Parronley for it." He rubbed his face. "Wexin must be watching the coaching inn."

The fear felt like a hard rock inside her. "When can we leave?"

"Tomorrow, the stableman assures me." He reached across the table and took her hand.

She squeezed his fingers. "We can wait a day, can we not? We can hide in this room. Bram will warn us if anyone comes."

He lifted her hand to his lips. "That is the wisest course, I believe."

She poured his tea and placed some ham and cheese on his plate. She listened with only half an ear as he told her more particulars about the horse and his thoughts of what route they could take to avoid the more travelled roads.

"I spoke to Bram and he will draw us a map." He took a bite of ham.

Her heart began to pound faster. She tried to keep her voice calm. "Bram said he knew you from Waterloo, that you were in Brussels after the battle. He spoke of your heroic work with the wounded."

"Heroic?" He shook his head. "I assure you, I merely helped a little. There was nothing else to do."

What Bram described had been considerable, but Marlena did not argue the point.

"What were you doing in Brussels?" she asked instead.

The newspapers during that time had reported that some of the English had considered Brussels somewhat of a social event, the place to be, until Napoleon decided to be there as well.

"Pure accident, I was there." Tanner took a sip of tea. "I'd been at the Congress of Vienna. Assisting Castlereagh, you know. When he went back to England, I stayed. Helped Wellington for a bit and went on to Brussels when his Grace was called there."

Her jaw dropped. "You were at the Congress of Vienna?"

After Napoleon's first abdication, all the powers of Europe gathered in Vienna to decide the fate of the Continent. If Tanner had been there, someone must have considered his assistance very important indeed—important enough to be a part of deciding the fate of nations.

"Just helping out a bit. Castlereagh talked me into it." He chewed on a piece of bread.

She supposed Wellington had "talked him into" helping him as well. Marlena leaned back in her chair and stared at him. "Goodness, Tanner, what else have you done?"

"Done?" His brows rose. "I did not *do* anything. I merely assisted."

"Why you?" She lifted her cup.

He shrugged. "I suppose the Duke of Clarence suggested my name to Castlereagh."

"The Duke of Clarence!" The King's son. The Prince Regent's brother. She nearly spilled her tea.

"Friend of mine." He pierced another piece of ham with his fork and popped it in his mouth.

Although it seemed as if she could no longer breathe, she coaxed more out of him. He leaned his chair and balanced it on its back legs as he told her about his activity in the Lords.

His efforts seemed considerable to her, although he spoke of them as trifles. He shrugged his work off as no more remarkable or important than wagering on a horse race or playing at cards. Merely another means to relieve boredom.

The more he talked, the tighter the knot grew inside Marlena, the harder each breath came. It was plain as a pikestaff that Tanner did not see what was so very evident to a common man like Bram and to her. Tanner was a man capable of great achievement, not only because of the title he bore, but more so because of the man he was. He was capable of befriending Whigs and Tories alike, princes and common men, to charm them all with his affable manners, influence them with the sheer force of his personality.

Marlena swallowed against a rising sense of despair. If Tanner took her to France, if he remained with her, connected to her, what would happen to all those people he might have helped, the other men who might perish if he were not there to assume their burdens?

She choked back a sob.

He let the chair right itself again, peering at her with concern. "What is it, Marlena?"

"Oh." She blinked away threatening tears. "I suppose I am afraid."

He reached across the table and grasped her hand. "I'll make certain no harm comes to you. We'll make it to Edinbugh and to Paris."

You cannot let him do this, Marlena, the voice of Eliza seemed to warn.

I know it, she replied inside. *I know it.*

He smiled at her, eyes like a warm caress. "What shall we do to pass the time today, Marlena, confined to this room as we are?"

Her heart swelled with love for him, for his ready desire

to ease her fears. What frightened her now was more than her capture, however.

She tried to smile back. "I do not know, Tanner."

He rose from his chair, still holding her hand. "I shall think of something."

Wexin waited in the breakfast parlour, finishing his meal, while his lackeys had been dispatched to Kilrosa to discover if Marlena was indeed in residence there. Wexin had roused himself early and called his men to him to apprise them of his suspicions, ordering them to find her without delay. Now he had no choice but to wait for their report.

Wexin hoped his men would not tell him that she had fled already. The thought of her being so close and yet slipping through his fingers would drive him into a real fury. He wanted this business concluded quickly.

He took a deep breath, cautioning himself not to think in such a depressive vein. Marlena was in Kilrosa. He could sense it. All that was required now was a plan to capture her.

It was unfortunate that Tannerton accompanied her. Such a man would be a formidable enemy, one powerful enough to convince others of Marlena's innocence. And Wexin's guilt. Obviously, Tannerton must be killed, but the death of a marquess would arouse a great deal of undesired attention.

Wexin picked up a newspaper fetched for him by a footman the previous day. He supposed it would be several days old, having come from Edinburgh, but he needed the distraction.

A report caught his eye. *Packet Boat Wrecks.*

Wexin half-rose from his chair as he read the report of the boat Marlena had been on. Tannerton must have been on the packet boat, too. He nearly whooped with glee. Rapp said Tannerton and Marlena had been using false names.

Perhaps no one knew that the Marquess was alive. Wexin could dispose of him here in Scotland where no one would be looking. They'd assume he drowned.

The butler entered and Wexin refolded the newspaper quickly. "Well, what is it?" he snapped.

"Your men to see you, m'lord." The old man bowed.

Wexin straightened and gestured at the remnants of his breakfast. "Get rid of this and tell them to come in."

The butler bowed again and stacked up the plates in his hand. He reached for Wexin's tea cup.

"Leave me my tea, you fool." Wexin shooed him away.

Two of his men entered the room. Wexin signalled them to wait until the butler walked away with the dishes.

"What news, then?" Wexin asked, unable to suppress the eagerness in his voice.

Smith, as stout and solid as a powder keg, spoke up. "We've got nothing for certain, m'lord."

Wexin pounded his fist on the table.

The other man, Jones, shorter and leaner, but in a way that made him a good scrapper, broke in, "We are certain the woman is at the inn, m'lord. It is just that no one is talking about her."

"We saw the gentleman, though," Smith added. "He went to the stable. The man has two horses there, so she must be with him."

This sounded promising. "You left someone to watch the inn, I hope."

Jones nodded. "Oh, we did that, sir. Williams is watching the place."

Wexin stifled a laugh. Smith. Jones. Williams. Not real names, he'd wager a pony, but these were the sort of men who would get results, not incompetent asses like Rapp. He was well rid of that fellow.

He frowned again. They would be much too conspicuous, all of them, waiting and watching in the village. He must come up with another plan. "Can they be spotted leaving the village?"

"Unless they leave on foot," Jones replied. "There is only one road in and out."

Wexin leaned forward. "Here is what we do. Two men watch the road, one man watches the inn. We must attempt not to be conspicuous, however." His brow furrowed in thought. "I will accompany you." He would ensure they did not make some stupid mistake.

Smith piped up, "I overheard the stableman talking to the gentleman. One of their horses almost went lame and cannot make the trip until tomorrow. I think they won't go anywhere until then."

"We must assume nothing. We must watch them." Wexin drummed his fingers on the table. "If it were me, I would leave under cover of darkness." He felt energised with excitement. "Just in case, one of you must watch the inn all day; the others, the road, but when darkness falls, the real vigil begins."

Chapter Eighteen

The day with Tanner was a delight. They rarely left the room and did not leave the inn at all. Most of the time they remained in bed, making love or merely talking.

Marlena was hungry to know all about him, asking endless questions about his childhood, his thoughts, his secret wishes. He insisted his only wish was to be with her, but that statement only made tears prick her eyes again.

She soaked up tales of boyhood escapades, various larks that always seemed instigated by his friend, Pomroy, which took Tanner's cleverness to extricate them.

She told him about herself, about living at Parronley and leaving there for school, never to return. She told him about Eliza, how they were school friends and débutantes together. She told how Eliza took her in when she'd run to her, making Marlena a part of her Irish home, keeping her safe until Eliza's brother came to visit. Marlena talked about Eliza and her children becoming ill, and how Marlena tried so hard to keep her dear friend alive. Marlena talked about Niall, about his death, and the death of her nephews. Tanner held her when she finally could cry for them all and for herself.

And for him.

Time hung suspended, giving the illusion they would have all the time in the world to lie abed, talking. Loving. Then in an instant it was night, and desolation replaced the joy of her all-too-brief marriage to the Marquess of Tannerton.

The path she must take stayed in her mind while they talked and made love.

She knew better than to merely run. Tanner would find her and protect her, no matter what. Her only choice was to turn herself in, and he must not be a party to that. She must do it alone and never let it be known that Tanner had helped her.

The prospect of death lost some of its terror, at least. She had lived a lifetime in a few short days, more than some people live if they reach one hundred years. She'd known Tanner. She'd known love.

She wrote a letter to him in snatches, whenever he left the room to get them food, or to check on the horses. What he would think or do when he read it, she did not know.

In the letter she asked for his promise not to reveal that he had helped her, to give her the gift of knowing he would not share her fate.

She explained why she was leaving, to free him to do the good he was destined to do—nay, *obligated* to do with his personality and position. She reminded him of all the people they had met on their journey who needed him to look out for them. The innkeepers and stable boys, the blacksmiths and tavern girls, the caretakers at Dutwood, Bram and Fia, everyone who had helped them. She asked him to care for them in her name.

She wrote that it grieved her to know how much her leaving would wound him, but the more bound she felt to him, the more right it seemed. They had been born to duty, and his duty was to care for those who needed him. She would not allow him to sacrifice those people for her alone.

She closed the letter saying how much she loved him, and how grateful she was to have been his wife.

When they made love for the last time, each caress, each kiss brought pain as well as delight. She savoured every moment of the experience for herself, but there was more to it than that. This lovemaking was like a prayer, a prayer to give him happiness, to help him remember how greatly she loved him.

She lay in his arms afterwards, listening to his heartbeat and to each breath of air he took in. She could feel him drift to sleep as his breathing slowed. It was so tempting to close her eyes and join him in sleep, but she forced herself to remain awake.

She had watched the window, waiting for a glimmer of light. When it came, all too soon, she slipped from his arms and dressed herself. Her bag was already packed with her clothing, each item reminding her of Tanner. When all was ready, she placed the letter on the table where she knew he would see it, and took one long, last look at him, so peacefully unaware, his hair mussed, his handsome face still wearing a hint of a smile.

"I shall love you always, my husband," she whispered so quietly she was not certain she hadn't merely thought the words.

Turning the knob slowly, she opened the door, and walked away from the man she loved.

In the hall of the inn, she paused to don her cloak. As she stepped into the street, she saw a person rushing towards her. Marlena drew back to hide in the shadows.

It was Fia, hurrying to the inn's door as if she were being pursued.

Marlena stepped into the light. "Fia? What is wrong?"

The girl gave a sharp cry. "Lady Corland!"

"Has something happened?" Marlena looked at the girl with worry.

"Och, m'lady." Fia tried to catch her breath. "It is me that's wrong and I could not sleep for it."

"I do not understand." She took Fia's arm and led her away to where their voices would not so easily carry through the inn's windows.

Fia looked at the bag she had slung over her shoulder. "Are you and Lord Tannerton leavin' so early, m'lady? Because you need to hear what I say before you go."

It was too much to explain to the girl. "What is it, Fia?"

"I came to tell Bram I'm goin' to the laird. I'm going to tell Laird Hay what happened that night. I do not know what he can do, but he's the magistrate and I'm going to tell him." Even in the near-darkness, Marlena could see the resolute set of Fia's chin.

She held the girl by the shoulders. "No, Fia. It is too dangerous. Wexin—"

"I'm done with being afraid of Lord Wexin, m'lady," Fia cried. "It is wrong that he can go free and you have to hide." She paused, glancing towards the inn. "I cannot ask Bram to love me if I don't do something to stop this. Bram would do it in my place. I know he would."

"Fia, Bram would love you no matter. It truly is too dangerous." She gave her a little shake.

Fia twisted out of her grasp. "Nae, m'lady. I would not be worthy of his loving me. I woke my sister and told her I was comin' back. I'm asking Bram to take me to the laird. He'll believe us, I know he will. He's a good man, the laird is."

Marlena could hear the blood roaring through her body, ringing in her ears. She did not know if it was fear or excitement. She did not know if they could dare test the truth. Or dare to hope.

"I'm waking Bram for him to take me as soon as it is light. You cannot stop me." She leaned towards Marlena. "You should come with us—Lord Tannerton, too—the laird is sure to do something, if his lordship tells him to."

She gave Fia an agonised glance. "I'll go with you," she told Fia. "But Lord Tannerton must not be part of it. If this does not work, he could hang along with me."

"His lordship would not like you going without him, m'lady," Fia said.

They started to walk back to the door of the inn when two men jumped out of the shadows and seized them, clamping huge hands over their mouths. Marlena felt the point of a knife against her throat.

His breath foul with rotting teeth, the man holding her sneered, "You are coming with us. Do not make a sound or you both will be sliced to bits."

The other man made a high whistle and, as they were dragged behind the building and past the stable, two more men emerged from opposite directions.

One of them whispered, "Do you have her?"

"Take a look," Marlena's captor said, stuffing a dirty handkerchief in her mouth so that she thought she would gag.

The man came closer and peered into her face. He smiled, his teeth glowing white. "My dear cousin."

Wexin.

Her nightmare had come true, and Fia's, as well.

The knife still pointed to her throat, the man bound her hands.

"This other one said something about going to the laird," Fia's captor said.

Wexin turned and strode over to Fia, bound and gagged as well. Wexin gasped and squeezed Fia's face in his hand. "My good fortune is boundless this day." He turned to the men. "Quickly, before someone hears. Let us be off."

The men carried Marlena and Fia over their shoulders and quickly made their way out of the village. Marlena struggled to keep her wits about her, to look for an opportunity to escape and to free Fia.

The men had hidden horses outside of town. Marlena was thrown over a horse's back and bounced painfully against its withers as its rider put the horse into a gallop. She presumed they headed towards Parronley, to the home she had not been inside for over thirteen years.

She could see little but the horse's shoulder and the ground and she only glimpsed the entrance of Parronley when they passed through the wrought-iron gate and on to its cobbled road. She lifted her head and caught a glimpse of the house in the distance, lit from behind with the glow of dawn.

"This way," called Wexin. "The day grows light. We will lock them away until I decide what to do. Finding the girl puts this entire matter in a new light."

Marlena tried to keep her wits about her to make out which wing of the house the men were taking them, using the lightest part of the sky to tell her which way was east.

One of the men opened a door that creaked on its hinges. She and Fia were carried into pitch blackness.

"We need light," Wexin said.

She had not been able to determine exactly where they were. She had been so long away, and there were so many parts of the house unused even when she lived there.

Finally torches were lit and they were carried down a stone staircase and into what looked like a dungeon.

"In here." Wexin led the men to a room with a stone floor and stone walls and the smell of damp and decades of disuse. He put the torch in an iron bracket on the wall.

She and Fia were dumped on the floor like sacks of flour. The young woman thrashed against her bindings.

Marlena managed to sit up. She glared at Wexin.

He laughed. "I will remove that disgusting cloth from your mouth, my dear cousin. You may remember that no one can hear you in this place." He pulled out the handkerchief and held it in two fingers away from his body, dropping it on the ground. "There you are, my dear. I am certain that feels much better." He turned to the men who had captured them. "You have done an excellent job. Wait for me outside."

While their footsteps receded up the stone stairway, Wexin walked over to Fia. He pulled her hair, and she stopped struggling. Marlena could make out Fia's glaring eyes in the light of the torch. Wexin leaned down into Fia's face.

"It *is* you." His voice was triumphant as he removed Fia's gag. "You change everything, my sweet little maid. Who would have guessed I would find you here with her? I'd hoped you'd landed in a Cheapside brothel and died of the pox, but I could not depend upon it, you realise."

Fia twisted away from him.

"Why does she change everything, Wexin?" Marlena asked, more to take his attention from the girl than anything else.

He turned back to her. "I may be able to take you back to London for your trial and to weep for your wickedness as you walk to the scaffold, after all."

"What had you intended otherwise?" she asked, knowing he was capable of treachery much greater than taking her back for a sham of a trial.

"Well, to kill you, of course." He sauntered over to her. "I thought perhaps you might vanish, once and for all." He put a finger to his cheek. "Although that would delay the wealth of the barony passing to me. No, if you are hanged, then I shall have all of the Parronley lands for raising sheep. I assure you, I am in great need of the revenue that will earn. I just need to get rid of the crofters, but that is the fashion, I hear."

Marlena felt sick. What would happen to Parronley's crofters? Where would they go?

She glared at him. "Perhaps I shall escape again and deny you the pleasure of my death."

He tilted his head. "Believe me, it is no pleasure, cousin Marlena. It is a necessity, however. You and the maid."

She made herself laugh. "You have been so clever, Wexin. I never would have guessed it of you." Perhaps if she kept him talking, Fia could free herself from her bindings. Marlena worked on her own. "I always thought you merely followed in Corland's shadow—"

Wexin grabbed the front of her dress, lifting her off the floor as he put his face into hers. "I follow in no man's shadow." He dropped her back on to the floor. "Least of all your husband's. Corland was a fool and not at all a gentleman."

Marlena could not disagree. She sat up again and tried to keep him talking. "Is that why you killed him? Because he was not a gentleman?"

He laughed. "Yes. Yes. It was." He stared down at her. "Do you know what he threatened to do?"

"Beat you at cards?" she taunted. "Steal your mistress?"

She glanced at Fia and saw her trying to free her hands.

Wexin's eyes flashed. "Worse than that, Marlena. He threatened to call in my vowels." He looked skyward, as if remembering. "He'd gambled even more excessively than usual. He'd gone to the moneylenders and he could not meet their payments. So he called in my debt to him, so he would have money to pay the moneylenders. I did not have it."

Her eyes widened. "You killed Corland because you owed him money?"

He leaned close to her face again. "I killed him because he threatened to spread the word that I reneged on my duties as a gentleman. Lord Strathfield, you know, would look with great disgust upon any man who failed to pay a debt of honour. He'd refuse my offer of marriage to his daughter." He leaned back again. "That was a risk I was not prepared to take."

Marlena shook her head, unable to believe her ears. "You killed Corland because a man might consider you less of a gentleman?"

"That is the right of it." Wexin laughed. "But Corland's life had negligible value."

She tried to rise. "What of my life, Wexin? Did my life have no value? From the start you planned it so I would be blamed."

He sighed and rubbed his palms together. "Now that I do regret, but there was nothing else to do. I could not risk anyone thinking it was *me,* could I? Corland had given you so many reasons to do him in; you were the most logical choice." He turned to Fia again. "All would have been well if this little chit had not shared his bed that night."

He took a step towards Fia, but she lashed out, kicking her bound feet at him. He backed off again.

"I think I must kill you both." Wexin sighed. "I am too impatient to wait for a trial. I merely must ponder the best means of doing so." He sauntered to the door, then turned and touched his forehead. "There is the matter of Lord Tannerton, as well. He must also die."

Marlena went rigid with rage and it was all she could do to disguise it from Wexin. Her death mattered little, but Tanner and Fia must live.

Wexin paused again in the doorway. "I am not a heartless man, Marlena. I shall leave you the torch so you will not have to spend all of your last hours in darkness."

He closed the door behind him and turned a rusty key in the lock.

"My lady," Fia cried from the corner of the room. "Bram will try to stop him and he will get killed, too! We must escape from here."

Tanner, in that delicious moment between sleeping and waking, reached across the bed, expecting to pull Marlena's warm soft body next to his. He felt only cool sheets.

His eyes instantly flew open.

She was gone.

He sat up, heart pounding, knowing he would not find her in the room. "Blast it, Marlena. Why run from me now?"

He continued to swear as he jumped out of bed and reached for his clothes. When he pulled on his shirt, he saw the paper folded on the table. He grabbed it and read.

Forgive me, my love, the letter began.

Forgive her? He'd throttle her for putting herself in so much danger.

He read only far enough to see she was going to the laird. He threw the pages down and finished dressing, pounding his boots on to his feet as he rushed out of the door.

He ran down the stairs and into the taproom, looking for Bram. He needed the man's help.

Bram's stepmother jumped, dropping a spoon into a large pot of porridge. "Mr Henry, ye gave me a fright!"

"Where is your son?" he bellowed, scaring her more.

She placed a hand on her chest. "I do not know."

Tanner caught sight of the door to the back of the building and ran outside that way, rather than retrace his steps through the inn. As he reached the yard, Bram came towards him.

"Have you seen Fia, m'lord?" The man was white-faced. "She's left her sister's house."

"Lady Corland is gone," Tanner said, not answering him.

"Lady Corland!" Bram's stepmother stood in the doorway. "Bram, what is this? The baroness?"

Her stepson said only, "Mam, check if Fia is in the inn and be quick!"

She ran inside. Bram and Tanner followed, falling in step with each other.

"I walked to Fia's sister's house, wantin' to see her." Bram was breathing hard. "She'd left before dawn, her sister said."

"Lady Corland has gone to the laird."

They hurried through the kitchen when Mrs Gunn ran up to them. "Her room is the same as when she left it."

"They've both gone to the laird, then." Bram frowned, pushing his way towards the inn's entrance.

"What is it, Bram?" his mother cried. "Why do you talk of Lady Corland?"

"I cannot explain, Mam," Bram said as he and Tanner reached the door.

"To the stables," Tanner said. "We'll ride."

If Marlena and Fia had taken the horses, he would simply commandeer whatever horse was there. Both horses were there, however, already saddled as Tanner had requested of the stableman the previous day.

"Your steed is right as rain today, sir," the man said.

Good, Tanner thought. He might need to run the horse hard.

He lengthened Marlena's stirrups to fit Bram and within two minutes they were off.

"Show me the way," Tanner said.

As they rode, Tanner told Bram about Marlena's letter.

"I told Fia I would take her to the laird." Bram frowned. "I told her she must tell what she knows."

"What she knows?" Tanner asked.

Bram faced him as they rode. "She witnessed the whole

thing, m'lord. She saw what Wexin did to her lady's husband, and Wexin saw Fia."

"My God." Both women were in danger. "Let us hope they made it safely to the laird's, then."

Why the devil had Marlena left this time? Tanner fought against the pain of her running from him again. He needed first to know she and the maid were safe.

There was no sign of Marlena and Fia on the road. Bram led them to a comfortable country house with a well-tended park and good land around it.

They left the horses at the laird's front door. A footman answered the knock, greeting Bram by name.

"Has Fia Small and another lady come this day?" Bram asked the man.

"Fia?" The footman looked puzzled. "Call upon the laird?"

"Never mind that," Tanner said, striding into the hallway with Bram in his wake. "Tell the laird the Marquess of Tannerton wants to see him immediately.

The footman's eyes widened. "The who?"

"Do it. *Now,*" Tanner barked.

It still seemed like precious minutes passed before they were ushered into a drawing room where an elderly man was still buttoning a brocade waistcoat, a white wig askew on his head.

Tanner strode up to him. "I am Tannerton. We need to know if Lady Corland and Fia Small have called upon you."

The man straightened his wig. "Lady Corland? Do you mean *that* Lady Corland? The murderess?"

"The accused murderess." Tanner tried not to lose patience. "We have reason to believe she and Miss Small intended to call upon you."

"Fia?" The laird shook his head in confusion. "No one has called this morning, I do not believe." He walked to the door.

"Lamont," he said to the footman. "Check with the staff if Fia Small has been here."

He glanced back at Tanner. "You are the *Marquess* of Tannerton?"

"Yes," Tanner replied.

The man's eyes looked uncertain. "May I offer you refreshment?"

Bram spoke up. "We cannot tarry, sir. We need to find them."

Tanner took the laird's arm and leaned close to him. "We may require your assistance. I must apprise you of this whole matter…"

As concisely as possible, he explained Marlena's situation, Fia's involvement and Wexin's treachery.

"Dear heavens." The laird collapsed into a chair. "Wexin dined with me two days ago. He seemed a decent fellow."

Tanner stood over him. "Are you saying you do not believe what I have told you?"

The man lifted his hands. "Oh, dear me, no. Who am I to dispute a marquess?"

"It is true, all of it," Bram put in. "Fia would not tell it false."

The footman returned. "No one has come here this morning."

"M'lord?" Bram turned to Tanner, his face white.

Tanner started for the door. "We are going to Wexin, Laird. I would be obliged if you would mount some men to come after us in case we need assistance."

Laird Hay stood. "I will do it."

Tanner and Bram ran out to the horses and were soon back on the road.

"Parronley is about seven miles, m'lord," Bram told him. He shot Tanner a pained look. "He has them, doesn't he?"

"I fear so."

Tanner prayed they would reach Parronley in time. He had no doubt in his mind that Wexin intended to kill both Marlena and Fia.

God, he prayed. *Do not let me have Marlena's death on my conscience. Save her. Take me, but save her.*

They set a fast pace, but had to slow down as they rode through Kilrosa; its people were now awake and busy and crowding the road.

"Where are ye goin'?" some shouted to Bram.

"I cannot explain now," Bram answered them.

Once out of Kilrosa, they put the horses to a gallop. Over a rise, however, a horseman approached.

Rapp, the Bow Street Runner.

"Whoa, there!" Rapp turned his horse sideways to block the road. "Not so hasty." He held a pistol and aimed it directly at Tanner. "You are not going anywhere."

Chapter Nineteen

Marlena struggled at the ropes that bound her wrists. "We *will* escape, Fia." She looked about their dungeon, trying to fix some memory with it. "Somehow."

The ropes were too tight to free her hands. She moved across to Fia. "See if you can untie me."

Fia wiggled her way closer to Marlena and they sat back to back, Fia trying to loosen the knot. "I cannot do it, m'lady."

"Perhaps I can untie yours," Marlena said. She found the knot and worked at it with her fingers. It would not loosen. "Let me try my teeth."

She manoeuvred herself so that she lay on the stone, her face in reach of Fia's hands. At least she could see the knot this way. It had been knotted several times. She pulled at the top strand with her teeth.

It formed a loop. She tugged at it until the loop loosened more. Quickly she swung around again and was able to get a finger through the loop, pulling one of the rope ends through it. She worked on the rest of the knot, first with her teeth, then with her fingers, until it came undone.

Fia hurried to untie her legs and then she worked on Marlena's bindings. In a moment, they both were free.

"I remember playing in the dungeons," Marlena said. "Niall and I. Wexin, too." She closed her eyes, trying to see it clearly in her memory.

When she was small Wexin had threatened to toss her in one of these rooms and throw away the key if she did not leave him and Niall alone. She later begged Niall to promise never to lock her in. Niall had hugged her and reassured her he would hide a key in all three of the dungeon rooms so she might never be locked in.

Did you hide the key, Niall? Marlena said to herself. *Show me. Please show me.*

She walked around the room, touching the wall, examining it, picking at stones that looked as if they might be dislodged.

"There should be a key hidden in here," she told Fia, who immediately began to search the other wall.

Niall would have made it easy, Marlena thought.

She ran to the door and examined its thick wood. There in a niche between two boards was a key. "Here it is," she cried. She could not pry it out with her fingers. The damp had rusted it and it was well lodged in its hiding place. "We need something to tease it out."

She pulled a hairpin from her hair and used it to pick around the key.

"Can you pry it out?" asked Fia, pacing behind her.

"I will," Marlena responded determinedly.

A sliver of wood broke off, giving Marlena sufficient space to hook the hairpin under the key. She pulled and the key moved enough so that she could grasp its end with her fingers.

It pulled free. "I have it!"

She put the key in the lock and turned, her heart leaping as the sound echoed in the chamber. Now if the old door would not creak so loud that their captors would hear it, they would be free.

Holding her breath, she pushed on the door. Its creaking sounded as loud as a demon's scream, but no one came.

Marlena turned to Fia. "There might be a guard at the outside door. We will have to go another way."

The dungeons hid a tunnel through the cliffs out to a tiny cove where the water was deep enough and still enough for a boat. It was a secret escape route for the laird should he need to get away by sea. Her old grandfather used to boast that his father had been prepared to use the tunnel to aid in the escape of Bonnie Prince Charlie, had the Prince come to Parronley. Marlena and Niall had been forbidden to play in it, so, naturally, they had explored the tunnel whenever they could.

Marlena grabbed the torch from its bracket on the wall. It was already burning low. "We must hurry."

She led Fia out of their prison chamber and turned away from where light peeped in from the top of a stone stairway.

"This way," she whispered. "There is a tunnel."

"A tunnel." Fia's voice was fearful but resolute.

As if Marlena had been there yesterday, she led Fia to the hidden entrance. Now they need only hope that the tunnel was still clear, that over the years the walls that had remained passable for three centuries had not collapsed. Debris that Marlena dared not try to identify crunched under their feet, and they heard the skittering of tiny animals, rats or mice, probably.

"How much further?" Fia gasped.

"I think not far," Marlena said, although there was nothing but darkness up ahead and the torch was burning out.

"I cannot believe my good fortune," said Rapp, still aiming his pistol at Tanner. "And, in case you decide you must play the odds that I will shoot and miss, I should warn you, this pistol has rifling in the barrel."

The man was reading Tanner's mind. Rifling made the ball shoot straight and true. "Rapp, stand aside and let us through. It is a matter of life and death."

"Life and death? Your life. Your death." Rapp leaned forward in his saddle. "I do not feel inclined to let you go, Mr Lear or whatever your name is. You have been harbouring and abetting my fugitive and I am going to see you pay the consequences. Now, where is she?"

"You ought not to speak to him that way," Bram cried, moving his horse closer.

Rapp gave Bram a fierce glance. "You had better stay where you are, or I will shoot him."

"Don't be daft, man," Bram went on. "It is a marquess you'd be shooting."

Rapp laughed. "Impersonating a peer, are you now? That will get you in more difficulty."

"He *is* a marquess," Bram said.

Tanner started to remove his glove. "I will show you my signet ring, if you wish."

"Bah." Rapp waved the pistol. "What do I know of rings? Besides, you may have stolen it."

Tanner lost all patience. He needed to find Marlena, to stop Wexin. "Listen, Rapp. I *am* the Marquess of Tannerton, and you will put that pistol down now. I need your help, not your interference."

Rapp frowned. "Do not try to trick me. I worked for Tannerton once. I would know—"

Tanner cut him off. "And you never met me, did you? You worked for me a year ago last summer, was it not? What was your task? To go to Brighton to find the whereabouts of Lord Greythorne? Or into the rookery to learn who might have killed two people? Or, perhaps you were one of those guarding the Vauxhall singer? Perhaps you were on duty that night when she and I were abducted from under your noses, but then, if you had been one of those men, you should recognise me now."

Tanner waited, glaring at Rapp, so furious, he felt like playing the odds and charging directly into the man. The ball might not hit a vital part of him. He ought to chance it.

Marlena's life depended upon it.

"Tannerton?" Rapp's arm lowered. He immediately raised it again. "It cannot be. You are not dressed like a marquess."

"Fool," Tanner bellowed. "I was in the shipwreck. Do you not remember me? I remember you. I remember you pushing your prisoner aside so you could take her place in the boat. You left her to die. May you be damned for it!"

Rapp bowed his head. "God help me." He glanced up again, but the pistol swayed in his grip. "You must understand. I have a wife. Children. She would have died anyway."

Tanner advanced on the man, moving his horse in slow, steady steps. "She will die now, if you do not let us through. Wexin has her. Wexin is the real villain. Wexin killed Corland—"

"Wexin?" Rapp's eyes widened.

Tanner nodded. "He made it look as if Lady Corland did it. She is innocent, Rapp. You saved yourself on the packet, leaving an innocent woman to die."

Rapp's face contorted and he let his arm drop completely, his shoulders shaking.

Tanner brought his horse next to Rapp's. "I need your help, Rapp, not useless bawling. Come with us to stop Wexin. Save her life now."

Rapp straightened his spine and nodded. He stuck his pistol back into his pocket, and turned his horse around. Bram started forward and shouted, "Let us go."

The three men galloped towards Parronley, and Tanner prayed they would not arrive too late.

The butler appeared at the door of the drawing room where Wexin was taking a cup of tea. The old man opened his mouth, but Jones pushed past him.

"Leave us," Wexin told the butler.

Jones watched until the man closed the door. He turned back to Wexin. "They are gone."

"Who is gone?" Wexin asked.

"The women."

"What?" Wexin jumped to his feet, knocking over the small table upon which sat his tea cup. "How could that happen?"

Jones slapped his hands against his sides. "I do not know. Williams went to check on them. The door was open and they were gone."

Wexin's fingers curled into fists. "You were supposed to be guarding them."

"We were," Jones protested. "We sat at the top of the stairs, right outside. They could not have got past us."

"Well, they did get past you, obviously." He started for the door. "We must search for them."

Wexin grabbed his top coat and the two loaded pistols he'd carried with him earlier that morning. He patted a pocket of the coat, feeling the knife he had also carried.

He and Jones hurried outside and around the house to the wing where they had imprisoned the women. Wexin descended the stone stairway and examined the room that ought to have kept them prisoner. Their bindings lay on the stone floor of the dungeon. The torch was gone.

He climbed back up the stairs. When he stepped outside to where Jones waited for him, Williams came running towards them from across the park.

At still some distance, Williams stopped and shouted, "We've found them!" He pointed in the direction of the cliffs and gestured for them to follow. Wexin ran, with Jones close behind.

The cliffs were nearby. Wexin soon saw Marlena and the girl silhouetted against the sky. They froze when they saw Smith and Williams advancing on them. They turned and ran back towards the edge of the cliff.

Wexin's worries were eased. The cliffs were at least twenty feet high, with nothing but water below. He had them trapped. There was nowhere for them to go.

He laughed in triumph as Williams and Smith caught up with the two women, but Marlena fought off Smith, and Wexin frowned again. If Smith released her, Wexin would have the man's head put on a pike. He wished like the devil that he'd killed the women right away. Their bodies could have rotted in that dungeon for as long as he needed to decide how to dispose of them. When he got his hands on them again, Wexin would not make the mistake a second time.

To his horror, Marlena, her hair loose now in the struggle, dug her fingers into Smith's eyes. Smith screamed and let go, clutching his face. She rushed to her companion and started fighting with Williams.

Wexin quickened his step. "Hurry, Jones. They must not escape."

Williams was teetering near the cliff's edge, trying to hold on to the maid, while Marlena was hitting him and pulling on his clothing. Wexin reached the struggle and, with a surge of strength borne of his anger, seized Marlena by the hair and pulled her off Williams.

"This shall be the end of you, cousin." He caught her in a firm hold.

"You idiot." She struggled. "How many servants do you think are watching from the windows?"

He glanced over at the house where the windows sparkled in the sunlight. Curse her, she was probably correct. If he was being watched, he'd have to keep them alive.

But not for long. Marlena and her maid would never reach London.

Williams now had a good hold on the maid and was dragging her back towards the house.

Wexin, sick of Marlena's nonsense, pulled out his knife and held it against her throat. "Come nicely with me, my dear. You know my skill with a sharp blade."

"I know it well." She ceased her struggling, but stood her ground. "Does your wife know this side of you, Wexin?" she taunted. "Is she as bloodthirsty? Your Lady Macbeth, perhaps?"

He pushed the point of the knife into her skin, drawing blood. He did not care how many servants watched. "Do not speak of my wife!"

At that moment, horses' hooves thundered in his ears. He looked up to see three horsemen advancing upon them. Jones turned and ran, one of the men on horseback turning to pursue him. Another made straight for the maid, and a third headed directly towards him.

Tannerton.

Tanner instantly took in the tableau in front of him, but his gaze was riveted on Wexin, who held Marlena at knifepoint close to the edge of the cliff.

When they had ridden up to the house, an elderly manservant had run out and yelled for them to head for the cliffs. They had barely broken speed to do so.

Tanner saw Marlena's hands gripped around Wexin's wrist, and she managed to break free of Wexin's knife as Tanner approached.

Tanner leapt off his horse, knocking Wexin to the ground, but the momentum sent Tanner rolling dangerously close to the cliff's edge. When he looked up, Wexin was advancing on him, eyes wild with fury.

"Give it up, Wexin," Tanner said, scrambling to his feet. "Your game is over."

Wexin, no longer holding the knife, reached in his coat and pulled out a pistol. He pressed the weapon against Tanner's chest.

"It is your game that is over, Tannerton," Wexin cried. "I will blow a hole through you."

Tanner lifted his arms and glanced over the cliff to see that the sea was a good twenty feet below them. Its waves sounded a steady rhythm, like a battlefield drumbeat. Tanner edged closer to the precipice.

"You will never get away with this," Tanner warned, his voice low with rage at this man bent on destroying Marlena. Tanner's feet were close enough to the edge to knock pebbles over the side.

Wexin's face was red. "I will take you to hell with me, and my cousin, too." He moved the pistol to Tanner's heart and straightened his shoulders.

"No!"

Tanner heard Marlena's cry the same moment she barrelled into him. As a shot pierced the air, Tanner and Marlena flew off the edge of the cliff.

"Mar—" Tanner managed before they hit the icy water and plunged into its depths.

It was as if a nightmare repeated itself. Tanner felt the same bone-numbing cold as the night of the shipwreck, the same disorientation, the same desperate need for air. He thrashed in the water, one hand still gripping Marlena's clothing. He'd be damned if he'd allow the sea to take her now, not after all they had been through. This time, daylight shone through the water like hope. Tanner kicked towards it.

They broke the surface and both gasped for air. Still holding on to her, Tanner swam in the direction of the tiny sliver of beach at the opening of what looked like a cave.

As they stumbled out of the water, Tanner took her in his arms and held her tight against him. "Marlena. We might have been killed."

"No." Her teeth chattered as she spoke. "I knew. Used to swim here. We escaped through the tunnel, Fia and I." She shivered. "So cold."

She made no sense, but Tanner could only think that he might lose her yet if he could not get her warm and dry. He glanced around, searching for a way out.

Wexin leaned over the edge of the cliff. "No! It cannot be!"

Marlena tried to pull away at the sight of him. Tanner covered her with his arms and backed towards the mouth of the cave. There were more shouts from above and the sound of a pistol shot rang through the air.

It is not over yet, thought Tanner.

At that moment, a man in livery, carrying a torch, appeared at the entrance of the cave. "This way," the man said.

Tanner lifted her into his arms. "I'm so cold, Tanner," she murmured. "I'm so cold."

Marlena woke in a familiar place, but one as disorientating as if she'd been transported to Van Diemen's land. She was in the room of her childhood, its walls and furniture the same as the day she had left it.

"Are you feelin' rested, m'lady?" Fia leaned over her, placing a hand on her forehead.

Events came rushing back.

"Tanner?" She sat up.

"Fear not. He is here. Below stairs with the laird and Bram and some others. They are sorting matters out."

"Wexin?"

Fia averted her gaze. "He is dead, ma'am. Shot himself after you and Lord Tanner climbed out of the water."

Marlena put a hand over her mouth, remembering Wexin's face the moment she knew he'd decided to shoot Tanner, the moment she ran and she and Tanner flew off the edge of the cliff.

Her memory was hazy after that. She recalled the icy cold water. She recalled Tanner pulling her on to the beach and carrying her through the tunnel. He'd carried her up the stairs to this room and had undressed her while shouting for dry clothes and blankets.

She looked down at herself. She was wearing an old nightdress that still smelled of cedar. "Are there clothes for me? I want to get up." And find Tanner, she could have added.

"Right here," Fia said. "I'll help you."

Fia helped her don a dress that might have once been her mother's, an old velvet gown in deep green.

"I'll help with your hair," Fia said, sitting her down at her old dressing table where Marlena's maid once plaited her hair and told her stories of Shellycoat and Selkies.

She opened the drawers of the table and found a forgotten ribbon in one and a comb in the other. Fia combed out the tangles in her hair.

"Tell me what happened, Fia."

Fia's brows knit. "Well, after you and Lord Tannerton went off the side, Lord Wexin ran to the edge. Bram was fighting the fellow who had me, and there was another man helping. A Bow Street Runner, Bram said."

"Not Rapp." Marlena's eyes widened.

"I do not know, ma'am, but he was helpin'." Fia worked the comb through a strand of Marlena's hair. "Lord Wexin must have seen ye come out of the water, because he yelled and then he took a pistol to his head and fired it." The girl shuddered. "It was an ugly sight, but I'm glad of it. I'm glad he is dead."

Marlena touched the cut on her neck, a small reminder of her cousin. "Is it over, then, Fia?"

"Aye, it is over and done, and we have naught to worry over. The laird came and I told him everything. Those men helping Wexin were all tied up, and some of the laird's men took them away. Lord Tannerton and the laird and some other men from Kilrosa are all below stairs talking about what is next to be done."

Marlena's cut stood out an angry red against her pale skin. "And you, Fia, were you hurt?"

Fia shook her head. "Nothin' to speak of, ma'am."

"And Bram?"

Fia's face filled with colour. "He is very well, ma'am."

Marlena smiled. "I am glad."

Fia's eyelids fluttered. "I am going to marry Bram, m'lady. He asked me after they took Wexin's body inside. He took me aside and kissed me. He knows all about me and still says he wants to marry me."

Marlena reached up to clasp her hand. "He is a very lucky man to have you."

Fia's face flushed with colour again as she tied the ribbon around Marlena's hair. Marlena slipped her feet into a pair of old silk shoes that must have also been her mother's. She and Fia walked down the stairway to the hall of Parronley House, another familiar site.

An elderly man approached her, bowing deeply. "Baroness."

"Forbes!" She recognised the old butler and threw her arms around him. "It is so good to see you."

When she let go of him, she saw tears in his eyes.

"It is good to see you, my lady." His voice was thick with emotion.

"Where are they?" she asked him.

"The drawing room, ma'am." He led the way, stepping inside the room first. "The Baroness Parronley," he announced.

A murmur went through the room as the gentlemen stood. Marlena caught a glimpse of Rapp, who averted his face from her. She would ask about Rapp later. When Bram stepped forward to take Fia's hand, Marlena smiled inside.

Then her gaze found Tanner.

He stood at the far end of the room, the apex of the group. The clothes he wore were old fashioned and even more ill fitting than those they had purchased in Liverpool, but, still, he had the air of command. The other men showed deference to his authority.

The other men bowed and addressed her as Baroness as she crossed the room. Tanner's gaze followed her progress, his expression a mixture of both tension and relief. As she reached him, his eyes glowed, warming her more than a blazing fire could do.

His arms opened to her and she stepped into his embrace.

"Gentlemen," she heard Tanner say, his voice deep and full of emotion, "may I present you to the Marchioness of Tannerton." His arms tightened around her. "My wife."

Heedless of their audience, Marlena wrapped her arms around his neck. "My husband," she murmured before his lips closed on hers.

Home, again. To stay.

Epilogue

March, 1819

Tanner stepped out of the Palace of Westminster, weary of sitting all day listening to the debates, tired to death of looking at the red walls, red chairs, red carpet. He was heartily sick of red. The bland beige of the buildings in the street was a welcome relief.

He chatted with Lords Heronvale and Bathurst. Lord Levenhorne walked by and nodded to him. Lord Levenhorne was Heronvale's brother-in-law and the heir presumptive to Wexin's title and property, waiting only for the widow Lady Wexin to give birth to the child she carried. Tanner did not know if Levenhorne cared much whether he inherited or not.

It was said Levenhorne was deeply affected by the scandal around Wexin's death, but the person for whom Tanner felt the most sympathy was Lady Wexin. She had withdrawn from society, from the prying eyes and loose tongues so quick to condemn her by association. Tanner had heard she was in debt, but she had turned down his offer to assist her.

Bathurst was in danger of rehashing the entire day's debate

if Tanner did not stop him. He turned to Heronvale. "I have heard horses from your brother's stables are fetching top dollar."

Heronvale beamed. "Indeed. If you've a fancy for a race-horse, you should pay him a visit."

Tanner held up a hand. "Not at the moment, but I would not be averse to placing a wager now and then."

"A wise bet," Heronvale said. "Devlin's breeding pro-gramme promises to produce winners."

Bathurst recalled seeing one of the horses race and he launched in to a stride-by-stride description. Tanner spied his carriage finally appear at the end of the queue of carriages waiting to transport the lords from Westminster to their homes in Mayfair. He begged leave of his companions and walked to the vehicle rather than wait for it to reach him.

He greeted the driver and the footman who jumped down to hold the door open for him. Tanner climbed inside.

"Hello, my darling."

To his surprise, Marlena sat inside, looking beautiful in the light that filtered into the carriage. She wore a splendid carriage dress in deep blue with a pelisse to match. Her lovely face was framed by a matching hat with a tumble of white feathers on its crown.

"Ah, you are a feast to my eyes," he said, leaning over to give her a long, hungry kiss. When he broke contact, he murmured, "What the devil are you doing here? You must have been waiting an age."

She touched his face and lightly kissed him again. "Not that long, I assure you. I was pining to see you and took it in my head to ride in the carriage."

He wrapped his arm around her and held her close. "Very nice for me."

"How was the session today?" she asked.

He groaned. "The whole day was spent on the consolidated funds. Tedious in the extreme."

She looked at him with sympathy. "I am certain there was some good reason for such a discussion."

Tanner well knew that Marlena considered his activity in the House of Lords to be of very great value. He'd never thought much about it. It was an obligation, like signing papers, attending balls, answering a summons from the Duke of Clarence. If he was lucky, he had the chance to speak up about something worthwhile. Occasionally the debates became so loud and rancorous that bets were taken whether fisticuffs would break out. Those were the fun days. Mostly it was a boring obligation.

"The cursed bill was good enough," he told her. "To increase funds available for public service, but why they had to prose on about it all day was beyond me." He shook his head.

She laughed softly. "My poor husband."

He grinned at her then and tasted her lips one more time. "How has my wife been today?" He pressed a hand on her belly.

She covered his hand with her own. "I've felt splendid today. No queasiness at all. I even received callers."

To Tanner's great delight and Marlena's astonishment, she was with child. That physician who long ago pronounced her unable to conceive had been proven utterly wrong. There was a baby growing inside her. Tanner's baby. A son, a daughter, he cared not which. To have a child with Marlena seemed nothing less than a miracle.

Tanner asked her who had called upon her, and listened with half an ear as she told him about the ladies, most new to her acquaintance, those she liked, those she suspected of wanting merely to befriend London's newest marchioness, those who came to see the notorious Vanishing Viscountess.

Tanner enjoyed the sound of her voice. He had no right to feel so happy, to have so much to live for. His wife. His child.

After Wexin's death, they had travelled back to London, to clear Marlena's name once and for all and to do what needed to be done for her to assume her title as Baroness Parronley. One of Tanner's first tasks had been to dispatch his secretary to procure a special licence. Within a week of their return to London, he and Marlena were married by clergy at St George's Church in Mayfair. Many members of the *ton* witnessed the nuptials, as well as the Duke of Clarence and Tanner's much-relieved cousin, Algernon. Tanner wanted it very clear that he was really and truly married to Marlena, in the sight of God and everybody else.

Even before the wedding Tanner had taken Marlena shopping. Not at open clothes markets like in Liverpool, but at the finest shops Mayfair had to offer. He bought her jewellery at Rundell and Bridge, perfume at Floris, confectionery at Gunter's. He took her to all the best modistes—Madame Devy, Mrs Walters and others—and the best milliner, Mrs Bell. Marlena ordered a wardrobe of fine gowns and Tanner paid extra for them to be made for her as quickly as possible. Gloves, stockings, there was no item he did not wish to share in the purchasing, to make certain she knew she could have anything she desired.

To think he used to leave the purchasing of gifts to his secretary. He'd never enjoyed more what his money could buy than when using it to indulge Marlena in shop after shop after shop.

A lesser woman might have been overwhelmed by his attention and the attention of all of society upon their return. It had been somewhat like being plunged into the icy sea water, totally engulfing, hard to breathe. The newspapers carried the story and everyone from Mayfair to Cheapside was talking about the return of the Vanishing Viscountess. Marlena withstood the furore with the same fortitude she'd shown on their journey to Scotland, and Tanner was fiercely proud of her.

The consolation of all the tumult had been spending their nights together, full of lovemaking, full of joy, a haven in the midst of a storm.

"You are not listening!" she accused him.

He gave her a chagrined smile. "I was woolgathering, I admit." But what precious wool. "What did you say?"

"I had a letter from Laird Hay, with a message from Fia and Bram. Fia is increasing, too. Is that not splendid?" She squeezed his hand.

"Very splendid."

Tanner had had his secretary send money to all the people who had helped them during their flight to Scotland. When he took Marlena back to Parronley this coming summer, to await the birth of their child, he would find out what else he might do for Bram and Fia. Their own house, perhaps. Their own land.

He closed his eyes as Marlena sighed and relaxed against him. The carriage swayed as it rolled along, reminding him of the rocking of a ship.

Tanner thought back to standing in the cuddy of the packet boat from Dublin. He thought of his despair, his lamenting of his useless life. He had no doubt he would have let the sea take him if he'd not needed to save Marlena. He held her tighter.

She had saved him.

He lifted her face and his lips touched hers once more. He poured all the love in his heart into the kiss. Afterward he pulled her on to his lap and clung to her.

"What is it, Tanner?" she murmured, caressing his cheek, undoubtedly sensing his emotion.

"Nothing," he said. "Everything." He fixed his gaze upon her. "Thank you, is all. Thank you, Marlena."

They rode the rest of the trip to their Mayfair townhouse in contented silence.

REGENCY
Collection

*Let these sparklingly seductive delights whirl
you away to the ballrooms—and
bedrooms—of Polite Society!*

Volume 1 – 4th February 2011
Regency Pleasures by Louise Allen

Volume 2 – 4th March 2011
Regency Secrets by Julia Justiss

Volume 3 – 1st April 2011
Regency Rumours by Juliet Landon

Volume 4 – 6th May 2011
Regency Redemption by Christine Merrill

Volume 5 – 3rd June 2011
Regency Debutantes by Margaret McPhee

Volume 6 – 1st July 2011
Regency Improprieties by Diane Gaston

12 volumes in all to collect!

MILLS
BOON

www.millsandboon.co.uk

REGENCY
Collection

*Let these sparklingly seductive delights whirl
you away to the ballrooms—and
bedrooms—of Polite Society!*

Volume 7 – 5th August 2011
Regency Mistresses by Mary Brendan

Volume 8 – 2nd September 2011
Regency Rebels by Deb Marlowe

Volume 9 – 7th October 2011
Regency Scandals by Sophia James

Volume 10 – 4th November 2011
Regency Marriages by Elizabeth Rolls

Volume 11 – 2nd December 2011
Regency Innocents by Annie Burrows

Volume 12 – 6th January 2012
Regency Sins by Bronwyn Scott

12 volumes in all to collect!

MILLS
BOON

www.millsandboon.co.uk

"To say that I met Nicholas Brisbane over my husband's dead body is not entirely accurate. Edward, it should be noted, was still twitching upon the floor..."

London, 1886

For Lady Julia Grey, her husband's sudden death at a dinner party is extremely inconvenient. However, things worsen when inscrutable private investigator Nicholas Brisbane reveals that the death was not due to natural causes.

Drawn away from her comfortable, conventional life, Julia is exposed to threatening notes, secret societies and gypsy curses, not to mention Nicholas's charismatic unpredictability.

www.mirabooks.co.uk

MIRA

HISTORICAL

Regency
MORE THAN A MISTRESS
by Ann Lethbridge

Merry doesn't need a man—no matter how handsome he is! Sadly society takes a different view and she is to wed Charles Mountford. The Marquis is more than happy to make her socially acceptable, but only if she acts publicly as his betrothed and privately as his mistress!

Regency
THE RETURN OF LORD CONISTONE
by Lucy Ashford

Miss Verena Sheldon is more than a little surprised when Lord Conistone—notorious womaniser and the man who broke her heart—returns from London. Even more surprising is the effect he still has on her. But Lucas has returned with a secret that will surely drive Verena from his arms for ever...

SIR ASHLEY'S METTLESOME MATCH
by Mary Nichols

Determined to overthrow a notorious smuggling operation, gentleman thief-taker Sir Ashley Saunders will let nothing stand in his way! Until he runs up against spirited Pippa Kingslake, who's just as determined to protect her own interests...

On sale from 6th May 2011
Don't miss out!

Available at WHSmith, Tesco, ASDA, Eason and all good bookshops

www.millsandboon.co.uk

0411/04a

HISTORICAL

THE CONQUEROR'S LADY
by Terri Brisbin

To save her people and lands, the lady Fayth is forced
to marry the commanding Breton knight, Giles Fitzhenry.
The marriage is as unwelcome as the deep desire which
stirs each time she looks at her husband's powerful,
battle-honed body...

SURRENDER TO AN IRISH WARRIOR
by Michelle Willingham

Tortured soul Trahern MacEgan is a born warrior, forever
scarred by a lost love and untameable by any woman.
Yet can Morren Ó Reilly, who is no stranger to suffering
and still shrinks from a man's touch, be the one to
bring light to his dark world?

MAIL-ORDER GROOM
by Lisa Plumley

Fleeing scandal, stage sensation Savannah Reed swaps
sparkles and satin for calico and wool to be Morrow Creek's
telegraph operator. Through the wires she finds her new
leading man, but when he arrives shot and left for dead on
her doorstep Savannah suspects she's jumped out of the
limelight and into the fire...

On sale from 6th May 2011
Don't miss out!

*Available at WHSmith, Tesco, ASDA, Eason
and all good bookshops*
www.millsandboon.co.uk

04a

0411/04b

England's Forgotten Queen

Anne Neville is the heiress and daughter of the greatest powerbroker in the land, Warwick the Kingmaker. She is a pawn, trapped in an uncertain political game.

When the Earl of Warwick commits treason, his family is forced into exile. Humiliated and powerless in a foreign land, Anne must find the courage and the wit to survive in a man's world.

www.mirabooks.co.uk

"The arrogance! To think that they can come here with their town bronze and sweep some heiress or other to the altar."

When a feudal law requires all unmarried ladies to wed or surrender half their wealth, the quiet village of Fortune's Folly becomes England's greatest Marriage Market.

Laura, the dowager duchess, is determined to resist the flattery of fortune hunters. Young, handsome and scandalously tempting Dexter Anstruther suspects Laura has a hidden motive for resisting his charms…and he intends to discover it.

www.mirabooks.co.uk

Immerse yourself in the glitter of Regency times through the lives and romantic escapades of the Lester family

Now the news was out that the Lester family fortunes had been repaired, Harry Lester knew the society matrons would soon be in pursuit, so he promptly left London for Newmarket.

Fate, however, proved more far-sighted, having arranged for a distraction in the person of Mrs Lucinda Babbacombe. Lucinda is a beautiful, provocative but unwilling conquest – who to Harry's irritation cannot be ignored.

MIRA